Fated for Love

The Bradens

Love in Bloom Series

Melissa Foster

ISBN-13: 978-1-941480-01-4
ISBN-10: 1941480012

FATED FOR LOVE

MELISSA FOSTER® is registered in the U.S. Patent & Trademark Office

Cover Design: Elizabeth Mackey Designs

WORLD LITERARY PRESS
PRINTED IN THE UNITED STATES OF AMERICA

A Note from Melissa

Get ready to fall hard for fearless rancher Wes Braden. Wes thinks he's the luckiest guy on the planet when Callie Barnes, the sweet, sexy librarian from his hometown, shows up at his ranch. He is more than willing to convert sweet Callie from chick lit to a world of erotic romance, but Callie ties sex to love, and Wes avoids commitment like the plague. Read on to see if this rough and rugged rancher has what it takes to win the love of the only woman who has ever stolen his heart—sweet, love-infused, Callie. If this is your first Love in Bloom book, all of my love stories are written to stand alone, so dive right in and enjoy the fun, sexy adventure!

The best way to keep up to date with new releases, sales, and exclusive content is to sign up for my newsletter.
www.MelissaFoster.com/Newsletter

About the Love in Bloom Big-Family Romance Collection

The Bradens at Trusty is just one of the series in the Love in Bloom big-family romance collection. Characters from each series make appearances in future books, so you never miss an engagement, wedding, or birth. If this is your first Love in Bloom novel, you have many more loving, loyal heroes and sexy, sassy heroines waiting for you!

Download a free Love in Bloom series checklist here:
www.MelissaFoster.com/SO

Get **free** first-in-series Love in Bloom ebooks and see my current sales here:
www.MelissaFoster.com/LIBFree

Visit the Love in Bloom Reader Goodies page for downloadable checklists, family trees, and more!
www.MelissaFoster.com/RG

Be sure to check out my online bookstore for pre-orders, early releases, bundles, and exclusive discounts on ebooks, print, and audiobooks. Ebooks can be sent to the e-reader of your choice and audiobooks can be listened to on the free and easy-to-use BookFunnel app. Shop my store:
shop.melissafoster.com

Chapter One

CALLIE BARNES PICKED through the new releases in the Trusty Town Library, where she'd worked as the assistant librarian for the last four weeks. She snagged the last copy of Kurt Remington's newest thriller, *Dark Times*, and put it on top of the two others she was carrying. The cover depicted the silhouette of a man at the edge of a cliff, holding a bloody knife that glistened in the eerie moonlight. She turned the book over. She couldn't even *think* about those types of situations, much less read about them. Callie's first love was fairy tales. She loved the idea of knights on white horses and happiness coming when a person least expected it. Fairy tales were safe, and the princesses were always loved for who they were, flaws and all. Her second secret love was women's fiction, specifically, chick lit and light romances, where the worst thing that a character encountered was a broken heel during an interview and all the sex scenes were left up to the reader's imagination—*as they should be*. She didn't need to read about some hunky hero touching a woman's thigh…with his tongue. She felt her cheeks flush at the thought and wished she hadn't worn her hair pinned up in a bun so she could hide behind it. She hugged the books to her chest, closed her eyes, and inhaled deeply. *Puppies. Kittens. Ice cream. Brownies. Chocolate syrup...oh yes...all over his—*

"Hey, Callie. You okay?"

Cripes! She clenched her eyes shut. Wes Braden's voice sent a shudder through her entire body. Of course he'd come in when she was thinking about chocolate syrup all over...*Stop, stop, stop!* This was the best—and the worst—part of Thursdays. She mustered a smile and turned around. He stood a few inches away, which brought her face oh so close to his broad, muscular chest. She could press her cheek to it and hear that big heart of his pounding beneath all those layers of muscle.

Holy cow.

She lifted her gaze and met his slightly amused dark eyes.

"Hey." His eyes landed on the books she was still clutching against her chest. "Those for me?" Wes came into the library every Thursday to pick up the latest thrillers and an occasional biography.

Callie's body pulsed with anticipation over the few minutes they shared each week—so much anticipation that when she was alone in bed in the dark of night, it was Wes's face that appeared in her mind and his voice that whispered in her ear. It was his full lips and his piercing dark eyes that made her heart race and her body so hot she couldn't help but satisfy the urges he stirred deep within her.

Callie opened her mouth to answer, but his masculine scent surrounded her dirty thoughts, shooting her hormones into overdrive and gluing her tongue to the roof of her mouth, which she was pretty sure was a godsend, because otherwise she might have drooled all over him. She shoved the books into his hands and was rewarded with a grateful smile that made her legs turn to wet noodles.

Wes's eyes lingered on her high-collared blouse, which was

buttoned up to her neck; then he lifted his eyes to hers again.

She felt her nipples harden under his hot stare, and of course her cheeks flushed again. She wished she could disappear into one of those books right there and then.

"Thanks, Callie. Any interesting plans this week?" He'd asked the same question every week for the past four, and each week she answered with the titles of the books she was reading, which was not only all she could manage, but it was also the truth.

There were no two ways about it. Callie's life was boring. She heard it from her girlfriends all the time; of course, that was because none of them lived in the tiny town of Trusty, Colorado, where she'd moved to take her dream job of working in a library. They still lived in Denver, where Callie and her friends had grown up and gone to college, but after four years of working in jobs she didn't enjoy, she'd jumped at the assistant librarian position that had opened up in Trusty. And while it might be miles away from her real-life friends and family, at least she was surrounded by more fictional friends than she could ever hope for. Besides, when Alice Shalmer, the head librarian, finally retired, she'd be next in line for the position. She hadn't expected the added weekly bonus of being able to ogle all six foot something of delicious Wes Braden, the hottest man she'd ever set eyes on.

Totally worth being away from my friends.

Finally she was in a position to give Wes a more exciting answer.

"My friends are taking me to a spa for a few days." She bit her lower lip to keep from grinning like a kid going to Disney World. She couldn't wait to spend a few days with her friends, where being pampered meant plenty of reading time. It would be a perfect long weekend.

Wes arched a thick, dark brow, leaned one hand on the bookshelves beside her head, and gazed down at her with a sexy, dark stare. "A spa? Now, that does sound interesting. Which one?"

She could barely breathe with him leaning in like that, bringing his clean-shaven, chiseled face, full lips, and…Her heart went a little crazy.

"Yeah," she whispered. Callie's stomach fluttered, and she realized she must be gazing at him with a horrifyingly dreamy look in her eyes. She turned back to the books—and away from the badass guy who taught hunting and fishing and made her sharp mind numb.

"Um." She tried to remember what the question was. *Spa. Which spa.* "I'm not sure which one, or even where it is. They're surprising me." Her girlfriends had scheduled this trip before she began working for the library, and Alice was kind enough to give her the time off even though she'd been there for only a month.

"What do girls do at a spa for a long weekend?" he asked over her shoulder.

Did he really expect her to think with him standing so close? She could feel his hot breath on the back of her neck. "Um…Massages." *Jeez! I might as well have said,* Have strangers touch us all over! She took a deep breath, which helped exactly none since his scent took shelter in her nose and lungs.

She forced herself to finish answering. "Uh…read, take walks." She stumbled back a step and knocked a book from the shelf. When she bent to pick it up, her darn too-tight pencil skirt trapped her knees together halfway to the floor. She made a mental note to stop eating ice cream as a replacement for those dirty things she was trying not to think about.

Wes retrieved the book, and their eyes met and held for a long, hot beat. He handed it to her and rose to his full height again. "Well, that sounds a lot more relaxing than spending a week with a group of people who are probably afraid of heights, spiders, and snakes." He tucked the books she'd given him under his arm, ran his hand through his short, dark hair, and shrugged, causing all those hard muscles in his shoulders to flex beneath his tight shirt.

"If you add *deep water* to that list, you've described me perfectly." Callie didn't know much about Wes, other than he liked thrillers and biographies, he turned the heads of every female in the library, and he taught alpha male stuff, like hunting, fishing, and…She had no idea what else, but the thought of guns and deep water made her dizzy. Or maybe that was a side effect of being around him. She wasn't sure.

"Wes?" Tiffany Dempsey ran her eyes up and down Wes's body with an appreciative smile, like a mountaineer revisiting a familiar peak.

It had taken Callie a week to realize why Tiffany appeared in the library every Thursday but never took home a single book or said a word to Callie.

Wes smiled at Tiffany in a way that made Callie blush. His eyes were as seductive as his voice. "Hey, Tiff."

Tiffany flipped her long blond hair over her shoulder and ran her finger down his forearm. "How's it going? Oh, I see Callie picked out some good books for you again."

Callie was surprised that she knew her name.

"Callie knows her books." Wes smiled down at Callie.

Knows her books. Callie watched him walk away with Tiffany, then banged her forehead against the bookshelf, wishing she could be anyone but the girl who *knew her books*. No, that wasn't really true. She loved books—everything about them, from the weight of them in her hands to the smell of the pages and the worlds they held between their covers. The world she loved to climb into, live vicariously through, and where she hid away from the world. She had no idea *what* to wish for. She was who she was and she liked who she was, even if she'd never be the type of woman a guy like Wes Braden would be interested in. She glanced around the quiet library. There were two women sitting at a table staring at Wes like he was made of gold. In the reference aisle, she noticed another woman, who, she realized, also came in only on Thursdays. She was peering out of the aisle at Wes, too. And then there was Tiffany, stealing every ounce of Wes's attention in three seconds flat. Callie sighed. She'd never be like Tiffany. Callie sucked at the whole one-touch-turn-on thing that Tiffany had down pat. Tiffany was tall and lean, and every outfit she wore was tight and revealing in the all the right ways. Callie would feel silly in the tight, black minidress Tiffany wore like a second skin. She somehow managed to look sexy *and* strong, which was probably nothing more than her brazen personality. Callie was petite and far from athletic. Even though she did her Jillian Michaels DVD religiously, she could never do the things she imagined Wes doing, like wrangling cattle or riding bulls.

I wouldn't mind riding him, though.

She shivered with the painfully unrealistic thought. She needed that damn massage, and she hoped the masseur was tall, dark, and handsome. Maybe she'd throw caution to the wind and do all those behind-closed-doors dirty things she wished she could do with Wes and had been trying not to fantasize about.

Her damn cheeks flushed again.

She looked up at the ceiling and wondered if there was a handbook for nerdy girls who fantasized about badass men to learn to take the reins and land their men.

Stick to fairy tales, Callie.

WES SHOVED A stack of papers to the side of his desk, yanked open the file drawer, and weeded through the hanging file folders. *Shit. Where are they?* He didn't have time for this. Wes and his partner, Chip Shelton, owned The Woodlands, a dude ranch about an hour outside of Trusty, in the Colorado Mountains, and he was meeting a group there just before dinnertime. If he could only find the itineraries he'd put together, he could get out of his office and on the damn road so he wouldn't be late.

He moved around the desk and looked down at the fifteen-week-old bloodhound sleeping soundly beneath his desk. "Hey, Sweets. Any idea where I put those itineraries?" He hoped he hadn't left them at his house. Wes split his time between his house in Trusty and his cabin at The Woodlands, and the last thing he needed was to make an additional trip before getting on the road to the ranch.

Sweets turned sad eyes up at him and yawned, then laid her head back down on her cushy bed. Wes had found Sweets a few weeks earlier on the side of a remote mountain trail, all skin and bones and sick with distemper. With the help of his brother Ross, the Trusty veterinarian, he'd nursed her back to health and fell in love with probably the only bloodhound on earth that had no sense of smell. Zero. None. A bloodhound that couldn't track a lost person would be of little use if a client turned up missing, but he loved her so damn much that even her missing sense didn't make her any less amazing.

Wes leaned down and loved up Sweets; he scratched her belly and pressed a kiss to her forehead. Then he sat in his chair and rubbed his eyes with his forefinger and thumb.

"What's that piss-ass look for?" Chip stood in the doorway, his shaggy blond hair hanging in his eyes. He'd been Wes's business partner since they opened the dude ranch doors eight years ago and Wes's best buddy since second grade.

Wes sighed and set a dark stare on Chip's annoyingly amused baby blues. They were two peas in a pod—no risk was too big, no job was too difficult, and no woman was worth more than a night or two. Chip knew as much about Wes as his five siblings did, and Wes loved him like a brother, but love wasn't the emotion that was currently brewing in his gut.

"Have you seen my itineraries for the new group?"

Chip flopped into the chair across from Wes's desk, the amused look in his eyes now coupled with a smirk. He stretched his long legs and clasped his hands behind his head. "How can a guy who's overprepared for anything outdoors be so frickin' unorganized with paperwork?"

"Either tell me where they are or get out." Wes went to the file cabinet near the window and tugged the top drawer open.

"Dude, you do this every other week. Just admit it: You have an aversion to paperwork."

"Shut up." Wes slammed the file cabinet closed. He peered out of his office and hollered down the hall, "Clarissa?"

"I don't have them!" Clarissa Simmons, their secretary and bookkeeper of three years, hollered.

Chip laughed.

Wes slid him another narrow stare. "If you're not going to help me look for the damn things, get out."

Chip pushed to his feet. "Did you look in your put-off-until-later pile? That would be my guess." Chip lifted his chin toward a pile of papers currently holding down the edges of an open map on top of a table in the opposite corner of Wes's office.

Wes stalked across the floor and snagged the top file in the stack. The itineraries.

"I'll refrain from telling you I told you so." Chip snickered as he glanced over the map, checking out Wes's trail for the overnight with his group. "You're all set for your days in female hell?"

"Yeah. You want to take them?" Wes loved running the dude ranch and he enjoyed taking charge of the outings, but they'd recently lost Ray Mulligan, a key employee who ran a third of the overnight trips, which left Wes and Chip to pick up the slack until the position was filled. They had flipped for the lead on this group, and Wes had lost.

Chip held his hands up in surrender. "I'm taking the day trips, remember?" He tapped his finger on his chin. "I'm thinking big burly broads who are out to show you how little you know." He shrugged. "You know, out for a week of fun."

"Or four women who think that I'm part of the package." As much as Wes loved women, fending them off during the outings had lost its charm about two months after they opened The Woodlands. He realized exactly what women must feel like when guys like him sized them up for a quick lay.

Wes slapped his leg twice, and Sweets lazily stretched, then scampered out from under the desk and came loyally to his side. She tried to climb up Wes's legs.

"Down, Sweets." Wes placed the pup's paws on the floor and loved her up again. "See you up there," he said to Chip.

He stopped by Clarissa's desk on his way out.

Sweets's nails clicked on the hardwood floors as she walked around Clarissa's desk. Clarissa glanced up from the spreadsheets she was studying and eyed the file in Wes's hand. Her dark hair curtained her serious eyes. Though she was seven years younger than Wes's thirty-two and probably weighed about a hundred pounds soaking wet, she ran the administrative side of The Woodlands with an efficient iron fist.

"Found them, I see." She bent to kiss Sweets.

Sweets tried to scale her legs and climb into her lap.

"No, Sweets." Wes shook his head. "I found the file in my procrastination pile."

Sweets whimpered, then sat at Clarissa's feet while she petted her.

Clarissa sighed and leaned back in her chair. She was smart as a whip and cute as hell, with long dark hair and a slim figure. More importantly, she was organized and efficient, and though Wes's siblings thought they'd hook up—given his penchant for cute females—she was a little too tough for his liking, and he'd never seen her in an amorous way. Not to mention that she seemed to have eyes only for his anally efficient partner, who happened to saunter into the room as if on cue.

"You're still here?" Chip sat on the edge of Clarissa's desk, and her eyes took a slow roll down his torso.

"Heading out in a sec."

Chip glanced at Clarissa, and their eyes held for a split second too long.

Clarissa lowered her eyes and began shuffling papers on her desk. "All set for the group?"

"As ready as I'll ever be." Wes ran his eyes between Clarissa and Chip. The air practically sizzled between them, but every time Wes brought up the possibility of Chip going out with Clarissa, Chip refused to acknowledge there was even a spark of interest. "Do you have my cheat sheet?"

Clarissa grabbed a piece of paper from the corner of the desk and pushed it across to Wes.

"Kathie Sharp, Bonnie Young, Christine Anderson, and Calliope Barnes, midtwenties, three married, one single, all experienced with high school sports and hiking, yada, yada. No medical concerns, no worries." She looked up at him from beneath her long bangs. "You're doing the overnight, right?"

"Yeah."

Her eyes widened. "Four twenty-something women and one hot wrangler, tents, moonlight, margaritas…"

Wes didn't live by many rules. And though it wasn't an official rule, he refrained from hooking up with Woodland guests, much to several sexy guests' dismay. He slapped his thigh, and Sweets came to his side again. "Have a little faith. The last thing I need is some woman suing me for my trust fund, my resort, *and* my dignity. No, thanks."

She rolled her eyes and pointed her pencil at him. "Wes, what if one of them is your soul mate? I wish you'd at least leave that door open a crack."

"Colorado's a big state. Too many pretty horses in the corral to be roped to just one." Wes turned and headed for the door with Sweets on his heels.

Sweets jumped onto the front seat of Wes's pickup truck and settled onto the plaid blanket he'd bought the first night after he'd found her. She rested her head on the books he'd gotten from Callie and looked up at Wes with another yawn.

Wes picked up the book on the top of the stack. *Dark Times.* He ran his hand over the cover, thinking of Callie and knowing he'd never have time to read three books with the busy days ahead of him. He usually got through at least one of the books she chose for him. She had good taste, and even if he didn't get through a single book, he couldn't stop himself from going back for more. He smiled as he set the book back down, thinking of her curvy little body in that tight black skirt and how flustered she became every time she saw him. She was sweet and proper and nothing like the women he was usually attracted to, and as he drove out of Trusty and headed into the mountains, he couldn't help but wonder what it might be like to take her hair down and run his fingers through it—and he was powerless to quell his desire to climb beneath her conservative facade and help her move from women's fiction to erotica.

Chapter Two

"THIS IS INCREDIBLE. I've never seen a spa like this." Callie stepped from her friend Kathie Sharp's Toyota FJ Cruiser and stood beside Bonnie Young. Bonnie was tall and blond and had been Callie's roommate in college her freshman year, and when they pledged their sorority, they'd met Kathie Sharp and Christine Anderson. The four of them had been best friends ever since.

Kathie and Christine exchanged a look. Christine tucked her short, pin-straight blond hair behind her ear and grabbed her bags from the truck.

Bonnie gripped Callie's hand.

"Honey, this spa is a little different," Bonnie explained in the calm, mother-hen tone she was known for. She was their voice of reason and the chosen one of the group to dole out bad news.

Callie took a hard look at the property. Acres of pastures and paddocks surrounded a cedar lodge. She turned back toward the road and noticed that they'd driven beneath a wooden arch. As she turned back toward her friends, she caught sight of two log cabins set up high on a hill. At the foot of the hill, horses grazed by a wooden bridge crossing a stream.

"What exactly do you mean by *different*?" Callie asked. "Are we staying in the cabin instead of the lodge? Because I totally don't mind."

"Oh, that's great. Yes, that's what she meant." Kathie picked up Callie's quilted bags and handed them to her, then slung her own designer bag over her shoulder and carried the smaller one. "Christine, Bon, why don't you check us in and we'll start up toward the cabin? The reservations are for cabin two."

Kathie stopped on the bridge to admire the view. She was a historical fiction novelist, and she found inspiration almost every place they went. "This would make a great writing retreat, wouldn't it? I could sit right here with my laptop and write about the Wild West."

"Or the perfect reading retreat, although the Wild West isn't really my thing." Callie took a deep breath of the crisp mountain air. "I can't wait to get a massage and lay out by the pool. They have a pool, right?" Callie surveyed the grounds again, cataloging the barns just beyond the lodge.

"Kath? Where *is* the pool?"

Kathie flipped her dark hair over her shoulder and pressed her crimson lips together. "Oh, they definitely have someplace to swim, not to worry."

Callie breathed a sigh of relief and smoothed her skirt. "Good. It'll be nice to relax. I miss you guys so much. Thanks for planning this trip for us. I swear this doesn't look like a spa at all. Must be a Colorado thing to look ranchy."

"Oh, look, here they come." Kathie pointed to Christine and Bonnie heading in their direction. She smiled at Callie. "We miss you, too, Callie."

Bonnie held her camera up to her eye and stopped to take pictures every few steps. She was a nature and wedding photographer, and she was forever documenting her surroundings. She waved at them, and Kathie and Callie waved back with ready smiles for the pictures they knew she'd take.

"I feel a little overdressed. You guys are all wearing jeans."

Kathie narrowed her baby blues again. "We had time to change before picking you up. You did bring clothes for the outdoors like we told you, right?"

Callie ran her finger along the wooden railing. "Of course. I brought sundresses and my bathing suit, oh, and that cute little skirt you gave me for Christmas last year. I love that. And I brought sandals and boots. I finally have someplace to wear my regular fun clothes instead of my work outfits. Is there a town near here? It might be fun to go shopping. Since you refused to tell me where we were going, I couldn't even Google it, but I thought Christine said there was a town nearby."

"Oh boy." Kathie picked up her bags when the others joined them and crossed the bridge.

"Oh boy? What? Is there *not* a town nearby?"

Kathie flashed her an *oh-shit* look that made her stomach lurch.

"They're here. Hey, Bon!" Kathie plastered a fake smile on her pretty face.

Oh God. What am I in for?

"You were right. Cabin Two, on the hill." Bonnie pointed up the hill toward a log cabin. Bonnie had grown up on a farm, and like Kathie and Christine, she had grown up camping, fishing, and doing all the outdoors things Callie never had.

Callie wondered if they'd picked a spa that looked like a ranch on purpose because it reminded them of all the things they loved. When Callie wasn't working, she was usually in her apartment experiencing life through the pages of a novel. The idea of a cabin was a little nerve-racking, but with her girl-friends' woodsy expertise, she was sure they'd take care of creepy crawly things that gave her the willies.

Bonnie dropped her bags and held the camera at arm's length. "Selfie! Gather around."

They huddled together as Bonnie clicked off a few shots.

"I bet all you got was boobs." Christine was a stand-up comic, and she never missed an opportunity to make them laugh.

"That only happens when I take the pics because I'm so short," Callie said.

"Boobs or not, this is going to be awesome." Bonnie slung her camera strap over her shoulder. "They said there's a welcome barbecue down that dirt path by the big barn in an hour."

"Barbecue? That sounds fun," Callie said.

"Yeah…" Christine had a round face with flawless, ivory skin, and as they walked up the hill toward the cabin, her ever-present smile turned serious. "Maybe we should go over the *amenities* with Callie."

"We will. They're supposed to give us itineraries at the barbecue when we meet our *wrangler*." Bonnie stopped in front of the cabin.

"Wow. This is a real log cabin. Check out the front porch." Callie mounted the steps onto the wide front porch and dropped her bags. "Did you say, *wrangler?*"

"Yeah." Kathie pushed her dark hair from her shoulder and glared at Bonnie, then turned and flashed a smile at Callie. "I think they call him a wrangler to keep it, you know, authentic to the mountains and the woodsy feel of the lodge…resort."

"Makes sense." Callie followed them inside the cozy, rustic

cabin. "Oh my gosh, this is adorable. Look at those book-shelves." She pointed to two floor-to-ceiling bookshelves packed full of books. She crossed the hardwood floor to a leather couch near the shelves and flopped onto it.

"You have to check this out. It's so soft." She kicked off her heels and put her feet on the coffee table. "You'll find me right here reading if you need me."

"I'm going to unpack." Bonnie headed for the stairs.

Kathie hoisted a bag onto the counter in the kitchen. "I brought nutrition." She withdrew several bottles of alcohol.

"It's a spa. They'll feed us," Callie said.

"Yeah, but we need our Skinnygirls." Kathie held up two bottles of Skinnygirl margaritas.

"Kathie, can you come up here a sec?" Bonnie called from upstairs.

"Pour yourselves a drink," Kathie said as she ascended the stairs.

"I'll just go make sure there are no Norman Bates bodies left behind." Christine followed Kathie upstairs, bags in hand.

Callie settled into the deep couch cushions. She was in no hurry to check out the bedroom when she had all those titles to consider reading. Callie surveyed the room. The cabin was more rustic than the spas they had gone to in the past, with real log walls and chunky wooden tables that might be found in any Colorado farmhouse. Callie went to the picture window that overlooked a small deck. Just beyond was a view of the forest. She felt as if she were nestled among the mountains, and she realized that she liked that cabin better than the fancy rooms at the other spas they'd visited. Not that they'd visited more than a handful over the years for their annual girls' trips.

A deep leather recliner sat at an angle beside the window

with a reading light arced over the back of the chair. *That's where they'll find me reading.* She went to the bookshelves and ran her fingers across the titles, cataloging them in her mind. She bit her lip, fighting the urge to alphabetize them. *All About Horses, Cattle Driving, Colorado Wilderness Guide.* She was bummed that there were no women's fiction titles. *A man definitely filled these shelves.* It was a good thing she never left home for an overnight trip without her books—or her Jillian Michaels DVD. She looked for a television and realized there wasn't one. Her stomach clenched momentarily until she remembered that she'd brought her laptop and could watch the DVD on that.

Low voices filtered down from upstairs. Callie picked up her bags and went to join her friends. She found the three of them huddled in one of the two bedrooms.

"Hey, what's the big secret?"

They turned deer-in-the-headlights eyes to her.

"Uh-oh. What is it?" They'd been friends for so many years that she knew something was up, and the fact that she was the only one not whispering made her stomach lurch. She sank to the bed and took a deep breath.

"Okay, tell me. What's wrong?" She tucked her hands beneath her thighs, steeling herself for whatever it was that had her friends looking so worried. "You guys would only keep something from me because you think I can't handle it. Oh no, please tell me no one is getting divorced, because you guys are the happiest couples I know. I couldn't take that." She lifted worried eyes to her too-damn-silent friends. She'd always been the most emotional of the group, and through the years her friends had tempered bad news—like when the sorority house cat got hit by a car—and she loved them even more for it. But no one had a cat at the moment, and she feared something worse might be waiting in the wings.

Bonnie pulled her back down to the bed and sat beside her. "It's not anything like that. Kathie, I'm going to just tell her."

"Tell me *what?*"

"Fine." Kathie waved a hand in the air as if she'd forfeited an argument, then sat beside Callie.

Christine sank to her knees in front of Callie. "I think it's time to give our little girl *the talk.*"

"Oh dear Lord. By the looks of you guys, I need that margarita…or the whole bottle."

"You might." Bonnie shot a narrow-eyed look at Kathie.

"Okay, here goes," Kathie began. "Now that Christine is married, you're the only single sister left in our little group."

"Yeah, so?"

"So, we know how you hate to step outside your comfort zone, and now that you're living so far away from us, we can't exactly kidnap you once a week like we used to, to go out for drinks or dancing or to meet guys." Kathie kicked Christine's knee lightly.

"Right," Christine added. "So, we wanted to help you a little, you know? Get you out and about and show you how strong you really are, so you wouldn't be afraid to go out and get in trouble—"

Kathie kicked her again.

"I mean, do things by yourself in your new town." Christine glared at Kathie.

"I'm missing something here. How will being at a spa make me stronger or want to go out by myself?" Callie looked at Bonnie, hoping to figure out what they were *really* telling her.

"Cal, this isn't a spa. It's a dude ranch. And we're here for a few days of toughening you up." Bonnie held tight to Callie's hand.

"Toughening? Wait. What?" Callie pushed to her feet and went to the window. "So, there are no massages? No pool and no cabana boys to drool over?"

Kathie went to her side. "No, but there are hot cowboys, and you'll learn that you can do so much more than you ever thought. I scheduled a bunch of fun things that you'd never do on your own."

"There's a reason I don't go to places like this." Callie stalked away, irritated and feeling duped. "I happen to like my life as it is. A dude ranch? Really, you guys?"

"Yeah, we know you love the library, and you love your apartment." Kathie picked up Callie's bag and dug through it. She held up a romance book and her Jillian Michaels DVD. "Cal, you've slept with exactly three men in your life, two of whom were nerdy math students. Your sex life is fictional and your exercise is…" She eyed the DVD. "Okay, it's tough and efficient, but it keeps you locked in your apartment. We just want you to be happy, and we want you to meet a guy who will adore you. And you can't exactly do that in a library."

"I meet men."

Kathie rolled her eyes. "Where? Because last I heard, your daily pattern was pretty much apartment to library to apartment. Rinse, wash, repeat." Kathie pulled her down to the bed again. "Sweetie, we love you. You're a beautiful twenty-six-year-old woman, and we don't want you to end up a beautiful fifty-six-year-old cat lady having fictional sex. Especially when all it takes is knowing you can handle anything so you're confident enough to go out without us and meet real men who give real orgasms."

Callie felt her cheeks flush. "I'm allergic to cats, so no worries there, and you know I hate the whole idea of going out to meet men." She couldn't dispute the rest, and it had been way too long since she'd had an orgasm that wasn't self-administered.

"We do know that, Cal, but it's not like many young, single guys hang out at the Trusty Town Library. This is all going to be fun," Bonnie assured her. "We're going horseback riding, fishing, shooting."

Callie didn't care if many men hung out at the library. The only one she wanted did, and that was enough for her. Even if she never did more than talk to him once a week, a few minutes of Wes Braden was enough to fuel her fantasies at least seven days.

Callie flopped back on the bed. "All of which you guys will do really well and I'll stink at." She threw her arm over her eyes. "Just take me home. You can enjoy your little dude vacation, and I'll go back to work, where I should be."

"No way." Kathie pulled her back up to a sitting position. "You've spent years hiding in your books, Cal. We love you, but just because our parents were more rural and yours were more academic doesn't mean you'll stink at these things. You just haven't been exposed to them."

"I hate being around deep water. You know that. I've never even ridden a real horse. A pony on a lead years ago, but..." Callie sat up and gave Kathie a deadpan stare. "And shooting, Kathie? Just the thought of guns makes my stomach hurt."

Callie wondered what her parents would think about her being at a dude ranch, much less shooting a gun. They'd supported her move, but she knew they missed her. She was an only child, and they'd always treated her more like a mini adult than a child. They'd taught her to play Scrabble when she was eight, and the three of them used to read in the evenings when other kids were watching Nickelodeon. It never even would have occurred to them to vacation at a dude ranch.

Christine went to the window. "Cal, come here."

Callie tried to fall back on the bed again and Kathie and Bonnie dragged her from the bed to Christine. She had to admit, the view was spectacular, and the horses were beautiful, but the serenity she'd thought about downstairs was blown apart by the image of guns and fishing and whatever other crazy things they wanted to torture her with.

"Look how serene it is out there. You can sit on the front porch and read all evening if you want." Christine turned to face her. "All we want is a few hours of each day to get you out of your shell. They have live music at night, campfires, beautiful horses…and every ranch has sexy cowboys."

"Can't I get out of my shell at a real spa, without fish hooks and guns?" She remembered what Wes had said about spiders and snakes, and her stomach plunged again.

"I'll tell you what. Give us twenty-four hours. Just one day of whatever they have planned for us, and if you truly hate it, we'll leave and you can go home and bury your nose in a book and fantasize about Mr. Darcy, Prince Charming, or that *Shades of Grey* guy." Christine's big brown eyes held the hope and love only a best friend's could. She saw the shiny side of a rusty dime, and she brought that positivity to the group. There was no way Callie could turn her down.

"Fine," she relented. "One day." She put her DVD and book back in her bag and carried it to the other bedroom. *A dude ranch.* What the heck was a dude ranch, anyway? She pulled out her computer to research The Woodlands while the girls showered and dressed for the barbecue, and of course, there was no Internet. She pulled out her iPhone. *There's more than one way to skin a cat.*

She typed in the name of the ranch and the search results began to populate. Then stopped. She did it again, and again it stopped. She held the phone up toward the ceiling, hoping for service, and paced the floor. Bonnie returned from the shower wrapped in a thick towel.

"The service here is really spotty, almost nonexistent. They told us that when we registered. Actually, I think their exact words were, *Might as well not even try.* Sorry, Cal." She unpacked her bags while she spoke. "We didn't mean to dupe you."

Callie glared at her.

"Okay, we did, but out of love. When you were in Denver, you had a life. You went to the park; you met us for drinks and to go shopping. And now that we're so far apart, and we're all married…We're worried about you in that little town all by yourself."

If she was honest with herself, Callie would admit that she'd been a little worried, too. She missed her friends, and she missed their nights out. Texting and talking on the phone helped, but they all had husbands, and she knew that when they weren't working, they didn't need her bothering them all the time—sometimes, maybe, but not every night. She was a little lonely, even with her book boyfriends.

"The town is really cute, and the people are nice. I like it there." That much was true. She liked Alice, and the people she'd met in the library—and ogling Wes every week. She hoped that she'd settle in and eventually meet a girlfriend to hang out with, maybe find a place outside to replace her favorite spot at the park in Denver. And when she was really feeling generous with her bucket of hope, she allowed herself to hope Wes might see her as something more than a girl who *knew her books*.

Callie enjoyed the small-town feel of Trusty, maybe even more than she liked Denver. If her friends were there—or if her dreams about Wes ever came true—she would definitely put Trusty ahead of Denver. "It's typical small town, you know? Everyone waves to each other on the street, and in the diner they ask after family members." She shrugged. "It's like they've known each other forever. It's nice and quiet, too, which you know I love."

"Oh yeah, I know. How about guys? Last time we talked, you hadn't really met anyone who was even slightly appealing." Bonnie began brushing her hair. "Well, unless you count that guy you refuse to make a move on."

She thought of Wes and sighed. "He's so out of my league, it's crazy. I've never seen anyone like him, at least not in real life."

Bonnie pointed her brush at Callie. "First of all, no guy is out of your league. You're gorgeous and smarter than all of us put together." She flicked on the hair dryer and yelled over it, "He's really that yummy? So what's the problem?"

Callie shrugged as she unpacked her bags. The reality of having not packed jeans or even shorts and being stuck at a dude ranch settled heavily on her shoulders. "Probably that I turn into a bumbling idiot around him."

"Who's yummy?" Christine came into the room wearing a black shirt with *SINGLE SLAYERS* emblazoned across her chest.

"What is that?" Callie pointed to Christine's shirt.

"They're called boobs." Christine's eyes widened in feigned

surprise as she pointed at Callie's chest. "Look! You have them, too."

"Did I hear yummy?" Kathie joined them, wearing an identical *SINGLE SLAYERS* shirt.

Callie turned, and sure enough, Bonnie wore a matching one. "What the heck is this? Did you hire a guy for me, too?"

"Damn. We should have thought of that," Kathie said. "No. We're just having fun. You're the last single one of us. We're just going to help you cut loose, so you can move forward and slay as many single men as you want."

Callie shook her head. "I am not going anywhere with you dressed like that. You can just forget it."

"Oh, come on. It's all in fun," Kathie urged.

"Slay men? I don't slay men." Callie shook her head. "Nope. I'll leave right now if you plan on wearing those stupid things. You might as well have shirts that say, *Please help us find a man for my loser friend.*"

"First of all, you're definitely not a loser." Kathie whipped her shirt off. "Second of all, this is definitely not a man-seeking mission. This is just the opposite."

Christine and Bonnie took off their shirts and tossed them on the bed. All three of them now stood in their bras and jeans with their hands on their hips, like Charlie's Angels without the guns.

"This is a confidence-building mission so you can take Trusty, Colorado, by storm," Kathie explained.

"Yeah. Then you can go after Mr. Hottie…What's his name again?" Bonnie asked. She picked up her camera and clicked off a shot of the pile of T-shirts. "Gotta have memories."

"Wes. Wes Braden." Her stomach fluttered as she said his name.

Charlie's Angels shared another glance that made Callie sweat. "Oh no. What?"

A loud bell rang in the distance, and Christine gasped. "Calling all fillies! That's the dinner bell. We gotta get dressed, and, Callie, you haven't showered. Hurry."

She ushered Callie toward the bathroom.

THE RUSTIC LODGE was made of logs and stone, with exposed-beam ceilings, hardwood floors, and wooden railings that led up to the guest rooms. The Woodlands had a small staff, including a receptionist, a housekeeper who also helped bartend, a barn manager, and two ranch hands who assisted on outings, cooked, took care of the animals and the ranch, and pitched in just about anywhere they were needed.

Wes greeted a young couple by tipping his Stetson. He amped up the Western hospitality that folks from out of town loved so much. *Howdy, ma'am. Yes, sir. Y'all enjoying your stay?* Then he headed out to the barbecue area by the barn to meet the women he'd be guiding over the next few days. As he crossed the lawn toward the barn, with the sun setting behind the mountains and Sweets trotting by his side, his mind drifted to Callie.

He wondered what she was doing at the spa with her friends. He imagined her dressed primly, sitting poolside and drinking froufrou cocktails. He wondered if she wore a bikini or a one-piece bathing suit. He'd bet his bottom dollar on the one-piece, given all those tiny buttons that ran up the center of the blouse she'd had on that morning. His mind immediately retrieved the image of her nipples becoming taut peaks beneath the sheer white material of her blouse. He had to stop thinking of her like that. She was definitely not the kind of girl who would want him to rip those buttons off with his teeth. He stifled his desirous thoughts as he came to the picnic area.

The twelve-foot barbecue pit was built of indigenous rock at the base of a hill on the east side of the entertainment barn, where the barn dances were held. Wes spotted four women talking to Cutter Long, the barn manager. At twenty-eight, Cutter had a youthful face and a rich tan. In his leather chaps and Woodlands T-shirt, with a perpetually unshaven face, piercing blue eyes, and pitch-black hair he wore a little long, women flocked to him. Wes shook his head at the common sight. The employees knew how he felt about hooking up with guests, and as far as he knew, they respected that thin gray line.

Wes joined Butch Armstrong, one of the ranch hands, by the barbecue pit.

"Hey. Butch. How's it going?" Butch had worked for Wes for six years, since his wife of thirty-seven years passed away. He'd since sold his property in a neighboring town and moved to the lodge full-time. Butch was even-tempered, known for seeing and hearing everything that went on at the ranch, and the spitting image of Ed Harris—nearly cue-ball bald on top with a few sparse white hairs above his ears. He had vibrant and wise blue eyes, weathered skin, and a quiet way about him.

Sweets stood beside him, completely oblivious to the delicious aroma wafting around her.

"Mighty fine evening, Wes." Butch patted Sweets on the head. "Looks like you have a fine group." Butch nodded toward the women talking with Cutter. He added barbecue sauce to the chicken and steaks on the grill. It sizzled and popped from the drippings.

"Smells amazing, like usual." Wes bent down to pet Sweets. "Tonight you're really missing out, Sweets."

"I'm still not used to a dog who can't smell and doesn't beg for food." Butch stirred the vegetables in an iron pot and shifted the foil-wrapped biscuits to the outside of the fire. He took a piece of chicken and set it to the side to cool before holding it out for Sweets to gobble up.

"Thanks, Butch. Time to meet the girls." Wes did a quick visual survey of the women as he approached. Two blondes, two brunettes. All but one wore jeans and boots, the fourth, the petite brunette—*with sweet curves*—wore a moss-green dress that stopped just short of her knees, belted at her narrow waist and accented by a fancy pair of cowgirl boots. Simple. Sexy. *Off-limits.*

Cutter met his gaze and cocked a crooked smile. Over the years, Wes had learned to read Cutter's looks as accurately as Cutter could read his. The way he was eyeing the girl in the green dress told Wes that she was just as hot from the front as from the rear.

"Here's Wes now. Wes, these are your—" The rest of Cutter's introduction was white noise as the women turned to greet Wes. *Callie? Calliope Barnes.* He replayed their earlier conversation. *Spa. Girlfriends. Surprise.*

Holy hell.

Callie's eyes widened and she bit her lower lip. Her fingers began doing the fidgety thing he'd noticed her doing at the library, playing with the fabric of her dress.

Sweets bounded forward.

"Aw, look at the puppy." The blonde with the short, straight hair knelt to pet Sweets. "What's your puppy's name?"

Wes couldn't look away from Callie. "Sweets."

"Sweets? That's her name?" she asked.

"Yeah." Wes was still trying to wrap his mind around the buttoned-up and intricately bunned librarian he knew from the library and the woman before him being one and the same. She looked even more beautiful with her hair framing her face in silky waves and that sexy dress with the open neckline, revealing a path of milky skin that looked good enough to taste. His pulse accelerated at the thought.

"Hi," the other, taller brunette said. "I'm Kathie Sharp. Your ranch is gorgeous."

"Oh, I'm Christine, by the way," the short-haired blonde said as she petted Sweets.

"Oh my God. She's so cute." The other blonde, who had thicker, wavier hair, took pictures of Sweets as she fell to her knees. "I'm Bonnie. She's so cute. I hope you don't mind if I take a few shots."

Sweets rolled over on her back, giving them better access to her belly.

Wes tipped his hat with a nod. "Not at all."

Callie was still nibbling on her lower lip.

"Callie, I didn't expect to see you here." He was damn glad she was there, but equally as worried. How in the hell was he supposed to suppress what he felt every time he saw her? Talking with her for a few minutes in the library wasn't easy, and he'd been lucky that there was always someone there to distract him when he felt himself wanting to reach out and touch her. He'd begun to need a Callie fix on Thursdays the way addicts needed drugs.

"You know each other?" Kathie ran her eyes between them.

"Callie works at the library where I live," Wes explained.

Bonnie gently nudged Callie. "You didn't tell us you knew Wes."

"Yes, I did," she said quietly.

"I guess it's not exactly the spa you were expecting." He wondered why her friends had thought this was a good trip to surprise her with. Callie didn't come across as the adventurous type.

She shook her head and licked her lips, then trapped her lower lip between her teeth again.

Good Lord. You're adorably sexy.

"How old is Sweets?" Christine asked as she rose to her feet.

"Our best guess is around three and a half months. I found her abandoned on a mountain trail."

That earned him a collective *Aw* and drew them all back down to shower Sweets with love and kisses—except for Callie, who was standing still as a statue. The last thing he wanted to do was make her uncomfortable. That wasn't exactly true. He could think of plenty of positions he'd like to put her in that might make her a little uncomfortable, none of which included her being speechless or looking like she wanted an eagle to drop from the sky and swoop her away.

She's off-limits.

Very off-limits.

Wes forced himself to shift his focus away from her and pulled the itineraries from his back pocket.

"These are your itineraries for the week. You'll see that you have plenty of free time, and if you can't, or don't want to, take part in any of the activities, you're welcome to hang out here at the ranch. There's always someone around to talk to." When he handed Callie her copy, she finally released her lip. He didn't think it was possible for her to look even more alluring, but her high cheekbones gave the impression of a slight smile even when he was sure she wasn't trying. Her nose wasn't perky or perfect, but rather plain and small. It enhanced her Cupid-like mouth and full lips, reeling him right in. Callie had thinly manicured brows and slightly wide-set brown eyes, which gave her a refreshing hint of innocence that had drawn him in since the first day he'd met her a month ago and made Wes want to wrap her in his arms and remind her to breathe.

"I'm not staying." Callie dropped her eyes to her fidgeting fingers.

All three of her friends shot her incredulous looks.

"Why?" Wes asked.

She nibbled on her lower lip again and then drew her delicate shoulders back. "I think…"

"Callie, you said you'd give it a day," Kathie reminded her. She touched Wes's arm. "She's just a little surprised because she thought we were taking her to a spa."

That wasn't new information, but the way his heart was hammering against his ribs and the way his mind screamed, *Please don't leave*, was new.

"I hope you'll give it a chance, Callie. The ranch is a lot of fun. We might not have the same accommodations as a spa, but we have a pretty nice lake on the other side of the barn, and we have a hot tub. Even horse wranglers need TLC."

"Hold your horses," Kathie interrupted. "You have a hot tub?"

"Sure. We're not still in the eighteenth century. We just enjoy pretending like we are…most of the time." Wes nodded to the lodge. "Out on the back patio."

Kathie slipped an arm around Callie's shoulders. "See, Cal? A hot tub. And I brought Skinnygirls, so we'll be just fine."

Skinny girls? What the hell are skinny girls? Sweets lay down at Wes's feet and huffed through her nose. Wes shook his head in an effort to stop himself from picturing Callie in the hot tub.

"I'll leave you ladies to enjoy your dinner. The saloon in the entertainment barn is a great place to get to know the other guests, and we've got a local guitarist playing tonight." He patted his thigh. "Come on, Sweets." He would have liked to give Callie a private tour of the hot tub, but she was a guest on his ranch and that made her even more off-limits—and for some strange reason, even more enticing. Since he couldn't even begin to try to think, he forced himself to walk away.

Cutter joined him at the pit. "Need any help on the overnight with this group?" He glanced back at Callie.

Wes's gut clenched. "Not this time. We need you here."

"Yeah, sure. If you change your mind, I'd love a shot."

Wes knew Cutter wanted to take over where Ray left off, but he was hesitant to shift his position. It would mean promoting someone from beneath Cutter to replace him and then retraining at a lower level. Cutter ran the barns as if they were his own. He took care of the animals, kept detailed inventory and budgetary reports, and managed the ranch hands with firm, well-respected authority. Promoting him would leave many of those duties unattended, and unfortunately, retraining another person in those areas would be more difficult than hiring a person to lead the treks. And now, as he watched Cutter stealing peeks at Callie, there was no way in hell he'd let him go overnight with her anywhere—no matter how much he trusted him.

Cutter took another long look at Callie. "Sometimes I hate your rules."

With full plates, they headed to a picnic table. "You know

it's not an official rule. But yeah, sometimes I hate my own rules." Like now, when his mind was playing tricks on him and making him want to coddle a woman instead of fucking her. Hell, he wanted to coddle her and be *intimate* with her. The F-word didn't even sound right in his head where Callie was concerned.

"What's skinny girls?" he asked Cutter.

"What do you mean what's skinny girls? They're girls that are skinny."

Cutter eyed Callie, and it sent a zing of jealousy through Wes.

"She's off-limits," Wes said too gruffly, then tried to cover the jealousy he'd heard in his words. "I think we're missing something with the whole skinny girls thing. Maybe it's code for something else." *I brought skinny girls, so we're all set. What the hell could that mean?* Wes shoveled down his food and headed out to check on the horses with Sweets before he became too tempted to break his own not-a-rule.

Chapter Three

KATHIE LOOPED HER arm through Callie's as they walked back to the cabin after dinner. "You've been holding back on us. Maybe you don't need this trip after all."

Or maybe I need it more than I ever realized. "I thought I was home free when you guys didn't give me an inquisition during dinner. Silly me."

"Girlfriend, we're jonesin' for some details. We just didn't want to embarrass you." Christine took Callie's other hand, essentially trapping her in between her two most inquisitive friends. "Where have you been hiding that delicious man? And exactly why have you been hiding him?"

"He's not mine, remember? I barely know him."

"But you said you did at the cabin," Bonnie reminded her.

They went into the cabin and Kathie grabbed two bottles of Skinnygirl margaritas. "Bon, can you get glasses and we'll go out front and chill for a while?"

"Sure." Bonnie found glasses shaped like horses' heads in the cabinet. "Guess we're drinking from Mr. Ed tonight."

They settled onto rocking chairs on the front porch with their drinks. "It is pretty out here," Callie admitted.

"I personally think the view at The Woodlands is far hotter

than the view in Denver." Christine nodded at two stocky men on horseback riding across the lawn by the lodge.

"Oh yeah." Bonnie grabbed her camera and took a few pictures. "Much hotter."

"Speaking of views—details, Callie. No more stalling." Kathie kicked her feet up onto the porch railing.

Callie looked at her glass. She was a lightweight when it came to drinking, which had come in handy with her friends because they always had a designated driver. Maybe her plan to throw caution to the wind was a good one after all. She guzzled her drink, then set the glass down with a loud, "Ahh."

"Whoa. The details are that good?" Bonnie asked.

Callie shook her head, smacking her tongue on the roof of her mouth to get rid of the sour aftertaste. "Nope. They're that lame. Fill it up if you want me to talk."

"Oh yeah, baby." Kathie refilled her drink and topped off the others'.

"You're going to be disappointed." Callie picked up the glass, tossed back her head, and guzzled the second glass. "Ugh. It tastes so much better when I don't gulp it down."

Christine laughed and patted her on the shoulder. "Don't worry, hon. You'll be numb in a few minutes and won't care about the taste."

"I like it." Kathie refilled Callie's glass.

"So, here goes. He comes into the library every Thursday to pick up books. Three usually, thrillers and biographies." She sipped her drink.

Kathie leaned forward. "And?"

Callie shrugged. "That's it. Told you it was boring. I had no idea he owned this place. I only know a handful of people in town, so it's not like I have the dirt on anyone yet."

"He looked at you like he knew you pretty well," Christine said.

"He looks at all women like that." *Sort of.* There was something very different about the way he looked at her, although in her fuzzy-minded state, she couldn't pinpoint what it was.

Kathie sat back, shaking her head. "Bull. He didn't look at us like that. I think he looked at you like he'd like to know you better."

"Better? *Intimately.*" Bonnie refilled her own glass and topped off the others', then opened the second bottle.

"You guys, I think I know how well we know each other. You saw how I couldn't even talk around him." *Or think. But I can feel. Oh man, can I feel.*

"Yeah, that's not like you, either." Kathie rose and paced the deck. "You might not be the center of the conversation, but you aren't usually so flustered around guys, which either means that you really want him or…" She stood in front of Callie and cocked her head one way, then the other. "Nope, it can only mean you want him." Her mouth spread into a wide smile. "Which means we have a project for the next few days."

"No. Oh no. I live in the same small town as him. It's not like Denver, where you never see the same person twice unless you try to. We are so not doing this." Callie shook her head. Even though she had yet to run into Wes outside of the library, she knew it was just a matter of time. The town was too small for them not to cross paths sooner or later. "You remember when you tried to set me up with Charlie Zucker our freshman year? He turned out to be a real jerk. No way, no how. I don't do setups and definitely not with a guy like him."

"I'd do him in a heartbeat," Kathie said.

"Yeah. Me too," Bonnie agreed.

FATED FOR LOVE

"Sorry, Cal. I would, too." Christine patted Callie's leg.

"You guys are sick. You're all spoken for, and you have great guys. I'd kill to have any one of your men as my boyfriend." She covered her face with her hands. "Ugh!"

"We wouldn't *really* do him; we just mean that you should," Bonnie explained.

Callie sighed loudly.

"Jesus. Why not?" Bonnie asked. "You're both single. He's hot. You're gorgeous."

"Yeah, and you're out here in the wilderness. You could go all Tarzan and Jane with him," Christine said with an eager nod.

"How about…no. Every woman who sees him wants him. I see it every time he walks into the library, and you know a guy like that has been around. I mean, please, what is he? Thirty…something?"

"Oh, who cares? You're not sixteen. He could be fifty and it would be okay," Kathie said.

"You're a little sick, Kath." Bonnie raised her glass with a nod.

Kathie let out a long breath. "You know what I mean. So what if he's a few years older? She's fishing for reasons to stay in her shell, and we're here to drag her out of that shell, remember?" Kathie's gaze softened. "Fine. No setups. Just tell us why you aren't going for him and we'll leave you alone."

Callie looked at their expectant faces and shook her head. "You've known me forever. You know I'm not the kind of girl who makes the first move. I'm barely the girl who makes the hundredth move." *Except in my fantasies, where I let myself go a little wild.* "If he was interested, he would have asked me out." There it was, the truth. She'd been trying to ignore that hurtful

37

nugget for weeks, and now that she'd said it aloud, she had to face it.

"That's bullshit. Guys are clueless most of the time. You have to give him some indication that you like him other than going mute. Let's go to the saloon, loosen up, and strategize." Kathie rose, and Bonnie and Christine followed. "Come on, Cal."

"I don't suppose you'll let me sit and read for tonight?"

The three of them shared another eye roll before Kathie and Christine reached for her hands.

"I think I'm already pretty loose." She followed them across the wooden bridge feeling a little light-headed. "Do you guys hear that? It sounds like someone's singing."

"I hear it. That must be from the barn." Kathie pointed to a group of horses in the distance. "I love how the animals aren't penned up all the time. Don't they look peaceful?"

Callie realized that her friends must have spent a fortune to rent the cabin and pay for her trip. She probably couldn't have afforded it on her own, and they must feel very strongly about wanting her to climb out of her shell—the shell she was quite comfortable in. For her friends, she'd do just about anything, as she knew they'd do for her.

"I'm sorry for being such a dolt, you guys. I really appreciate all you've done. This is wonderful, and it was really sweet of you." Callie opened her arms. "Group hug. Come on in here."

They fell against one another.

"Is this the alcohol talking? Will you still be here when we wake up tomorrow?" Christine asked.

"I said I'd stay for a day, so let's see how tomorrow goes. With Wes as our guide, I'm not sure I'll be able to think, speak, or move."

"Aw. Hon," Bonnie said. "Like Kathie said, we'll figure out a way to get past the stupor that hunky cowboy throws you into. Maybe we'll give you a few shots of vodka in your orange juice each morning." Christine draped her arm over Callie's shoulder.

"Not a bad idea," Kathie agreed.

They followed the sound of singing to the barn. Inside, the saloon was dimly lit and decked out in full Western fashion, with a rustic wooden bar, stools topped with saddles, and several round tables with chairs adorned with faux bullhorns. At the front of the bar, a dark-haired man wearing a cowboy hat played a guitar and sang a Blake Shelton song.

Kathie walked ahead of the others. She spun around with wide eyes and whispered, "Oh my God! Look! A mechanical bull." She pointed to the rear of the bar, where there was a padded ring with a mechanical bull in the center. "I'm so riding that."

"And I'm so taking pictures." Christine held up her phone. "I think the mechanical bull was invented by someone who really wanted to be a dentist, but couldn't make the grade, so he created a contraption that would *knock* your teeth out."

"So I'll wear a mouth guard," Kathie said with a curt nod.

"Mark would love a picture of me lying on it. Wearing lingerie." Bonnie's husband, Mark, was an attorney. To those who didn't know him well, he appeared to be all business with his perfectly coiffed hair and three-piece suits. But Callie and her friends knew and loved the real Mark Young. He could shift from staunch conservative to sexy frat boy in the blink of an eye, and he adored Bonnie, which in their eyes was his most important attribute.

"Smile." Bonnie turned the camera on them.

Callie felt completely out of her element, and all the talk about Wes made her even more nervous about seeing him the next day. She turned to avoid being in the pictures.

"Come on, Callie," Bonnie urged. "We have to do a CD of our trip. We always do."

"Well, I hope you brought a cardboard cutout of me to carry with you, because I'm not getting on that crazy thing." Callie pulled a chair out from a table in the middle of the room, and they settled in. "Although, I have to admit that this place is really cool. I love how everything is so rustic and ranchy."

"Ranchy? Yeah, you totally didn't grow up on a farm." Bonnie leaned across the table. "What's it like living in a farming town, having come from suburbia?"

"I'm going to order drinks so I can drool over the bartender a little." Christine headed to the bar.

Callie shrugged. "Not much different. It's not like I have to get my milk from the dairy farm or anything. It's like a little piece of a larger city, that's all." *Except better because Wes is there.*

Christine returned with drinks, and they talked about Denver and Trusty, their jobs, and their husbands. Callie spent the time watching the door, hoping Wes would suddenly appear, then in the next breath, hoping he wouldn't.

An hour later, Callie was still watching the door and feeling like a loser for doing it. She was enjoying being with her friends, but she needed to get her mind off of Wes or she was going to drive herself crazy.

"If you guys don't mind, I'm going to turn in and read for a while." Callie pushed to her feet, feeling light-headed.

"Want me to go back with you?" Bonnie asked.

"No. I'm fine. Have fun, and I'm really glad you dragged me out. This was fun." *Even if I was distracted.*

The chilly night air brought Callie out of her buzz. She stopped in her tracks at the path toward the cabin. It was pitch-black and reminded her of all the reasons she didn't read thrillers. She looked toward the lodge, where the lights shined brightly against the starry sky, illuminating the lodge in a romantic haze. *Let's see. Creepy path or fairy tale lodge? Easy peasy lemon squeezy.* Callie headed for the lodge instead of going straight back to the cabin.

The interior of the lodge was brightly lit, and like the rest of the buildings, it had a rustic feel. The lobby was outfitted in distressed leather chairs and sofas. There were wooden end tables and a massive glass coffee table with an intricately carved wooden base. Cathedral ceilings and a stairway that curved around a wooden pole gave the lobby an open and airy feel. Callie noticed a sign on the reception desk next to a telephone that read:

Hunkered down for the evening. Emergency? Call #0 and we'll come right out. See y'all in the morning.
The Woodlands Staff.

A wooden placard shaped like an arrow with the word LI-BRARY painted on it pointed down a hallway to her right. Drawn like a horse to water, she followed the hallway to a set of double doors. She pushed the door open just enough to peek inside and see that it was an enormous conference room. She closed the door and continued down the hall to the next room. The door was open, and Callie smiled as she entered the small library with inviting armchairs and plush carpeting. She was drawn to the bookshelves. With her head tilted to the right, she scanned the titles of thrillers, biographies, women's fiction titles, and of course, books about horses and all things pioneering. She wondered if Wes had chosen the books. Her mind wandered as she began organizing the books, first by subject matter, then by author. It was a habit that soothed her nerves, which had been bundled into knots all day. Callie was crouched on the floor, organizing the last few books on the bottom shelf, when two familiar, scuffed boots and a pair of jeans-clad legs came into view, followed by a pair of brown paws and a wet tongue on her cheek. She drew in a deep breath and Wes's masculine scent, mixed with hint of puppy, filled her lungs.

She felt his hand on her shoulder, and a flash of heat seared through her entire body. There was no way she could stand on burned legs. Surely they'd crumble under her weight. She remained there, crouching by the bookshelves, silently taking one deep breath after another and telling herself, *He's just another guy.*

Wes crouched beside her, one knee to the ground; the other thick thigh grazed her back. "You're supposed to be on vacation." His breath was hot across her cheek, his voice deep and sensuous.

Callie looked at him, and those darn butterflies took flight in her stomach again. Wes was definitely not just another guy.

"Sorry," she managed. "Habit."

He slid his dark eyes to the books, then back to her. "There are worse habits to have." He rose to his feet and held out a hand to help her up.

Callie stared at his hand for a beat. She finally set her hand in his, and he closed his big, rough, calloused fingers around it and lifted her to her feet. Her heart galloped in her chest, which made her cheeks flush.

"Enjoying your stay so far?"

She sighed dreamily—she couldn't help it. Every damn thing about him, from his sensuous voice to his chocolate-brown eyes and his too-hot-to-think-about body, made her go weak. *Oh, hell.* She had to pull herself together. It was now or never. She couldn't spend the next twenty-four hours acting like a silly fan girl. She drew in another deep breath...of him. If he hadn't been holding her hand, she'd have crumpled back down to the floor.

"Yeah, it's really peaceful here." She couldn't believe it. She was actually talking, breathing, standing...and he still held her hand.

"I like to think so. Your friends really pulled a fast one on you. Are you okay with this?"

She looked down at their hands, and his eyes followed. When he let go, she missed his touch and wanted it back.

"They meant well," she said.

He glanced at the books again. "Were you looking for a book? I have a few that a friend picked out for me." He smiled, and it set her body on fire again.

"No, I just...I'm just sort of drawn to them. I can't pass a bookshelf without stopping to look." Her pulse quickened, and she worried her ability to speak might be short-lived. "I should probably get back to my cabin."

"I'll walk you out. It's pretty dark by the cabins." He patted his thigh, and Sweets trotted along beside him.

"Do you bring Sweets with you everywhere?"

He smiled down at the loyal dog. "Yup. I can't stand to think about her alone after what she went through before I found her. I can only imagine how scared she must have been, and I never want her to feel that way again. I want her to know she can count on me, you know?"

"Yeah." Her breathy voice took her by surprise. She knew exactly what he meant, and she wished he'd found *her* out on the trail.

Once they were outside, Callie filled her lungs with the crisp night air and breathed a little easier, despite her churning insides. They descended the hill at a lazy pace.

"I was surprised to see you. Your application said Calliope Barnes, and I never put two and two together. I don't think I even knew your last name before today. I'm glad you're here, though."

You are?

His eyes were warm and honest, and one look at them nearly stole her ability to speak again. She forced words from her lungs to keep the flow of oxygen moving.

"Calliope is my given name. I have no idea why my friends put my full name, but…an application? We had to apply to come here?"

"Yeah. Everyone does. That way we know about experience levels, medical concerns, that kind of thing. Your group is pretty experienced. You all did high school sports and have been hiking and riding for years, so you shouldn't have any trouble."

If by hiking he meant walking from one end of her college campus to another, she was very experienced, but hiking in the woods? Never. Not once. Not even close. She should fess up to her lack of experience, but she was enjoying his company too much to inflict something that would only spark a discussion about either how lame she was or how her friends had lied on the application—neither of which was worth ruining what little time she had in his company.

"Did you always want to be a librarian?"

"Pretty much. I spent a lot of time in the library in elementary school, after school, when I'd wait for my parents to pick me up, that sort of thing. Every day I'd choose a new book, read a few chapters, and disappear for a while." She smiled at the memory, realizing her nerves were finally, thankfully, settling down.

"How about you? Did you always want to own a dude ranch?" *Dude ranch.* The term made her smile.

"I don't know. I was an adventure guide for a few summers, but I missed the animals. My partner, Chip, and I grew up together and went to college together. With a double major in engineering and biology, I was in this strange place with degrees in fields that I was really interested in but that didn't really complement each other. I couldn't be strapped to a desk—that much I knew—and field research wasn't really my thing. One night Chip and I were talking about what we *really* wanted to do for a living." He shrugged. "We both wanted jobs we would enjoy, you know? We love animals, and we love ranching and the outdoors, but we wanted to build something, too. Something that we'd be excited about years from now." An easy smile formed on his lips. "My cousin Treat owns resorts all over the world and lives over in Weston. He knew Chip and I were debating opening a ranch, and when this property came on the market, he told me about it. Two months later, Chip and I owned nine hundred acres. That was eight years ago."

"And do you still wake up happy to go to work?"

"So far so good. My sister, Emily, is an architect, and she designed the lodge, the cabins, the whole deal. She's since opened a design-build firm, but we were her first client, so the whole place means even more to me."

She loved knowing his sister designed the property and that this wasn't something he bought and continued but something he and his friend had conceptualized and brought to fruition. He was much more than the adrenaline junkie she'd thought he was.

"Hey, are you too tired to take a walk? I'd like to show you something."

Sleeping was the last thing on her mind. "No. I'd love to."

He put his hand on her lower back and guided her up a hill, past outcroppings of rock and through a path in the woods. Her eyes finally adjusted to the darkness as they moved around trees and over rocks and sticks. Focusing on moving forward instead of concentrating on how good his hand felt against her back was a good distraction.

"I come out here sometimes." He led her deeper into the woods. "Do you have any place that you go to be alone?"

"Well, in Trusty, I don't really know anyone yet, so there's no need to go anywhere, but back in Denver, where I'm from, there was this park I would go to on Saturday afternoons. I'd sit and read for hours." She hadn't been there in ages, and she wondered if there was a similar place in Trusty.

"I can see you doing that—reading for hours, I mean."

They came to a mountainous boulder, and Sweets put her paws up on the side of it.

"Doesn't she ever bark?"

"Not much. I think she probably barked a lot when she was left alone on the trail, because she was hoarse when I found her, but she's never barked much around me." He placed a hand on her shoulder. "Give me a sec." Wes scaled the boulder in three easy steps, then crouched and reached for her hand.

"Take my hand. I'll help you up."

She looked down at her boots and back at the boulder. "I'm not very good at climbing. Or heights." She looked up and swayed backward, dizzied by the sight.

"You don't have to climb. I'll lift you up, and I promise not to let you fall."

His confidence and eager reach curtailed her fear and made her want to touch him again. With her stomach twisting in knots, she took a deep breath, closed her eyes, and thrust a shaky hand up toward his. He grasped it tightly, and in one swift move, she was on top of the boulder—and folded in his powerful arms. His chest was just as hard as she imagined it would be, and—*oh gosh*—she could feel his heart pounding against her knuckles as she clutched his shirt for dear life.

"Callie, I've got you," he said in a calm, soothing tone. "Open your eyes."

No, thanks. I'll just stay right here plastered against you and pretend we're on the ground. She shook her head and felt him lowering them both to a seated position. His arms remained around her, holding her pressed to his side.

"Better?"

If I say yes, will you let me go? She had a death grip on his shirt, and she wasn't taking any chances. "Still a little nervous."

"Okay. We'll just sit here until you feel safe."

"I do feel safe," she admitted before she could stop herself.

"You just said you were nervous."

With eyes still closed, she answered, "I am nervous, but I also feel safe."

"Fair enough." He kept her close. "You know those books you give me each week? Sometimes I read them right here on this rock, when I'm taking a break or just need a few minutes to breathe."

Breathe? Oh yeah, almost forgot. She gasped a deep breath, forcing herself to try to breathe normally again. Nope. She'd have to settle for simply breathing, even if shallow and thick with desire.

"I really appreciate that you take the time to choose books for me. Not many people would do that."

She opened her eyes at that. She thought of the way he'd asked her to collect books for him all those weeks ago, as if the person who had held the position before her had been doing it forever. "Didn't the last assistant do it?"

He laughed and drew one knee up. "Patricia Olson? No. Never."

"Really?" She realized she was still clutching his chest and dropped her hand to her lap. As long as she didn't look down, she'd be okay. Maybe.

"Do you do that for everyone?"

She considered lying, but she had never been a good liar. "No. Just you."

He smiled, and it sent her pulse wild again.

"Just me?"

"Yeah."

He nodded at that, and she wondered what he was thinking. The silence stretched between them. Every second felt hotter than the last. She tried to fill the gap.

"You don't have to hold me. As long as I don't look down, I'll be okay."

"You sure?" He held her tighter.

No. "Yeah. I think so."

He took his hands off slowly. "You okay?"

She nodded, though she wished she hadn't said she was okay.

"You don't really have a lot of outdoor experience, do you?"

"Only if you count all the time I've spent in the park." She fidgeted with her dress.

"This should be interesting."

He said it with an arc of amusement in his voice that made her stomach lurch again—and made her want to prove she could do it. *Or run away.* Maybe running away was better.

"I'm sorry they lied on the application, but I won't stay and ruin it for everyone." She pushed to her feet and stumbled toward the edge of the boulder with a shriek. He shot to his feet and caught her, and in the next second, she was wrapped in his arms again.

"I've got you," he assured her.

Panting and clutching his shirt—and a handful of muscular pecs—she looked up at him and stumbled backward a step.

"Stop. Don't move."

She froze at the seriousness in his voice. He took a step backward, bringing them both away from the edge.

"Okay, now take a deep breath."

She did. Then another.

"Callie, I don't care that you're inexperienced. I meant it would be fun to help you learn what you need to know, but you can't react like that out here. You could really hurt yourself."

He used his finger to tip her chin up until she had no choice but to meet his gaze, which sucked her right in. She felt like putty waiting to be touched, molded, *taken.*

"Okay?"

"Okay."

He stared down at her, and she wondered if the heat of their embrace sent the same lustful rush through him as it did through her. She was suddenly certain he could feel—or see— how much she wanted him to lower his mouth to hers. Just one kiss. One kiss would calm her nerves, satiate her greedy desire.

"I shouldn't have brought you up here." His eyes darted away.

And just like that, her hopes deflated. *I'm an idiot.* How could she respond to that? She'd blown any chance she had with him. Not that she'd had any chance to begin with, but she'd thought—*hoped*—that his bringing her here was a sign of something more.

"Why…did you?" She had to ask. She had to know.

"I'm not really sure. We were talking, and it felt right to share this place with you."

"Then you realized I'm afraid of heights and socially moronic around you? I could have saved you lots of time." She pushed away from him, stumbled backward, then clutched for him again.

"Sorry. Sorry." *I have to leave. Forget staying a day. I need to call a cab and get the heck out of here tonight. Maybe out of Trusty, too.*

"What? No. Neither of those things." He lifted her face again, and this time there was no misreading his annoyed and slightly angry dark eyes. "I meant *on top of this boulder.* Christ, Callie. You're afraid of heights. Why'd you let me pull you up here?"

Because you're hot and I'm stupid. She swallowed her words and dropped her gaze.

"God, I'm an idiot." He lowered her to a seated position again. "Don't move. Don't stand. In fact, don't breathe for a second, okay?"

She managed a nod at his careful command as he climbed down the boulder, stopping midway. He held his hands toward her, and she wondered how the hell he wasn't falling backward, because she definitely would have.

"Callie, scoot forward on your butt. Don't stand up." Another command.

She scooted forward, and when her feet were inches from the edge, her heart raced again. Goose bumps chased the hair on her arms upright, and she stopped cold.

"I...can't."

"Just get your legs off the edge, and I'll take you down."

"How about...you leave me here and come back with a ladder. Or firemen. Yes, firemen would be even better. Three, please."

He cracked a smile. "Firemen? To climb down an eight-foot boulder?"

"Hundred foot. Not eight. There's no way it's only eight feet, and I'm not going to look over the edge to find out, but I remember. It's at least fifty." She crossed her arms to keep him from seeing her tremble.

"Look me in the eyes, Callie."

She did, feeling embarrassingly silly.

"Do you trust me?" he asked with a soft, thoughtful gaze.

She nodded.

"Can you come a little closer? I promise I won't let you fall. You can even pretend I'm a fireman."

She laughed a little and bit her lip again.

"You're incredibly cute when you do that."

Cute? Cute! "You find scared women attractive?" She scooted forward, and he grabbed her just above her knees, on the bare skin below her dress, sending another shot of warmth to her naughty parts.

He let out a soft laugh under his breath. "I find attractive women attractive." Their eyes met and held for a hot second. "I..." He shook his head and his eyes grew serious again. "I need to get you down from here."

"I can stay right here. Really. If I lay back and don't move, I'll be okay."

He sighed, and she realized that he was probably wishing he'd never run into her.

She closed her eyes. "Okay, tell me what to do."

"If you scoot forward a little more, I can get a good grip on you and carry you down. You're safe with me, Callie."

She scooted forward with her eyes closed, trusting him as he gripped her hips and lowered her against him. She wrapped her arms around his neck, and in two of his giant steps, they were on level ground again.

"You can open your eyes now."

"No, I can't," she said in a croaky voice. *When I open them, I have to unlock my arms and pull away, and you feel way too good to do that.* She felt him shake his head, and she forced herself to open her eyes. Oh boy. There was no misreading the desire in his eyes or trapped behind his zipper, which was currently pressing against her belly. For another hot second they stared into each other's eyes, before he pulled back and stepped from her embrace.

"Come on. I'll make sure you get home safely."

She couldn't move as the reality of his pulling away struck her. *He pulled away.* She definitely needed to leave.

They walked in silence out of the woods with Sweets beside them, and Callie felt him distancing himself even further, which didn't surprise her in the least. She knew she was far from his type, and she'd just spent their time together proving it.

As they crossed the bridge, she forced her thoughts into words. "I'm sorry, Wes. I'm sorry they lied. I'm sorry I freaked out back there. I just—"

He took a deep breath and blew it out slowly, stopping halfway across the bridge and pinning her in place with a piercing stare. "Callie, you didn't do anything wrong. So you're afraid of heights?" He shrugged, and something else flashed in his eyes before he shifted them away.

Desire.

Oh Lordy. I must be dreaming.

He shoved his hands in the pocket of his jeans and looked in the direction of her cabin. "Come on. We've got an early ride tomorrow. You'd better get some rest." He stopped at the bottom of the porch stairs, hands still deep in his pockets. His eyes darted to the dark cabin, then back to the trail, everywhere but at Callie.

She got the message loud and clear. "Thanks, Wes." She took a step toward the stairs and felt Wes's hand gently touch her arm. She turned and found his dark brows knitted together. He was leaning forward, as if he'd been intent on kissing her or whispering in her ear. She hoped for the first.

"Callie," he said just above a whisper.

He felt it, too. He had to, regardless of the conflicting messages he was sending. She saw it in his eyes, felt it in the heat that swirled around them, sending shivers down her back. Her lips parted in anticipation. His Adam's apple jumped as he swallowed, then licked his lips. His mouth was a breath away from hers.

A light flicked on in the cabin, and his eyes shifted to the door.

He looked down at Sweets, sitting beside his feet, then back at Callie. With a nod, he turned and walked away, leaving Callie to stumble up the stairs, wondering what the hell just happened.

Chapter Four

FRIDAY MORNING WES paced his cabin floor, beating himself up for taking the walk in the woods with Callie. He'd liked talking with her and hearing about why she'd become a librarian, and once she'd begun to relax, he'd enjoyed being with her even more. It felt natural to share his most private place with her, the spot he'd never shared with anyone. *Christ.* He'd made a big mistake. Seeing her as the shy, intriguing girl who picked out his reading material went right out the door. One look in her sultry dark eyes and he'd lost his ability to think clearly. Suddenly, he'd felt the soft pillows of her breasts pressed against him and the curve of her hips filling his palms. He'd smelled her fresh, feminine scent, and that was it. He was a goner. If that damn light hadn't turned on, he would have taken her in a kiss that would have led to God only knew what else. He needed to get his emotions in check before the trail ride today.

The trail ride presented another issue. He had a feeling she had no experience on horseback, and given that she nearly climbed under his skin at the height of the boulder, he had concerns about how she'd do riding a horse.

A few minutes later, he and Sweets headed down to the

stables, where Cutter had already saddled the horses and packed the supplies for their ride. Usually Wes joined their guests in the saloon at the end of the trail ride, but this morning, with the sun high in the sky and the crisp mountain air promising a warm day, his gut clenched at the thought. He wasn't sure he'd be able to hold himself together when he was near Callie without everyone else seeing how she turned him on. He didn't trust himself to be around her in a situation where they were drinking. He'd need all of his mental faculties in order to keep from reaching out to her. There was no way he'd be at the saloon tonight.

He heard Cutter's voice before he saw him come around the side of the barn.

"Here you go, ladies. Your wrangler awaits you." Cutter waved to Wes.

Bonnie's camera hung from her shoulder like an extra limb. She, Kathie, and Christine all wore shorts and sleeveless shirts with the telltale signs of bikini straps tied around their necks. Callie wore a short skirt and—*sweet Jesus*—a bright blue bikini beneath a blousy white top that stopped just above her waist, revealing two inches of toned stomach sweet enough to eat off of.

Wes shifted his eyes to Cutter, who raised his brows in quick succession before heading into the barn. He cleared his throat in an effort to concentrate on something other than running his hands up Callie's thighs and tasting every inch of her. He settled his hat on his head to distract himself from the thought.

Focus on the activity and do your damn job.

"Good morning, ladies. Ready for the trail?"

Callie's eyes were trained on the ground.

"You know it." Kathie's hair was pulled up into a high ponytail. She walked up to Chestnut, a red-coated mare, and
stroked her side. "Can I just climb up?"

"In a minute." He hated to embarrass Callie, but after last
night, he needed to know exactly how much experience she had.
He no longer trusted a damn thing on her application. "Have
all of you ridden before?"

"I grew up on a farm." Bonnie wiggled her fingers in the air.

"I had a thing for cowboys at a young age. Riding lessons at
six years old." Christine adjusted her red sun visor on her
forehead.

"Me too," Kathie said. "Plenty of experience."

*Just what I thought. Callie is the only one with little or no
experience.* "Callie?"

Her cheeks flushed, and she nibbled her lip again. Damn it.
Why did he want to hold her every time she did that? The way
her girlfriends watched her with bated breath, as if they'd all
stopped breathing in anticipation of her answer, didn't escape
him.

"I've ridden," she said quietly.

Right. Never ridden a day in your life. Great. If she'd mentioned that last night, he could have given her a private lesson,
but now he'd have to take her at her word or risk embarrassing
her further.

"Super. Why don't you take Chance?" He patted the white
horse with black spots. "She's a gentle girl."

Callie drew her shoulders back. "Which one is the least
gentle?"

Bonnie stepped closer to her. "What are you doing?"

"I don't need the most gentle horse." Callie held Wes's
stare.

That would be Glory, and there's no way in hell you're riding her. He nodded to a brown mare. "That would be Jazz." What the hell was she trying to prove?

"Okay, Christine, you'll be on Flash, and, Bonnie, you can take Brownie. It looks like Kathie's already made friends with Chestnut." Wes glanced at Kathie, who had her cheek pressed against the horse's neck.

"Brownie. Yum." Bonnie brushed her hair from her face and went to Brownie's side.

"Today we'll be riding up the mountain. We'll take it at a nice, slow pace so you can enjoy the views. We'll be stopping for lunch by a creek, and then we'll head back. There are riding helmets right inside the barn, and if you have to use the ladies' room, I suggest you do it now."

"Oh, bathroom. Good idea." Kathie put her hands on her hips. "Anyone care to join me?"

Bonnie and Christine flashed quick smiles at Callie and followed Kathie into the barn. Wes had a feeling he and Callie were being set up, which meant that she had told her friends about their little trip into the forest last night. *Fucking perfect.*

He came around Chance's side and found Callie fiddling with the stirrup. "Hey."

"Hi." The bravado she'd shown in front of the others was gone, and shy Callie was back in full adorable blush.

"Listen, Callie, I hope I didn't make you uncomfortable last night. I'm sorry I took you up on the boulder. I should have picked up on your hesitation, and…" *I'm sorry I almost kissed you.* Only he wasn't sorry. He still wanted to kiss her.

"I'm fine, Wes."

She took a step toward the back of the horse and he grabbed her arm. She whipped her head around.

"When's the last time you were around a horse?" He held her arm tightly as she tried to pull away.

"Why?"

"Because if you walk behind even the most docile horse, you take a chance of being kicked into tomorrow." He closed the gap between them and lowered his voice. "Callie, I can delay the trail ride and give you a quick lesson. Twenty minutes, that's all it'd take."

She pressed her lips together, and he could see her contemplating a response. She looked down at his hand gripping her arm and he released her.

"Safety first, okay?" Goddamn it. He wanted to protect her from getting hurt, like he would any guest, but the way she was looking at him, like she was angry and hurt all at once, nearly brought his arms around her again—and that was *nothing* like he felt toward other guests.

She sighed. "I've ridden once, okay? A pony at a county fair. On a lead. But how different can this be?"

He was glad she trusted him enough to be honest. "Night and day. Do your friends know?" He shoved his hands in his pockets to keep from reaching out to her again.

She nodded.

"Great. Then give me twenty minutes. Please. I don't want you to get hurt, okay?"

She rolled her eyes and he knew he'd won. She took a step toward the horse's rear again and he took her by the shoulders and turned her around. Callie was too smart to have forgotten the recent directive, which meant he had the same effect on her that she had on him.

He liked that. He liked it a lot.

Ten minutes later, Christine, Kathie, and Bonnie sat on the

fence watching as Wes gave Callie a quick lesson in horse etiquette.

"Okay, before we begin, are there any other surprises I should know about?"

Callie fidgeted with the stirrup. "I told you in the library that I didn't like deep water, or heights, or spiders, snakes, or—"

"Christ, you did." He shook his head. "I'm sorry. I should have known that you wouldn't like being on top of the boulder. I won't make the same mistake again." He explained what each piece of equipment was used for and talked to her about using her body to give the horse direction. "Remember, a sharp kick will send her running, and she'll pick up on subtle movements like pressure with one leg harder than the other, leaning, and easing or tightening of the reins."

"I've got it. Okay."

He lowered his voice and leaned in close. "Callie, are you sure? If you're nervous, the horse will pick up on it, and you'll be more likely to make sudden movements."

She pressed her lips together. "I'm fine." She'd show them that she could do more than read books or be the girl who *knows her books.*

"Okay, let's get you on the horse." He looked down at her thin cotton skirt. "You sure you don't want to put on jeans or even shorts?"

"I didn't bring any."

"You didn't—"

She rolled her eyes again. "They said we were going to a spa, remember? And they offered to share, but I'm smaller, so…"

"What size do you wear?"

She pressed her lips together like he should know better than to ask that question.

"What is it with women and sizes? If you said twenty-eight or two it wouldn't mean anything to me. I was just going to see if one of the women on my staff had a pair you could borrow."

"I'm a petite four and no, thank you. I'm fine. It's not like anyone's going to be looking up my skirt."

He felt his lips curl up and she pushed his chest playfully. Oh yeah, he was totally in over his head. Even that little touch had his groin tightening.

"ARE YOU GOING to get on the horse today?" Kathie hollered.

"Trying," Callie answered. Last night, when she'd finally gone inside, her friends had bombarded her with questions. She'd been too upset to tell them much, and admitting that she'd recognized the moment when Wes had gone from considering kissing her to putting space between them had shifted her mind-set. She'd be damned if she was going to be a weak girl who fawned over some guy. That's how she was able to stand firm and demand a tougher horse.

Now, as she lifted a foot to the stirrup and tried to hoist herself up in the way the girls had told her to during their how-to-ride-a-horse lecture this morning, she promptly faltered and landed back on the ground with a *thud*.

Without a word, Wes's hands found her hips and lifted her easily into the saddle.

So much for standing firm.

"Okay?"

Oh, heck yeah. Maybe I should fall off again just so you'll do that again. "I could have done it."

He leaned in close, one hand on the thing that stuck up in the front of the saddle—dangerously close to her crotch—and the other on the back of the saddle. "I know you could have, but your friends sounded anxious to get started."

Callie imagined that low, husky voice saying her name in a dark bedroom. She looked away to avoid embarrassing herself any further, and Kathie gave her a thumbs-up.

Being up on the horse wasn't so bad. It had a wide, stable back, and Callie was surprised at how confident she felt. Wes settled the reins in her hands and kept one hand on her thigh.

"Remember what I said about not pulling back too hard. Nice, easy movements. She'll take her cues from you." He looked down at his hand on her leg. "You're shaking. Do you need more time?"

It's from your hand, not the horse. "I'm okay."

"I'm going to take a step back, and you can lean forward a little to give her a cue to walk, and remember, not too—"

"Ow!" Callie jerked her heels back and leaned to the side to swat at something on her leg. It stung her again, and as she jerked her heels back again, the horse took off running.

"Help!" She was flying—literally. Her butt lifted off of the saddle as the horse bolted across the pasture.

She heard Wes and the girls yelling, but she had no idea what they were saying. Her mind was screaming, *Holy shit! Holy Shit! I'm going to die!* She tried to remember what to do, and when the horse turned and headed back toward the barn at full speed, she just held on tight and screamed some more. They flew by the barn so fast her friends were a blur. She saw Wes mounting a horse as Jazz took another lap. Tears streaked her cheeks. She dug her heels into the horse's side in an effort to keep from falling off, which made the horse run faster. In the next breath, Wes's horse was neck to neck with Jazz. Wes was in complete control, while she was hysterical, clutching the saddle for dear life and praying she didn't die as they sped around the arena.

"Pull back on the reins, lower yourself to the saddle, and relax your legs," he hollered.

"I...can't." It was all she could do to hold on to the reins and the leather thing that stuck up in the front of the saddle. She tried to sit back down, but it was a futile effort. She popped back up every time the horse's hooves hit the ground.

The horses rounded the curve and began the long run back toward the barn again. Wes leaned toward her, his arms outstretched. His eyes were locked on Callie.

"Let go and lean toward me."

"No!" *Are you freaking crazy?*

"Callie, I've got you."

"Hell no!" She gripped the saddle for dear life. Suddenly Wes's big, strong hands clutched her waist.

"Let go!" A command.

She slammed her eyes shut, released the reins, and in the next breath she was suspended in midair. She landed hard on his horse, and her eyes shot open.

"Hang on to me!" With one powerful arm wrapped around her middle, he grasped the reins and the horse slowed its pace.

Callie could barely breathe. Tears streaked her face, and her heart beat so fast she thought she was going to pass out. Wes's heart thundered against her back; his thighs were pressed to the outside of hers.

"You're okay, Callie. I've got you. You're safe," he said in a low, confident voice that reassured her.

She saw her horse walking at the other end of the arena, and it made her cry harder.

"Callie!" Kathie yelled as Wes guided the horse back toward the barn.

"Oh my God!" Christine said, clutching Bonnie's arm. "Oh my God. Oh my God."

"Shh. She's okay. God, Callie, you're okay." Bonnie reached up and touched Callie's leg. "Wes, Jesus, thank you."

Even after the horse stopped, Wes didn't loosen his grip around her. It was all she could do to keep breathing as she tried to calm her racing pulse and stop the flow of tears.

"I've got you," he whispered against her cheek. "You're okay. Breathe, Callie. Just breathe. You don't have to do anything else. I've got you."

She focused on his reassurance and let out a breath. Without thinking, Callie sank back against him. He was big and strong, safe and warm. So warm. She closed her eyes and tuned out everything except his calming heartbeat. She'd never been so scared in all her life, and she'd never felt so safe in someone's arms.

"Oh my God. I was so scared." Kathie came to the side of the horse. "Thank God you're okay. Thank Wes, actually. We'll skip the trail ride."

"No." Callie opened her eyes. It was a gut reaction, and she had no idea what she was thinking. There was absolutely no way she'd climb onto another horse, but she wasn't going to be the cause of a ruined day after everything her friends had done for her. "No. I'm not ruining this trip for you guys. No way."

"Callie, it's only a horseback ride. We don't have to—"

Wes cut Bonnie off. "She can ride with me."

Callie froze.

Kathie was the first to crack a smile.

"Really?" Christine asked. "You don't mind having sweet, sexy Callie between your legs?"

"Christine!" Bonnie chided her.

Wes shook his head. "If Callie's okay with riding with me, I'm fine with it. I don't want her on a horse by herself until I have a chance to work with her." He lowered his mouth to just beside her ear again. "Are you okay enough for me to bring you down off the horse?"

No. Please keep holding me. Forever. One look at her friends' worried faces brought a nod of her head.

"I'm going to get off the horse and help you down. Don't flinch. Don't kick. Don't scream. Don't…breathe." He slid his hand around her waist and trailed it across her back as he dismounted, one hand on her at all times. From the ground, he settled his hands on her waist and lifted her off the horse.

She held tightly to his wrists.

"Okay?" He searched her eyes.

She nodded, feeling a million things—hot, flustered, embarrassed, still a little scared, but definitely not okay yet.

"You must have kicked her with your heels." He sounded as if he were working out the logistics of what happened. His hands were still on her hips, his eyes full of compassion.

"Something bit me." She looked down at a swollen red bite on her leg. Her pulse was finally calming down.

"Oh, hon, didn't you put on the bug spray I gave you?" Christine took her hand. "We'll be right back. I just want to clean her up and make sure she's okay." She guided her toward the barn and whispered, "Holy shit. That was brilliant!"

Callie glared at her.

Kathie and Bonnie ran after them, leaving Wes alone. Callie

was still in a frightened fog. She looked over her shoulder, wanting to be back in his arms.

"Did you see him? That was like the hottest thing I've ever seen. He fricking rescued you." Kathie's eyes were wide as she pushed the bathroom door open.

"*Hot* isn't the word for him." Bonnie wrapped Callie in her arms. "Oh, honey, you're shaking all over."

"I almost died on that horse, and then he…He's like the Lone Ranger, and after last night?" She buried her face in her hands. "I'm mortified."

"Oh, hon. He probably goes through this stuff all the time. Really. Did you see how easily he did it? The man didn't hesitate. He knew exactly what to do." Christine hugged her. "We don't have to take the trail ride."

"Yeah, we can totally skip it," Bonnie agreed.

Callie lowered her hands from her face. "Skip it? I'm mortified, not stupid." A smile spread across her lips. "No way am I missing out on riding up the trail with him."

"Ha!" Kathie clapped her hands together. "That's my girl!"

"So our pep talk last night worked?" Bonnie asked.

"Sort of. I just…You guys, I really like him, and not like you guys do, where all you think about is how sexy he is. I mean, yeah, there's that, but…" She sighed and grabbed a tissue from the sink to pat the tears from her cheeks. "He's…"

"Total alpha badass male," Kathie said.

"Sexy as hell," Bonnie added.

"Looks at you like you're dessert all wrapped up in a pretty little package?" Christine offered.

"Sweet."

"Sweet?" they asked in unison.

Callie shrugged. "I think so." She knew he was a badass, and of course he was sexy as hell. She'd have to be blind not to see that. *Sweet* wasn't a reflection of what she saw; it was the person he was, his very nature. He was a caring and compassionate man, and to Callie, that was much more important than sexy or badass ever would be. Sexy and badass could turn her on, but caring and compassionate could love her through sickness and gray hair and look past a few extra pounds. A compassionate man would want to help her through the harsher aspects of life and make her strong enough to deal with them in case he wasn't around when she stumbled upon them. Yes, Callie had no doubt: Wes was a deeper man than just a sexy badass, and she'd made up her mind. She was staying for the duration of the trip to get to know him better.

Chapter Five

THERE WAS ONE thing Wes hadn't taken into consideration when he offered to let Callie ride with him up the trail—how uncomfortable the ride would be with a hard-on. Hell, who was he kidding? There were at least a dozen things he hadn't considered, like how there was no way in hell he'd be able to hide from the intense feelings he had for her, but when the horse took off with her, his heart had leaped into his throat, and once he had her safely in his arms, he didn't want to let go.

She stopped trembling about fifteen minutes into the trail ride, and he was surprised that she wasn't freaking out by the way the mountain fell away to the right in ripples of yellow flowers, outcroppings of rocks and brush, interspersed with occasional pine trees. The view never failed to take Wes's breath away, and it was even more beautiful with Callie pressed up against him. He reached around her and pointed at a creek up ahead and just off to their left.

"That's where we're going to stop for lunch." The creek was about fifty feet wide, and Wes knew that it ran fairly deep in the center. The shoreline was covered with leaves and a few large rocks. The tree line stopped about ten feet from the shore, giving them plenty of space to sit and enjoy their break in the warm afternoon sun.

"Sorry I'm such trouble," Callie answered.

It was that sweet, caring side of her, he realized, that made her so different from the women he was used to. She wasn't feigning helplessness, and she was far from helpless. She was trying to keep up with her friends in an unfamiliar world with her pride intact, and he respected the hell out of her for it.

"You're no trouble at all." He held the reins in one hand and tightened his arm around her waist. "We're going to move up this hill, so hold on."

She gripped his forearm as they climbed the slight incline with Sweets trotting along beside them.

He glanced over his shoulder and found the others smiling and happy, riding along like they'd been born on horseback. He wondered what Callie's life was like when she was growing up and what her parents were like. Did she have these fears because of past experiences, or had she never been given the chance to face the things that scared her? Had they gotten blown out of proportion in her mind? He hoped he'd get to know her well enough to find out.

At the creek, they dismounted and stretched from the long ride.

"I haven't been on a trail ride for so long. I forgot how freeing it feels." Bonnie came to Callie's side. "What did you think?"

"Breathtaking."

Callie flashed Wes a smile that made his stomach do something weird. He focused on filling a water bowl for Sweets, then walked the horses over to the creek while Callie's friends *ooh*ed and *aah*ed over the views. He noticed that Callie stayed far back from where the mountain sloped. Sweets hurried over to her and rubbed against her leg. Callie held on to a tree as she crouched to pet her.

"Cal, come look at the pastures in the valley. They're incredible." Kathie held a hand out toward Callie.

"I can see from here." Callie remained beside Sweets, and Sweets ate up the attention, rolling onto her back with her legs pointed up toward the sky and her tongue lolling from her droopy lips. "You like that, huh, girl?"

He knew he shouldn't eavesdrop, but he loved hearing her with Sweets, and he wondered what she had to say about their ride up the mountain—and about him.

Kathie crouched beside Callie. "Are you sure you're okay?"

"Mm-hm."

"The creek's beautiful. Let's lay out in the sun." Kathie rose and pulled Callie to her feet.

Callie's eyes shifted toward the slope of the mountain, and Wes could tell by the way she threw her hands behind her and latched on to a tree that she'd gotten a good look at the miles of space between where they stood and the mountain range across the enormous, seemingly bottomless gap in between. She slammed her eyes shut.

He took a step toward her, then hesitated, aware of how hard she'd tried to appear brave in front of him and her friends. He reluctantly turned back to the horses. He didn't want to overstep his bounds or smother her.

"Callie?" Kathie asked after her.

Bonnie stopped taking pictures and went to her. "Uh-oh. Cal, how did you get up here if you can't even look out at the view?"

"I had my eyes shut," she said in a loud whisper.

Wes fought the urge to whip his head around at that. He

clenched his jaw. *Eyes shut? Good Lord.*

"The whole way?" Bonnie asked.

"Mm-hm."

He heard twigs and leaves crunching beneath their feet as they walked deeper into the woods. He chanced a glance. They were huddled together beside a tree, with Sweets pressed against Callie's leg. *Lucky Sweets.*

A few minutes later, he said, "Okay, ladies. Ready for lunch?" He drew everyone's attention except Callie's, whose eyes were riveted to the ground.

Aw, Christ.

He should have known better than to bring her on the trail. *Hell, she should have known better than to go.* He wondered why she'd agreed to come along if she had to ride up with her eyes closed. *Maybe she's as drawn to me as I am to her.* He chewed on that for a few minutes, and it tasted damn good.

He forced himself to continue speaking. "In the leather bag on your saddle, you'll find lunch and drinks."

"I'm starved," Christine said to Kathie as they headed to their horses. "Let's eat by the water. I could use some sun." Christine took off her tank top and draped it over the saddle, revealing a yellow bikini top that barely covered her small breasts. "Let's give the horses an eyeful."

"I think they'd rather have a mouthful of oats. But sitting in the sun sounds good." Kathie and Bonnie took their tops off.

Wes purposefully kept his eyes to himself, but he couldn't help stealing a few glances at Callie as she finally pried her hands from the tree and made her way toward the creek. She stared at the ground, he assumed to keep from looking at the edge of the mountain, and settled onto a log. A few minutes later, he brought Callie her lunch and found Sweets resting comfortably at her feet. He wondered when the pup had become so attached. *Probably the same time I did.*

"Thanks." She squinted against the sun. "Where's yours?"

"I forgot to grab it from the other horse, but I'm fine. Enjoy." She was too tempting. If he sat beside her, he wouldn't be able to stop himself from putting an arm around her or reaching for her hand. "Come on, Sweets." He slapped his thigh, and Sweets came to his side.

"Can we swim here?" Kathie asked as she shimmied out of her shorts.

"Sure, but watch for snakes."

Kathie's eyes widened as she pulled her shorts back on. "I think I'll just sit on the log next to Callie."

"Snakes?" Callie jumped up.

"They're more afraid of you than you are of them," he assured her.

Callie took a deep breath and nodded. She was so far out of her element that he couldn't help but be impressed as she tried to hold her own.

"You rode up with your eyes closed, Cal?" Christine sat on a nearby rock.

Callie's eyes shot to Wes. He turned and walked away to spare her embarrassment and found a log to sit on overlooking the mountainside. Hot from the ride—and from being so close to Callie on the horse—he took off his shirt and draped it over his shoulder, then leaned his elbows on his knees and hoped Callie would stick around for another day.

"CALLIE, YOU ARE quite possibly the luckiest girl in the world today," Kathie said around a mouthful of turkey sandwich.

"Really? You think it was fun when I had the crap scared out of me on that horse?" Callie nibbled on the crust of her sandwich.

"No, but you just spent two hours pressed against *that*." She nodded toward Wes's bare, tanned, and incredibly muscled back.

"Okay, now, y'all know my hubby is hot, but damn, girl." Christine shook her head. "I have to agree with Kathie. I'd jump on a runaway horse willingly if it earned me his attention."

Callie gazed at the man whose image she'd conjured up during the last few weeks when ice cream didn't satiate the desires that he stirred in her and she'd had to take things into her own hands. At those times she saw the way he looked at her in the library, with appreciation—and, she liked to think, something more. A girl had to dream, didn't she? His muscles rippled and flexed as he stroked Sweets's back, and she remembered the emotion in his voice when he'd realized she'd never taken a horse out alone. She felt the warmth of his arms around her, holding her tight and keeping her safe. She felt the brush of his breath against her neck as he reassured her. And then, as much as she tried to fight it, she remembered the way he looked at Tiffany, and she couldn't help but wonder if he had ever held her close or spoken to her with the same enticing emotion.

"Callie? Callie?" Kathie poked her arm. "Cal!"

"W-what? Sorry."

"You were practically drooling." Kathie gathered the trash from her lunch. "Want to dip our feet in the water?"

"Snakes." Callie looked down at her sandwich. "I'm going to give this to Wes. I'm not hungry, and he has no lunch."

Bonnie sidled up to her. "Oh, good idea. Go. We'll stay back here." She gave Callie a little shove, and although Callie wasn't watching, she would bet Bonnie was taking pictures.

"Wait." Christine grabbed Callie and yanked her shirt over her head, revealing Callie's bright blue bikini top.

Callie crossed her arms over her chest. "Christine!"

"Oh, please. If it were any other guy, you wouldn't think twice about wearing your bathing suit. Get over him already. He's hot, but you're hotter. Know it, baby. Go." She shoved her again.

"Good luck!" Bonnie whispered after her.

Callie felt like she was moving in slow motion as she crossed over fallen leaves and sticks that crunched beneath her boots. If she'd been in her right mind, she might worry about snakes and spiders and other creepy things that lived in the woods, but her mind was focused on Wes. Her friends were right. If Wes had been any other man, she wouldn't care that she was wearing a bathing suit. She knew she looked good enough. *Thank you, Jillian Michaels.* It wasn't that. It was *him.* He made her whole body hum.

Sweets lifted her head and wagged her tail.

Wes turned, and for a nervous second their eyes caught. He dropped his gaze to her bathing suit just as she shifted her eyes away and realized he was sitting close to where the trail sloped away.

Oh boy.

She forced herself forward and sat on the log beside him, facing the opposite direction. She stared at the creek and tried to ignore the fact that just behind her the mountain dropped six thousand—or million—feet.

"Here. I'm not hungry." She held the lunch bag behind her.

Sweets licked her legs and, with her paws on Callie's knees, tried to reach her face. Callie leaned in for a puppy kiss, thankful for the distraction.

"You should eat it, Cal. I'm fine."

"I'm really not hungry." *How can I eat with a family of butterflies living in my stomach?*

He straddled the log with one thigh behind her and the other so close to hers she craved the feel of it.

"Did you really have your eyes closed the whole way up the mountain?" he asked quietly.

She bit her lower lip and nodded.

He rested his forehead on her shoulder. "Callie," he whispered.

She could barely breathe with the intimate gesture. When he lifted his head and looked at her with tenderness and compassion, she was powerless to look away.

"What am I going to do with you?" His mouth kicked up in a little smile that melted her heart.

She could think of a million things she'd like him to do. "Sorry?"

He shook his head, and the smile never left his lips. His bare chest rose and fell in an alluring stretch of lean muscle and masculinity. *Just one touch*, that's all she wanted. One touch that she could remember for the rest of her life.

"No, not sorry, Cal."

She shook her head to clear the salacious thoughts that were clearly clouding her hearing. It didn't work. Sweets rested her chin on Callie's leg, and she focused on the dark area around the pup's muzzle, the sad circles around her eyes—anything to keep her eyes from Wes's body.

"Callie, this whole trip is so far from what you're used to. Are you sure you want to be here? I can drive you back to Trusty." He lifted his hand, and she froze, anticipating the feel of it on her leg, but he petted Sweets instead.

"Do you want me to go back to Trusty?" *Why, oh why, did I ask that?* Of course he did. Then he could have fun on these outings and not have to babysit her. *Please say no. Please say no.*

He touched her jaw and drew her face toward his. Her lips parted on a sigh. His dark, soulful eyes searched hers.

"What I want…"

OhGodohGodohGod.

"Is for you to be happy and comfortable."

Comfortable? She was anything but comfortable.

"And if that means you don't want to be here, then that's what it means. I'd like nothing more than to help you *become* comfortable with all of this. Horses, trail riding, the mountain itself. There's a world of beauty out here that I think you could love if you were able to push past your fears." His eyes dipped to her chest—stealing her breath—then lowered to her lap, where Sweets had fallen asleep. "But I won't force it on you."

There *was* a world of beauty out there. Callie might not be able to stare at it, but she wasn't blind. She'd seen it when she'd peeked at him. She heard the beauty around her, as unique as the barely audible crackling sound the spine of a book made when it was opened the first time. The mountain had its own unique and refreshing sounds of animals scurrying on the forest floor, leaves rustling in the wind, and the breeze as it swept up the mountainside against the long grass. Even the sounds of the horses' hooves on the earth were different on the mountains than in the paddock. She didn't need to see the scarier side of it to know how beautiful it was, just as she didn't need to be told that the look in Wes's eyes was more than just the look of a guide talking to a guest.

"I've read a lot about fear of heights and deep water and all the things I'm afraid of, and I haven't been able to conquer my fears yet."

His hand slid from Sweets's head to her hand. "Maybe you just need the right person to help you."

Her breath hitched. "You're so busy."

"I'll make time."

"Why?" *Oh my gosh. Isn't it enough that he will? Shut up!*

His mouth tilted into that heart-melting smile again. "I'm not exactly sure."

A soft laugh escaped her lips, and she bit her lower lip again to hold it in.

"But I'm pretty sure it has something to do with how damn cute you are."

She felt her whole body flush with heat.

Wes inched closer, one thigh against her back, the other pressed against her leg, and that bulging zipper was dangerously close to her hip. He brought his cheek to hers again—God, she loved the feel of his clean-shaven cheek.

"I've never met anyone like you, Callie. You're fearless and fearful at the same time, and it confuses the hell out of me."

Fearless? Me? She held her breath.

"You make me feel things no woman ever has, and you don't even try."

I do? She couldn't move.

"I hope you'll stay."

Her entire body tingled. The sound of blood rushing through her ears tangled with his words and somehow—she had no idea how because her brain was not functioning—she must have nodded, because his forehead fell to her shoulder again and he whispered, "Thank you."

Chapter Six

"I DON'T CARE if he's slept with the entire town of Trusty," Kathie said as they headed for the hot tub later that afternoon, wearing their bathing suits and carrying fluffy towels. "That man is definitely looking at you differently than he would look at someone he only wants a one-night stand with."

"I think he is, too, but what if I'm wrong?" Callie had spent the day tangled in a web of thoughts, mulling over Wes's words. She didn't want to get her hopes up, but no matter how much she tried to force herself to believe he was looking for a quick lay—because after all, he was sexy and sweet and everything she and every other woman could ever hope for in a man—she wasn't buying it.

"Oh, so what?" Kathie snapped. "Why do you have such a hard time with casual sex? I've never really understood that. You've made out with tons of guys. We all have."

"Yeah, but kissing is way different from sex." Callie leaned against the railing, thinking of Wes. "I like sex as much as the next person, but for me, it's connected to my heart. You guys know that. It shouldn't come as a surprise."

They walked across the grass toward the back of the lodge in search of the hot tub.

"It's not a surprise," Kathie explained. "It's just that you keep yourself so carefully protected, Cal. Don't you want to cut loose and just see what it's like?"

Callie stopped cold. She stood in front of her friends with her hands on her hips. "Why did you bring me here? To find a guy or what?"

"No. Of course not," Bonnie replied. "We brought you to show you that there is more to life than the library and your apartment. So you could find other things you liked to do and maybe expand outside your little nest."

"Right, and I totally appreciate that. That's why I'll stay, but as much as I want to let myself cut loose, grab Wes by the collar of his shirt, and throw him to the ground…" Yeah, that's exactly what she wanted to do.

"Um, Cal…" Christine said.

"No, let me finish, because you're right. I do want to cut loose. I want to tear every shred of his clothing off—with my teeth—and I want to lick every inch of his glorious body." She closed her eyes. "Mm. You know that would be amazing."

"Callie!" Kathie said.

Callie opened her eyes, facing the three of them, who were wide-eyed. Of course they were. She'd never said anything remotely close to this with such vehemence. She was the good girl, the careful girl, the *librarian*. She held her palms up to shut them up as weeks of pent-up sexual frustration tumbled forth.

"No. You started this, so let me finish. As much as I want to ride that man like the stallion he is, regardless of how many other women have been there before me, or might be there after me—which makes me sick to my stomach, by the way—I just can't. My heart has a direct line to my…you know what…and where one goes the other follows, and you know he's not like that. Cripes, he's probably slept with every woman who's ever come to this place, with the exception of us, so—"

Bonnie ran up and covered Callie's mouth with her hand. "Okay, Cal," she said through gritted teeth. "Enough."

The seriousness of Bonnie's voice shut Callie up long enough for her to really read the look in her friends' eyes as they stared over her shoulder. With a sinking feeling in the pit of her stomach, and Bonnie's hand securely over her mouth, she turned.

Wes stood before her in snug-fitting jeans and an open button-down shirt with a T-shirt beneath, looking utterly handsome and excruciatingly hurt. He drew his shoulders back, cleared his throat, and spoke in a hoarse tone. "I was just coming to see if you wanted to uh…" He ran his hand down his face and looked away. "You know what? Never mind."

Bonnie's hand dropped from Callie's mouth.

"Fuck," Kathie whispered.

"Oh my God." Callie watched him stalk away. "Oh my God." *No. No. No.* Her legs trembled. "You guys. Shit. Oh my God."

Bonnie put her arm around Callie and she shrugged her off. "I'm an idiot."

"No," Kathie said. "We're idiots. I'm an idiot for pushing you to do something you weren't comfortable doing and then not stopping you before he heard what you were saying."

"I have to go apologize."

"Maybe you should give him a little time," Christine suggested.

Or maybe I should just go home. No. She couldn't just leave things like that. "I'll be back." With her heart in her throat, she sprinted after Wes.

FUCK. FUCK. FUCK. Every determined step seared Callie's words into Wes's head. What was he thinking? He never led with his heart. Ever. But when they were up on that mountain on the trail ride, he'd asked her to stay. He'd desperately wanted her to stay, and that was one hundred percent driven by his heart, which blew him away and confused the hell out of him. *She wants to ride me like a stallion?* The sexual words coming from Callie seemed so out of place that he had trouble connecting them to her. The thought made his body white-hot. When she'd said, *But I can't,* he realized he'd been holding his breath. If she were anyone else, he wouldn't care if she thought he'd slept with every girl on the planet. Why did he care?

Fuck if he knew why, but he *did* care. A lot. Her words sliced through him like a knife as he headed into the barn and climbed on the back of the first horse he saw. He didn't even know where he was headed as he rode out of the barn, determined to get the hell away from everyone.

Callie stood just outside the barn doors wearing nothing but her bikini and the saddest frown he'd ever seen. One arm hung loosely by her side, as if all the oomph she'd possessed only moments before had disappeared. In her other hand, she clutched a towel. Sweets stood beside her with a matching goddamn frown. Wes's chest constricted. He wanted to wrap his arms around her or shake her. He wasn't sure which.

She didn't say a word, just looked up at him with sad brown eyes that made his heart ache. He watched her walk silently to his side, slip the towel around her neck, and reach her arms up.

Well, hell. Wrapping his arms around her won out over

shaking her—and he knew it always would.

He lifted her easily onto the horse in front of him and felt her trembling. *My heart has a direct line to my…you know what.* His heart squeezed a little more. He draped the towel over her legs, then wrapped his arm around her and pulled her close. She gripped his forearm, and he wondered if her eyes were open or closed. Somehow, she'd lassoed his heart and roped him in. She'd said all those passionate things about him, and for a guy who could handle the toughest of situations, he was a jumble of nerves. His chest tightened again, and as unfamiliar as the sensation was, he could pinpoint the cause this time. She'd opened his heart, and it had been closed for so damn long that it ached.

Sweets ran back and forth beside the horse, and with one flick of Wes's heels, they rode out of the pasture and toward the setting sun.

Wes tried not to think as they rode through the meadow. He didn't try to figure out a way to fix whatever was going on between them. He let the horse lead them, and as the sun settled behind the mountains and the horse slowed his pace, he breathed Callie in. When he'd seen the muscles in her back tighten and heard unbelievable passion and conviction in her voice, her words had reached into his gut and fisted tight. By the time he'd realized she was talking about him, his nerves had tangled into knots and he could barely think straight.

He needed to be closer to her, to hold her, talk to her, and figure out what the hell was going on. He brought the horse to a halt and slid from its back. He reached up for Callie, and though she didn't meet his gaze, she leaned forward and he lifted her off the horse. He couldn't have taken his hands from her bare waist if she'd begged him to. It was all he could do to look into her beautiful, sad, trusting eyes.

Why the hell did she still look like she trusted him? He didn't deserve to be trusted. Part of what she'd said was true.

He grabbed the towel, then took her hand and walked up the hill with Sweets trotting happily by their side. Wes laid the towel on the ground; then he took off the button-down shirt he wore over his T-shirt and draped it around her shoulders. It hung to her knees, and that endeared her to him even more. As strong as she'd tried to be all afternoon, she was still fragile. He was beginning to wonder if he had a bit of fragility in him as well because he felt as if he'd cracked wide open when she'd said she thought he probably slept with all the guests. And until he set that record straight and saw that she truly believed it, he feared pieces of himself would fall through that crack and he might never be whole again.

He sat with his feet flat on either side of the towel, knees up, and drew Callie down between them. He pulled her close again, to the spot that was beginning to feel like it belonged to her, and folded her into his arms. He worried she might push him away, and when she sank against him, he breathed a sigh of relief.

Sweets whimpered.

"Lay down, Sweets." His voice was raspy, emotionally spent.

Sweets stretched her long legs before her, and with a noisy yawn, she rested her head between her paws.

Wes knew how to flirt, and he knew how to handle the most treacherous situations Mother Nature had to offer. He could hunt and fish with the best of them, but this—these unfamiliar, protective urges that were bubbling up inside of him toward Callie—this was new and unfamiliar territory. He didn't even know where to begin.

"Callie," Wes said at the same time Callie said, "Sorry."

"I'm sorry, Callie." He tightened his arms around her. He leaned his chin on her shoulder and closed his eyes, thinking of the things he wanted to say. The emotions that swelled inside him and filled every crevice, making him feel full and scared at the same time, were so unfamiliar that as he tried to form them into words, he felt like his mouth was full of pebbles. He felt Callie's hand on his knee and he opened his eyes. She was gazing into the distance and looked beautiful and pained.

"You don't have to say you're sorry. Ever." He didn't recognize the thin voice as his own. Callie closed her eyes, and he felt her withdrawing from the safety of his arms. He tightened his grasp. "Before you pull away, I need you to know that I haven't slept with every guest who has come to the ranch. I haven't slept with any of them."

Her neck bent forward, and a flush rose on her cheeks.

He wondered if it was driven by her desire to *lick every inch of his body*—even the thought made him hard—or by the words that followed, *he's probably slept with every woman who's ever come to this place*—which took care of his hard-on altogether.

"I shouldn't have said that. I'm sorry." Her voice quivered. "I was just trying to convince myself to stop thinking of you and me...of us..." She turned away.

Us. She was protecting herself from her feelings for him. That was something Wes could relate to, and it was what drove him to gently shift Callie so she was sitting sideways between his legs. He didn't want her to hide from her feelings, and he was damn sure that he didn't want to hide from his anymore, either. He stroked her cheek, drawing her eyes to his. It took everything he had not to try to kiss the pain away. His and hers.

"I..." He swallowed hard. Talking to women had never

been difficult for him, but he felt the need to be careful with Callie. He smiled at that, because after hearing what she wanted to do to him, he was having trouble seeing her as the innocent young woman he'd thought she was, and it made him wonder about that protected heart of hers and whether he was worthy of it.

"Callie, I—"

"Wait." She silenced him with a serious tone, then pressed her palms flat against his chest, as if she might need to hold him back. "Before you say anything else, I need to know how much you heard."

Her flash of determination almost made him lie to ease her worry. But Bradens weren't liars. If his mother Catherine's lessons about honesty weren't enough, his three older brothers continuously driving it into his head were. So he took a deep breath and hoped for the best.

"I don't know what you said before wanting to ride me like a stallion," he began.

Her hands fisted against him, yanking his chest hair right along with them.

"But I pretty much heard everything after that."

She pressed her lips together and nodded. Her hair fell around her face, and he could tell by the way her brows drew together, relaxed, and then repeated the movements several times, that she was struggling with the urge to flee.

He tucked her hair behind her ear and smiled up at her. "Feeling trapped?"

Her mouth curved up at that. "A little."

"Want me to take you back down the mountain and pretend I never heard it?"

Callie's eyes dropped to her hands, still clinging to him as if she could steal the strength from his body. "You'd do that?"

It was the last thing he wanted to do, but yeah, he'd do it. He shrugged.

She nodded and drew in a deep breath. "No. I don't want you to."

Wes stilled. Her hands tightened again. His mind was reeling with her admission about sex being tied to love, and it should have held him back, but he couldn't stop himself from sliding his hand beneath her hair and stroking the soft hairs at the base of her neck, then pressing his lips to hers.

IN THAT INSTANT, when weeks of heady anticipation met reality, Callie forgot to breathe, and when their lips came together, his breath filled her lungs. Her body warmed and tingled all at once as his tongue hungrily swept her mouth. Lost in the most earth-shattering kiss she'd ever experienced, she was barely aware of his other arm drawing her closer. He smelled like soft leather and prairie wind. She slid her hands over the arc of his chest and wound them around his thick neck, bringing them chest to chest. With two soft kisses, his lips slid to her cheek, and he embraced her. His arms were strong and safe. *Tender. So tender.*

"Callie." A soft, hot whisper against her neck stole her breath.

Sweets shoved his nose along Wes's waist and beneath the button-down shirt Callie wore and pressed his furry face against her belly. She felt herself smile, and as much as she didn't want to move one inch, how could she not? She pulled back with her lower lip held tightly between her teeth and looked down at Sweets with another noiseless laugh.

The look Wes gave Sweets wasn't quite as forgiving. His eyes met Callie's, and he pressed another kiss to her lips before dropping one hand to Sweets's head and stroking it gently.

"Guess she's a little jealous," he said.

Callie let out a shaky breath. *Kiss me again. Please kiss me again.* She watched him stroking Sweets's head, and she understood the puppy's desire for more of Wes's attention, because even after that incredible kiss, she wished he were still touching her, too.

Wes gently lifted the dog's head from his lap, settled her beside them, then placed his hands on Callie's cheeks and looked thoughtfully into her eyes.

"You'll have to guide me, Cal, because all those things you said you wanted to do? I want to do them, too, and I don't want to cross any lines you might regret."

I want you. Kiss me. Touch me. Take that darn shirt off so I can feel you against me. She knew she hadn't said a word. She could barely admit those things to her girlfriends—and only had because she was so darn mad at herself for being shy. But to say them now? To him? Just looking at Wes made her damp, and kissing him nearly made her—

In the next breath, he captured her mouth with his again like he'd read her thoughts. She didn't think as she brought his big, strong hand to her breast. She moaned against his lips when he brushed his thumb over her nipple, sending a sharp titillation of need through her. Callie's hands slid beneath his T-shirt to his hot, hard abs. *Oh God. You feel so good.* He drew her legs around his waist. His thighs were taut beneath hers, and as he pressed himself to her, she couldn't ignore the pressure of his arousal against the thin, damp material of her swimsuit.

Completely lost in the sensation of Wes's full lips as they slid to the corner of her mouth, then followed her jaw to the base of her neck, Callie exhaled and arched her neck back. The cool evening breeze brushed over the wet memory of his kisses along her bare shoulder as he slid his shirt from her arms. His hand moved down her back and cupped her rear. Tight. Her body shuddered, and she arched farther back, opening her chest to him. Thankfully, blissfully, his head came back to center, and he kissed the chilled skin above her breasts. His other hand was splayed across her upper back, sending warmth to chase the chill away. With every breath, she felt his fingers touch the tie of her bikini, and oh how she wished he'd just tug those strings free. She didn't need to go all the way; at least that's what she told herself. She could wait until she was sure what all the tangling of her nerves and swelling of her heart really meant before they went that far, but she wanted—*needed*—more of him. He smelled so damn good, and as he kissed her, his neck was right there, inviting, taunting, looking so gloriously delicious that it might as well have been covered in chocolate frosting. She settled her lips over the curve at the base of his neck and couldn't help but sink her teeth into his hot, salty skin and suck it in against her tongue, earning a deep, guttural groan from deep within him. She felt his neck arch back—she couldn't open her eyes if her life depended on it. He tasted too good, felt too warm and hard—*oh so hard.*

"Callie." A breathy plea that drew her lips to his.

Finally, she felt his fingers grip the tie of her bikini top. *Yes, please, yes.* They were both breathing hard, so hard they had to draw away with the need for oxygen. Wes pressed his forehead to hers, eyes closed as they both sucked in air. When his eyes fluttered open, they were nearly black, full of desire. How could words be so unnecessary? She lived her life by them, swore by them, devoured them, and followed them to so many magical places, and yet when she looked into the dark pools of Wes's eyes, not a single word was needed. A silent nod and a press of her fingertips against the back of his biceps had him gently pulling the tie of her bikini top free. His hand slid down her back, and another tender tug sent the thin material to their laps. His eyes held hers as the hand on her rear sank a little lower, his fingers splayed. His fingertips brushed the damp material between her legs, and his eyes—those smoldering dark eyes that enraptured her with every glance—traveled slowly to her lips, lingering just long enough for Callie to suck in a breath before they sank lower and came to rest on her breasts. He drew his eyes back to hers.

"You're exquisite."

Exquisite. Not beautiful. Not pretty. *Exquisite.* A careful, well-chosen word that had her arching back again and drawing his mouth to her breast. She sucked in a jagged breath as his tongue washed over her nipple; then he took her breast fully into his mouth and stroked it with his hot tongue. Not fast and hard, but slowly, erotically, sending pinpricks of anticipation through her limbs. She held the back of his head. His hair was soft; the muscles in his neck bunched beneath her palm as he sucked and laved her breasts. Soft kisses drew his lips back. His teeth grazed her sensitive nipple, causing another trembling inhalation.

"Wes." The whisper came without thought.

Palm on her ass, his fingertips pressed against her center, stealing any chance she had at coherent thoughts, he caressed her through the thin material. She was wet, swollen. Needful.

Callie had never felt so needy, so filled with desire and white-hot lust. She pressed her hands to his cheeks and took him in a deep, greedy kiss. Sexy, aggressive, wanton noises filled the air around them. It took a moment for her to realize they were coming from her. When Wes's finger slid beneath her bathing suit bottom, the first touch of his fingers nearly did her in. Her tongue, her lips, everything stilled for a breath from the sheer pleasure of it. She didn't stop him—she didn't want to—and in the next breath she kissed him again, harder, deeper, as he slid his long fingers inside her, in perfect rhythm to every stroke of his tongue. He took over. He had to. She was having trouble breathing, much less leading their passionate kiss. One hand pressed to the middle of her back, the other working its magic down below, and his mouth, that magnificent, luscious mouth of his drove her right up and over the edge. Her body flashed hot, every muscle flexed, as her head fell back and her eyes slammed shut. She clung to him for dear life as he held her at the peak until she thought she might faint from the force of the explosions inside her. He drew her close, held her against him, his fingers still buried deep inside her, as she came down, her body shuddering against him.

Holy cripes. She rested her head on his shoulder, panting—and desperately wanting more.

He kissed her softly, and when he withdrew his fingers, she gasped a breath and held it as her insides ached for his return. Without severing their connection, he shifted them both to their sides, legs stretched along the towel. He slid one thick thigh between her legs and pressed his body to hers. She closed her eyes and buried her face in his warm, broad chest, feeling safe and probably far too comfortable after all the things he'd heard her say. He ran his fingers along her back, and they stayed like that for a long time, until he pulled back and kissed her forehead, then shifted her hips so she was partially beneath him.

His gaze was soft, his body a warm blanket above her. He was propped up on his elbow, fully dressed, and, Callie realized, she was bare-chested and wearing a damp bikini bottom. She felt her cheeks flush again.

"Callie." His brows knitted together. "Stopping was the most difficult thing I've ever done."

She wasn't sure if she was thankful he stopped or disappointed. Her brain was still reeling from the intensity of the orgasm he'd given her using nothing but his fingers. That was definitely a first. She pushed away the shy girl who was coming back to the surface and forced her shaky voice from her lungs.

"Why did you?" She slipped her finger beneath the edge of his T-shirt.

His eyelids were heavy, and when the edge of his lips curled up into a sweet smile and he ran his index finger down her cheek, she wondered if she'd actually said anything at all.

"Because I'm not who you think I am. I have been with a lot of women, and if we ever decide to go that far, I want you to know that I'm clean. I've been tested. I'm not stupid enough to try to lie to you, but I wanted you to know that I haven't been with women here, Cal. Not at my ranch. I steer clear of mixing business with pleasure."

"Then why...?" Okay, so he'd been with a lot of women. She knew that without having been told. A man couldn't look like him and flirt the way he did without having followed up on it a few hundred times. She silently cringed at the number, so she modified the thought. *A handful of times.* That was better, even if it might not be true.

He sighed loudly and ran his hand along her arm. "I've been

asking myself that since I offered to ride up the mountain with you."

Oh, great.

"Hey, look at me." He lifted her chin so she had to look at him.

He did that a lot, and Callie was beginning to like the silent demand that she allow him to look into her eyes, as if it would make her hear him more clearly. Maybe he put as much value in words as she did.

"I don't have all the answers, but I'm going with it. You're unlike anyone I know, Callie. In a good way. And I'm drawn to you. So drawn to you." He rubbed her arm again. "I love your femininity and your strength."

"That would be a great line if it were true, but I'm not strong." She stared at his chest again to keep from falling into his eyes.

"Not many women would move away from everything they knew to follow their dream. Maybe *strong* is the wrong word. *Brave. Courageous.* Moving to a small town where you know nobody? That takes a hell of a lot of courage."

Courageous? Brave? She'd never thought of herself as courageous. Even her friends didn't think she was courageous. Did they? Or did they think she was weak for not being aggressive with guys and for being careful with her heart *and* her body, but maybe brave in other ways? The power of the words he chose intrigued her.

He placed his hand on her hip and ran it down the length of her thigh. "And I'm not sure if there's a gym in your library that I've missed the last few weeks, but your body is strong, Cal."

"Um…I have Jillian Michaels to thank for that, actually."

"Jillian Michaels? Like *The Biggest Loser* Jillian?"

She nodded. He smiled and pressed a soft kiss to her lips. "Okay, that just makes you so much cuter."

She rolled her eyes. "Loserish, I know."

"What? No way. Those DVDs are hard as hell. My sister, Emily, tried them for a few days and was so sore that she quit doing them." His eyes slid down her body. "Jillian must know her stuff, because you are the perfect combination of femininity and strength. But I have a feeling it has less to do with Jillian and more to do with who you are."

She turned her head from side to side, shielding her eyes as if peering into the distance.

"What's the matter?" His hand gripped her hip protectively.

"I was just checking to see if I'd died and gone to heaven."

Chapter Seven

CALLIE CLOSED THE cabin door behind her and leaned against it, finally free to let out the dreamy sigh she'd been holding in.

Kathie stood at the top of the stairs and hollered into the bedroom, "Flushed and sighing."

Christine and Bonnie followed her down the stairs.

"We thought he'd abducted you for the night," Bonnie said. They'd changed their clothes, but Callie was still wearing her bathing suit and Wes's button-down shirt, which he'd insisted upon her keeping.

Kathie grabbed her hand and dragged her to the couch. "So? Spill. He heard it all, so…"

Christine snagged a bottle of Skinnygirl piña coladas and filled a glass for each of them. All three of them stared at Callie with wide, expectant eyes. She traced a distressed vein in the leather couch.

"Yeah, he heard all of it. Maybe next time you could, I don't know, jump up and down and tell me to shut up?"

"In all fairness, we tried to give you hints, but, girlfriend, you were on a roll." Christine took a drink. "Wow. That's good."

"Yeah, well." Callie *had* been on a roll, and she knew it would have taken exactly what Bonnie had done to shut her up.

"Well?" Kathie straightened her glasses and tucked her dark hair behind her ear and leaned in close.

"We rode off into the sunset, sat on the crest of a beautiful flowery meadow for a while, then made out like horny teenagers."

Kathie hugged her. "I knew it! You guys owe me so bigtime."

"You bet on it?" Callie smiled at the thought. They would bet on her sex life. In fact, they'd done it in college a handful of times, until they realized that she'd meant it when she said she wasn't going to sleep with her dates.

"Nah. Bon wouldn't let us." Kathie rolled her eyes in Bonnie's direction. "But I would have won."

"See? I have your back." Bonnie patted Callie's leg. "So? Did you lick every inch of him?"

Callie felt her cheeks flush. "No."

"Oh, stop it. It's us, Cal." Kathie moved closer and draped an arm over her shoulder. "You're wearing his shirt. That's got to mean something."

"Yeah. It means it's cold on the mountain when the sun goes down."

Christine and Bonnie nodded at that.

"And?" Kathie narrowed her eyes.

"And let's just say the man knows his way around a woman's body." *Did he ever.* Surprisingly, she didn't blush this time. "But we didn't. You know."

"Hm." Kathie sat back and pressed her lips together.

"Your choice or his?" Christine asked.

Callie shrugged. "Both, I guess. Gosh, you guys. We don't

have to cram everything into one perfect night." It was a perfect night, at least once she was in his arms.

"True." Kathie finished her drink. "So what's your plan?"

"I didn't think we needed one, but apparently he did. He asked me again to stay. Did you guys know we're supposed to learn to shoot skeet tomorrow and go on an overnight camping trip?"

"Yeah. It's on the itinerary," Kathie reminded her.

"Right. I didn't read that far. I was leaving, remember?"

"But now you're not. Right?" Bonnie asked.

Callie took a drink. "There is no way I'm leaving now."

Christine squealed and pulled her into a hug. "I'm so glad. This is so good for you. *All* of it." She wiggled her eyebrows.

Callie ran her finger along the couch again, following the path with her eyes. "I might just break my heart-and-you-know-what rule." As the words left her lips, she wondered if she'd need to break that rule. She'd felt something for Wes for weeks, and it was way more than lust.

Christine gripped Callie's knees. "Callie."

Kathie scooted up against her. "Really?"

"Babe, don't do anything because of us. We're idiots." Bonnie sat beside her on the couch. "You need to do what you feel is right."

"She's right, Cal. We'll all go back to our husbands, and you have to go back to the library, where you'll see Wes every week." Kathie finished her drink and then continued. "Unless you guys decide to see each other after you go back home. Is that a possibility?"

"We didn't talk about that, so I don't know. I mean, I hope so. I don't even know if we'll do anything more than we've done, but kissing him was like…" She looked up at the ceiling, remembering the way her body tingled with desire, the way his tongue made her body melt and her brain numb, and she hoped—damn, did she ever hope—that they'd come together again.

"You know that feeling when you've been thinking about kissing someone forever, and the anticipation alone is enough to steal your breath? And your heart beats so hard that you're sure the minute your lips touch, you'll die, right there on the spot? And when your lips finally do come together, and he breathes air into your lungs, you wonder if you'll ever want to breathe on your own again?" She sighed just thinking about it.

"Wow," Kathie whispered.

"I'm sure it was like that with Mark at some point, but I can't remember it as clearly as you described." Bonnie patted her hand over her heart. "Wow is right."

"I know what she means. Billy still takes my breath away," Christine said. "Of course, maybe that's because when we're kissing I sometimes pretend he's Chris Pine or Josh Holloway."

Bonnie rolled her eyes. "That doesn't count."

"Cal, maybe there's more here than just, you know, a good time," Kathie said hopefully. "I mean, you rode off on his horse. If Wes was just looking for a good time, he'd have probably tried to do the deed tonight." She looked at Bonnie and Christine. "Right?"

"Good point," Bonnie said. "So?"

"I hope you're right. I don't want to think right now. I just want to wallow in the memory of being with him and take a nice warm bath. I've got to get up in the morning to do my DVD." She headed for the stairs, stopping when she came to the bottom step. "Do you guys think I'm brave?"

They exchanged a glance.

"What do you mean?" Kathie asked.

"Never mind." She headed up the stairs, wondering if Wes saw something in her that even her closest friends didn't.

WES'S CABIN WAS built up the hill from the guest quarters with views of the mountains, the forest, and the lodge. Tonight he sat out on the covered deck with a fire in the stone fireplace, thinking about Callie. Was she thinking of him the way his every thought was consumed by her? Would she tell her friends what they'd done tonight? He took a sip of his beer and reached down to pet Sweets, who was gnawing on one of her toys.

Wes had no cell service at his cabin, which normally was fine, as he'd never loved the idea of being that accessible twenty-four seven. But on a night like tonight, when he couldn't take his mind off the woman he was just with—and hadn't wanted to part from—talking to one of his brothers would have been a nice distraction. There were landlines down at the lodge, but he didn't trust himself enough to make the effort. If he headed down that hill, he knew his legs would carry him directly toward cabin two.

Sweets lifted her head and barked, a single low *woof*.

The land in front of the cabin was level for about twenty feet before it sloped toward the guest cabins and the lodge. In the moonlight, his visibility was limited to that short distance.

Sweets ran down the steps and into the darkness.

"Hey, girl." Chip came into view and crouched to pet Sweets. Sweets may not have been able to smell, but her hearing was damn sharp.

"Beer's in the fridge." Wes held up his beer bottle.

Chip grabbed a beer and then sat beside him.

"How'd the day trip go?" Wes asked.

"Fine, you know. Normal day on the trails. Did you look at the new applications for Ray's position yet?" Chip took a pull on his beer and crossed his legs at the ankle.

"No time yet. I'll check them out tomorrow."

Sweets went back to chewing her toy.

"Sure you don't want to reconsider Cutter? He has the skills. He's willing and able."

Wes thought about the way Cutter had looked at Callie. "Positive."

"I think it's a mistake. You should think about it. Anyway, I heard you took off on Willy with a chick." Chip shook his head, and his wet hair stuck to his forehead.

Wes took a long drink. "You go to the hot tub?"

"You can't avoid the question. Yes, I was at the hot tub. How do you think I knew about you and the girl? Her very attractive bikini-clad friends were there."

Wes could still feel Callie's fingers pressing on the back of his arm, urging him to untie her bikini top. He could still feel the weight of her breasts in his palms, her nipples hardening beneath his thumbs. *Christ.* He was getting hard again. He shifted in his chair.

"Why ask if you already know?"

"They said it was Callie, the girl from the library."

"Yeah. So?" He met Chip's gaze. "You got something to say? Go ahead."

"Cutter said she rode the trail on your horse." Chip leaned forward, knees on his elbows.

"She's afraid of heights. I didn't want to make her sit it

out." Wes knew from the way Chip met his stare that he saw right through the bullshit. "Okay, whatever. Yeah, I'm attracted to her. What do you want me to do? Walk away?"

"Yes," Chip said in a flat, serious tone.

After those intoxicatingly sweet kisses and the memory of her luscious curves against him? Jesus, after the way she'd opened up to him and the way she'd looked as she came apart from his touch? There was no way in hell he was walking away. He couldn't wait to learn more about her, to teach her the things he'd promised, so she could enjoy the rest of the trip without fear. Hell, he could barely get from one minute to the next, waiting to hold her in his arms again.

"Why the hell should I?"

"How about you tell me? In eight years, you've never ridden the trail with a woman on your horse." He took another drink of his beer. "Remind me again why you never have."

"You know damn well why."

Chip shrugged. "I rest my case. Plus, she's from Trusty. Dangerous, Wes."

"You think I don't know that?" He'd been over it in his head a hundred times. Was he just fucking around with her? Hell if he knew for sure, but it certainly didn't feel like it.

"Then what gives? First you have her pull books for you that you never read; now you ride off into the sunset like you're goddamn Clint Eastwood?"

Wes stood and paced with Sweets on his heel. "I read the books she gives me."

"Right."

"Most of them, anyway." He usually made it through at least one each week. "Shit, Chip. Don't you think I would walk away if I could? You said it yourself. Eight years and I've never ridden up the trail with a woman. I have no idea what the hell's going on, but…" *I don't want to walk away.*

"You know Clarissa will have a field day with this if she finds out. She'll have you married off by next week." Chip laughed.

"Then keep your mouth shut." Wes sat back down and petted Sweets. "What's with her, anyway? Why does she want me to get tied down so badly?"

"Aw, come on. You know why."

"No, dude. Seriously, I have no clue." Wes finished his beer and set the bottle on the deck. "Enlighten me."

Chip shook his head. "How often does she tell you it's a waste for you to keep sleeping around?"

"Right, but why? Chicks say some weird shit."

"All I know is that she says she sees something in you that tells her you should settle down. That you'd make a great husband or some shit like that. It's like she's talking about some other guy." Chip shrugged. "You know how she is. She believes she knows things about people that they can't see. Who knows? Maybe she does."

"So, why haven't you ever given in when she's made a play for you?" Wes held his stare.

"First of all, the whole dipping the pen in the company ink thing, and second of all, she doesn't make plays for me."

Wes laughed, startling Sweets into a *woof*. Wes stroked her head. "Right, you just keep believing that."

"Listen, I came up to see if you wanted to swap. Want me to take the fishing and overnight and you can take the day trip?"

"Isn't that big of you now that you've seen three pretty women in bikinis?" Wes shook his head.

Chip held his hands up. "Hey, I'm trying to save you from

regrets you might have next week when you're not on the trail, but back to real life, in the library every Thursday, looking at the assistant librarian instead of a group of girls gone wild."

Anger brewed in Wes's gut. "She's not…They're not the girls-gone-wild type of chicks."

"Yeah, I know. At least her friends aren't. They're hot, but *very* married. Even with me and Cutter in the hot tub, all they talked about was their husbands and Callie. And you, of course, but they spoke in code, like, *that guy who loves to read* and shit, as if we wouldn't put two and two together."

The thought made Wes smile. "Hey, speaking of code. What does it mean when a girl says to another girl, *I brought skinny girls?*"

"Depends. Are they at an orgy?"

Wes belted out a laugh. "No, man. They're talking here at the ranch."

"There's an orgy at the ranch and I missed the memo?"

"You're an idiot."

Chip rose and stretched. He tugged at the collar of his hoodie. "You sure you don't want me to take the overnight? I know Cutter's dying to come along."

"That's reason enough for me to say no." Wes had never been a jealous man, and he trusted Cutter to respect his boundaries, but he couldn't deny the claws of the green-eyed monster scratching at his spine with the thought of Cutter going on an overnight trip with Callie.

"All right. If you change your mind, I'll be at my cabin tomorrow night." Chip patted Sweets's head. "Just tell me this. What is it about her, and where'd you take her tonight?"

"Everything, and none of your business."

"Oh yeah," Chip said as he stepped off the deck. "Clarissa

will love this."

Wes knew Clarissa would love it because, when he hadn't been able to reach Emily when he'd called earlier, he'd called Clarissa and asked the favor of her instead. It was a big favor, and she'd practically salivated at his request, but he wasn't about to tell Chip that. He'd have enough teasing to deal with once Chip talked to Clarissa. Until then he'd try to make it through the night without crawling through Callie's window.

Chapter Eight

CALLIE DREAMED ABOUT Wes all night. Sweet, erotic, naughty dreams that she'd awoken from, panting and hot, several times throughout the night. She woke early Saturday morning and climbed silently from the bed, trying not to wake Bonnie, who was fast asleep, sprawled out on top of her covers, wearing her Single Slayer T-shirt and boy-shorts underwear. Callie changed into her exercise clothes and went into the bathroom. She stared at herself in the mirror as she brushed her hair, thinking about Wes. She loved kissing him more than anything else she could think of. Even reading. That was a first, she realized as she set her brush on the marble countertop.

"What is it about him?" she whispered to her reflection. Her pulse kicked up just thinking about him. Today he was going to give her a private riding lesson so she would feel more comfortable when they rode out to the backcountry, where they would be camping. Wes was rugged, which was different from the guys she usually dated. Callie was usually drawn to academic types, men who pondered, not men who lifted her from moving horses to rescue her. Then again, no one had ever done that before. Wes was smart, and that was evident in all that he'd accomplished and the way he spoke, but it was also present in his eyes every time she looked into them. And then there were his kisses. *Boy, can he kiss. And touch.* Her cheeks flushed and turned away from the mirror. Her stomach fluttered nervously, and she drew in a deep breath. *Okay, Callie. Get it together.*

Callie went through her morning routine with renewed energy. After finishing her Jillian Michaels workout, she made coffee and took it out on the front porch to sit in the sun—and stumbled over a gift-wrapped box.

"What the…?" She was surprised to see her name written in pencil on a small rectangular gift card envelope. Hoping it was from Wes, and knowing that was a stupid thing to hope for after one evening together, she sat down on the porch steps and read the card.

Cal, petite four. Hope they're okay and glad you're staying. Wes.

Callie stared at the card. "No way." She wondered if her friends had orchestrated a gag, but one look around told her she was all alone. If they had done this, Bonnie would be taking pictures. She tore open the box. Inside were two pairs of petite, size four, boot-cut jeans and a pair of cutoff jeans shorts. She pressed them to her chest and closed her eyes for a beat.

Wes Braden took thoughtful to a whole new level.

TWO HOURS LATER, Callie and the others headed down to the lodge for breakfast.

"Let me get a picture of all of you guys on the bridge." Bonnie lifted her camera.

"You're like the paparazzi. We're going to have to start

dodging you." Christine fluffed her stick-straight hair, as if it might actually fluff instead of falling flat beneath her visor. "Farrah Fawcett I am not."

Callie looped her arm into Christine's, feeling confident on the wings of her budding romance and in her new jeans. "You're gorgeous."

"Agreed." Kathie held Christine's other arm. "I still can't believe he bought you jeans, Callie. I mean, come on. Really? How did he even manage that? Wasn't he here the whole time?"

"Can you guys smile instead of talking?" Bonnie directed.

"Sorry," they said in unison and plastered smiles on their faces.

Bonnie took a few pictures. "Those were great."

"Okay, now get in here and I'll take the picture." Kathie held her hand out to Bonnie, and Bonnie reluctantly handed over the camera.

"Put on the strap." She draped it over Kathie's neck. "Okay, just push that button when we look clear."

"I think I can handle a camera." Kathie held it up to her eye. "Wow! You guys look great." She turned, scanning the grounds through the lens. "Oh, baby, we have to make a quick stop before breakfast."

"Kathie!" Bonnie reached for the camera.

"Wait, wait. Okay, I'll take it." Kathie laughed. "I just got sidetracked by the hot cowboys."

"Take the darn picture already. Then we can all see the hot cowboys," Christine said.

Kathie forced a serious face. "Smile."

"I'm only interested in one hot cowboy," Callie said.

"Yeah? Well, I'm only interested in one hot accountant by the name of Paul Sharp, but a little eye candy never hurt."

Kathie lowered the camera after taking the pictures. "Inspiration for my Wild West novel."

"Is that what we're calling it? Inspiration?" Christine asked as they crossed the bridge.

"You laugh. Just wait. I'm going to write the next hot cowboy historical romance. You guys will be able to say, *I knew her when.*" Kathie grabbed Callie's arm and tugged her in the direction she'd been scanning with the camera. "You have to see this."

They followed the sounds of hooves on dirt, and a moment later Wes came into view, sitting atop a large black horse and swinging a lasso over his head.

Cutter leaned against the wooden fence, cheering him on. "Come on, Braden. Get in there."

A handful of cattle ran beside the horse. Beneath Wes's leather cowboy hat, his eyes were locked on one brown steer. His thick, powerful legs held him to the horse. The muscles in his arms bulged and flexed as he swung the lasso, then expertly threw it toward the steer, looping it over the steer's head.

Cutter let out a *whoop!* Sweets ran back and forth along the fence. When she noticed Callie and the others, she bounded over to them, drawing them all to their knees to love her up.

"Holy cow." Callie's eyes remained on Wes. She grabbed Bonnie's arm. "Pictures. Get pictures."

"Already on it." Bonnie lifted the camera.

Wes looked virile and focused. There were no two ways about it; he was the most valiant and handsome creature Callie had ever seen.

"Breathe, baby. Breathe," Christine said in her ear.

"Right. Breathing. That would be good."

"Told you that you needed to see this." Kathie pulled Callie toward the fence.

"Hey, ladies." Cutter lifted his cowboy hat in greeting. "He's getting a little roping practice in."

Callie tried to concentrate, but she could barely think past her tingling nerves and the desire that coiled down low at the sight of Wes as he flicked the rope off of the steer and watched it run free.

"Why didn't he jump down and tackle it like they do in the movies? And what's the steer got around its horns?" Bonnie asked, continuing to take pictures.

"You only tackle the steer if you're steer wrestling. And the leather contraption is a horn protector. It protects the skin and hair at the base of horns, keeps 'em from getting chafed," Cutter explained. "He's practicing loop and catches. He loves roping, and as you can see, he's damn good at it."

Damn good is right, but deliciously appealing might be a better choice of words.

Wes rode over to them. Callie thought she'd get used to his striking good looks, but apparently, her brain didn't get the memo, because she was hot and bothered and struggling to remember how to speak.

"Hey," Wes said casually. His eyes drifted over the others and settled on Callie. "I see the jeans fit."

She followed his eyes south. "Yes, perfectly. Thank you. That was so nice of you. You didn't have to—"

"I wanted to. You look great." He smiled, and she grabbed the fence to remain upright on her weakening knees.

"What am I missing here?" Cutter asked.

Wes slid him a narrow-eyed look.

"I'll just…uh…go take care of the cattle." Cutter tipped his hat and went into the riding arena. Sweets wriggled beneath the fence and ran after him.

Wes joined Callie at the fence, and Bonnie turned her camera on them. Callie wondered how they looked together and whether she looked any different now that they'd become so close.

Kathie tugged Bonnie and Christine away. "Why don't we grab breakfast? Callie, we'll meet you at the lodge, okay?"

"Yeah. Sure."

Wes covered her hand with his, then leaned over the fence and kissed her softly. "Hi," he said just above a whisper.

"Hi." She'd like to have one of those kisses every morning.

"I'm glad you liked the jeans. I wanted you to be comfortable when you rode."

"Thank you. No one has ever bought me jeans before, I mean except my family and girlfriends."

"You mean no man has ever bought you jeans before." He kissed her again. "Good. I like being the first. Are we still on for a private riding lesson later? I really want to help you get comfortable on a horse, unless you've decided that you'd rather not. No pressure."

"You're so considerate. Thank you."

"Is that a yes?" He brushed the back of her hand with his thumb.

God, yes! "Yes."

Wes ran the back of his hand down Callie's cheek. "I thought about you all night. Any regrets?"

God, no. She shook her head, and he kissed her again, sending a shiver down her back.

"Good. Me neither." He smiled. "We're skeet shooting today, and I know you said you don't like guns, so you can sit it out if you'd like."

Callie stepped closer to the fence. She'd climb right over it to be closer to him if she wasn't afraid of the steers on the other side, though she knew Wes would protect her.

"I'll try it."

"Yeah?"

She nodded again.

Wes lifted a foot to the bottom rung on the fence, and in two quick moves he landed on the other side beside Callie and drew her into his arms. He was holding her right out in the open, where Cutter or anyone else could see them, and she felt like the luckiest girl in the world.

"Aren't you worried about what your employees might think?" she asked.

"Nope. It was too hard to stand on the opposite side of the fence from you." He drew his thick brows together. "Of course, if it bothers you…" He released his grip on her.

She hooked her fingers into the waist of his jeans and pulled him against her again. "No. I was only worried about what you said yesterday. You know, not getting involved with guests."

"I never have." He lowered his forehead to hers. "I guess you've just claimed a first for me, too."

She hoped a last, too, though she'd never say that out loud.

"I'm glad you stayed and that you're willing to give some of these things a shot." He pressed another soft kiss to her lips, lingering just long enough to steal her breath. "I'm glad you're willing to give *me* a shot."

A shot? I'd give you the whole arsenal.

Chapter Nine

WES WAS TALKING on the phone to Emily when Chip came into the office in the lodge and sat down across from him. He clasped his hands behind his head and stretched his legs as if he had nothing to do for the rest of the day. Wes glanced at the clock. Chip was due to guide a day trip in fifteen minutes. He held up one finger, indicating he'd be just another minute, and Chip shrugged.

"Emily, Chip just came in, so I have to run in a sec. I'll be gone for the next day and a half, but you can come anytime. You can stay at my place or the lodge, whichever you want."

Emily sighed, and Wes pictured her leaning over her architectural drawing table, her forehead wrinkled and her long, dark hair curtaining her face. She had a habit of hiding behind her hair when she was stressed, which wasn't often, and it was why he'd so readily offered her his cabin when she'd called to say she needed a break from reality. "Thanks. I'm not sure if I'll come out, but it's nice to know the option is there."

"Whatever you want to do is cool with me. You're working too hard, Em. You deserve a vacation." He briefly wondered if her being at his cabin might somehow derail an evening with Callie, but he quickly dismissed the idea. Callie would probably never leave her friends overnight, and he wasn't even sure they'd move to sleeping together that quickly. He wanted to leave the pace of their relationship up to Callie, even though he wasn't sure he'd be able to hold back. The anticipation of seeing her, touching her, and kissing her made for a hard day in more ways than one.

"When are you coming back into town? Jake's coming in for the weekend next week, and we're all going to Luke and Daisy's for a barbecue. I think they left messages on your cell, but I know you can't get reception there. Can you make it?"

He hadn't seen his older brother Jake in three months. He was a stuntman in Los Angeles, and his filming schedule made it difficult for him to visit. "I'll make sure I can. I have to run, Em. Love you."

Wes hung up the phone and splayed his hands on the desk. "If you're here about the applications, I've already gone through them."

"I'm not, but what did you think?" Chip leaned forward, and his shaggy hair flopped into his eyes.

"Nothing overly impressive. What *are* you here for?"

"It's none of my business, but—"

Christ. Cutter must have mentioned seeing him and Callie together, or he'd found out about the jeans. Wes pushed himself to his feet. "Then keep it to yourself. Come on, Sweets." He slapped his thigh, and Sweets crawled out from under the desk.

Chip rose and met him eye to eye. "Wes, you're putting yourself out there in the open for all the employees to see. She's been here a day or two, and suddenly you're willing to let the employees see that you don't follow your own advice? Eight years of holding back, gone—just like that?"

Wes clenched his jaw.

Chip lowered his voice. "I've known you since we were yay high." He held his hand waist high. "I'm just protecting you here, man. Tell me this is something more than a fling, and I'll back off. But if it's not, we have to protect our business reputation—and you're the last person that I should have to say that to."

"No shit. You think I don't know that? You're like a broken record." Wes pushed past him, and Chip grabbed his arm.

"Think with the head on your shoulders, not the one in your pants. If it's real, fine. As I said, I'll back off. But we've spent eight long years building a business we're proud of. And we've had some hot pieces of ass in here. Too many to count. Think before you…" Chip searched Wes's eyes, then blinked several times and released Wes's arm. "Holy shit. You have feelings for her."

Wes had been thinking about how quickly his brother Luke had fallen for Daisy and how Luke had known without any hesitation that she was *the one*. Wes hadn't believed it at first. In fact, he'd just about told Luke as much, and as his stomach went all weird and desire coiled deep in his belly at the very thought of Callie, he was beginning to think he understood what Luke felt.

"Hey, Wes, if you do, it's cool, man." Chip took a step back, allowing Wes to pass.

Wes trusted Chip with his life and his secrets, but he didn't understand what was going on with his emotions, and he wasn't about to let anyone else contemplate his feelings until he had a handle on them.

"I've got a skeet shooting lesson to give."

CALLIE HELD THE property map as they went in search of the shooting range. "It says it's near the goat barn. Do you remember seeing a goat barn?" The receptionist at the lodge told them to walk past the picnic area and follow the dirt path to the goat barn. She'd marked it on the map, and Callie felt like they'd been walking forever.

"Look. Behind the trees. There it is." Christine pointed to a group of trees. "I guess the goats need privacy."

"Turn around, you guys," Bonnie called to them.

Callie and Christine turned, and Bonnie took a picture. "I want a copy," Callie said.

"Me too," Christine added.

"You know I'll send each of you a CD of the whole trip and put them on Flickr, so chill." Bonnie handed the camera to Callie. "Take one of me and Kathie so you know we were here, too."

"Remember the trip to Cape May that spring break when we got home and didn't have a single picture of Bon?" Kathie winced. "Good thing you were good at Photoshopping."

"We looked extra slim in those pics. Did you notice?" Bonnie smiled. "Like I said, I've got your backs."

As they came upon the goat pen, they found Cutter feeding a baby goat with a bottle.

"Aw, look how adorable he is," Callie said.

"The goat or Cutter?" Kathie asked.

"Both, in my opinion." Bonnie took a picture. "Come on. Let's see if we can feed them."

Cutter looked up as they came to the fence. "Hi. Looking

for the shooting range?"

"Yeah, but we saw these babies. Can we come in and pet them?" Christine asked.

"Sure." Cutter opened the gate and handed her a bottle. "You can feed them if you'd like. We like our kids to get as much love as they can."

Callie petted a small brown goat. It *baa*ed and they all *aw*ed.

Kathie pulled a handful of grass from the ground and held it out to one of the baby goats.

"That one's name is Buster. He's really sweet." He went into the barn, and a few minutes later he brought out baby bottles for each of them to feed the goats.

"This is as good as finding a new author I love." Callie could practically hear Christine's eyes roll.

Bonnie held a bottle for a baby goat. "Almost makes me want a baby."

"Whoa, not me. I've got a lot of books to write before I give up all my free time." Kathie repositioned the bottle for the goat. "Although, they are pretty darn sweet."

Callie sat on a log and fed the goat. She loved listening to her friends. She could guess each of their reactions to most things, and as much as she probably should resent them for lying to her about the trip, she'd had a better time the last two days than she could ever remember—even with the runaway horse. They did know her well, and she'd bet that if asked again, they might even call her brave, because she knew in her heart that they'd never have let her move away if they didn't think she could handle it. They loved her that much.

Cutter sat beside her and watched over them with an easy

smile.

"How long have you worked at The Woodlands?" Callie asked.

He took off his hat and wiped his brow, squinting against the bright sun. "Few years."

"Do you like it?"

His smile widened and his eyes lit up. "Every second of every day." He drew in a deep breath and brought his focus back to Callie. "What about you? What do you do for a living?"

"I work in a library." She watched his eyebrows lift in surprise. "Why does almost every person I meet have that same reaction?"

"You want the truth?"

She laughed. "Sure. That would be nice."

"Because usually librarians are old fuddy-duddies, not…"

"They didn't start out old. Maybe fuddy-duddy, but not old." She was used to the generalization, and for whatever reason, it didn't bother her. She had to admit, as she'd packed for this trip she'd been excited to wear something other than her work clothes. She wouldn't call the clothes she wore to work fuddy-duddy, though. At least she hoped she leaned more toward proper and quietly sexy than fuddy-duddy. "I feel as lucky as you do."

Callie remembered the look Wes had given Cutter earlier that morning, and she wondered if it was because of the way Cutter had been eyeing her or if there was some other rift between them. She didn't know where her courage came from, but she sat up a little straighter and asked, "Do you like working with Wes?"

Cutter looked down at the baby goat she'd been feeding. "I

can't imagine ever working for anyone else. He's honest and fair handed." He met her gaze. "He's a great boss. A good man."

A good man. She'd had that sense the minute she met him a month ago. Obviously, there wasn't any bad blood between Cutter and Wes, which could only mean that the look she'd seen was Wes staking claim to her. She recognized the fortitude it took for Cutter to refrain from using her question as a chance to belittle Wes and make himself look good. She respected that and she wondered if Wes knew that Cutter held him in such high regard.

"See you got sidetracked."

Wes's deep voice drew both Callie and Cutter's attention toward the gate, where Wes stood in a Woodlands shirt and a pair of jeans that rode low on his hips and tight across his muscular thighs. His dark eyes ran between Callie and Cutter, and she realized they were still sitting side by side.

The air grew tense under Wes's gaze, and Callie knew she was the cause. She glanced at Bonnie, who was clicking pictures again. *Of course.* Kathie gave her an *oh-shit*, wide-eyed look.

Callie handed the bottle to Cutter. "Thanks for letting us feed them. They're so sweet." She took a step toward Wes. "Sorry. But look at these babies. How could we pass by without petting them?"

Wes opened the gate. "Stay," he said to Sweets before shutting the gate. Sweets wagged her tail and obediently remained on the other side. "They are pretty damn cute." He pet one of the babies. "I'm glad Cutter was here to let you in. Thanks, Cutter."

Maybe she'd misread the tension between them. As the others returned the bottles to the barn, Wes slid a possessive hand to Callie's lower back.

117

Nope. I didn't misread you, and I kind of like it.

She felt a little guilty for enjoying the silent male one-upmanship.

Chapter Ten

AT THE SHOOTING range, Wes had a hard time pulling free from the jealousy that gripped him at the sight of Callie sitting shoulder to shoulder with Cutter. It was stupid, and he knew it. He wasn't a jealous guy. Hell, he'd dated women who were dating other men at the same time they were seeing him, and he'd never given a rat's ass. But the minute he'd seen Callie with Cutter, his gut fisted and his chest tightened. What made it worse was that he'd seen a flash of recognition in Callie's eyes, and he hated that he was weak enough to feel jealous in the first place, much less be so struck by it that Callie had recognized it, too. He tried to push the ugly emotion aside, but as he gave the girls a lesson on gun safety, he realized that he was having a hard time meeting Callie's beautiful eyes.

He handed each of them a shotgun. "Even though these are not loaded, remember never to aim them at anyone. We're just going to practice tracking shots first."

"Are you sure you guys don't want to learn to rope cattle instead of shooting skeet?" Callie held the gun as far as she could from her body with the barrel pointed toward the sky.

Kathie held the butt of the gun against her shoulder and pointed the barrel up. "Are you kidding me? To be able to go home and tell Paul that I can shoot? That's priceless."

Christine tossed her visor to the ground and handled the gun like she'd been doing it her whole life. "I don't understand the thrill of shooting a piece of clay. Now, if it were my last boyfriend, I could get behind that one hundred percent."

"No shooting ex-boyfriends." *Christ Almighty.*

Bonnie shouldered her shotgun. "Sorry to tell you this, Kath, but I doubt your accountant or my lawyer husband will be too impressed by this."

Wes taught them the correct grip and showed them how to move the gun in an arc to track the shot.

"The targets move fast. Even experienced shooters have to develop some muscle memory in order to hit them. This is not an easy thing to do, and it's more about the mechanics of following the skeet and shooting ahead of the target than it is about aim, so don't be surprised if you don't hit any." Once the others had the hang of holding their guns, he went to help Callie.

She nibbled on her lower lip and held the gun with a rigid grip. She looked at the gun like it might explode at any second. He stifled the urge to take the gun out of her hands and hold her. Jesus. He needed to get a handle on his emotions. He was supposed to be helping her, not falling for her. He forced himself to concentrate on his job rather than his heart.

"Here. Let me show you." He stood behind Callie and helped her lift the shotgun. One breath of her sweet scent quickened his pulse.

"Like this?" She held the butt of the gun to her shoulder. She was leaning forward too far, and her ass pressed against his crotch.

Not that Wes minded, but he was still struggling with jealousy and having a hard time thinking straight. What if he'd totally misread Callie and she was interested in Cutter? Even a little? Who was he to assume she'd see only him? Shit. He hadn't even realized he was thinking about that until just now. That was exactly it. He *wanted* her to see only him. He *did* give a shit. And, by God, he wanted to see only her.

How the hell did he get here so fast?

Callie's eyes narrowed, intent on aiming the gun that looked out of place in her delicate hands, and his heart opened even more. Yeah, he wanted her. *Only her.* And he had no idea how to get from here to there. He was practiced at avoiding monogamy, not asking for it.

"Wes?" Callie looked to him for direction.

"Sorry." *Shit. Focus.* He tried to push away the jealousy and the realization of what he wanted and focus on doing his job. *Yeah, right.* He stepped back to relieve the pressure of her perfect ass from his crotch, which was rapidly swelling with desire.

"Bend your front leg a little, and place your weight on your front foot."

She adjusted her footing.

"Good. Perfect." Unable to stay away, he stepped in closer again—telling himself he had to in order to position the gun correctly. He pressed his cheek to hers and settled one hand on the curve of her hip. "Keep the gun in tight. Good. Perfect."

"Really? Yay."

She was too damn cute. "Okay, good. Now tell me you'll only date me." *Holy shit. Where the fuck did that come from?*

"Okay. Wait. What?" She shifted confused eyes to him, still holding the gun in place.

He gulped a deep breath. His nerves pinged throughout his

body like electrical shocks. He felt like a teenager asking her to go steady, only this was so much bigger. He held his breath, and out of his peripheral vision, he noticed Bonnie had set down her gun and begun taking pictures of them. *Great.* He couldn't deal with that right now. He had to finish what he'd started.

Callie turned toward him with the butt of the gun at her shoulder, the nose lowered to his thigh. He shifted the gun away with his hand.

"Wes?" she whispered.

"I realize that this isn't the time or place to say that, and I'm sorry. I have no idea how it slipped out. The last thing I want to do is pressure you." He lowered his voice, unable—or maybe unwilling—to stop what he'd started. "I saw you with Cutter and…Callie, I've never been jealous, but…" He glanced at her friends, who were now thankfully talking among themselves, which meant he was doing a shit job of leading the group. *Christ.*

He drew his attention back to Callie. "You saw it. I know you did, and I'm not proud of that. Cutter's a great guy, and if you're interested in him, I'll back off, but I really like you, and I'd like to see only you. And if you're interested, then I'd like it if you'd see only me."

Holy shit. He couldn't believe he was asking her to see only him. Was that even how it was done? He had no idea.

Callie placed her dainty hand on his forearm—damn, she felt good—and she smiled up at him. "I'd like that."

He let out a loud breath and nearly lost his balance as he dodged the barrel of her shotgun. He slipped it from her grasp and wrapped her in his arms—right there in front of her friends and Bonnie's big-ass camera lens. He felt like doing a fist pump and exclaiming, *Yes!* Even though his heart was galloping at full speed, he somehow managed to keep his cool. He drew back and couldn't help but kiss her quickly.

"Okay?" He didn't know what else to say. *Thank you? I'm the luckiest guy on earth? I want to kiss you again?*

She nodded with a wide smile that lit up her eyes and told him everything he needed to know.

"I feel like I just captured a big moment on film," Bonnie called.

"You did," Callie yelled back.

"Care to share?" Kathie asked.

Callie flushed pink.

"You would get a straighter answer from a corkscrew," Christine hollered.

Wes was sidetracked for a few minutes while he reveled in the thrill of their new relationship status. He realized the group was waiting on him and forced himself to focus on the activity at hand.

"Ready to shoot some skeet?" He went over the directions again and made sure they were each comfortable with the movements and positioning before he loaded the guns.

"Can I go first?" Callie stood with her shoulders back and one hand on her hip.

"Whoa. What did you do, Wes? Inject her with confidence? You get that, Bon?" Christine hollered again.

Huh. Now, there's a thought. Callie did look and sound more confident.

"On it." Bonnie set down her gun and lifted her camera.

"You sure, Callie?" Wes saw a glint in her eyes that hadn't been there before and instinctively knew that she was as thrilled as he was with their decision.

"I'm not sure. I think I can do this, and I promised I would try." She lifted the gun to her shoulder. "What am I supposed to yell again?"

"Pull." Wes reminded her. He sidled up to Bonnie and lowered his voice. "Can you get a few close-ups for me?"

"Absolutely." She focused her camera.

"Remember, the gun has a kick to it, and whatever you do, don't drop it. Ready when you are, Cal." He expected her arms to tremble and her stance to falter, but Callie stood with her weight perfectly distributed, her hands positioned firmly in place. With his thumb on the remote control, Wes watched Callie draw in a deep breath and waited for her to say *pull*. And waited.

He was about to ask her if she wanted someone else to go first when she finally said, "Pull."

The skeet went up, and Callie shot—amazingly without shutting her eyes or dropping the gun when she pulled the trigger—and hit the target.

"Holy shit."

Callie screamed and jumped up and down, waving the gun. "Oh my gosh! I did it! Did you see that?"

Kathie and Christine cheered and ran to Callie while Bonnie took pictures. Sweets barked at their excitement.

"I had no idea you were a relative of Annie Oakley. Damn, girl." Christine looked up at the sky.

Callie swung around with the gun at hip level. Wes snagged it before she shot someone. He didn't want to interrupt Callie's celebration with her friends. He refrained from swooping her into his arms for a congratulatory kiss.

"Get in there, Bon," he said. "I'll take the pictures." Seeing the pride in Callie's eyes made his heart swell. He captured beautiful images of Callie and her friends laughing and squealing so loudly that Sweets howled.

When he lowered the camera, his eyes caught Callie's for a beat, no longer than a breath, and the feeling it birthed inside of him was unlike anything he'd ever felt before, like he—*they*—were on the cusp of something new and exciting. A beginning. Their beginning.

Our beginning.

Chapter Eleven

WES HEADED DOWN to the barbecue pit for lunch before meeting up with Callie for her private riding lesson.

"How's it going, boss?" Butch filled a bun with pulled pork and set it on Wes's plate beside a mound of vegetables. He slid his pointy-toed boots to the side, making room for Sweets to lie at his feet. He smiled at the pup and tossed a hunk of meat to her, then wiped his hand on a rag that hung from the pocket of his jeans.

"Can't complain. How did the cattle run go?" Butch and two other ranch hands had driven the cattle up the mountain to a new grazing spot earlier in the day.

"You know, long ride up, short ride down." He made himself a sandwich and joined Wes at a picnic table. The sun glared off of his bald head. He gazed out at the mountains as he spoke with a slow drawl. "Heard you're giving a riding lesson this afternoon before you take off for camp." Camp, or what they sometimes referred to as backcountry, was a level spot near the river where they set up tents for overnight pioneering adventures like the one he was taking Callie and her friends on later that day.

"You heard that, huh?" Wes took a bite of the sweet pork

barbecue. Butch's cooking never disappointed.

"Heard more than that." He took a bite of his own sandwich and stared straight ahead.

I bet you did. Wes let the comment rest. He was in too good of a mood to deal with questions or opinions on why he shouldn't get involved with Callie.

Butch took another bite and ate in silence for a few minutes. "I was thinking about Roxy the other day." Roxy was his dearly departed wife.

Wes knew how much Butch missed Roxy. When he spoke of her, his voice became low and thoughtful and his eyes shifted away from whomever he was talking with, as they did now.

"I was thinking about how she used to look at me, like I was her whole world one minute, and then I'd say something stupid, and she'd roll her eyes and look right through me, it seemed. Like she was thinking something like, *You're an asshole, but, God, I love you.*" He nodded. "You know that look? Ever see it?"

"I think I grew up with it. That's how my mom used to look at all of us, and I'm sure I saw it from Pierce and Ross a few dozen times."

Butch shook his head. "Nah, this is different. This couldn't come from anyone but a woman who loved you like a lover, not a mother or a sibling." He took another bite of his sandwich, and when he was done eating, he sighed. "I'd give anything to see that look again."

Wes draped an arm over his shoulder. "I'm sorry, Butch. I wish I could bring her back."

"So do I, Wes. So do I."

"How did you know Roxy was the right woman for you?"

He shrugged. "I didn't know she was the right one. I knew she was the only one."

Wes could see from the sadness in Butch's eyes that he was having a hard time today. He loved Butch like family, and he hated seeing him sad.

"Do you want to have a drink or something later, before I leave for camp?"

"Nah. You have a pretty little filly waiting for you. I appreciate the thought, though." Butch splayed his hands on the picnic table and pushed to his feet. He set a hand on Wes's shoulder. "Have a good time on that overnight, Wes. And for the record, I trust your gut as much as I trust my own."

After Wes finished eating, he checked on the horses and found Cutter going over the budget and inventory in the barn office. Wes stood in the doorframe watching him. He was meticulous about the work, and Wes was thankful for his willingness to do the work Wes knew he could never do. He was smart and he could be detail oriented, but Chip was right—he had an aversion to paperwork that he just couldn't shake.

"Hey," Cutter said.

"Hey." He felt guilty for not promoting Cutter, and as he watched him drag his finger across the color-coded lines he'd constructed, he began to reconsider his position. "Thanks for doing all you do around here, Cutter."

Cutter cocked his head and nodded. "Sure. Do you need me to do something? I saddled Trina for your lesson."

"Great, thanks. I don't need anything. I just wanted to say thanks."

A smile spread across Cutter's face. "No problem. Glad I could help."

Ten minutes later, Wes was still thinking about Cutter's dedication to the ranch as he climbed the porch steps to Callie's cabin. He heard the girls talking around back.

"Every time I tried to date a man who wasn't a cowboy, I was disappointed. A man who doesn't smell like he can roll in the hay just isn't right for me."

He recognized Christine's sarcastic tone and followed it around the cabin to the back deck, where they were stretched out on Adirondack chairs in their bikinis.

"So you're married to a cowboy?" He arched a brow at Christine.

Sweets bounded onto the deck with her tail wagging and licked Callie's legs. Callie smothered her with kisses.

"No. Billy's a carpenter," Christine answered. "But he puts on chaps at bedtime and lets me call him Tex."

"Ride 'em cowboy," Kathie cheered.

Wes couldn't tear his eyes from Callie in a yellow string bikini that rode high on her hips. Her belly was narrow along her hips and curved up a little along the center in a sexy, feminine, barely there pillow that was so inviting, Wes wanted to lay his head down on it and wrap his arms around her. His eyes slid north, and he was a little envious of the triangular pieces of stretchy material clinging to her breasts. He drank her in as she sat there with one knee bent and the other stretched out in front of her, loving up the dog he adored. He wanted to feel her against him, run his tongue along every inch of exposed skin, then slowly make his way to the hidden parts.

Callie's cheeks flushed, and he realized he was staring. He shifted his eyes away.

"Ready to go for a ride?"

All of the girls laughed.

Christ. He shook his head to brush off the sprinkle of embarrassment. "I'm kind of outnumbered here. I have a feeling that anything I say will be twisted into a double entendre." Wes ran his hand down his face, but his smile refused to be quelled.

Callie rose to her feet and, good Lord, seeing her stand before him in that barely there bikini made a certain southern region of Wes rise, too. He shoved his hands in his pockets.

"Let me get changed and I'll be right down." Callie went inside.

"Sit. Enjoy the shade." Bonnie patted the empty chair.

"Why aren't you lying on the grass in the side yard, where it's sunny?"

"You mean there's no sun here?" Christine asked with wide eyes. "No wonder I'm not getting tan."

"The sun was perfect until about ten minutes ago, when it slipped behind the trees." Bonnie lowered her voice. "So, you're going to teach her how to ride?"

"Hopefully." Although after seeing her in that tiny bikini, his body had other things in mind.

"And you're going steady?" Kathie locked eyes with Wes.

"Kathie." Bonnie swatted her arm.

"What?" Kathie swatted Bonnie back.

"Yeah, I guess you could call it that." Jesus, were they going to rib him like his siblings would?

Kathie leaned closer to him. "So, tell us the truth. Do you read the books you ask her to pick out for you each week, or did you ask her to do that just so you could get to know her?"

Did all women know what men were really up to, or did they just fish until they got the answers?

"Okay, I'm ready." Callie stood in the doorway, wearing a three-quarter-sleeved light blue shirt that clung to her curves and, he assumed, the cutoffs he'd bought for her. Her toned legs disappeared into a pair of cowgirl boots, heightening her allure.

Damn, you are scorching hot. Her timing was perfect to rescue Wes from her friends' inquisition. He reached for Callie's hand, which she took with a quick glance at her girlfriends. He didn't miss the way her eyebrows lifted or the excited smile she was trying to mask.

"Enjoy your downtime because we leave in a few hours for camp."

Kathie and Christine lay back with a sigh and closed their eyes.

"Good luck, Cal. Remember, you can do this. You're strong and brave, and you've got your own personal wrangler, so no excuses." Bonnie made a shooing motion with her hand. "Go. Have fun."

WALKING THROUGH THE property with Wes made everything feel different. His hand was big and warm, and Callie's heart had forgotten how to pitter-patter altogether. He sparked a combination of frenetic heartbeats and tingling of her nerves, and she loved every second of the sensations that had quickly become familiar. They were crossing the footbridge at the base of the hill when Wes stopped and folded her into his arms.

He leaned down and kissed her softly. God, she loved his tender and sweet kisses, especially knowing that behind that tenderness, passion brewed. She felt him holding back when she rocked her hips into his. When their lips parted, she almost pulled him into another kiss; then she remembered that this beautiful place, this perfect, romantic spot, with the creek rippling beneath them and the horses grazing in the fields, was his workplace.

"You look cute as hell in those shorts." He took her hand, and they continued across the bridge toward the barn.

"Thanks. They were a gift from a secret admirer." She glanced up at him, and he smiled.

"I'm afraid you've ruined any chance I had at being a secret anything." He squeezed her hand. "No one here has ever seen me with a girlfriend, so we should probably expect a few strange looks."

Girlfriend. She tucked that simple word that made her head spin into a secret place to swoon over later.

Two men on horses waved to Wes as they crossed the grass toward the riding arena. He waved back and tightened his grip on Callie's hand.

"Are you sure you want to be so open about us? I don't want to cause any trouble for you." Callie thought of her own job. She couldn't exactly stop shelving books and give Wes a passionate kiss in the middle of the library or hold his hand as she moved from one task to the next. Prim and proper Alice would have a heart attack. *She* might have a heart attack.

"As sure as I've ever been about anything." He lifted her hand to his lips and kissed it.

Wow.

They walked the rest of the way in silence, passing the main riding area to a small round pen that couldn't have been more than sixty feet in diameter. A white horse was waiting for them, saddled up and ready to ride. The smell of horses and leather wafted through the air. Wes drew in a deep breath and smiled.

"You really love the ranch, don't you?"

"So much it's hard to put into words. I can't imagine not being able to look at that view or not knowing that at any moment I can jump on a horse and ride up the mountains or down to the river. I can sleep under the stars, and if I had to, I could forage for food and live in the wilderness." He ran his hand through his hair. "It's freeing. No walls, hard work." He shrugged. "I guess I'm simple."

"That's hardly simple." She thought of him roping the steer and fearlessly saving her from the horse she'd been unable to control.

He placed his hands on her arms just below her shoulders and gazed into her eyes. "I know you're nervous about all of this, the horse, camping… But I hope you'll see how serene the wilderness can be and how every breath can feel different and invigorating once you get past your fears."

She breathed harder at his words, his passion, and the thought of seeing the things she feared through new, braver eyes. Then reality set in.

"What if I can't get past my fears?" She'd been trying not to think about it all afternoon, and she was careful to hold back the question she really wanted to ask. *Will you stop being interested in me?*

"Then at least you've tried. There's no shame in not being able to get past your fears, Callie. You're willing to face them, and that's all that matters. Fear drives me to push myself further, because if I don't try to overcome it, I might miss out on the best things in life and never even realize it." His eyes grew serious. "Holy shit." He let out a loud breath and looked away.

"What?"

"I was thinking of something my bookkeeper said to me before I left town." He shook his head. "Clarissa Simmons, she's been our bookkeeper for three years. Anyway, she said I might meet my soul mate out here." His eyes searched Callie's.

Soul mate. Yes, that's exactly what you feel like. She liked Clarissa already.

"*Huh.*" Wes smiled. "Let's get started so we can get to camp before dark."

As they neared the tall, powerful horse, the memory of having no control over the other horse consumed Callie and stalled her thoughts.

Wes slipped his arm around her waist and stepped between her and the horse, which was behind the fence, but she was still glad for the barrier.

"I'm not going to let anything happen, Callie. I'll be right there with you, but you have to keep your eyes open, and no startling your horse. Your heels are like gas pedals. If you dig them in, she will react. Okay?"

She managed a nod.

He glanced over his shoulder. "This is Trina. She's a sweet, calm horse. It's like she eats Valium instead of horse feed. Callie, you look like you're ready to run away. If I didn't think you could learn how to ride with complete control, I wouldn't let you up on her. The other horse took off because you kicked her with your heels. You can control that."

Callie inhaled a sharp breath. She clutched his forearms and drew strength from them. She tried to push past the fear that screamed *Don't climb on that horse!* But the memory of the horse galloping and the fear it incited in her was too much. She felt her arms tremble and dropped her eyes to his chest. That was much better.

Concentrate on him, not the horse.

With his index finger, he lifted her chin. "Why don't we just stand here a minute and get used to Trina." He guided her to the fence, and the horse pressed her muzzle into his chest.

She wanted to bury her face in his chest.

He stroked the horse's cheek and kissed her on the muzzle. "Hey there. Trina. You'll take good care of my girl, won't you?"

My girl. She pushed her fear a little farther away.

Wes took her hand and brought it to Trina's cheek. He guided it down the firm muscles of her jaw. Callie could see only one of Trina's eyes from where she stood. The horse looked enormous, but the way she looked at Callie, with inky lashes any woman would kill for and a kind gaze, brought Callie a step closer. Wes lowered his hand to the small of her back. She felt safe knowing he was there with her. Trina shifted her head toward Callie, and she stumbled backward.

"She wants to get closer to you. It's okay. This is how horses connect with us." He slipped his hands around Callie from behind. Trina's nostrils flared as she sniffed Callie; then she lowered her head and pressed her muzzle just below Callie's chin.

It felt like a hug. She didn't know she could feel anything like that from a horse. She petted Trina. "Hi. She is sweet, isn't she?"

"She is. She likes you." Wes pressed his cheek to hers. "She feels what you feel. If you remember that, you'll connect with her. If you're fearful, she'll be fearful. If you're calm, she'll be calm."

She was trying to be calm, but his warm breath brushed against her neck, and she had no chance at being calm with that going on, or with his arms wrapped around her middle and his hips against her butt. *Oh boy.*

Callie turned around, hands pressed flat against his chest. *Oh, that's worse!* "Wes, I'm not sure I can calm down with you teaching me to ride."

He grinned, and his head fell back with a deep, sexy laugh that made her smile and feel a little silly.

"Well, then, we just might have a problem." He kissed her forehead before she banged it against his chest.

"What am I going to do?" He was laughing, and she was so damn turned on that her nipples were hard. This was not good. She had to get past this crazy desire to tear his clothes off so she could function like a normal woman. *Serious. Be serious.* She looked up at him and—*damn it*—between his playful smile and the desire in his eyes, she was a goner.

"I can't do it." She took a step back and regretfully peeled her hands from his chest. He took a step forward and she held her palms out. "No. Stay there. Just...stay there. And if you could somehow become uglier, that would be good."

He arched a brow.

She ran her eyes down his godlike body. "Ugh. And can you maybe get fat or something?" She spun around and looked at the horse.

"Cal."

She heard him take a step toward her, felt heat radiating from him. "No. Stop. Don't come closer. I can't be calm with you near me. Can't you have someone else teach me?"

His hands found her hips, and she closed her eyes. His stubbly jaw pressed against her cheek, and she breathed him in.

Okay, forget it. *Just stay right here forever. I don't need to ride the darn horse.*

"I can get someone else to teach you," he whispered.

She heard regret in his voice, cushioned by a thin layer of understanding. She should be adult enough to deal with this, and as much as the rush of new feelings excited her, this

FATED FOR LOVE

particular issue made her feel weak. She might be shy, but Callie didn't like feeling weak. This wasn't fear that was holding her back; it was lust. She could handle lust.

Couldn't she?

Damn it. She had to be able to.

She faced him again, and the feel of him against her drew a disastrously wanton groan from her lungs.

No I definitely cannot do this.

Wes laughed again and brushed away the hair that had fallen into her eyes.

"Let me get Butch."

"No. This is stupid. I should be able to calm down. Do you really think the horse will feel a difference?"

He looked at Trina. Callie swore the darn horse was smiling.

"I think it's more about you than the horse. You need to be comfortable and confident when you climb on her. If you can't focus, and you startle or kick her in the ribs, she probably won't run like the other horse did, but she'd definitely pick up her pace."

"Okay. You know what? This is stupid. I can totally handle this." *I think. I hope.* She pushed away from him again and drew her shoulders back. "I can do this. I don't need Butch." She glanced over her shoulder at Wes. "I need you. I just need to get my own...thoughts"—*desires, lust*—"under control. I can do this." With determination, she concentrated on the horse.

"You sure?"

"More than sure." *I think.* "Just don't look at me like you want to kiss me."

He arched a brow again.

She rolled her eyes. "Come on, or it'll be dark by the time I get up on that horse."

After a few embarrassing minutes, Callie made it up onto the saddle. Wes stood sentinel beside her, and surprisingly, Callie felt confident. The round pen was too small for the horse to take off at full speed—or at least she hoped it was. She reminded herself not to dig her heels into the horse's ribs and to hold the reins loosely.

She could do this. She refused to be the girl who needed a chaperone on a horse forever. So what if she was in the library club throughout elementary school, and while her friends were taking horseback riding lessons she was making lists of her favorite authors and pretending she was Snow White or Cinderella? That didn't mean she *couldn't* learn to ride. Even if it wasn't her favorite thing to do and it wasn't as safe as books and reading chairs or walking in a park on solid ground. It was something Wes loved, and for him, for them, she could do this.

"Are you ready? I'm going to walk with you. Remember to handle the reins gently. When you want her to turn, you need to guide her, give her the clues she needs. Your body is the steering wheel. Tighten the leg on the side you want her to veer toward, lean slightly that way with your head and shoulder, and loosen the reins on that side."

Callie nodded. "Look, lean, ease up in the direction I want to turn, give a little squeeze with that leg and tighten up the reins on the other side. I can do that."

"Impressive. Ready?"

Not really. "Yes."

"You've got this, Cal."

She didn't think as she leaned down and kissed him. "Thank you."

"I think I should be thanking you."

"Not for the kiss, silly, for this. For believing in me enough to put up with my ridiculous fears to help me."

His smile softened. "Put up with? I hope you're kidding, because if this is the worst thing I have to *put up with* where you're concerned, I'm a lucky man." He glanced at Cutter heading toward the barn. "I have a feeling that watching men gawk at you is going to be far more difficult than helping waylay your fears."

A lucky man. That sent a little thrill through her. The muscle in his jaw twitched, and she knew he had been referring to Cutter.

"Wes, Cutter didn't act inappropriately with me. He was telling me about how much he loves working here and how much he respects you."

Wes knitted his brows together again. He shifted his gaze to Cutter, and when he brought his attention back to Callie, his eyes were dark and serious.

"Let's walk," he said.

Trina was a graceful horse. Callie could feel the power beneath her, the shifting of the horse's muscles even with her slow gait. Callie felt more in control of her body and her actions. Wes's eyes shifted between the horse and Callie as he walked alongside them, and she knew her confidence was bolstered because of his faith in her and his desire to help her experience more than the inside of a library and expand her world—*with* him. It occurred to her how similar that was to the reasons her friends had brought her to the ranch in the first place, and the similarity comforted her.

"I think I'm okay." She watched his eyes turn serious again. "Really. I feel good about her, and I think I can do it."

"I *know* you can." He went to the edge of the riding ring

and watched her.

Callie sat up tall, and as the minutes passed, her confidence grew. She guided Trina to the left, then to the right, just to be sure she had the motions down, and half an hour later, with Wes beaming up at her with pride in his gorgeous dark eyes, she leaned forward and hugged Trina's thick, powerful neck.

Thank you.

She felt empowered and proud that she'd taken the chance to get up on the horse. As Wes lifted her down from the horse, her newfound confidence and excitement coalesced. She jumped into his arms, wrapped her legs around his waist, and kissed him. She didn't hesitate as she deepened the kiss, and when his hand slid to the curve of her butt, she shivered with the thrill of it all. She drew back and ran her hands along his cheeks.

"I did it." She felt her cheeks stretched tight with a smile.

"You did it." He kissed her again. "I never had any doubt."

"I didn't really want to do it on my own when it was so much fun riding with you wrapped around me."

"I have a feeling I'll be wrapped around you for a very long time, Callie Barnes."

When she kissed him again, she felt as though she'd loved him for a hundred years, and when he tightened his grip on her, she wanted to love him for a hundred more.

Chapter Twelve

CALLIE COULD BARELY believe she was riding a horse, much less riding it down a mountain. Granted, the trail was wide and felt more level than sloped, and she was nowhere near the edge of the mountain, but still. She was actually riding a horse. She'd always thought she was happy with her life. She had a job she loved and friends she adored, parents who loved and protected her, and a peaceful life in general. What she hadn't taken into consideration, and apparently her friends, and now Wes, had, was how much more there was to life than the safe corner where she'd tucked herself away. Her world was expanding right before her eyes, with activities and with Wes, and she found herself wondering how she could have closed herself off for so long.

She thought about her parents. Her mother worked in the administrative offices of an oil company, and her father was the director of a health care company. Family vacations were two weeks of city travel, where they'd visit museums, libraries, and historic institutions. They weren't outdoorsy people, but they were a happy and loving family. Callie had never felt as though she were missing out on anything. But as she rode down the mountain on a horse that seemed to enjoy the ride as much as she was, surrounded by miles of wildflowers, brush, and tall trees, with the scent of pine and earth filling her lungs, she realized that there was much more out there to experience. Wes had been right. If she'd given in to her fears, she'd never have known what she was missing.

Wes glanced over his shoulder and smiled, and she knew there was more she couldn't ignore. She was falling hard for him, in a way that had the feel of permanence. That should scare her into hesitation, but instead, it filled her with hope.

They followed the trail around a bend, and a line of white tents came into view.

"Look! We made it!" Christine hollered.

Callie wondered if she'd thought they might not and wrote it off to Christine being Christine. Always the jokester. She felt like they were riding into a postcard with the sun riding low in the sky, casting its last streak of sunlight through two mountain peaks in the distance. The trail gave way to a field of grass, beyond which were acres of tall grass and a forested mountainside to their left and a glistening lake, complete with a rocky shoreline, to their right.

Callie guided the horse across the grassy area between the lake and the mountains to a dirt clearing, where four thick tree trunks, stripped of their bark and cut to ten feet, served as benches around a rocky fire pit. At one end of the clearing was a long picnic table. An enormous orange cooler sat on the ground beside the table, and on the far side of the clearing, constructed against a backdrop of thick forest, were several tents. Some tents were built in the style of tepees; others were rectangular in shape with a tall peak in the center. The flaps of the tents were tied open, and where there might be metal poles on a typical structure, there were thick branches secured to the canvas tents with rope. There was a cot in each tent, and as the horse strolled closer, Callie noticed that some tents had two cots.

Callie glanced at her friends, then at Wes, who was a living, breathing fantasy sitting in profile on a black horse. She hadn't connected the idea of camping to sleeping—or rather, not sleeping—in tents with the overnight trip. She thought of the naughty possibilities. Slipping into his tent after dark, or maybe he'd sneak into hers. She glanced back at Kathie, who flashed a knowing smile that made Callie's heart beat faster. Obviously, she was a little slow on the uptake, because when she looked at Christine and Bonnie, they also had a look of mischief in their eyes. Callie ran through a quick mental checklist, just in case they decided to take their relationship to the next level, and boy, did she ever hope they would. She was on the pill. She was wearing lacy panties and a matching bra. Who was she kidding? She only owned lacy panties and bras. They were her guilty pleasures. She should buy stock in Victoria's Secret. Callie liked to feel feminine, and she liked the lace and frills that Victoria's Secret was known for. She had never been a thong girl, like Kathie and Christine. Even the idea of a thong up her butt crack was uncomfortable.

She was so lost in thought that she didn't notice everyone else had dismounted their horses until Wes was standing beside her with his arms outstretched.

"Ready, babe?"

She nearly fell into his arms at the sound of *babe* in his deep voice. He made the word sound sexy and rugged at once. When her feet hit the ground, she was still thinking about the tents—and Wes. Naked. *Oh, good Lord.* Her body flashed hot.

Wes leaned down and whispered, "You're blushing."

She whimpered a little, and that made her cheeks heat even

more.

He held her against him. "You seriously cannot make those sexy little noises, or I'll never be able to keep my hands off you."

Holy. Cow. There was so much promise in his voice that Callie had to clench her eyes shut to keep from whimpering again.

"Okay, lover boy. What now?" Christine stood by her horse with her arms crossed, tapping her foot.

Callie stepped back, giving Wes room to do his job. And giving herself room to remember how to function. How would she make it until tonight with that promise in her head? And what if he didn't come to her tonight?

She'd never wanted to be touched and to touch a man so desperately in her life.

"Tents, food, drinks." He pointed to each area as he spoke. "You can choose whichever tent you'd like. The cooler is full of food and drinks, and we'll cook over the fire tonight. Tomorrow we'll go down to the river to go fishing, and if you're up for it, we'll go for a hike." He pointed to the far corner of the camp. "There are chemical toilets behind the tents."

"Chemical toilets?" Kathie asked.

"We used to have outhouses. I think you'll like these better. Don't worry. They're not that gross, and they're emptied after every trip." Wes was obviously used to this reaction.

"It's better than using the woods, Kath," Callie offered with a shrug. She didn't think anything could spoil the idea of a night under the stars with Wes. She saw Bonnie walking toward her with a serious stare.

"Hey, Cal, come with me." Bonnie grabbed her by the arm and dragged her away. "I just want to talk to Callie a minute. Go ahead and dole out the instructions," she called over her shoulder.

"What are you doing?" Callie tried to focus on Wes's voice as he told Christine and Kathie to choose a tent and let the horses graze in the grass, but after that his voice fell away as she stumbled along beside Bonnie.

"You're holding me so tight it hurts."

"Oh, sorry." Bonnie let go and crossed her arms. She wore a plaid sleeveless shirt tucked into jeans and secured with a thick leather belt.

"You look like you're going to string me up in a tree. What did I do?"

"Nothing." She stared past Callie at the others.

Callie watched Wes helping the others untie their packs from the horses. She wanted to be over there with him.

"What, then?"

"Okay, mama hen here." Bonnie turned her back to others and guided Callie to do the same.

"Oh God. You're making my stomach hurt." She had no idea what Bonnie was going to say, but her mouth was pinched tight and her eyes were narrow and serious, and that couldn't be good.

"I just wanted to say something without the others around. I tried to tell you at the cabin, but we were packing and running late, and the girls were in and out of our room. I can see that I won't have a second with just you here before nightfall, so I had to drag you away. I'm sorry."

"What's so private that the others can't hear?"

Bonnie's eyes softened. "I just wanted to talk to you alone. Look, we all tease a lot about how hot the guys here are and what we'd like to do to them. I know that you know we're just being goofs and having fun. We'd never actually do anything.

We adore our husbands. God, you've known us forever—of course you know that—but I felt like I had to say this, between you and me. I really respect you, Callie. We tease a lot, but you've never fallen for peer pressure, and Lord knows we've put you in situations where a weaker girl would have given in. But those were college days. You know, fun kid stuff. This is real life, and when I see the way you look at Wes and the way he looks at you." The tension in her shoulders eased on a sigh. "Oh, Callie. I just wanted to be sure you weren't caving on your beliefs because of peer pressure."

"Thank you for worrying, but if I didn't cave as a naive freshman when you guys were egging me on night and day, I sure as hell wouldn't cave now." She drew in a deep breath. "I really feel something for him, Bonnie, and I want him more than I've ever wanted anything in my life." She covered her face and took a step away. "Oh God, I sound desperate."

Bonnie pulled her into a hug. "No. You sound like a girl who's falling for a guy, and I'm pulling for you, Cal. On a bigger scale than *hey, let's bang the hot wrangler.* I thought you looked like your heart was so tied up in him it's practically clawing its way out of your chest to get to him."

"You can see that?" *That means he can, too.*

"Yup. I just wanted to be sure. I'd hate myself if we pushed you into doing something with a guy that you really didn't want to." Bonnie glanced behind her at Kathie and Christine pointing at the tents. Christine pulled off her visor and pointed to a tent in the middle. "I better go over there before they pick the best tents."

Callie couldn't love Bonnie more than she did for everything she'd ever done for her, but now she worried that if Bonnie could tell how much she liked Wes, he could, too, and that made her fifty shades of nervous.

Bonnie rolled her eyes. "You're blushing again. I bet when you're fifty you'll still blush."

"Bon, I don't know if we're going to...you know, or not." *But I hope we are.* "But this is the guy that I dream about at night." She lowered her voice. "I mean, I think about doing all sorts of things and not waiting for him to make the first move. Do you think *he* can see that, too?"

"I think it doesn't matter what he sees. Do whatever feels right at the time. There's no right or wrong if you both want it. I'd better join the peanut gallery."

"Thanks, Bon." She watched Bonnie jog toward the tents. Wes stepped into her field of vision, and like pen to paper, she was drawn right to him.

Thank you, Bonnie. Thank you so freaking much for giving me the okay to follow my heart, because I'm not sure I can hold back much longer.

Chapter Thirteen

WES WAITED WHILE the girls chose their tents. He liked privacy, and on overnight trips he usually claimed the tent that was farthest from the group. Tonight he wanted that distance for an entirely different reason. He was going to climb out of his skin if he had to stay away from Callie much longer. She was like a drug, and damn, did he ever need a hit.

He watched as she, too, held back on choosing her tent. When the other three girls moved to the tents at the far side of the camp, Callie took the next in line. *Closer to me.* He wondered if she was thinking that, too.

Callie sat on the cot in her tent. She hated spiders and snakes, and he imagined her worrying about those things while she bounced up and down, palms to the thin mattress, like she was testing out its durability. Was she thinking about the two of them coming together on one of those mattresses later that evening, like he was?

He was so proud of her for riding Trina like a champ, and when she'd jumped into his arms earlier in the day, he'd wanted to carry her up the hill to his cabin and love her until she forgot how to read. The way she looked at him, the way she touched him, hell, everything she'd been doing lately felt like she was ready to move forward, and he was goddamn nervous. *Nervous.* He'd never wanted to *not* fuck something up so badly in his life. He knew that being intimate with Callie couldn't be anything short of mind-numbing. Jesus, just watching her come was ecstasy. It was the whole *taking-the-good-girl-to-bed* thing that was messing with his head. Her words sailed through his mind. *I like sex as much as the next person, but for me, it's connected to my heart.* If that wasn't pressure, he didn't know what was.

Wes grabbed his leather bag and slapped his thigh, bringing Sweets to his side. He filled food and water bowls for her before stowing his bag in the most outlying tent.

While the girls talked, he checked on the horses and led them to the lake to drink. Sweets was sacked out beneath the picnic table when he returned to start the fire.

"Those toilets aren't bad," Kathie hollered. She'd pinned her hair up into a ponytail and had put on a blue hoodie.

What'd I tell you? "Beats the hell out of outhouses."

Bonnie came out of her tent wearing a gray zip-up sweatshirt. "Can we help?"

"Callie's an amazing cook," Christine chimed in.

He lifted his eyes to see Callie's reaction. She'd changed into a cream-colored sweater with a scoop neck. It was slightly transparent, and he could see the outline of her pink bra. One sleeve was mint green, the other was peachy pink, and both covered her knuckles. The edge of her sweater hung loosely over her cutoffs, leaving only the fringe of her shorts visible. She looked so sweet that he wanted to fold her into his arms and snuggle with her.

What the hell is wrong with me?

Snuggle?

Holy hell, you've brought out a whole side of me I never knew existed. And, damn, if I don't love it.

The realization brought him to his feet. Callie laughed at something Christine said and covered her mouth with her hand. Her eyes darted between Christine and Kathie.

"Ready to hand the cooking over to the best cook this side of Kansas?" Christine asked.

He'd hand Callie anything she wanted. "That's up to Callie. Butch already seasoned the steaks and prepared everything we need. It's just a matter of heating it up over the fire."

"That's okay. I'll cook for you some other time." She hooked her index fingers in her pockets and flashed an innocent smile.

"I'll look forward to that." He loved that smile. He loved all her smiles, from the innocent to the shy and the bold, like he'd seen earlier in the day when she'd jumped into his arms and wrapped her legs around him. He needed to snap out of the daze she'd propelled him into, and as she blinked a few times and her smile turned more heated, he forced himself to continue.

"Okay, ladies. I'm going to get dinner rolling. There are margaritas in the cooler, and if you want to take a walk, don't go far, because it'll be dark soon, and take Sweets with you to scare off the bears."

"Bears?" Callie stepped closer to him with a panicked look in her eyes.

He cataloged that reaction for later. Not that he'd need a ruse to get closer to Callie, but he was trying to remember all the things she was afraid of.

"We are in the Colorado Mountains, Cal," Christine reminded her.

Wes touched Callie's arm and felt a zing of electricity course

150

between them. "We don't worry about bears. Keep a clean camp, keep Sweets around, and we'll be fine. They won't bother us if we don't bother them."

"Unless they're superhungry," Kathie said. "Then we might look like a tasty meal."

"Kathie!" Bonnie shook her head. "Callie, if they had trouble with bears, do you really think they'd do these camping trips? Tell her, Wes."

"Tell her you do and she'll end up in your tent tonight." Christine raised her eyebrows in quick succession, causing Callie's cheeks to heat up.

"Christine." Callie glared at her.

"Okay, fine. I'm kidding." Christine poked at the fire with a stick. "Sort of."

Wes laughed. "I swear you guys act like sisters. Don't worry, Cal. Bears aren't going to bother us." He was tempted to whisper, *But you can still share my tent.*

She nodded, but her eyes were now shadowed with worry. Without concern about her friends, who clearly knew everything there was to know about them, he draped his arm over her shoulder and pulled her close. "I won't let anything happen to you. Relax, okay? Just take a deep breath and let's enjoy the evening."

She pressed her palm to his stomach. "Okay."

Holy Christ. How many more hours until your friends are asleep?

They ate dinner around the campfire, and Sweets enjoyed the scraps of meat tossed her way. The margaritas were cold, the meal was tasty, and the stars shone like diamonds against the black sky. With Callie by his side, the cool breeze, and the sounds of the forest surrounding them, Wes couldn't think of anywhere he'd rather be.

"Tell us the truth, Wes. Do you ever get tired of taking these trips?" Bonnie sat between Kathie and Christine, leaning her elbows on her knees, holding her drink in both hands.

"You're married, right, Bonnie?"

"Yeah, the three of us are." She pointed to the others. "Why?"

"Well, do you ever get tired of coming home to your husband?" He watched Christine's eyes light up and knew she had a joke on the tip of her tongue.

"Nope," Bonnie said. "I love everything about Mark, from his stinky feet to his anal need to keep things orderly."

"You just love his anal needs," Christine teased.

They all laughed.

"Sorry. I couldn't help it." Christine took a drink of her margarita. "So you love it. What about when you're not on trips? You live in Trusty, right? Do you miss being here when you're there?"

Wes reached an arm around Callie. "Not on Thursdays."

That earned him a collective *Aw* from her friends.

"What about you guys? What do you do for a living? And do you like what you do?"

"I'm a writer, and yeah, I like it too much." Kathie gazed into the fire. "I think I need a twelve-step program."

"Oh, come on. You're not that bad," Bonnie said.

Kathie glanced up at her. "Yeah, I am. That's one reason I didn't bring my laptop on the trip. It's like an obsession. I think sometimes Paul feels slighted by the attention I give my writing."

"Aw, Kath." Callie tilted her head. "I'm sure Paul doesn't feel slighted. He adores you, and he knows how important your career is."

"Yeah, he does, but still." Kathie took a long drink. "I think I'll plan a trip away like this with Paul. He'd love it."

Christine put an arm around Kathie. "Why don't you plan something more extravagant? Pamper him a little."

"Not that I know much about this, Kathie, but have you thought about defining the hours that you write, like when he's at work? I know it's hard when your work is there with you every second, but maybe treat it more like a job and less like something you love?" Callie shook her head. "That sounded horrible. Less like something you love? Everyone should love their job."

Wes set his drink down and held Callie's hand. He loved her thought process. "You know, from a guy's perspective, I think it's great that you love your job so much, and I have no idea what Paul is like, but I know with my job, and with most of my siblings' jobs, if we don't draw a line, we could easily have no life at all. Sometimes you have to create your own boundaries."

"What do your siblings do?" Callie asked. "For that matter, how many do you have?"

"Five." He waited for the typical wide-eyed response.

"Five?" Callie's eyes widened.

And there it is. "Yup."

"Do they live near you?" Callie asked. "I'm an only child. I can only imagine how great it would be to have a big family."

"Yeah, most of them do. My oldest brother, Pierce, owns casinos and travels a lot, and my third older brother, Jake—he's almost two years older than me—he's a stuntman in L.A. The others live in Trusty. Ross is a vet, Emily is an architect, as I mentioned the other day, and Luke, the youngest, owns a ranch and breeds gypsy horses."

"Hold on." Christine held her palms up. "You have a brother who's a stuntman? Like jump-off-cliffs and tumble-over-moving-cars stuntman?"

"Like all those things and more." He was proud of his family, and he'd be just as proud if they didn't have such well-respected careers.

"What about your parents?" Kathie asked.

Wes finished his drink. "My mom lives in Trusty. My dad took off when I was three." He shrugged.

"I'm sorry," Kathie said.

Callie squeezed his hand. "That's awful. I'm so sorry." She scooted closer to him.

"It's not awful. Really. My mom is amazing, and my brothers and sister and I are close. I don't think you can miss someone you never really knew." He looked up at Kathie, who was watching him intently. "But you can miss someone you know and love."

Kathie nodded.

"So, Kathie, you're a writer. Bonnie, you must be a photographer."

Bonnie had her camera up to her eye, and when Wes looked over, the flash blinded him. "Yup. Nature and wedding photog."

"She's amazing." Callie put her cheek next to Wes's. "Take our picture."

Wes was still seeing spots from the first picture when Bonnie snapped a few more. He kissed Callie, and through closed lids he saw the flash light up.

"I get dibs on copies of those pictures," he said to Bonnie.

"I wouldn't have it any other way," Bonnie answered.

"And, Christine, you're obviously a comedian."

Christine drew her barely there brows together. "What? Why would you think that? I'm a serious person." She slapped her thigh. "A real taskmaster." She turned and shouted, "Hubby, put those chaps on. Brown boots, Stetson too, and get that cute little ass of yours in the bedroom."

Sweets sat up and howled.

"Come here, Sweets." He patted his thigh, and Sweets came to his side. "It's okay." He patted her back. "So how did you get into comedy? Do you do stand-up or...?"

"I sort of fell into it. I was a pharmacist and I used to make jokes a lot, you know, just passing the time. One night I went with a friend to a comedy club and they had an open mike. Four drinks later, I was the ten-o'clock show. The owner of the club gave me a gig and I never looked back."

"That's incredible. So many comedians struggle for years before they find real work. Callie gave me a biography on Charlie Kent, the comedian, and he said it took him nearly ten years before he could earn a living."

"You *do* read the books she gives you." Kathie's eyes widened and jumped between Callie and Wes.

"Callie goes to a lot of trouble to pick them out. Of course I read them. Or at least I try. I don't always have time to get through all three, and I have to admit that I've been too distracted to read at all the last few days."

Callie scooted closer to him. "Some distractions are worth setting books aside for."

"I never thought I'd hear those words from your lips," Bonnie said.

They made s'mores and talked for a long while, until all that was left of the fire were glowing embers. An owl hooted in the distance, and Sweets's ears perked up. She huffed a breath and closed her eyes again. The sounds of crickets and tree frogs sang out in the darkness.

Bonnie rose to her feet. "Well, guys, those margaritas did me in. I assume we'll be up at the ass crack of dawn tomorrow?"

"We have no set schedule, so feel free to sleep in." Wes's pulse sped up at the thought of finally being alone with Callie.

"I'm exhausted, too." Christine rose and stretched.

Callie fidgeted with the edge of her shorts, and he knew that she was expecting Kathie to suddenly be *exhausted*, too. He stifled the urge to lift her into his lap. It was one thing to be close in front of her friends, but another to openly settle his mouth on that tempting neck of hers and take his fill until neither of them could see straight. He was getting hard at the thought and quickly gave the others instructions to urge them along.

"There are flashlights in the baskets in your tents, and you'll see jugs of water, a washbasin, and hand towels in each tent. It was really nice getting to know you guys better."

Sweets got up and swung her head between Christine and Wes, as if she were deciding if they were going for a walk or staying by the fire pit.

Christine crouched to pet her. "I enjoyed our chat, too. You two kids don't stay out too late, now, ya hear?" She reached for Kathie's hand. "Come on, sugar. Time to get our beauty rest."

"Good night, Cal. Good night, Wes." Kathie took a few steps and then turned back. "You know, Wes, I think you're right. You can't miss something you never had, but you really can miss something, or someone, you know and love. I think I'll take Callie's advice and work out a schedule. I love Paul, and I don't want him to feel hurt because of my obsession for writing."

Callie hugged her. "He knows you love him, Kath. He loves you so much. Don't worry. Just have an honest talk with him, like you do with us. He gets you. He married you because of who you were, and that included working crazy hours and talking to people who don't exist."

Listening to Callie assure Kathie with such empathy and love tugged at Wes's heart. Not only did she have wonderful, warm, funny, and endearing friends, but she was as much of a rock for them as they were for her. He wanted to be that person for her.

Chapter Fourteen

CALLIE SAT DOWN beside Wes again and nervously ran her finger along the seam of his jeans. Her breathing was jagged. Her eyes followed her finger as it trailed along the side of his thigh. He wanted to calm her nerves, but words weren't enough, and he was still thinking about the warmth she'd shown Kathie. He covered her hand with his, a silent assurance that he wouldn't move too fast.

"I love the person you are," he whispered, then kissed her temple.

She looked at him with desire in her eyes, and when she placed her hand to his cheek, he turned in to it and kissed the center of her palm. He covered that hand with his, pressed it to his lips again, and kissed it. He couldn't help but take a quick taste with his tongue. Callie's eyes darkened, and she sucked in a quick breath. He wanted to be that breath, to be enveloped by her. He'd thought about her lips, and the taste of her sweet mouth, all afternoon. Wes cupped the back of her neck and brought his mouth to hers in a long, sensuous kiss. Kissing Callie was so much better, hotter, wetter, than his fantasies.

"I could kiss you for hours," he whispered against her lips before taking her in another greedy kiss. "Callie." One long, heated breath was all he could manage.

Her eyes were closed, her lips slightly parted, and her hands, those delicate, feminine hands that he wanted to feel wrapped around his hard length, were pressed against his abs, making it impossible for him to think. Her eyes fluttered open and her tongue swept across her lower lip, leaving it slick and enticing. Wes took her cheeks in his hands and licked the glistening streak, then followed the swell of her upper lip to the corner of her mouth.

"You taste sinful," he whispered.

She was breathing hard, and as he moved in to kiss her again, she whispered, "Let's *be* sinful."

Holy hell. He thought he'd dreamed those words up in his mind, but in the next breath, Callie climbed onto his lap and straddled him, breathing fast and hard. Her breasts pressed against his chest, her arms circled his neck, and he had to kiss her again. There was no holding back the pent-up passion as they kissed and touched, moaned and craved. She wasn't the fragile girl he'd thought when he'd first met her. Shy at times, and with that came a sense of vulnerability, in contrast to her strength and sensuality. She was sexy as hell. *Intoxicating.*

And she was his.

The thought brought him to his feet with her in his arms. She tightened her thighs around his middle as he carried her across the clearing, guided by instinct and the faint light of the stars, to his tent. Their lips never parted. Callie ran her fingers through the sides of his hair, then fisted them tight, deepening their kiss and pulling a hungry groan from him.

He carried her into the tent and drew his lips back long enough to whisper, "I have to…" He kissed her again. "Close the tent."

She eyed the open tent and nodded as he lowered her to her feet. Wes worked quickly to draw the tent flaps closed. He felt Callie's hands slip beneath his shirt and run up his back; then the soft warmth of her lips met his spine, drawing all the air from his lungs. Her hands slid around to his abs, lightly trailing over them. He was rock-hard and wanted to be inside her, feel her velvety center wrapped around him, and at the same time, he wanted their first time to be something she'd never forget. He spun around and gripped her wrists, fighting the fire in his belly, panting out each breath. He opened his mouth. *Slow.* The word wouldn't come, but he was damn ready to. He tore her sweater over her head, unable to control himself, and laid her down on the cot. She reached for him as he ripped his own shirt from his body and came down over her.

"Kiss me," she whispered.

Their lips met in an erotic collision of tongues and teeth. Their bodies gyrated, hip to hip, his hardness against her center. He gripped her sides, and when he came up for air, her eyes remained closed, and he drank her in.

"Christ Almighty, Callie."

Her breasts were trapped beneath a pink lace bra. He ran his tongue across the scratchy material and over her dark, hard nipples and felt her shudder beneath him. With his teeth, he dragged the straps from her shoulders until they lay loosely over her arms. Then he licked a path between her breasts and unhooked the simple clasp. Her skin was warm, her breath hot, and he loved the way every stroke of his tongue caused a sharp inhalation. Using his teeth, he slid the cups of her bra off her breasts, freeing them for him to devour. He filled his palms, sucking first one nipple, then the other. He caressed the taut peaks with his thumbs as he moved between them. Callie rocked her hips into him. She gripped the sides of the small cot as he kissed his way down the center of her body to her belly button, then ran his tongue around the sensitive skin while he adeptly worked the button on her shorts and slid them down to her knees.

She tried to push them down, and he caught her hand in his and brought it to his mouth. Callie's eyes shot open. She held her breath as he sucked each finger in and let it out sharply as he drew them out slowly. Wes slid her shorts off, and as she lay in her lace panties, completely open to him, he forced himself to slow down. This was Callie's decision to make, and he wanted to be one hundred percent certain that she wanted to be with him as much as he wanted to be with her. He slid up her body and looked into her eyes.

"Callie, we can stop."

Her eyes darkened, narrowed.

"I won't be upset. I'm happy just being with you, and I know how you feel about intimacy." He searched her eyes, and although he saw her desire as clear as day, he needed to hear her tell him it was what she wanted. He didn't want any misinterpretations.

She nodded.

He touched his forehead to hers. "I need to hear it. I can't risk making a mistake and blowing this. I already care about you too much."

A sweet smile spread across her heated cheeks. "Wes Braden," she whispered, "I want to be with you in the most intimate way imaginable. Are we clear?"

"Crystal."

He sealed his mouth over hers, and even though he'd love to tease her into oblivion, he didn't think he could manage that long.

"Hurry," she said with a seductive grin, jolting him out of his careful movements.

He made quick work of removing her pretty pink panties and his own clothes. All her precious curves lay naked before him. Her breasts heaved with each breath, and when he lowered his mouth to the skin just above her damp curls, she made a low, sensual sound that spurred him on. His fingers found her center, and she arched against him, urging him deeper. She was so wet, so hot, that when he brought his tongue to her sensitive folds and tasted her sweetness, he nearly came apart. He teased her with his tongue as his fingers found the spot that made her insides clench tight; then, with his other hand, he brought her slim fingers to her center. She hesitated, but her eyes told him this wasn't new to her. He covered her hand with his.

"You're safe with me, Callie. It's just you and me."

She closed her eyes and touched herself tentatively at first, then more fervently, and it was the most erotic thing he'd ever witnessed, watching the woman who filled his heart show him what she craved as they took her over the edge.

"Wes," she panted.

He dragged his tongue over her wetness as she stroked herself and her knees fell open wider. She was so beautiful, touching herself so openly, sharing her most intimate self with him. He drew her fingers into his mouth and sucked them clean, pulling another loud, needy moan from Callie. He held her hands in his as he used his mouth to give her the pleasure she needed, to take her over the edge again. Her body pulsed and thrust against his mouth as she stifled a cry of pleasure and dug her fingernails into his palms. She came down slowly, panting and reaching for him again. He grabbed his wallet from the floor and fumbled in the dark for a condom.

"I'm on the pill."

Holy hell, he felt like he'd waited his whole life for this moment.

She reached for him again, and he settled his hips over hers and kissed her deeply, pushing into her until he was buried deep in her warmth. He stilled, wanting to stay with her as long as he could.

"Callie." He held her sweet face in his hands as they gazed into each other's eyes. "I want you to know that my heart is in this, too."

"I know," she whispered. "I can feel it."

His forehead met hers, and they both closed their eyes. Love swelled in his heart and three powerful words tumbled in his mind. He opened his eyes again, confused by the speed of his feelings but not wanting to fight the bliss that ran through his veins like blood. Callie wasn't a girl he could *like*. She was a girl he could *love*. She pressed her fingers in to his hips, pulling him from his thoughts, and they moved together in perfect rhythm. She wrapped her legs around him, taking him deeper, driving him out of his mind and stealing his last shred of control. He thrust hard and fast, taking them both up, up, up, biting, sucking, clawing, until they gasped for air. He felt Callie's thighs flex beneath him. Her head fell back and she called out his name. He captured her cry in his mouth as their bodies quaked with simultaneous earth-shattering releases.

CALLIE DIDN'T WANT to breathe, or think, and she

definitely didn't want to move from beneath Wes. He exhaled heavily against her neck, his heart thundering against hers. His body shuddered with aftershocks as he came down from their earth-shattering lovemaking. The tent was quiet, save for their breathing and something else. Quieter breathing. Her eyes followed the sound to where Sweets lay sleeping by the tent flaps. She smiled and despite herself let out a soft laugh, causing Wes to lift his head. She pressed it back down to her shoulder, and he nuzzled against her.

"Sorry," she whispered. "I just noticed Sweets sleeping over there. I didn't even know she followed us in."

"She goes where I go." He kissed her neck and lifted his head again. Callie wrapped an arm around his middle, as if she were strong enough to hold him there.

"I'm not going anywhere, Cal. I just want to see you."

Thank goodness. "'Kay. Sorry."

He kissed her, and it sent a tingling sensation down to her toes.

"I don't want this night to end either." He stroked her cheek with the pad of his thumb. "I don't want us to end."

She heard a little mewing sound and realized it had come from her. She'd done that a few times now, and she had no idea how to keep from doing it. The things Wes said, the way he looked at her, like she meant something special to him, tugged at her heart in ways that made her want to crawl inside his world and have him crawl inside hers.

"Me either," she managed.

"Sleep with me tonight. Stay with me, right here, or we can sleep in your tent and I'll get up before sunrise and come back here if you don't want your friends to know. I just want to be with you."

She loved that he would do that for her. "I think they probably already know."

"I kind of got that idea when they all magically got tired at the same time."

Callie smiled. "They're the best friends I could ever have. They're like the sisters my parents never gave me."

"Are you sure you're okay staying? You might feel differently in the morning. Or when you see them." His voice was serious and compassionate.

"It's not like the walk of shame in college. I'm twenty-six, and you're…How old are you?" Gosh, she felt like she knew him so well, and she didn't even know his age. Heroes and heroines fell in love fast in all of the books she read, and she never fully believed it could happen in real life. Boy, was she wrong.

His brows drew together. "Thirty-two. Old enough to have sown my oats and know what I want in life." He looked at her for a long time, then whispered, "I want *you*, Callie. Just you."

She closed her eyes as the words sank in.

You have me. All of me.

Chapter Fifteen

WAKING TO BIRDS singing and sun warming the tent didn't begin to compare to the safe, loving feeling of waking up in Wes's arms. Wes came awake slowly, and when their eyes met, Callie's body warmed. Sweets licked their faces, and without a word, Wes let Sweets out of the tent and they made love again, slower and quieter this time, savoring every second of intimacy, before washing up and greeting the day. They hadn't heard a peep from the others, and Callie assumed they were still asleep. While Wes started a small fire and heated water for coffee, she tiptoed over to her tent, still wearing Wes's T-shirt and her panties. She drew the flaps open and found all three of her friends sitting on her cot, grinning like fools.

"Yay!" Kathie pretended to clap, then shot a fist into the air.

Bonnie clicked a photo—or twelve—and Christine blew her a kiss.

"Oh my God, you guys." She whipped around and pulled the flaps of her tent closed. "How long have you been waiting for us?"

"Long enough." Kathie wiggled her eyebrows. "Damn girl, you look...freshly fucked and something else."

Callie dug through her bag and changed her clothes, ignoring their banter.

"She looks like she's in that honeymoon stage," Bonnie said, still taking pictures.

"Do you have to take pictures of my butt?" Callie asked as she tugged on clean underwear.

"It's for the morning-after collage." Bonnie took a picture of Callie scowling.

"Honeymoon stage," Callie mumbled under her breath.

"You're right, Cal. It's not the honeymoon stage. It's too new even for that." Christine wore shorts and a pink T-shirt with JUST LAUGH ALREADY written across her chest. She already had her visor firmly in place, even though they were inside the tent.

Callie pulled on her shorts and a short-sleeved sweater.

"It's the lust stage." Kathie lay back on the cot. Her ponytail hung off the other side, and she crossed one leg over the other with a sigh. "I love that stage."

Callie brushed her teeth using the basin and bottled water, washed her face again, having already practically taken a sponge bath with Wes, and sat beside Kathie.

"It's more than that."

Kathie bolted upright. "More?"

Callie nodded. "Remember how Bon knew she loved Mark after their first date? You said you met the man you were going to marry before you even slept with him."

Bonnie turned the camera on herself and took a selfie. "Truth."

"And, Christine, you knew Billy was the right one for you when—"

"It was when he first wrapped his arms around me. Before our lips even touched." Christine met Callie's gaze. "He set those baby blues on me, and I died and went to hell because of all the dirty things I wanted to do to him."

Callie laughed. "And, Kath, you and Paul took a little longer, but when you knew, you knew, right?"

"We took eighty-four hours exactly. Two dates, third base, and one night when he sat and read his legal briefs while I wrote until three in the morning. I knew we were perfect for each other." Kathie hugged her close. "More?"

Callie nodded. "More."

She wasn't sure exactly what happened next. There was a flurry of squeals, hugs, and *Oh my Gods!* Then Sweets's nose poked through the flaps of her tent and she barked, and suddenly they were shouting over her barks.

"Did you tell him?" Kathie stood on the cot.

Still wrapped in Bonnie's arms, Callie answered, "No. God, no."

Sweets barked more, her head still sticking through the flaps.

"You have to," Christine yelled. She snagged the camera from Bonnie's hands.

The flaps of the tent flew open and Wes stood before them with worried eyes. "You guys okay?" He scanned the tent, and only then did Callie realize what they must look like.

Bonnie was hugging her beside the cot, atop which Kathie stood, bouncing up and down, and Christine was snapping pictures of Wes. He looked so serious, and she was so happy, that she burst out laughing, then tried to stifle it by covering her mouth, which made her snort. *Snort!* That set Sweets into another barking fit and sent Kathie to her knees with laughter. Bonnie crossed her arms, trying to refrain from cracking up, but she burst out laughing and grabbed hold of Christine, taking her down to the floor with her and catching the camera on the way.

"Sorry, sorry, sorry," Callie managed between laughs. She covered her mouth again.

"Tell him!" Kathie squealed, then fell back and tumbled off the cot.

Wes shook his head, but his smile told Callie that maybe he wouldn't turn tail and run from the crazy females in the little tent after all.

"Shh," she managed.

"Aw, go ahead." Bonnie held her camera to her eye. "I can get it on film."

Wes reached for Callie's hand. "Tell me what?"

That sobered them all up. Even Sweets stopped barking. She wagged her tail and shoved her big head into Bonnie's lap. Christine reached over and pulled Sweets toward her, freeing Bonnie to take pictures.

"Um." With her heart in her throat she glanced at her friends. Telling Wes how she really felt would be a big risk, even after what he'd said to her last night. That was said in the heat of passion, and she knew sex could skew people's feelings, even if it didn't skew hers. She was as sure as she'd been since day one, when he'd walked into the library and turned her stomach inside out with nothing more than a smile and a voice that still cut right to her core. Four weeks she'd waited for Thursdays with bated breath, choosing her outfits more carefully based on the day he would appear. Since the first day they'd met, every time she filled her car with gas or went to the grocery store, she secretly hoped she'd run into him. But Wes Braden wasn't everywhere. She never did run into him, except Thursdays, when he came to her.

He came to her.

You came to me.

His words swirled in her head—and her heart—*I love the person you are...I want you, Callie. Just you.* She could blow it. Tell him how she felt and be jumping the gun. Or she could lay it all on the table and...

He reached for her other hand and gazed lovingly into her eyes.

She knew. Even if he didn't.

It was now or never.

She shrugged. "Nothing, really. Just that I love you." She said it in the same vein she might say *I like the color blue* or *Let's take the bus.* And then her body betrayed her; her knees weakened and her limbs trembled.

She'd said it.

Aloud.

In front of everyone.

Wes held her gaze. He didn't say a word, and every second sucked a little more air from her lungs. Wes stepped closer, until they were thigh to thigh, his hands pressed against her lower back, and in an equally blasé voice, he said, "Yeah? Heck, I love you, too. Want some coffee?"

What? She couldn't have heard him right. She shot a look at Kathie, whose hands were clasped together in front of her. She lifted her chin toward Wes, and Callie turned back to him.

"You..."

"Yup." The left side of his mouth lifted into a smile. "Now that we have that out of the way..."

She jumped into his strong arms and kissed his entire face, eyelids and all. "You love me?"

He laughed, loud, deep, and filled with warmth. "You

snagged my heart, Cal. I never had a chance in hell of not loving you."

"I think I just fell into one of Callie's fairy tales." Christine patted her hand over her heart; then she bent over Sweets. "What do you think, Sweets? Can you share your man with this incredible friend of mine?"

Sweets let out one loud *woof,* and everyone laughed.

Bonnie grabbed Christine and Kathie's hands. "Come on, girls. I think these kids need a little privacy."

"Aw, Mom," Christine teased as she followed her out.

Wes's eyes never left Callie's as he lowered his mouth to hers and took her in a long, soulful kiss. He held her so easily, one hand under her butt, the other on her back, as if he'd been carrying her around for years. He looked into her eyes with a serious, narrow stare that nearly stopped her heart.

"Hear me when I say this, Cal. I've never said it to anyone other than my family before. It means something to me, and I hope it means something to you."

Her throat thickened.

"I love you, Calliope Barnes. I love the way you care about your friends and the way you nibble on that luscious lip of yours. I love your voice and the way you steal looks at me when you think I'm not looking. I love being close to you, and..." He glanced at her friends. "And more."

He rested his head against her forehead.

If he hadn't been holding her, she'd have slithered to the ground like melted butter. Callie wrapped her arms around Wes's neck and pressed her cheek to his.

"I love you, too, Wes. So much." Warm tears slid between their cheeks. She swallowed against the happiness that threatened to render her mute, and in an effort to lighten her thoughts so she was capable of standing on her own again, she added, "Now we can have coffee."

Chapter Sixteen

WES'S BROTHER LUKE had told him that falling in love with his girlfriend, Daisy, had changed his entire life, and at the time, Wes thought his brother had lost his mind. How can anything change a person's entire life? The way Luke painted it, he awoke feeling happier, and every task he did throughout the day seemed easier. He looked forward to Daisy's texts and phone calls, but nothing, he claimed, could compare to knowing he'd be with her every night and wake up beside her every morning. For a guy like his brother Luke, who was restless to start with, that was a tall order, and Wes was happy for Luke, even if he didn't quite believe his claims. After loving Callie last night—*loving*, he repeated to himself—not fucking, not banging, not using her as stress relief, but full-on, no-two-ways-about-it *loving* her, he believed the things Luke had said. Because this morning, and for the last several hours, his world had brightened, cheered, and simply become better.

Better. It seemed like a silly thought. One word was much too simple for such intense feelings. Surely there was a more accurate—more magnanimous—description for all that he felt. He glanced at Callie, sitting in the grass, reading, up the hill from the river where he and the others were fishing. She stroked

Sweets's head as the pup slept across her lap. He swallowed against the fullness he felt for her. He realized that it didn't matter what words he chose to describe what he felt. His world had evolved into something more, and there wasn't a chance in hell his feelings for her would change.

Callie glanced up, and their eyes met. She smiled and lifted her hand and wiggled her fingers in a wave. He remembered those fingers touching herself and stroking him last night, how sweet they'd tasted, and this morning when she had them wrapped around his…He pushed the thought away to keep from getting hard while he was supposed to be teaching her friends how to fish.

"I got one!" Christine stood on an outcropping of rocks above the river. She leveraged the bottom of the rod against her stomach and leaned back as she reeled it in.

"Set the hook," Wes directed.

"I did. This baby isn't going anywhere."

"Yay, Christine!" Callie yelled from her safe perch away from the fast-moving water.

"Get your butt down here and cheer me on," Christine yelled.

"No way. I don't like deep water." Callie looked back down at her book.

Bonnie hopped from one rock to the next, moving closer as she took pictures.

Christine pulled a nice-sized trout from the water. It arched and flapped at the end of her line.

"Aw, Christine, let it go." Callie came down the hill, clutching her book to her chest like it might soak up her fears. Sweets ran onto the rock, barking at the fish.

"Sweets. Back, now." Wes pointed to the grass.

Sweets continued barking at the fish.

"Christine, can you manage for a minute?" Wes picked up Sweets and carried her to the grass. "Callie, can you hold her collar?"

"Yeah, why?" Callie crouched beside her and wrapped an arm around Sweets.

"The water's too fast for her. She couldn't handle the current if she fell in." He returned to Christine and helped her hold the fish up for another picture.

"Let's throw it back." Christine glanced over her shoulder at Callie. "Callie hates seeing animals suffer."

"Does she?" *Something else we have in common.* He helped Christine take the fish off the hook and tossed it back in the water before joining Callie on the grass.

"Hey." She shielded her eyes from the sun.

He bent to kiss her. "Thanks for holding on to Sweets. You can let her go now that the excitement has died down."

"I want to learn to fish."

She said it with such determination that it surprised him. "I thought you just said—"

"I did. I hate deep water. I fell in once when I was little and I've hated it ever since, but I want to try the things that scare me. I did okay on the horse, and it doesn't look like I really need to go that close to the water, right?"

He reached for her hand and kissed her again. "Right. God, I love you, Cal." He pulled her to her feet and drew her to him. "You sure you want to?"

"Yes. I can stop if I get too scared, but if I don't try, I'll never know if it's something I'd love. You taught me that." She fisted her hands in his shirt.

"I love when you do that."

"Say I'll go fishing?" She tilted her head to the side.

"Touch me."

Her cheeks flushed.

"I'll never tire of seeing you blush. Come on. Let's get you a rod."

"I like *your* rod," she said just above a whisper.

He shot a look at her in complete disbelief.

"Oh, boy. I said that out loud, didn't I?" She batted her lashes at him.

"Jesus. You sure know how to surprise me." He grabbed her by the ribs and spun her around. Callie squealed in delight, and he kissed her again.

"Sheesh, you two. You make me want to run home and jump into my hubby's arms." Bonnie lowered her camera as Wes set Callie's feet back on the ground.

"And that's bad because?" Wes said as he prepared a fishing rod for Callie. When Bonnie didn't answer, he shook his head. "Your husband will probably send us a thank-you card. Can you get a few pics of Callie fishing for me?"

"I'd love to." She pulled her hair back and tied it with an elastic band she had on her wrist.

"Babe, why don't you take off your boots so you don't slip?" He watched Callie draw in a breath and eye the rushing water.

Callie removed her boots. "I would have brought sneakers if they'd told me the truth about where we were going."

"I would have bought you a pair of sneakers if I'd known you didn't have them, but I'm right here and I won't let you fall in. You know, I just realized that we'll be testing your fear of heights on the hike later. Are you sure you can handle both in one day?"

She shrugged. "I won't know unless I try. Just don't let me

fall in." Callie reached for his hand as she stepped onto the rock. "If there's ever going to be a day when I feel brave, it's today. Trust me on that."

"Today breathed new life into me, too." Their eyes held for a silent second full of emotion that only the two of them could hear. Callie had a dreamy look in her eyes, and he feared she might take a step in the wrong direction. As much as he hated to break the strand of emotion that tethered their thoughts together, he needed to bring her focus back to where she stood.

"Stay back from the edge of the rock and know where your feet are at all times, okay?"

She looked down and planted her bare feet firmly on the rock, hip distance apart. "Feet. Got it."

He released her hand and gripped her arm instead. *Just in case.* "I'm going to come around behind you and show you how to cast, okay? Don't move. Don't slip. Don't freak out and take us both into the water." With Callie safely tucked between his arms, he said, "I'm proud of you. I know this is scary, and you're doing great. I won't let anything happen to you. Ever."

"I believe you." She leaned back against him, and he knew she did.

He helped her pull the rod back, then pitched it forward.

"Wow, look how far it went." Callie held the rod so tightly her knuckles turned white. "It's heavier than I thought it would be."

"Jillian Michaels has got nothing on you, babe. You can do this."

Kathie reeled her line in and joined Bonnie by Wes and Callie. "Look at you, Cal. This is so much better than a spa, isn't it?"

"Only about a hundred times better," Callie called over her

shoulder. "Although I might need a little pampering after playing Davy Crockett."

"You're so damn cute that it's hard for me to keep my hands off of you. I'll be sure you get pampered. Don't worry."

"Hey, none of that dirty talk." Christine set her fishing rod on the ground and sat beside Sweets.

Wes laughed to himself. "You okay?" he asked Callie.

"Yeah. As long as I don't look down and if I pretend the sound of the rushing water is really a giant bathtub filling up, I'm fine."

She held her body so rigid that Wes knew she was struggling to remain brave. He debated giving Callie an out by saying it was time to head back to camp, but he had a feeling that as much as he loved taking care of her, she needed to do this for herself.

She fished for another thirty or forty minutes without catching a single fish. The afternoon sun glistened off the river. Bonnie and Kathie were sprawled on the rocks, soaking up the rays, and Christine and Sweets sat in the shade on the grass at the edge of the forest.

"My arms are getting tired." Callie shook her right hand.

Wes hadn't moved from his post behind her. He lifted the rod from her hands and held on to her as she moved from the rock to the grass.

"You did great. How do you feel?"

She stretched her arms above her head, and her shirt lifted up, exposing a strip of bare skin. Wes couldn't wait to kiss that sweet belly again and to feel her beneath him.

"Stiff. But happy."

Stiff. Christ, he had to stop thinking like that. She was so much more to him than a luscious body, but there was no denying the heat that flamed every time they were close. He wanted so much more with her—everyday things that he'd never even thought of doing with a woman before. He wanted to see where she grew up and the park she'd told him about. He wanted to sit and read with her, introduce her to his family and meet hers. He wanted to show her places she'd never seen. Hell, he wanted to make her dreams come true and he had no idea what they were.

AFTER EATING LUNCH, the girls changed into jeans for the hike, and they gathered around the picnic table to look at the map with Wes. Even after being out in the warm sun all day, he still smelled delicious. Like pine and musk and sheer masculinity.

Wes pointed to a line on the map. "We're hiking the Homestead Trail. It runs along the mountain. Then we'll take a break at the crest here." He moved his finger to another spot.

"We're going up the *side* of the mountain?" Callie cringed at the shakiness of her voice.

"Well, it looks like it, but not really. There's a wide trail that runs up this side. You'll probably feel like you're walking on a dirt road with a forest on one side and incredible views on the other. We're winding around the mountain, not scaling it." He covered Callie's hand with his. "As long as you walk on the inside of the trail, you will barely know you're up high."

"Except your ears will pop, and if you look to your right, you'll feel like you're falling off the edge of the earth." Christine's eyes remained trained on the map.

"Christine," Kathie hissed.

Christine lifted her eyes. "Callie, you know I'm kidding, right?"

No. "Yeah, sure."

"You don't have to come on the hike. If you want to stay here and read, no one is going to think badly of you." He brushed her hair from her forehead and smiled. "You've done so much that was outside of your comfort zone already, babe. We know how brave you are."

At first Callie had thought she was trying to push past her fears just for Wes, and for their relationship, but what she realized was that she was doing this as much for herself as she was for them. She wanted to try the things he enjoyed, and she *was* enjoying herself. She knew damn well she wouldn't go *in* deep water anytime soon, but she still felt like she was making strides, and she felt more alive than she ever had.

"I want to do this. If it gets to be too much, I can stop, or come back. I have to admit, I'm having fun."

Wes pulled her on to his lap, gathered her hair over one shoulder, and kissed her cheek. "I think that's all any of us wanted."

"I have a feeling that you wanted a little something more, Mr. Braden." Christine arched a brow.

"Do you blame me?" Wes asked with an arched brow of his own.

He tightened his grip on Callie's hip, and the memory of making love heated her cheeks.

"Actually, I couldn't think of a nicer guy for one of my best friends." Christine took off her visor and leaned across the picnic table.

Callie held her breath and covered Wes's hand with hers.

He slid his fingers out from beneath and placed them over the top of hers. Each of those intimate, protective gestures endeared her to him even more.

Christine spoke in a low, threatening voice. "Just don't hurt her, because I studied martial arts, and I'll go Jackie Chan on your ass."

Wes met her gaze. "I'd say that's enough to keep even the worst offenders in line. Callie's lucky to have you."

Christine smiled. "So you bought that, huh?" She put her visor back on. "Did I sound tough? I've been working on that for an act."

"I was shaking in my boots," Wes said with a nod.

"Yeah, I'm good like that." Christine stretched her arms out to the sides. "Ready to blow this taco joint?"

"Sure." Wes folded the map. "Be sure to bring your water and put on bug spray. You may want to tie your hair back, too. Use the bathroom if you don't like using leaves, and then we'll hit the trail."

Callie sat on the picnic table watching Wes check his gear as she pulled her hair back and secured it with an elastic band. His backpack was enormous and chock-full of gear. She tried to peer around him to check out the contents.

He lifted his eyes to hers and smiled. "Curious? Water, first aid supplies, flashlights, sweatshirt, radio in case of emergency." He came to her and stood between her legs, then leaned one palm on either side of her, bringing them eye to eye.

Her pulse quickened.

"Hello, gorgeous. Big day for us, huh?"

"Huge."

His mouth quirked up at the corners. "Huge." He leaned

his forehead against hers. "I've always been this regular guy, you know?" He gazed into her eyes. "A guy's guy. I never knew I was capable of feeling so much, or of wanting to put someone else ahead of everything in my life."

Everything around them fell away. All that existed was the two of them, and his words wrapped around them, binding them together like his powerful arms.

He sat beside her and held her hand.

"I want to know your hopes, Cal, your dreams. I want to go to the park where you used to read for hours, and I want to find a place that you love equally as much that can be ours, where we can sit together and read for hours. I want to take you with me on horseback rides and do silly things like lie beneath the stars and figure out which one we want to call our own." His eyes searched hers.

She laced her fingers with his just to feel closer to him. She never wanted to forget a single word he said.

"I never knew I could want any of those things until you."

She opened her mouth, wanting to tell him she felt the same way, but *me too* felt cheap, and *I love you* wasn't enough.

He searched her eyes again and asked with the most serious and thoughtful voice, "What's your favorite thing in the world?"

Sweets set her front paws on the picnic bench beside her.

He smiled at the pup. "Sweets wants to know, too."

"Do you mean besides you?" she asked.

He narrowed his eyes. "Yes, besides me. Before me."

Had she even had a life before him? Before the trip to The Woodlands? It seemed like a lifetime ago.

"High tea and happily ever afters. High tea is just so romantic, and happily ever afters, well…"

"I want to be your happily ever after."

The moment their lips touched, she knew what she wanted to say to him and wasn't brave enough to share.

You already are.

Chapter Seventeen

THEY'D BEEN HIKING for more than an hour, walking along a dirt trail, stepping through tall grass and over the occasional rock. The incline didn't feel as steep as Callie had feared it might, and she was sure to walk on the inside of the trail, close to the forest. But in her peripheral vision, she saw the way the trail fell away. She gripped Kathie's arm and braved a glance in that direction.

"Gorgeous, isn't it?" Kathie drew in a deep breath.

The edge of the trail gave birth to miles of forest below and a vast expanse of mountainous terrain in the distance. There were a variety of trees, some spiky and full in vibrant and deep shades of green, others bare, with branches that reached out like arthritic fingers. Brush bordered the edge of the trail, lush and plentiful, separated in spots with large rocks and set against a sky as clear and blue as a freshly cleaned swimming pool.

"It's staggering to think that we live so close to all of this beauty and that I almost missed it by going home." Callie sighed. "Thank you. You guys really changed my life. I never would have come here." She lowered her voice. "And I probably would have ogled Wes forever and never gotten any further."

"You are kidding, right?" Kathie looked her in the eye.

"That man could no easier stay away from you than I could stop writing. That's love in his eyes, Cal. True, honest, no-two-ways-about-it *love*. If we hadn't come here, it might have taken him some time, but he couldn't have ignored it for long."

"I know," Callie whispered. "I feel so lucky I can barely stand it."

"Yeah, well, stand it, because he's just as lucky to have you, and you deserve to be happy and loved by a man who treasures you as much as we do."

Callie pulled Kathie down so she could whisper to her. "I can't believe I'm in love. Love, Kathie. Me! And it's kind of scary, but not scary like that." She pointed toward the edge of the mountain. "More like…God, I don't know…my heart feels like it might burst scary. I know I don't know him very well, but…" She rolled her eyes up toward the sky and tightened her grip on Kathie's arm. "I trust him, and it feels right. And, Kathie, oh my God, making love to Wes is like…heaven."

"Smile," Bonnie said.

They lifted their heads and Bonnie clicked a picture. She turned the camera on Wes, and he grabbed Christine, who happened to be closest to him, and held up bunny ears behind her head for the next shot. Kathie jumped in front of them with her arms outstretched and a loud, "Tada!" Christine pulled off her visor and put it on Sweets's head, and Wes pulled Callie into his arms and kissed her—all of which Callie was sure Bonnie caught on film. She reached for the camera and shoved Bonnie into the group, taking several shots of Bonnie and the others. Then she drew the camera lens in tight on Wes's profile. She caught him midlaugh, head back, eyes to the sky. She lowered the camera, mesmerized by everything unfolding before her. Her friends and the man she loved coming together.

Kathie climbed to the top of a boulder at the edge of the trail and stood on top of it with her arms spread wide. "Take a picture, Cal." She thrust one leg straight out behind her.

"Oh my God. Kathie, don't fall. Please don't fall." Callie shoved the camera into Bonnie's hands and backed up against the forest. Sweets looked from her to Kathie and barked. "Wes, don't let her fall."

"I'm not going to fall, Cal. There's, like, two feet of rock on that side of me. Take a pic, Bon."

THE LOOK ON Callie's face brought Wes to her side. He slid his arm around her waist. "Hey, you okay?"

"Yeah. She just freaked me out a little. It's the whole heights thing. If I pretend there's no edge to the trail, I'm fine, but I can't really look over it." She turned and faced the forest, drawing in several deep breaths. "That's better."

"Do you want to sit down, babe?" He placed his hands on her shoulders and felt her trembling.

"No. I'm fine. Is she still up there?"

"Yeah, but Christine's with her. Guests do that all the time. I wouldn't let her up there if I thought she might fall. You need to trust me, Cal."

"I do. I trust you, and I trust her. It's my own issue, not hers. I'm sorry." She took another deep breath.

"It's okay. I just want to make sure you're all right. There's a grassy area just around the bend. Why don't we go chill for a while before hiking the rest of the way up?" He reached for her hand.

Around the bend there was no brush at the end of the trail and no large outcroppings of rocks. They sat far from where the land fell away. Wes knew that without the sharp divide of the trees and rocks, from Callie's vantage point on the thick grass, she would feel as though she were sitting by a hillside rather than the edge of a mountain.

"Better?" He covered her hand with his.

"Much. This isn't nearly as scary."

"It's an optical illusion. The slope is very close to the same, but the rocks and brush make it appear more drastic." He pulled her closer, and Sweets put her head on Callie's lap. "Looks like Sweets found a new pillow. I'm a little jealous."

She leaned her head on his shoulder. "I'm sorry I freaked out. I don't want to ruin the hike for you. My friends are probably used to me, but this is what you do, Wes." She shook her head. "I wish I wasn't such a chicken."

"Hey, look where you are." He lifted her chin with his finger. "Babe, you were feet from that river down there."

"The river's down there?"

"Yeah, of course. You can't see it because you haven't come close enough to the edge, but it's there."

She gripped his thigh.

"Callie, think about everything you've done. You shot a gun, and you were the only one to hit a target. You fished, you hiked, and you slept in a tent."

The way her eyes darkened, he knew just what she was thinking.

"Okay, well, maybe we didn't sleep much, but you know what I mean. Those are all things you weren't prepared for when your friends picked you up on Thursday. The truth is that if you never went hiking or fishing, I'd still love you. I know that here." He patted his heart. "Where it counts. I love who you are, fears and all."

"I do want to hike and I didn't mind fishing. The water scared me, but I enjoyed the fishing part. I want to do these things with you, but…" She dropped her eyes, and he could tell she was holding something back. He could feel it as she swallowed hard and refused to look at him.

"Hey." He rested his forehead against hers. "But what?"

"Does…seeing me get scared make you second-guess our relationship? Even a little?"

She closed her eyes as he turned his body fully toward her. He cupped her cheeks in his hands.

"Please open your eyes."

She did, and they were so full of worry it nearly killed him.

"If I suddenly couldn't read, would your feelings for me change?"

"Of course not," she said quietly.

He pulled Sweets into his lap and kissed her on her snout. "Sweets is a bloodhound who can't smell. Not much of a hunting dog, can't help track a damn thing. She'd rather kiss than bark, and some days she's about as energetic as a sloth. And I love her so much, that if she hurts, I hurt." He drew his eyes back to Callie. "And you? After a few weeks of counting the hours until it was Thursday again, so I could see you without feeling like a stalker, a few days of the most intense feelings I've ever felt, and coming together on every level, Cal, I know without a doubt that whether you can climb a mountain or go white-water rafting doesn't have any bearing on my feelings for you." He ran the back of his hand down her cheek. "Okay? Have a little faith in me as a person. Trust that I wouldn't let you or your friends get hurt."

She nodded. "You're so confident and so honest with your feelings."

The side of his mouth curved up. "Yeah, that's all new. It's all you. I don't know where all this is coming from. It's crazy. I get that, and I've never been a…this type of guy. But I feel it." He shrugged. "I know it's usually the woman who says that stuff, right?" He ran his hand through his hair. "I'm probably really freaking you out, aren't I?"

She shook her head without saying a word.

He fell back on the grass and closed his eyes. "Shit." He glanced at the girls lying in the sun with their eyes closed, blissfully unaware that he was spewing his feelings like a waterfall and probably making Callie's world spin on its axis.

Callie draped her arm across his stomach, laid her cheek on his chest, and closed her eyes.

"I love you, Cal." He couldn't stop the sappy truth from leaving his lips again.

Using his shoulders for leverage, he felt her pull herself up and kiss his lips.

"You don't freak me out. I believe what you say to me, and I've fallen head over heels in love with you, too. But I'm a little worried about when we go back home. I mean, I see you in the library each week, and those really pretty women practically invite you into their bedrooms with the way they look at you. I can see it, and you're…flirty, which is totally normal, but I don't know if you hook up with them, or—"

Wes bolted upright. "Callie, you think I've slept with the women who talk to me at the library?"

She shrugged. "Some of them are gorgeous."

He racked his mind, trying to figure out who she was talking about.

"I might be a little naive, Wes, but I'm not blind. Tiffany Dempsey comes in every week on Thursdays just to fawn over you, and I don't blame her. And I wouldn't blame you. She's impossibly gorgeous."

Wes rubbed his temples. He'd thought this relationship had come together too easily. She lived in Trusty. There was no way he could shield her from his past or the way it infiltrated his present, but he'd be damned if he wasn't going to be honest and do everything within his power to ensure the women who vied for his attention knew he was unequivocally off the market. "Cal."

"It's okay. I mean, if all those things you said were just, you know, because we're here and the moment felt right." She looked away but not before he saw the hurt in her eyes.

"Callie, everything I say to you is real. I'll never lie to you."

She clenched her eyes shut, sending his gut into a tizzy. How the hell was he supposed to navigate this? He stole another glance at her friends. They hadn't moved. This wasn't the time or place to say what he needed to say, but he knew waiting until after the hike would be torturous for both of them. He moved closer to her, shoulder to shoulder.

"Cal." He held her hand, rubbing the back of it with his thumb. "Babe, I grew up in Trusty. I've lived there forever, except during college. I went to school with everyone my age, so yeah, I've dated a lot of women who live there. If you can call it dating."

She tried to pull her hand from his, and he held tight. "Please try to hear what I have to say. I know it's not easy. It's not easy for me either. I'm thirty-two, and I'm not a saint. I've never claimed to be. I went out with Tiffany once, when I was home from college on a break. Jesus, I haven't thought about it in years. We didn't even go out. We were at a party, and we were both drunk. We made out. We were kids, Cal. You know, drunken kissing, groping, not sex."

The tension in her hand eased a little.

He debated taking the explanation further, and one look at her brought his heart to the forefront. "Callie, I might as well get it all out on the table. I've slept with...plenty of women. I don't know how many, and to be honest, I don't care. It's who I was, not who I am, and I always used a condom, so it's not like I was totally irresponsible. I wasn't lying when I said I've never loved a woman before, and I've never, not once, felt anything close to what I feel for you." His chest constricted at the thought that he could lose her over what he'd done in his past. It was the one thing he couldn't change. He let go of her hand and rubbed the tight muscles at the back of his neck.

She opened her eyes and slid her hand onto his thigh. "I don't need to hear more. I just wanted to know if you thought that when we went home you'd feel the same way as you do here. You know, when we're out of the moment and back to real life. When I'm just the girl at the library."

Her words pierced his heart. "Callie, you were *never* just the girl at the library. You want honesty? Here you go. The first week you worked there, I came into the library on a fluke looking for some book. I can't even remember which one."

"The *Colorado Guide to Birds of Prey*. You said you and your partner were battling over the flight patterns of birds."

"Holy Christ. You remember that?"

She nodded. "And I remember that you were wearing those faded jeans with the hole just above your left knee and you had a bandage on your hand that you said you got roping steer. You were wearing a green button-down shirt, and..." She lowered her eyes. "Now I sound like I'm a stalker."

"No, babe. Not unless I sound like one because I remember you were wearing the sweetest navy blue dress that zipped all the way up your back like a second spine." He'd thought about her in that dress night and day until he went back to retrieve the books she said she'd pull for him the following Thursday. He ran his fingers through her hair, remembering how he had wondered what her hair would feel like tangled around his fingers. "And it was the only Thursday when you didn't have your hair up in a bun. You had it pinned back with a...a...."

"Barrette."

"Yes, that's it. You asked me if I needed anything else, and you asked all sorts of questions about my reading interests. I remember thinking that you didn't look at me like everyone else did. You were interested in, I don't know, what I was interested in rather than my looks or who I was." He looked away again. "Loser, right? What kind of man says these things?"

She slid her hand onto his forearm and held on tight.

"The good kind." She smiled, and the tenderness he'd seen in her eyes so often lately returned.

"So I asked you to pick out books for me, and I was blown away when you agreed. Cal, I haven't been with another woman since the day I set eyes on you. I've been like a damn kid, getting turned on just thinking about seeing you, and then you showed up here, and..." He shrugged, but what he felt was so much bigger than a shrug. "When we get back to Trusty, I'm not going to feel any differently than I do now."

She nodded.

"Hey, I mean it."

"I believe you."

Her words should have reassured him, but he felt her holding back, and he heard the others moving around behind them.

"Ready to roll, Cal?" Bonnie crouched beside her.

"How far is it to the top?" Callie asked Wes.

"Another half hour, maybe a little less." Wes stood and patted his thigh. He had a nervous feeling in his stomach. Sweets stretched her front paws out in front of her and stuck her rear up in the air.

"Do you guys mind if I sit and read while you hike the rest of the way?" Callie shielded her eyes from the sun and squinted up at Bonnie.

"We can turn back if you're tired," Bonnie said.

"No. Don't be silly. You guys go. You'll get great pictures. I'm comfortable here, and I would really like to sit in the sun and read."

Wes knelt beside her, wishing her friends weren't standing so close so he could ask her what was really going on. "Are you sure you want to sit this part out?" *Shit.* This could only mean that she was upset. Maybe he'd been too honest.

She nodded and reached for her backpack. "Yeah. I made it pretty far, and I'll just freak out the higher we get. I'm fine right here. Do you mind?"

Hell yes. He wanted to stay right there with her. Damn it. How was he supposed to leave her by herself?

Kathie moved in front of Callie, casting a shadow over her face. "You sure, Cal?"

"Yeah. Go. Have fun. Besides, it's not like it's all day. Half hour up, a few minutes to jump on rocks and take pictures, and then you'll be back. I can read a lot in an hour."

Kathie shrugged. "If you say so."

Wes dug through his backpack and handed her the two-way radio. "This goes directly to the lodge. If you have any trouble,

193

use it." He showed her how to use it. "I'm going to leave Sweets with you, too. Are you sure you want to stay? I'd really prefer not to leave you alone."

Callie pulled Sweets against her. "I won't be alone. I'm fine, really. It's a little breezy with the hill, though. I didn't bring a jacket. Do you have one?"

"Always." He dug in his pack and handed her a Woodlands zip-up hoodie.

"Thank you. Go, have fun, and don't let them drive you crazy."

Every fiber of his being told him not to go, but this was his job, and Callie's friends were already heading back toward the trail.

He watched Callie slip on the hoodie, then leaned in close and lowered his voice. "Cal, are you staying because of what I said?"

She touched his hand, and her eyes softened. "No. Please don't worry. You were honest, and I appreciate that. I believe everything you said to me, Wes. I know myself well enough to realize that when I stand up and look over that slope, or when we're on the trail and Kathie or Christine do something that's totally fun for them, it'll petrify me. The last thing I want to do is ruin everyone's fun. Go. Let them have fun. I've got my book. I'm totally fine."

She was so damn thoughtful. Wes didn't think he knew of another person who was as selfless, except maybe his mother, who had raised him and his siblings on her own and devoted herself to them for so many years that now, as she climbed toward sixty, he wished she had someone who loved her the way he loved Callie.

"Okay. Use the radio if you need it, and keep Sweets with

you." He looked at the surroundings. She was out in the open, far enough from the edge that if she really just sat and read, she should be perfectly fine. Sweets would keep her safe from snakes and small animals, which he knew better than to mention to Callie. He folded her into his arms one last time. "I love you, Callie, and I'm sorry we didn't have more time to talk."

"Don't worry. We talked enough. I'll be fine, here and in Trusty."

How could she possibly know that he needed to hear that?

On the trail, he took one last look at Callie. She had one arm over Sweets's back, the other held her book, and he felt like he was leaving two-thirds of himself behind.

"She'll be fine." Bonnie clicked a picture of Callie and Sweets. "She did great, don't you think?"

"She's nothing short of amazing." *And I hope to hell I don't lose her.*

Chapter Eighteen

CALLIE WAS STILL reeling from her conversation with Wes when they disappeared up the mountain. She hadn't realized she was even worried about what would happen when they returned to Trusty or what it might be like to watch Tiffany pawing at him now that they'd become so close. But now that it was out in the open, it buzzed around her head like a horsefly waiting to sting. She trusted Wes, and she'd seen the honesty in his eyes and heard it in his voice. He hadn't tried to deny his past, and for that she was thankful. She hadn't expected him to be a saint. What she needed, he'd given her. Honest assurance. She knew he would do everything in his power to make sure she was comfortable, but she'd never been in love before, and she sure as heck had never been jealous before. She could only hope that *she'd* be able to handle it.

Her stomach twisted as she thought about Tiffany Dempsey trying to entice him into a date, or her bed, or whatever she had in mind each week. Heck, her stomach had done the same thing when Wes had been just a guy she was drooling over. That hadn't changed. What *had* changed was that now her heart was involved, and whether she wanted to think about it or not, Wes held her fragile heart in his very capable hands.

Callie sighed and set her book on her lap. "What do you think, Sweets? You know him. My heart is perfectly safe, right?"

Sweets opened one eye and blinked up at her.

"Not even worth opening both eyes? Good to know."

She heard a rustling just over the crest of the hill. Sweets's ears perked up. She stood on all fours with a low growl. Callie's pulse quickened.

"What is it?"

Sweets barked and darted over the hill and out of sight.

"Sweets!" Callie rose to her feet and got a little dizzy at the change in perspective. She sat back on her heels. "Sweets!"

Sweets barked a blue streak, but her barks were getting farther away.

Oh boy. What if Sweets didn't come back?

"Sweets! Here, Sweets! Come on, girl."

Sweets's barks sounded even more distant. Callie sank to her butt. What could she do? She could call her again. That didn't seem to help. *What would Wes do?* Darn it. She had never had a dog, much less been responsible for a dog in the wilderness. Sweets stayed so close to Wes, she doubted that she'd have left his side if he were the one reading on the hill.

Sweets began barking again. Callie scanned the area to her right, following the distant trail of Sweets's barks until they silenced. Callie's heart leaped to her throat. *Oh no. Please come back.* Sweets howled, then yelped—loudly—followed by a mix of yelping, howling, and whining that tore at Callie's heart. *Oh no, no, no. Please come back.*

She pushed to her feet, leaving her book on the ground, and took a few tentative steps forward. Wes's hoodie hung to her thighs. She thought about the radio in Wes's backpack, but that only communicated with the lodge, and she couldn't just leave

Sweets down there and wait for who knows how long for someone to get there.

"Sweets?"

Sweets continued yelping. Callie forced her trembling legs to carry her forward. *Oh God.* The ground fell away at a steep angle. Her stomach lurched. She crouched a few feet from the edge, breathing heavily and shaking like she'd seen a ghost. Sweets yelped again, and her yelps morphed into painful cries. Callie clenched her eyes shut. *I have to do this. Go. Just go look. Find her.* She crawled on all fours almost to the edge of the mountain.

"Sweets?" The late-afternoon breeze swept the word away. Callie forced herself to look down the treacherous mountainside. Low brush, dirt, grass, big, craggy rocks, and—oh God—the sight of the rushing river below sent her crawling backward.

Ohmygodohmygodohmygod.

She slammed her eyes shut and sucked in a breath.

Sweets yelped, and Callie forced herself to crawl forward again. Fisting her hands in the tall grass, she peered over the edge and scanned the brush for Sweets. Blood rushed in her ears, and her heart hammered against her chest. Sweets cried out again, and Callie forced herself to follow the sound. She spotted Sweets lying on the ground beside a rock, off to her right about twenty feet below. Callie's stomach lurched again.

"No. Oh God, no." She clenched her teeth together and crept along the ground until Sweets was directly below her. "I'm coming, Sweets," she said more to herself than to Sweets. "I can do this. It's just a hill. It's just a hill." The first step down made her dizzy. She plastered herself against the side of the mountain. How the hell did people do this every day? She lowered one foot, then the other, silently making deals with herself. *Do this and you can skip everything else. Save Sweets and you never have to see a mountain again.* She lowered her hand to a rut in the dirt and dug her nails into the earth. Another step down, followed by another grip of the ground. She didn't dare look down. The sound of rushing water broke through her thoughts. She clenched her eyes shut and forced herself to continue.

Sweets's whimpers were getting closer. Not once did she wonder what had caused Sweets to run. She was a dog. Dogs ran. Now, as she climbed down what felt like Mount Everest, she began to wonder. What if it was a snake? What if Sweets had gotten bitten? What if *she* got bitten? *Oh God.* She pushed away the thought as she lost her footing, slid down several feet, scraping her stomach against stones and grass, and cried out. Her hands grasped for purchase; she dug the toes of her boots into the dirt. *Please, please don't let me die.* Her foot hit something hard, and she clutched the closest thing she could reach—a prickly branch of a bush.

"Ouch!" Tears filled her eyes. She clenched them shut and took several sharp breaths.

Sweets yelped and whimpered again. Callie heard her moving around below.

"Stay, Sweets. I'm coming." With several loud grunts, or maybe whimpers or groans—she wasn't sure what sound was accompanying her shaking body as she continued blindly searching for footholds, taking one backward step after another. Sweets came into view to her left, and thankfully, she seemed to have tucked herself onto a level ridge beside big rocks a foot or so from where Callie was clinging to the mountainside. Callie reached her left hand over and grabbed a thick root that stuck out from the ground. Then she slid her foot along the mountainside until the ball of her foot hit the ridge beside Sweets.

Sweets whined in gut-wrenching pain. She lay on her side, her legs up, her front paws hanging limply, covered with quills that stuck out like dark, thick needles. Sweets snapped at them. Callie dug her boot into the dry dirt and walked her hands down the side of the mountain until she was crouched beside Sweets. Breathing hard and clutching the rock, she pressed one hand firmly on Sweets's stomach.

"Don't move." *Ohgodohgod.* Callie scanned the ridge for the culprit, which she could only assume was a porcupine. It was nowhere in sight—thank goodness. Spots of blood darkened the bottoms of Sweets's front paws. Callie's heart beat fast and hard. She knew she had to get the quills out, but she didn't know how, and she remembered reading they had painful barbs. Pulling the wrong way would be horrific for the dog—even worse than the pain Sweets was in as she struggled to reach the quills with her mouth. Callie could barely think past Sweets's painful pleas.

Callie forced herself not to look down the mountain beyond the small ledge where they were perched. She heard the rush of the river, and she feared that if she looked down, she'd probably pass out.

With a deep breath and a shaky voice, talking as much to herself as to Sweets, she said, "I have to carry you up."

She had no idea how she'd manage that, but with Sweets looking up at her with her big, sad eyes and her bloody paws, Callie's fear took a backseat to her need to help the injured pup.

"We can do this. I know we can." She scooped Sweets up under one arm like a football, careful to keep the quills from banging against her side. Sweets flailed, trying to get to her paws. *Oh God. Please don't let us fall.*

"This isn't going to work." She set Sweets down on her back

and rested a knee lightly on the dog's stomach to keep her from reaching the quills. She ripped off Wes's hoodie, and quickly tied the arms together, talking to the dog as she worked.

"A character in a book did this to carry her baby up a hill. I thought it was crazy…but it just might work." She shoved the loop of the arms over her head so it crossed over her body. Then she picked up Sweets and held her inside the hoodie while she zipped it up, careful to leave Sweets's injured paws hanging out the top. She took the elastic band from her hair and used it to secure the bottom of the hoodie so Sweets wouldn't slip out.

"I can't believe it. This might work." She kissed the pup's head, feeling hopeful and clinging to an ounce of confidence for her resourcefulness. With Sweets swaddled in the hoodie and pressed close to her body, she leaned forward, one hand against Sweets, and tested the contraption. Sweets's hammock swung out only a few inches, and the pup was zipped in so tightly that she couldn't reach her paws.

Callie's body shook and shivered. She forced herself to focus on finding footholds and gripping anything she could for purchase as she scaled the side of the mountain. She stopped every few feet to breathe—and remind herself not to look up or down. Sweets whined and whimpered against her. Callie had no idea how much time had passed, but as the sun crept lower on the side of the mountain, she knew it had to have been quite a while. She sweated despite the cool breeze sweeping across the mountain. Callie's neck ached from Sweets's weight, but she pushed past the ache and focused on her next fingerhold, her next breath. She brought a shaky knee up and dug the tip of her boot into the dirt. She pushed off to climb higher and her toe slid down the mountainside. Callie rolled to her side, shielding Sweets with one arm and reaching for a thick root with the other, panting, silently praying for strength and safety.

"It's okay. It's okay," she reassured herself. With a deep breath, she turned back to the mountain. She was *not* going to be defeated by a stupid mountain. She gritted her teeth and began her ascent once again. *One hand. One foot. I can do this.* The thought repeated in her mind, a mantra, a saving grace.

Fast footfalls fell upon her ears. "She's gone!"

Bonnie! "Help." A whisper. *Oh God.* She was in too precarious a position to scream, afraid the slightest movement might cause her to lose her grip. Words were her life, and she couldn't form a single one. She opened her mouth, willing herself to yell, and again, only a shredded whisper came out. Her heart hammered against her chest; her pulse raced. How could her voice betray her like this? She draped her arm across Sweets and swallowed hard, then forced herself to try again.

"Help!" Her head fell forward. Panting, she sucked in a breath and yelled again. "Help! Bonnie!" She chanced a look up and realized she was only a few feet from the crest of the hill. She dug the toes of her boots in deep and pushed upward with all her strength.

"Callie!" Wes's deep voice was laden with fear as his face appeared above her. He climbed down beside her with the ease of a mountaineer and pressed his chest to her back, straddling her legs like Spiderman webbing her to the mountain.

"Babe, I've got you. One step at a time. Follow my lead." He trapped her right hand inside his with his thumb pressed to her palm; then he did the same with her left.

She felt his knee push up against the underside of her thighs, first on the right as he moved one step up, then on the left. Her friends' worried faces peered down from above, reaching their hands over the edge of the mountain. They were talking, but she was too focused on saving Sweets—and herself—to register a single word.

At the top of the incline, Wes pushed Callie up from behind and with one arm around Sweets and her friends grabbing for her, asking after her, she crawled up to where her bag lay in the grass. She sat, shivering, with her arms wrapped securely around the dog and thanked the dear Lord that she was alive.

WES WIPED THE tears from Callie's cheeks. "You're okay. I'm right here." He folded her into his arms as best as he could without hurting Sweets's paws. Pain pierced his heart at the sight of Callie shivering in fear, her bloody and scratched hands clutching Sweets against her torn and dirty shirt. The quills sticking out of Sweets's bloody paws magnified the piercing pain. The pup had been through so much already in her short life. Wes had to work fast to get those quills out, and at the same time, he didn't want to release Callie.

"I have to get those quills out," he said over Sweets's cries. "You're okay, Callie." He dug through his pack. "Bonnie, please come hold Callie. Kathie, Christine, I need help with Sweets. This is going to hurt a lot." He kept his eyes trained on Callie. "Callie, you're okay. We're all right here." With needle-nose pliers from his pack beside him, he carefully unwrapped Sweets. She struggled to get at the quills, flailing her head and body from side to side. She whined and licked him, then whined again, craning her neck to reach the quills.

"I…didn't…" Tears streaked down Callie's cheeks.

Wes held Sweets with both hands as Christine and Kathie

joined him and helped restrain her. He lifted his eyes to Callie. "You did great. I'm so proud of you."

"They have…barbs." Her jaw trembled so hard, her teeth chattered. "I didn't know…how."

"Callie, it's okay. I'll get them out." He gripped her thigh. "Close your eyes, babe. You won't want to watch this."

Bonnie wrapped her in her arms.

"You're okay, Callie. I'm right here," Bonnie assured her.

Wes inspected Sweets's paws. The barbs went right through the webbing between her toes. He pushed them out backward as quickly as he could, causing her to howl in pain.

"Oh, it's okay. Shh. Shh, baby girl," Christine urged as she held the dog by her shoulders.

"She's lucky. The barbs went through. Only a few more." He gripped Sweets's paw and pushed the quills through quickly, trying not to focus on the sound of her pain echoing in the mountains. He shot a look at Callie wrapped safely in Bonnie's arms, and the magnanimous reality of what she'd done sank in. *I never should have left you.* Guilt tightened his chest. Holy hell. He thought he'd lose his mind when he saw her clinging for dear life to his puppy and to the side of a mountain that had scared her so badly that she'd had to stay behind.

He cleaned up Sweets's paws, then snagged the radio.

"Callie, I'll have Daisy—Dr. Honey—come and check you out," Wes said as he radioed the lodge. Daisy Honey was his brother Luke's girlfriend and the town doctor.

"No. I'm fine. Just…scared."

"Go ahead, Wes," Michelle, the front desk receptionist, said.

"Michelle, hold on." He lowered the radio. "Are you sure?" He did another quick visual assessment. She was scratched up and shaking but probably didn't need a doctor. He was being overprotective and he knew it.

Callie nodded.

He spoke into the radio again. "Call Ross and ask him to come out." He explained what he assumed had happened and asked her to send Butch up with a four-wheeler to drive them down. With Sweets tucked safely in Christine's arms, he tended to Callie. He took off his shirt and pulled it over her head, covering her torn top.

"I'm…sorry," Callie managed.

He drew her in close and kissed her cheeks, her lips, and finally, her forehead. "Babe, I don't know what happened, but I can guess that Sweets chased a porcupine, got stuck, and you saved her." He wiped her tears. "You have nothing to be sorry for. I do. I never should have left you here alone." He unfurled her fingers and inspected her cuts. "Let me clean you up. You can tell me about it later. Just breathe." He cleaned the cuts on her hands with his first aid kit, feeling guilty as hell. "I never should have left you alone."

"I'm…fine."

Fine. Are you ever not fine?

"Callie, you're a hero," Christine said, struggling to keep Sweets from running to them.

Kathie crouched behind her. "You deserve the purple heart of bravery."

She deserved a hell of a lot more than that, and Wes was going to see that she got it.

Chapter Nineteen

BACK AT THE ranch, Christine, Kathie, and Bonnie practically begged Callie to come back to the cabin with them to clean up and relax after her horrifying ordeal, but she didn't want to leave Sweets. At least that's what she told them. In reality, she didn't want to leave Sweets or Wes.

She and Ross Braden, Wes's older brother and Trusty's veterinarian, were crouched over Sweets in one of the offices at the lodge when Wes returned from taking a phone call. Dusk was settling in, stealing the last of the afternoon sun and casting a yellow-gray light through the window.

"She looks good, Wes. She was really lucky. Most pups end up with thirty quills in their nose and several in their limbs. I guess her inability to smell was actually a benefit in this case." Ross and Wes not only shared their height and muscular bodies, but their dark eyes and brows were also strikingly similar. When Ross lifted his eyes to Callie's, she noticed that his jaw wasn't quite as square as Wes's, and his hair was a shade lighter.

"It was a good thing you got to her as quickly as you did," Ross said. "She could have broken the quills off, and then it would have been more difficult to get them out."

Sweets got up on all fours and wagged her tail and licked

Ross's chin. Ross grabbed her face in both hands and kissed her snout. Callie recognized a hint of Wes in that move.

"I wasn't very quick. Wes could have gotten to her much faster." She petted Sweets, and the pup turned her wet tongue loose on Callie's cheeks, making her laugh.

Wes and Ross rose to their feet, and Sweets went to explore Ross's boots.

"Callie was incredible." Wes pulled her close and kissed her cheek. "She did what most people would never be able to do. You'd never guess she was afraid of heights."

Ross's brows drew together. His eyes darted between them.

She'd been so wrapped up in Wes since she'd arrived at the ranch that reality seemed a lifetime away. The last few days had felt like a year to them while they were falling head over heels in love, but the surprise registering in Ross's eyes brought reality rushing back. It had been only a few days. A few days ago, Wes wasn't a one-woman man. A few days ago, Wes didn't sleep with guests of The Woodlands, and here he was with his arm around her, kissing her.

Her body stiffened, and when she shifted her eyes to Wes, she realized that he wasn't picking up on his brother's surprise.

Ross shook his head, as if he realized that he was staring at them. "You're afraid of heights and you went down the side of Homestead Trail?"

Callie felt her cheeks flush. "Yeah."

"She didn't just climb down, Ross. She scaled it carrying Sweets in a sling she made out of a sweatshirt." He kissed her again. "She's a regular survivor woman in disguise."

"Wes." Between his raving about her and kissing her, she'd blush all day at this rate.

"That is pretty damn amazing." Ross eyed her arms. "Nasty

scrapes," he said.

"They're not bad. I'm just glad Sweets is okay."

Ross closed his medical bag. "Do you want me to look at those?"

"No. I'm okay, really."

"I wanted to ask Daisy to come check her out, but she refused." Wes kissed her again, and Callie leaned away a little. Wes looked at her with a questioning gaze.

She shifted her eyes to Ross. Wes's gaze followed, and his eyes widened as understanding dawned on him.

"Oh, shit. Ross, I should have said something. Callie's my girlfriend." He pulled her close again. "Sorry, babe. I feel like we've been together forever."

His honesty was further validation of his feelings.

"So I gathered by the possessive hold and the smooching." Ross smiled, and his eyes softened. "You coming to Luke's this weekend?"

Callie was glad they didn't remain on the subject of their new relationship for long.

Wes looked at Callie. "Can you make it?"

"To your brother's? Isn't that a family thing? I don't want to intrude." As much as she didn't want to intrude, she loved the idea of getting to know his family.

"It's been years since Wes has brought anyone to a family gathering." Ross slid a hand into his jeans pocket. "It's a welcome change."

Years. Wow.

"I want you to meet everyone." Wes tucked her hair behind her ear. "They'll love you as much as I do."

"How long have you guys been dating? And how did I not know about it?" Ross's brows lifted again.

It was a big day for surprises for everyone—most of all Callie. She never would have thought she could willingly go over the edge of the mountain.

To avoid embarrassment and to give Wes some space to talk with his brother, Callie crouched to pet Sweets. Sweets rolled over on her back and wagged her tail as she tried to lick Callie's hand.

"Well, bro," Wes began. "You know what Mom says about falling in love right?"

Holy cow. He's going to think we're nuts.

"Love?"

Callie felt Ross's eyes on her. She glanced down and realized that she was still wearing Wes's T-shirt, and her face and hair must be a wild mess. She cringed. Wes was wearing a different T-shirt, but she had no idea when he'd put it on. She thought back and realized that he'd grabbed it from a drawer in the office when they'd first come in, when her heart had still been in her throat. She wanted to jump up and explain. *I don't usually look like this. I'm much neater, and my hair is usually combed, and...*Oh heck, it didn't matter. None of that would change a few days into a few months, which might make his family feel better about their relationship.

"Yeah, love," Wes said.

Oh. My. Lord. Couldn't he have just started with the fact that they were dating? Did he have to bare it all to his brother right now? Callie held her breath, waiting for Ross to laugh or tell them they were crazy. But it was Wes who spoke next, and his tone held the familiar confidence that she'd come to rely on.

"She says, *Love will find you when it's damn good and ready and not a second before or a minute too late—and when it does, you don't have a chance in hell in getting away.* You know that,

Ross. She's only said it a million times."

Callie felt Wes's hand on her shoulder and pictured his warm brown eyes, serious and full of love, and it brought her to her feet. She slipped one arm around him. He took her other hand in his. When she met Ross's gaze, she didn't see judgment or disbelief. She saw compassion and maybe a hint of envy.

"We know it's fast," she said to Ross. "And I know right now I look like a mess, but I don't usually, and I never believed anyone could feel like this, either." She couldn't stop the words from falling off her tongue. "And I'm not one of those girls who's been chasing after him—"

"Hey, Callie, it's okay. Relax." Ross smiled. "I know who you are. You work at the library. And I know Wes well enough to know that if he's kissing you around here and bringing you to a family gathering, then he's serious about you."

Wes narrowed his eyes. "How did *you* know she worked at the library?"

Ross lifted his shoulders with a soft laugh. "It's Trusty. Do you really think a pretty girl can move into Trusty without everyone in town knowing about her?"

A pretty girl? People know about me and think I'm pretty?

"Trusty grapevine," Wes said.

"What does that mean? Trusty grapevine?" Callie ran her eyes between the two of them.

Ross crouched to love up Sweets. "Let's put it this way. Do you ever go to the Trusty Diner?"

"Sure, for coffee some mornings."

"How long did it take for Margie to find out where you moved from and that you were single and working at the library?" Ross shifted a knowing look to Wes.

"I thought she was just being nice." Margie had asked those

questions the first time she stopped in at the diner.

"Oh, she was," Ross agreed. "Margie is very nice, but she also can get the lowdown on someone in five minutes. According to Margie, once word got around that bozo here was in the library every week, the entire single female population of Trusty became avid readers."

"What?" Wes snapped.

"That makes total sense." Callie nodded. "I didn't have any comparison since I had only started when you came in that first week. Wes, that makes sense. Think about Tiffany and—"

"Dempsey?" Ross asked.

"Who else?" Wes answered.

"Shit. And Callie…" Ross laughed again and covered it with a cough. "Sorry. You're picking out books for him *and* watching women leach on to him? And you're still with him?"

Wes punched him in the arm.

Ross grabbed his arm. "Shit, Wes. Think about it. Would you like it if Callie came to the ranch and Cutter or Chip hit on her?"

Wes's jaw clenched. Callie felt him tighten his grip on her hip.

She crouched beside Sweets to escape the heated—and awkward—conversation. "It's okay, sweetie. The boys are just fluffing their tail feathers."

"Well, I'll put a stop to all that," Wes said in a serious voice.

Ross laughed. "Right. Good luck with that. I have to get back to town. I'll be sure to tell Margie you two are an item."

"Good. Thank you." Wes embraced him. "Thanks for coming out."

Ross opened his arms toward Callie. "Step on in here, Callie."

She moved into his arms, grateful for his easy nature. "It was nice to meet you, Ross."

"You, too. You did good with Sweets." He ruffled Sweets's head. "The webbing on her paws will be fine in no time. As you can see, she's no worse for the wear."

Wes reached for Callie's hand and drew her into his arms again.

Ross picked up his medical bag and shook his head. "My brothers are falling like flies. I'm going to have to stop drinking the water."

Wes planted a kiss on Callie's cheek. "Or maybe you should guzzle it."

Chapter Twenty

"THIS IS AWFUL, but I thought he'd never leave." Wes leaned his butt against the desk, and Callie stood between his legs. Her hair was disheveled, and she had dark crescents under her eyes. When she leaned her cheek against his chest on a restful sigh, the way her body melded to his told him she was flat-out exhausted. He gathered her hair in one hand and kissed her shoulder.

"Think your friends would mind if you stayed with me tonight?"

"Mm-mm."

"Butch is bringing our gear down from the camp. You can soak in my Jacuzzi tub and I'll spoil you."

"That sounds nice." Her voice was barely a whisper. "Can we stop by the cabin and let them know, so they won't worry?"

"Of course. Let's take the four-wheeler so you don't have to walk." He kissed her cheek. "I haven't gotten to thank you for rescuing Sweets." He glanced over her shoulder at Sweets, curled up and half asleep by their feet. "Thank you."

"I love Sweets," she whispered. "I love you."

Callie loving Sweets was huge to Wes, but nothing compared to her saving Sweets despite her fears.

They took the four-wheeler over to her cabin and found the girls drinking on the back deck, freshly showered and wearing shorts and sweatshirts. Sweets bounded onto the deck and covered them all with wet puppy kisses.

Bonnie hugged Callie. "How are you feeling? Are you okay? Wes, is she okay?"

"Yeah. Just tired." Callie pushed her hair from her face in that tired way that kids did using their whole hands.

"Do you guys want some Skinnygirls?" Kathie asked.

"What on earth are skinny girls?" Wes asked. "I heard you say that the other night, and not one man on this property has any idea what it is."

Kathie and Christine raised their glasses. "Drinks."

Bonnie grabbed the bottle. "Skinnygirls. It's a brand. Want some?"

Wes drew Callie into his arms again. "No, thanks. I'm a one-woman man."

"Aw, that's too cute." Christine took the bottle from Bonnie and shoved it at Wes. "Now take a drink so we can welcome you to our club. It looks like you'll be around for a while."

Wes took a swig from the bottle and shook his head. "Ugh, you guys like that? I think I'll remain a one-woman man, but thanks for the initiation."

"We like it, but most men don't. Now you know that temptation is never worth it." Christine nodded at Callie. "I've got your back, Cal."

A breeze swept through the trees, rustling the leaves. Callie wrapped her arms around herself. Wes rubbed his hands along her arms, warming the goose bumps.

"Would you guys mind if Callie stays with me tonight?"

"Not at all. We assumed she would," Bonnie said.

FATED FOR LOVE

"You're sure? Because I know you guys are leaving tomorrow night, and this is your girls' trip. I've sort of monopolized her."

"Oh my God. We're leaving tomorrow?" Callie clung to his arm.

"Jeez. I totally forgot, too," Christine said.

"Yeah, it kind of crept up on me, too, in all the excitement." Wes hugged Callie.

"All the more reason for you to monopolize her. Pass go, collect two hundred dollars, and enjoy your ride on the Reading Railroad," Christine said with a wave of her hand.

"Christine." Callie turned bright pink.

Christine laughed. "He knows I'm joking. Besides, you're not a railroad. You're more of a delicate flower petal sifting through life on a breeze."

"Oh please. Get rid of that purple prose." Kathie rolled her eyes.

Wes loved the dynamics between them, and he could see by the blush on Callie's cheeks and the smile on her lips that she enjoyed Christine's jokes more than she might want to publicly admit, even though they were a little racy. He loved her racy side, and the fact that she kept it tucked away made it even more special. "Cal, do you want to grab whatever you need for tonight?" Wes asked.

"Yeah. Good idea."

Once she was inside, Wes turned his attention back to her friends. "I've got a special day scheduled for all of you tomorrow, and the barn dance is tomorrow night if you have the energy for it."

"Callie's a hell of a dancer, Wes. She won't want to miss that," Kathie said.

215

"She is?" What other surprises did she have in store for him?

"Yup. She can dance, cook, and apparently scale mountains and shoot. Heck, she's a real pioneer woman." Christine leaned back in her chair and kicked her feet up on the arm of Kathie's chair. "Take care of her tonight so we don't have to hunt you down and make you drink Skinnygirls until you gag."

"No danger of that."

Callie joined them wearing a pink hoodie and carrying a small bag, which Wes took from her. They said good night, and with Sweets on their heels, went back to the four-wheeler and drove up to his cabin.

As they climbed the porch steps to his cabin, Wes felt tension leave his body like a valve had opened.

"This is beautiful." Callie walked across the decking to the screened porch. "You even have a fireplace out here? This is amazing."

"Thanks. It's not very big or fancy, but I like it. I split my time between my house in Trusty and the cabin." He opened the door. Sweets darted past Callie and jumped onto her bed beside the couch.

"Someone's glad to be home," Callie said.

Home. Yeah, it is home.

"When I realized that you owned the ranch, I wondered if you lived here or in Trusty."

"Well, with you in my life, I have a feeling I'll be spending a lot more time in Trusty." He kissed her again. "I used to think that this place was perfect, you know? I thought I was happy here. But now I realize that I wasn't happy. I was content. There's a world of difference between happy and content." He squeezed her hand. "Now that you're here, I'm happy."

She leaned in to him with her hands pressed flat on his

chest, one of his favorite positions. "I love the things you say to me."

He kissed her softly, and she pressed her body to his.

"I say the things I do because of how you make me feel. Why don't you relax, and I'll run a bath for us."

She raised her eyebrows.

"Unless you want to take a bath alone."

She fisted her hands in his shirt and shook her head with an adorably seductive look in her eyes; then she went up on her tiptoes and he met her halfway for another delicious kiss.

"Make yourself comfortable. I'll be right down." He went upstairs and filled the Jacuzzi with water, then dug through the linen closet until he found the bubble bath Emily had left there and the candles he kept in case he lost electricity. They'd have to do. He poured bubble bath into the running water, then lit a few candles and set them on the counter and the windowsill.

Passing through his bedroom, he realized that in the eight years he'd owned the cabin, he'd never brought a woman there. He felt a sense of pride for having stuck to his guns about not messing around with the guests—*until Callie.* Callie changed everything, and he was glad she did. He wanted her to feel good about being there and to know how special she was. He quickly stripped his bed and put on fresh linens; then he pulled a reading light from the nightstand drawer and set it on top. Not that she'd be doing much reading. In truth, he didn't care what they did, as long as he could hold her through the night and wake up with her in his arms.

They'd been so swept up in each other that they hadn't talked about how soon she was leaving. How could tomorrow be their last day together at the ranch, and why did it feel terminal? He had to stay until Tuesday evening to catch up with the staff and interview prospective employees. Suddenly twenty-four hours seemed not nearly enough time left before they had to spend a long twenty-four hours apart. How could the same amount of time feel like it existed on opposite ends of the acceptability spectrum?

He turned off the tub and went downstairs. Callie was curled up in his recliner, leafing through his photo album. Jesus, he could get used to this. She felt so right in his cabin. Like she belonged. She lifted her eyes and smiled a sleepy, half smile that drew him to her.

"I hope you don't mind." She closed the photo album.

He sat on the arm of the chair and opened the album. "Not at all. Let's look at it together." He flipped a few pages. "There's no rhyme or reason to the album, as I'm sure you noticed. They're just pictures I've kept over the years."

"I know. I had the urge to organize them."

"Alphabetize? Catalog by location? Person?" He kissed her again.

"It's a habit. I can't help it."

"We're quite a pair. I can organize my backpack for any situation, but give me paperwork, or photos, or basically anything other than a backpack or outdoor gear, and I'm a mess." He shook his head.

"I'll drive you crazy with organization and my fears." She looked down at the pictures.

"I love your organization, and, babe, you are the bravest woman I know."

"I'm a sure thing. You don't have to lie to me."

God, you're cute. "I promised I'd never lie, and I won't. Think about this. For a person who's not afraid of heights, scaling a mountain is easy. It takes determination and skill, but it doesn't take the same level of fortitude that conquering your fears does. For a woman who's afraid of heights to do what you did today? To do what you've done the entire time you're here? That's bravery. Callie, being brave isn't about if you can do something. It's about being willing to try to get from point A to point C when point B scares the hell out of you. It's about spirit and strength." He looked down at Sweets, sleeping soundly in her bed, healthy and safe, and his heart was so full that he had to take a moment just to breathe. He hadn't known that Callie's loving Sweets enough to risk her life and face her fears could make him love her even more. After a beat or two, he pushed past the emotions, and he continued.

"It's about loving someone enough to do what you don't think you can. Babe, you are the epitome of bravery." *Like following my gut and saying what I meant even when I was afraid you'd feel smothered.*

She touched his cheek. "You make me feel braver than I am. When Sweets yelped…Oh my gosh, Wes. I just about died. I mean, she's so little, and you should have heard her. I was petrified, but all I could think about was that if I was petrified, how scared was Sweets?"

He set the photo album on the coffee table. "That's why you are the most courageous woman I know. Come on. Let's take a warm bath so you're not too sore tomorrow. We can look through the pictures in the morning if you want." He held her hand as they went upstairs.

"So this is how you woo your women? Leave them alone on Mount Everest with a rambunctious puppy, scare the heck out of them, then lure them into your arms with promises of warm baths?" She said it with a glint of mischief in her eyes and a teasing smile.

"You're the first woman I've lured into my cabin." He led her into the bathroom.

"Wes," she said in a breathy voice. "You lit candles."

"Mm-hm." He drew her hoodie over her head and pressed a kiss to her lips as he wrapped her in his arms. "You took care of Sweets. Now it's my turn to take care of you." Trailing kisses along her shoulder, he unbuttoned the front of her shorts, then hooked his thumbs in the waistband of her panties and shorts and drew them down to her feet. She stepped out of them and he felt her body chill despite the steamy bathroom. It took all of his willpower to restrain from carrying her into his bedroom and loving her every which way he could. He helped her into the bathtub, then stripped off his clothes, stepped in behind her, and wrapped her in his warmth.

Callie sighed gratefully as she sank, neck deep, beneath the bubbles. "This...is bliss."

Her body slid against his, delicate and slight against his breadth. His inner thighs pressed against her hips, and her ass pressed against his groin, making him swell with desire. This wasn't his plan for their time in the tub. As much as he loved having her naked body against his, what he wanted more than anything was to help her relax, to take away the stress of the day, not to have her think sex was always on his mind...even if on some level, with Callie, it was. How could he help it? She meant so much to him, and sex was a natural part of their coming together.

Callie rested her head against his chest with another contented sigh. "Thank you."

"For?"

She ran her hands along his thighs, and he closed his eyes, relishing in her touch.

"This. For being you."

"Hard to be anyone else." He soaked a washcloth and washed Callie's shoulders; then he gently washed each arm. He brought her hands to his lips and kissed the scratches that marred her tender palms.

"I want to know more about you," he said honestly.

She leaned to the side a little and looked up at him with a sleepy smile. The arc of her breasts lifted above the bubbles. She looked devastatingly sexy.

"Like what?"

"Favorites? Dreams? Worst memory? Everything, Cal. I want to know what made you who you are." The question surprised him as much as it probably surprised her, although she didn't appear surprised. Her gaze was thoughtful, as if she were thinking about the question.

"Favorites? That's a broad question."

"Favorite authors or books? Is there a...I don't know, a literary place you wish you could go?"

"A literary place? Yeah, only every library in the world. I don't even think Kathie would ask me that, and she's a writer."

"There's a difference between a writer and a boyfriend." He ran the washcloth down her thighs, glad he was her boyfriend and not the writer.

"Yeah, I guess you're right. Let's see. Favorite authors or books? I really love Jane Austen, but I think everyone does, so that's kind of cliché, and her books aren't my favorite genre. I love Sophie Kinsella and Jane Green. Oh, and the Brothers Grimm, of course."

He had no idea who some of those authors were, but he mentally filed them away for future reference. "What's your worst memory ever?"

"That's a strange question. Don't you want to know my best memory ever?" she asked.

"No, because we haven't created it yet."

That brought Callie's hands to his shoulders and her warm, hungry lips to his. He drew her up onto his lap and guided her legs around his waist. Her skin was feathery soft as he cupped her rear. Her breasts pressed against him. The taut points of her nipples were hard against his chest as they kissed like they never wanted to part. Oh, how he wanted to make love to her, to lift her bottom and lower her onto his throbbing erection until he was buried to the hilt, but this—feeling her curves against him, her body open and willing, her desire raw in each stroke of her tongue—was too magnificent to rush.

Her skin pebbled with goose bumps. Without missing a beat, still lip to lip, tongue to tongue, Wes scooped warm water into his hands and brought it to her shoulders. The water trickled between them as he deepened the kiss. He ran his hands down her arms to her waist—to warm her, he told himself. But the feel of her shapely body only spurred his desire, and he was powerless to fight the temptation any longer. He tangled one hand in her hair and drew their lips apart. Callie's eyes closed, and she let out a seductive sound that brought his mouth to her neck. Kissing wasn't enough. He wanted to consume her. He settled his teeth on her neck and drew in a long, sensuous suck.

"Oh God, Wes." She arched her back, bringing her breasts away from his chest.

Two perfect mounds of beauty that he had to have. He brought his free hand up and cupped her breast while he sucked her neck and she writhed against his hard length. In one swift move, he laid her on her back, her legs still around his waist, and he pushed into her until he was buried deep, their bodies beneath the water, bound together with love and need. Callie clung to him, fingernails carving moons into his back as he loved her with all the fervor he'd been holding back. Moving masterfully, he gripped her ass in one hand, tilting her hips and angling his to hit the spot that made her eyes roll back and her neck arch. Callie panted, clawing at his back as he quickened his pace. Her insides tightened around him.

"More. Yes. More," she whispered.

He pressed his toes to the bottom of the tub for leverage and drove in hard, his shaft nearly numb with pleasure.

"More," she pleaded.

Her voice, her words, the erotic look of her parted lips and the feel of her velvety flesh swallowing him over and over sent him into a frenzy of thrusts as he took her over the edge and she cried out, filling the bathroom with an indiscernible cry. Her legs fell from his waist. Her hips bucked and thrust.

"Oh. Ye—" She opened her eyes into narrow, dark slits. "More," she demanded.

Holy hell. He felt her press her feet to the bottom of the tub and draw her knees up.

"Bed." One word was all he could manage. He stepped from the tub and picked Callie up in his arms. In a few determined steps, they were in the bedroom. With one hand, he drew the covers back, then laid her gorgeous, wet, naked body on the bed. His bed. Christ, she was beautiful. He'd dreamed about seeing her in his bed, and this was so much better than his dreams.

THE SIGHT OF Wes standing naked before her, all those glorious planes of muscle and power trapped beneath his tanned skin, made Callie's body vibrate with need. She was eager for his hard length to scratch her every sexual itch—and boy did she itch. As he came down between her knees, she pressed her palm to his chest, gathering the courage to tell him what she wanted.

"Wait," she whispered.

He froze. He was the perfect combination of sexual dominance and compassionate lover. He cared, and it was evident in every move, every stroke, and every time he stilled. She pressed his chest, urging him down on the bed beside her, flat on his back. *Oh, good Lord.* She could barely breathe at the sight of him. He had been the object of her bedroom fantasies for so many weeks, and none of them—not one—could hold a candle to having him here for her taking. Callie crawled over him and settled her knees between his massive thighs. She pressed her palms to his ribs, running her thumbs over the impossibly perfect ripples of his abs and feeling the heat radiating from his body—directly to the sweet spot between her legs. Callie brought her lips to the center of his stomach and kissed her way down those magnificent abs, dragging her tongue along the indentations between the muscles. She had to stop every inch or so to take a little suck of his skin and lave his shuddering body. *Delicious.* She wanted to love him, to give him the pleasures he'd given her—and to give herself the okay to be the person she had conjured up in her dreams—*If I ever had a man like that. If I ever had Wes...*Oh yes, she deserved to cast the hesitation aside. This was their last night at the ranch, and she wanted to remember it forever.

She ran her tongue along the curve of his abs as they drove south toward the heat of his desire. Wes drew in an uneven breath. Callie felt his hands tangle in her hair as she moved lower and dragged her tongue from base to tip, lingering there. She ran her tongue around the swollen edge where it met the shaft. His hands fisted, and his hips rocked forward. Oh yeah. She knew what he wanted, but he'd have to wait. She licked every inch of him until he was wet, then wrapped her slender fingers around his hard length and slid her hand up and down slowly, drawing a low groan from him as she took the tip in her mouth, teasing him as she pumped his desire to the edge.

"Callie." He panted.

She smiled around his shaft, feeling his body shiver with need, his thighs flex. Every muscle in his arms bulged, and she knew he was holding back from pushing her to take him in deeper. She drew her mouth away, pulling a needful groan from deep within him. Still working him with her hand, she licked his balls, feeling them tighten against her tongue. She'd never been so bold with any other man, and Wes's jaw clenched. He held her hair so tight she feared it might rip out—a pretty good indication that she was doing something right.

When she felt him swell within her hand, she finally took him in her mouth again, all of him.

"Oh, sweet Jesus," he said through clenched teeth.

She sucked, and stroked, until he was holding her back— literally. His fists tangled in her hair, holding her mouth away from his cock.

"Stop. I'll come, and I want to make love to you."

Before she could decide which she wanted more—teasing him until he lost control, or riding him like a bull—his hands gripped her hips and he shifted her onto her back. She lifted her hips, eager to take him in, and he shoved a pillow under them. Then another. She knew this would allow him to penetrate deeper. Her girlfriends had shared all their naughty tips with her over the years, and when he hesitated, she reached for the back of his neck.

He searched her eyes and a simple nod, a silent acquiescence, sent him plunging into her. *Holy cow.* Nothing could have prepared her for the scorching flame that seared her body with every thrust as he gripped her knees and pulled them up by his chest.

"Harder," she demanded.

His eyes bored into her soul, hypnotizing her into a world where only they existed, and she wanted to experience all of him, forever. She went a little wild, clawing, moaning loudly and hungrily, clutching his hips, pulling him deeper as he hit all the right places. Her body tingled and burned as the sensations rose in a seemingly endless crescendo of tantalizing pulses. On the verge of coming apart, he slowed and brought his teeth to her shoulder, sinking them into her flesh with a sinful mix of pain and pleasure. She sucked in a breath, and he tightened the bite and quickened his pace, taking her right over the edge in an explosion of cries, her body pulsating around him in a ceaseless rhythm.

"M-more," she managed.

He sucked where he'd bitten, then licked the tender spot, sending another rampant thrill through her. She dug her nails into his shoulders, then gave him the same exquisite pain he'd given her, teeth to muscle. He groaned and thrust and followed her right over the edge in a carnal frenzy that rocked them both from the pillows to the mattress in a shuddering tangle of tremors.

They clung together, breathing unsteadily, eyes closed. Callie felt his hand slide from her skin. *No. Come back.* He collapsed beside her, eyes still closed, and pulled her against him.

"No way..." He breathed hard. "We've only been...together a few days. It feels like we've been making love for years, and we know every single one of each other's hot spots."

"Way."

He shook his head. She loved that he felt as much for her as she felt for him. He drew the covers over them, and she wondered if her friends would miss her if they stayed right there in bed until it was time to go back home.

Chapter Twenty-One

MONDAY MORNING, SUN streamed across the front porch steps, illuminating Callie's bare legs as she read. She wore a crinkly pastel blue miniskirt, a white blousy tank top, and her boots. She looked sexy as hell and sweet enough to eat. Wes was watching her from the front yard, where he tossed a ball for Sweets to retrieve. They'd woken up before six with Sweets sprawled across the bottom of the bed, and to Wes's surprise, Callie reached down and pulled the pup between them, then showered her in kisses and love. There were no two ways about it. He was a lucky man. He'd stumbled across Sweets, and he'd stumbled across Callie. And he couldn't imagine himself without them.

He joined Callie on the steps, and she leaned against him.

"It seems weird that you're leaving tonight," he said.

Sweets brought the ball to Wes and climbed up Callie's legs with her front paws, craning her neck to lick her chin. Callie lowered her face so she could reach her. He loved that she didn't mind puppy kisses.

"Don't remind me. I'm pretending we're just going to blink our eyes, and the day we have to be apart is going to be over before it starts." She took the ball from Wes's hands and tossed it into the woods. Sweets bolted after it. "I'm going to miss Sweets, too."

"So, what's our plan after I'm back in Trusty?" He knew what he wanted—to see Callie every second that he wasn't working. But she had a life, too, and he also knew she'd pushed aside her morning rituals for him the last few days. He might not be organized with paperwork, but he had a memory like an elephant, and he knew she liked to do her Jillian Michaels DVD in the mornings. He was already thinking of her staying over at his house in Trusty. There was a television in the den that she could use for her exercise if he rearranged the furniture.

"Plan?" She set her book aside and tucked her hair behind her ear. Her face was makeup free and radiated with the warm glow of a fresh tan. He'd never seen anyone more beautiful.

"Should I call you and ask you on a date every night of the week? Because I want to see you whenever I'm not working. Or can I assume I'll see you? How does this dating thing work?" He'd like to move her right into his place, but he knew the reality was, a few days was just that, a few days, even if it came on the heels of four weeks of wanting. He didn't want to suffocate her. Well, he did, but he wouldn't.

"This dating thing?" She held her palms up toward the sky. "How am I supposed to know? I know I want to see you."

"Okay, so...can I assume you'll still come with me to the barbecue at Luke's on Saturday?"

"Yes. I would love to meet your family."

"And can I assume that when I'm back in town tomorrow afternoon, I can pick you up after work and take you home with me?"

She blushed, and he kissed her temple. "I'll take that as a yes? Is it safe to assume that maybe you'll take a drive with me

Saturday before the barbecue and let me show you my favorite park, so you can see if it's one you might like as much as you like the park in Denver?"

"You have a favorite park?" She narrowed her eyes like he was making it up.

"I do. I used to ride my dirt bike there when I was a kid. Unless you have a date?"

She squeezed his thigh. "I'll check my little black book, and if I don't have a date, I'd really like that."

Sweets bounded back to them with a giant stick in her mouth. She flopped on her belly, trapped the stick between her paws, and gnawed on it.

"And then I guess it's also safe for me to assume that after you check that little black book, I can burn it?" He was only half teasing. The thought of her with any other man made his gut burn.

"Now you're pushing your luck."

He grabbed her ribs, and she squealed, doubling over with laughter.

"How about…?" She jumped from the step, and Sweets popped up onto all fours. "How about I burn yours? It's probably as thick as a phone book."

He chased her around the yard with Sweets on their heels. Callie squealed with delight. When he caught her, she covered her ribs with her arms.

"Don't tickle. Please!" She laughed, and it shot love right through him.

"Oh, I'll tickle." He grabbed her ribs and she shrieked again. Sweets bit the bottom of his jeans and tugged. "Oh, now you're on her side?"

He pulled Callie into a kiss and cupped her butt, pressing

his hips to hers. "I don't have a little black book. I can barely remember my own schedule, remember?"

"You remember your schedule just fine." She arched a brow.

"Okay, truth is…I was never a dater." He shrugged. "I haven't had a girlfriend in years. No need to keep a book, because I don't call for dates." He shook his head, knowing how that made him sound. He never thought he was a player, but now he wondered if that term was accurate, and it made him feel a little sick to his stomach. He hoped Callie didn't think of him in those terms.

She narrowed her eyes again and wrapped her arms around his neck. "I'm sleeping with a guy who has never valued relationships. That should make me feel really bad." She held his gaze, and he clenched his jaw. "Well, I might be naive, but it makes me feel the opposite. It means that no one had this place in your heart before I did." She stood on her tiptoes and kissed him—while he recovered from a mini heart attack about her sleeping with a guy who never valued relationships.

Chapter Twenty-Two

"LET ME GET my sunglasses. That lovers' glow is blinding." Christine covered her eyes as she crossed the lawn in front of the cabin.

"Shut up." Callie pushed her playfully.

Wes was waiting for them at the lodge. Callie had no idea what he had in store for them today.

Kathie carried a notebook under her arm, and in her red T-shirt, short white skirt, and boots, she looked like she was ready to sit on a haystack and write for the afternoon.

Bonnie sidled up to Callie's other side and looped her arm into hers. "So? You look happy."

Callie sighed. "Yeah. I owe you guys big-time. I am so in love with Wes. I never even imagined that love could feel like this."

"I could have told you how it lifted you onto a cloud and held you there in disbelief." Bonnie sighed. "Until real life steps in and kicks you in the ass. Then you spend your life scrambling to find a way back up to that elusive cloud."

"Talk about a buzz kill." Callie scrunched her face. "What the heck?"

"Oh, I'm just missing Mark. I called him from the lodge last night, and he has to go to Idaho for a meeting today, which means he won't be home when I get home tonight." Bonnie released Callie's arm as they crossed the bridge.

"I'm so sorry, Bon. How long will he be gone?" Callie asked.

"Just until tomorrow night. I know it's silly, but it's been several days, and I miss him. I assumed he'd be home waiting for me. Besides, watching you and Wes made me miss him even more." Bonnie slung an arm over Callie's shoulder.

"I know. I'm so sorry." Callie leaned against the bridge, watching the horses grazing in the field. "This is where it all began. I just want to remember it."

Bonnie took a picture of Callie, then turned the camera on the horses. "I have so many pictures that you'll never forget."

"I know. I love that about you." Callie looked at her friends, and her heart swelled with gratitude. "Do you think I'm nuts for moving so fast with Wes?"

"We'd think you were nuts if you didn't. He adores you and you obviously adore him." Christine shoved her hip against Callie's. "How was the railroad ride?"

Callie rolled her eyes, but inside, she warmed with the memory of their lovemaking. She never imagined she could be so open and aggressive, but everything she did with Wes felt natural and safe.

Kathie closed in on her other side. "Earth-shattering or sensuous and sweet?"

Bonnie took a picture of the three of them. "Or both?"

Callie thought about the mind-numbing sex they'd had last night and the way they'd made love tenderly this morning. "Both. Definitely both. Can I ask you guys a serious question?"

"Always." Kathie climbed onto the bridge railing and sat

facing Callie and the others.

"He asked me about dating or assuming we'd see each other."

"Assume," Kathie said.

"Date," Christine offered.

"Both." Bonnie paced the bridge. "You guys remember what it was like. Think back to when you first started seeing Billy and Paul. You assumed. Kathie, you slept at Paul's place every night after you first did the deed, and, Christine, same with you and Billy. Heck, I'm not sure I ever left Mark's after we did that either. It seems like it just happens. Your lives meld together, and suddenly you're engaged and then married. So I think you should learn from us. Assume, because it's too hard to do anything else when you're in that ravenous I-must-have-you stage, but this next part is tricky, because *you* have to do it. Guys are clueless when it comes to these things. I think you should throw in a date now and again. A real date, where he picks you up at your place, so you can get that anticipatory shiver and worry about your hair and what you're wearing."

"Oh, I do like that," Kathie said.

"What if we're spending nights at his place? I just call one day from work and say, *Pick me up at six?*" That sounded sort of silly, although the whole anticipatory shiver thing sounded too good to pass up.

"Sure, or if you guys have an argument or something. It's just an idea to keep in your back pocket. When you want to spice things up a little or add a reminder of what it was like to fall in love in the first place." Bonnie put the lens cap on her camera and joined them leaning against the railing.

"Do you guys get bored now that you're married?" She couldn't imagine ever getting bored of Wes.

"Nope," Christine said. "But then again, with the chaps and the whole Tex thing, it's hard to get bored." She bumped her hip into Callie's again, and Callie smiled.

"Bored? Never. But I do love the idea of having Paul pick me up for a date. I think I'll call him and have him meet me somewhere one night. That's a great idea." Kathie opened her notebook.

"You're taking notes?" Callie asked.

Kathie tucked her hair behind her ear. "No. I'm putting it on the schedule I'm working on. My writing and pay-attention-to-Paul schedule." She lifted her eyes to Callie's. "Thanks to you."

"I sent Mark a key to a hotel room a few weeks ago," Bonnie admitted with wide eyes and a sinful grin.

"Really?" Christine turned to face her. "Do tell."

"Yup. Sent it with a courier to his office with a note that said, *Room 612, The Mayflower Hotel. Leave your briefs at home.*"

"Oh my God. That is the cutest thing I've ever heard." Callie wondered what Wes would think if she ever did that.

"It was a great night," Bonnie said. "Hey, look." She pointed at Cutter riding a horse toward the lodge, wearing leather chaps and a dark cowboy hat. "I don't think I could ever get bored of looking at handsome cowboys."

"I've got my own handsome cowboy," Callie mused. "Speaking of Wes, we'd better get in there. I wonder what the surprise is. Maybe I can jump off a cliff today."

"Not likely, considering the barn dance is this evening. He'd never let you break a leg when he knows you love to dance," Christine said as they walked up the hill toward the lodge.

"How does he know I love to dance?"

"A little birdie might have told him," Christine answered.

Bonnie pulled open the lodge door. "A little blond-haired birdie with a big mouth and a penchant for sun visors."

They walked inside. There was a couple standing at the registration desk and another couple sitting in the lobby.

"It's so quiet in here," Callie whispered.

"Not for long, it's not," Christine said. She pointed to Sweets running across the hardwood floor toward them. They all dropped to their knees to pet her. Sweets tumbled onto her back, allowing them to rub her belly.

"She's doing great, isn't she?" Callie said.

"Yeah. It's amazing how resilient puppies are." Bonnie lifted her camera and snapped a picture.

"Wes's brother Ross is a vet, and he said the webbing in their paws heals fast. I guess he's right." Callie heard the familiar cadence of Wes's boots behind her.

"Sweets gets all the babes." He reached for Callie's hand and drew her up for a kiss.

"Yeah, well, I think you got the best babe of all," Christine reminded him.

"Me too." He placed his hand on Callie's lower back. "Are you ladies ready for your surprise?"

"Heck yeah," Kathie said.

His eyes skidded over theirs, then lingered on Callie. "I know that when you brought Callie here, she thought she was going to a spa to be pampered, not to a dude ranch to be lasciviously loved by a...well, by me."

Lasciviously loved. There you go with those beautiful words again.

"I'm not sure she minds," Bonnie said.

"Neither am I, but she's been such a good sport, and you guys have generously shared her with me. I wanted to give you all a special thank-you. It's just the four of you for the next few hours."

The next few hours? She already missed him.

He took Callie's hand. "Follow me."

They followed Wes down the hallway Callie had explored her first night there, to the conference room. "Before I take you in, if you'd rather not do this, it's okay. Just tell me." He pulled the doors open and stepped to the side.

Gone was the conference table and chairs. The walls were draped in layers of silk and chiffon in pastel colors. There were four red velvet armchairs set around a fancy wooden table to their left with a tea set in the center, and just beyond, heavy red theater-style curtains hung beside the tall windows, allowing sunlight to bathe the room in a warm glow. Glittery silver stars dangled from the ceiling as if floating in midair.

"Oh my God." Callie took a step inside the room. Only then did she notice two massage tables and two manicure and pedicure chairs off to her right, and near the far wall there was a table draped in a deep red velvet tablecloth that matched the armchairs, with several leather-bound books between two wooden bookends.

Her eyes welled with tears. With trembling hands, she reached behind her, hoping someone, anyone, would take hold before her knees gave out. Wes's hands circled her waist.

"I don't know much about *spa* pampering," he said against her cheek.

She turned to face him and heard the girls talking, sensed Bonnie taking pictures, but her mind was draped in the elusive cloud of love that Bonnie had recently described—and she didn't need to scramble to find it.

"Wes."

He pressed his lips to hers. "Don't say a word."

"But how—"

He kissed her again. "If you keep talking, I'll keep kissing, and you'll never get pampered."

Callie had never felt so overwhelmed with emotions. She embraced him, and she would have stayed there for hours if he hadn't pulled away.

"I think your friends have already figured out what to do." He nodded at the girls as they removed their boots. "This part killed me, but I know it's part of the whole girl experience." His eyes narrowed, but it wasn't desire that Callie saw. It was something she didn't recognize, and it was gone in a flash. He lifted his chin and spoke loudly. "Okay, gentlemen, come on in."

Two tall, handsome, burly men burst through the chiffon, wearing dark slacks, loosely fitted white shirts with capped sleeves that ended just above their bulging biceps, open to midchest and belted with thick leather around their waists. Their faces were chiseled and tan, hair perfectly coiffed and sideswept. They could have been Chippendales dancers.

"Oh baby." Christine fanned her face. "Forget the mechanical bull. I wanna ride him."

Kathie stood beside a massage table and reached for the button on her shorts.

Wes put a hand on Kathie's shoulder. "We have changing rooms for that, and robes." He shot a look at Callie that clearly translated to *Don't even think about stripping in front of these guys.*

"You ruin all my fun," Kathie said. She patted him on the back. "I'm a happily married woman. I was just pulling your chain. This is amazing. Thank you."

FATED FOR LOVE

He leaned in close to Kathie and whispered, "I think they're gay."

Callie laughed.

"You wish," Christine said. "Want me to do the lick test?"

Callie swatted her.

The men stood with their arms crossed, pecs dancing, eyes smiling. They clearly enjoyed the attention.

Wes lifted his chin. "Ladies," he called out.

Two beautiful women dressed in sexy pink harem outfits complete with sheer, flowing pants and skimpy panty-like bikini bottoms joined the men.

Callie felt the claws of jealousy prickle her nerves. She glanced at Wes. His eyes were trained on her.

"I have no interest," he said knowingly.

Promise? Swear to God? Cross your heart and hope to die? She cringed at how quickly the jealousy hit her. How on earth would she make it through Thursdays with Tiffany Dempsey and the other women ogling him at the library?

"I can't believe you went to all this trouble. Thank you." Callie wondered how he could have gotten this all set up without her knowing.

"You deserve full-on pampering after the way you tore yourself from the claws of your fears and saved Sweets." He slid a worried stare toward the men.

She used her index finger to draw his chin in her direction, as he'd done so many times to her. "Why would I read a notebook when I have a leather-bound classic in my hands?" She kissed him and felt the tension she'd seen in his eyes and in the bunching of his muscles around his shoulders slip away.

239

Chapter Twenty-Three

BACK IN THE lodge office, Wes paced in front of the window. When they'd returned from the trail yesterday, he'd called and asked Emily to help him set up a spa afternoon and fairy tale evening for Callie, and when she'd asked if it was okay to send masseurs, he'd envisioned men with pasty skin from working indoors. Men who were more into manicures than muscles. What the hell had he been thinking? What man wouldn't want to massage half-naked women for a living? He eyed Sweets sleeping beneath his desk. If only he could push the jealousy away that easily. He felt like he might burst if he didn't get the worry out of his head. He needed a distraction, and calling his youngest brother, Luke, would have to do.

Luke answered on the second ring. "Hey, Wes. What's up, lover boy?"

"Christ. I see you spoke to Ross."

"Emily. She said you were setting up a *day of pampering and an evening of fairy tale wonder*, whatever the hell that means, for Callie Barnes."

"I should have known. She's got a mouth like a sieve. I told her not to tell anyone." Wes ran his hand through his hair.

"And you thought that would work? I guess your brain

really has turned to mush. It's Emily. She loves love. Daisy says Em's biological clock is ticking, so she's living vicariously through us."

Sweets yawned, and Wes scratched her head. "Great. Just what I need. Listen, I wanted to talk to you about the barbecue. You don't mind if I bring Callie, do you?"

"After what I've heard, I'd be surprised if you didn't."

He pictured Luke pacing in the field, watching his horses while he ribbed Wes. He was six three with dark Braden eyes and was almost the mirror image to their older brother, Ross, with hair a shade lighter than Wes's and worn longer on top.

"Okay, I'll bite. What did you hear? And before you say anything, I also wanted to tell you that I get it now, and I'm sorry I gave you crap about falling for Daisy so fast." He pulled Sweets into his lap and lifted the phone away from her pointy teeth as she tried to nip it.

"Not much. You're in love with the hot librarian all the single guys had pinned their hopes on."

Wes rubbed his temple with his thumb and index finger. "All the single guys?"

"From what I hear. Better get used to it. How do you think I feel knowing that half the guys who see Daisy are making up their symptoms?" Luke laughed. Daisy was the only family practice doctor in Trusty. She was a natural blonde with blue eyes and a killer body, and when she was growing up, she had fought against unwarranted rumors fed by jealous women. It didn't surprise Wes to hear that men would line up to take their clothes off for her. But he never imagined his brother being able to handle it so calmly.

"Really? No way."

"Yeah. She's good about it, very professional. But it's the

same shit as the girls who go to the library when they know you'll be there, Mr. Thursday."

"How the hell do you know about that?" Jesus, the Trusty grapevine was running faster than the river.

"How could I not? I have breakfast at the diner once a week. Margie sees all and knows all. By the time you get back, you and Callie will be the dish of the week."

"Good. Then maybe the guys will back off and the Tiffany Dempseys of the world will disappear. Luke, man…"

Luke laughed. "Callie?"

"Yeah. I just didn't expect to be so bowled over."

"Tell me about it."

"It's like someone punched me in the gut, turned me inside out, and somehow it is the best feeling in the world. What the fuck is that?" He petted Sweets, who was fast asleep across his lap.

"Love, man. I tried to tell you." He knew Luke was pacing by the cadence of his voice. "All I can tell you is this. That fucked-up feeling that makes you say all sorts of bizarre shit you never pictured yourself saying and do crazy stuff like create fairy tale nights? Get used to it, because if she's turned you inside out, it's the real thing."

Chip came into the office as Wes said goodbye to Luke. He leaned over the desk and stared down at Wes with his blond brows knitted together and his jaw clenched tight.

"What the fuck is going on in the conference room?"

Sweets lifted her chin from Wes's lap. "Look what you did." Wes set Sweets down on her bed beneath his desk.

Chip gazed at Sweets and his eyes, and voice, softened. "How are her paws?"

"Good. She's a tough girl."

Chip slid his butt onto the desk and crossed his arms. "What's all that fluffy shit on the walls in there, and how'd you get Butch to agree to help you set it up?"

"The man was married for over thirty years. He knows what love is. Besides, he and the guys were more than happy to help."

"*Pfft.* Yeah, right. Wait...love?" Chip arched a brow.

Wes ignored him and leafed through the papers on his desk. He didn't want to get into a long discussion about why he shouldn't be with Callie at the ranch. "Where's the file of people you wanted me to interview?"

"I left it on your desk."

Wes felt the heat of Chip's stare as he rifled through the papers again, then tugged open the desk drawers and looked through them.

"Dude, your girl is in there wearing nothing but a towel and some he-man's rubbing her body with oil." Chip smiled. "Not smart, man."

"I trust Callie."

"Yeah, but do you trust the dude who's rubbing her?"

Wes clenched his jaw. The guy was doing what he'd hired him to do, and he trusted Callie. That was all that mattered. He spotted the file beneath a stack of papers under Chip. "Move your ass."

Chip lifted his butt, then sat back down after Wes snagged the file.

"Did you come in here just to give me shit?"

"Nah. Giving you shit was just a perk. Before you interview the applicants tomorrow, I wanted to ask you again about Cutter."

Wes set a dark stare on him, but his conversation with Callie had crossed his mind several times, and he found himself considering Cutter more seriously for the position. Embarrassingly, he wondered if Cutter's interest in Callie had strengthened his resolve against considering him for Ray's position. He didn't want to believe that he could be the kind of guy who would let something personal affect his work relationships, but he'd been gnawing on that thought and it tasted like shit.

Unable to come to a decision, he shifted his eyes away from Chip.

"All right, whatever. For the record, I still think it's a mistake." Chip's gaze softened. "And the other reason I came in was, you know, I wanted to make sure you were doing okay."

"What do you mean? I'm fine." Wes came around the desk and sank into the chair in front of Chip. He skimmed over the applications in the file.

Chip sat in the chair beside him and kicked his feet up on the desk. "Well, you left our office on Thursday a single guy with nothing more than a pup on your mind, and now you're throwing massage parties and you're all googly-eyed."

"It's weird as shit, isn't it?" Wes closed the file and looked at the man who had been his best buddy forever. There was no judgment in Chip's tone and no hint of a tease. Wes realized that he'd been defensive about Callie from the moment Chip made the first comment about them the other day, and as he sat beside his best friend, he realized that he didn't need to be. Not with Chip.

Chip shrugged. "It was bound to happen to one of us sooner or later. I just didn't expect it to be you."

"That makes two of us." A relationship was the last thing he'd expected. But he hadn't expected to fall for a puppy that couldn't smell a damn thing either, and Sweets was one of the best parts of his life. Callie was a hundred times better. "I guess the best things in life really are the least expected ones."

"I guess." Chip laid a hand on Wes's shoulder. "Hey, man, you're happy, I'm happy. But I still think you shouldn't leave her alone half naked with those guys."

"Maybe you're right." He'd love an excuse to check in on Callie. It had only been a few hours and he already missed her. "By the way, the dance tonight…"

"Clarissa told me you've got something special planned. What can I do to help?"

"Help? Really? Thanks, Chip. If you could have Cutter or Butch get Ghost ready for me, and don't laugh when you see what I'm wearing."

Chip arched a brow.

"Don't ask. Wait. How did Clarissa know I had something planned?"

"Emily was running late for a client meeting, so she had Clarissa arrange for the shipment this morning. She already guessed that you'd fallen for some chick. Apparently, you had her ship jeans and shorts? Or did you forget?" Chip pushed to his feet.

Wes rubbed his temples. "That feels like a year ago."

"You've had a crazy few days, that's for sure. Listen, buddy, if you need me, I'm around."

"Hey, can I ask you something?"

Chip flipped his chin and his long blond bangs swung to the side, then fell back in his eyes. "Shoot."

"If I hadn't gone to the library every week, would you have known that Callie worked there?" He'd been thinking about what Ross had said.

"Shit. Everyone knew about the hot brunette working at the

library. But you had your sights set on her from the first day you saw her, so I never even bothered." He narrowed his eyes. "Maybe you had your sights set on her and never realized it yourself. You're kinda dumb like that."

"Ass."

"Whatever. I gotta run. I told Clarissa I'd go over the marketing figures with her tonight." Chip reached for the door.

"Is that what they call it now? Or are the figures foreplay?"

"I'll let you know." With a smirk on his lips, Chip sauntered out the door.

CALLIE SAT IN one of the armchairs by the window, sipping tea.

"I swear I could just stare at these guys all day. The girls, too. Have you ever seen such beautiful creatures?" Bonnie asked.

"Yes. He's about six three with dark hair, dark eyes, and has a sweet little puppy." Callie smiled and admired her freshly painted nails. "My body is so relaxed right now. I feel like I could slip from this chair like liquid."

"Maybe that's his evil plan. Get you all loosey-goosey so he can have his way with you." Christine raised her brows.

"Then why would he invite you guys?" Callie lifted her bare foot and rested it on Christine's knee. "Face it. He's just a nice guy."

"Yeah, he is," Christine admitted. "So he's staying tonight and you're coming with us? When will he go back?"

"Tomorrow night. He has to interview people tomorrow. I

thought about staying an extra day, but I've already taken off work, and I can't afford any more time off." And boy did she ever wish she could.

"Well, Cal, I'm proud of you. You stuck with everything we did. You rescued Sweets. You even fished. It wasn't so bad, was it?" Bonnie inspected her newly painted toenails.

"Not only was it not so bad, but I enjoyed it. Well, except for the climbing-down-the-mountain thing. That was so scary, but worth it to save Sweets. Sweets is so…sweet." She sighed.

"*Sweets.* Yeah, that's who I was thinking about, too." Christine rolled her eyes.

Kathie was poring over her notebook, writing page after page with a serious face.

"Are you still working on your schedule?" Callie asked.

"Oh God, no. I'm done with that. I'll work when Paul's at work. Done. End of workday." Kathie didn't lift her eyes as she spoke. "I'm taking notes about an idea for my next book. It's about a woman who loses everything and discovers that family's what matters most. How's that for a simplified plot? Lots of great heart-wrenching stuff will happen, of course."

"You amaze me, Kathie." Callie finished her tea and went to the window. "I can't wait to read this one, knowing you came up with it on this trip." The window looked out over the entertainment barn. The sun was going down, and the barn was lit up with white holiday lights. "Hey, you guys, come here."

Christine and Bonnie joined her by the window.

"They must be getting ready for the dance," Bonnie said.

"What are you guys wearing tonight?" Callie asked.

"Whatever. Jeans and boots. It's a barn dance, so it doesn't really matter." Bonnie's eyes widened. "Wait, for *you* it does,

Cal. Your first dance with your new man. Wow. How could we forget? What are you going to wear?"

"Probably that cute skirt that Kathie got me last year for Christmas." Callie ran her hands down the heavy curtains. "You guys, I saw this room the other night. Remember I told you about the conference room? This was it. These curtains weren't here. I know I've said it a hundred times since we got here, but I still can't believe he did all of this."

"Yeah, well, enjoy it now." Christine hooked her thumbs into her pockets, shook her shoulders, and spoke with a tough voice. "When you get back to Trusty, those bitches are gonna be hatin' your pretty little ass for taking the best horse in the barn off the market."

"Oh God, you're so weird." Callie bit her lower lip. "Wait. Do you think so?"

"You've got supersexy Wes Braden to come home to. What does it matter what anyone else thinks? Besides…" Christine fisted her hands and blew on her knuckles. "I've got your back. Just let someone mess with you. I'll take them down."

"Thank God for little favors." She smiled at Christine. "I think we'd better get ready for the dance, but I'm not sure how we tip these guys." Callie looked at Bonnie. "Any thoughts?"

"We didn't bring our purses," Bonnie pointed out.

"Okay, fine. I'll take a hit for the team and…you know." Christine wiggled her eyebrows in quick succession.

Callie smacked her arm. "No, you will not."

"I know. I just love to tease you because you get all prissy about that." She eyed one of the men. "I think Billy's going to be dressing like a prince tonight."

"I'm not prissy." *If you'd seen me last night, you wouldn't call me prissy!*

The doors opened, and Sweets darted in with something tied to her collar with a big red ribbon. Callie dropped to her knees, and Sweets padded right up into her lap, licking her cheeks and whimpering with excitement.

"What is that?" Callie tried to untie the ribbon, but every time she reached for it, Sweets twisted her head toward her hand, desperate for more petting. "Sweets, maybe you could sit still." She tried again.

Bonnie picked up Sweets and held her tight. "Go ahead. Untie it."

Kathie was still glued to her notebook.

Sweets wiggled in Bonnie's arms while Callie struggled to free the paper.

Callie laughed as she untied the ribbon with Sweets's tongue lapping at her fingers. "Let me see what you've got."

She unrolled the paper and her eyes widened. "Oh my gosh. No way. No way. No way." She looked at Bonnie. "Pinch me." She slammed her eyes shut. When no one pinched her, she opened her eyes again. "I said pinch me!"

"Fine." Christine pinched her.

"Ouch! Thank you. Whew, I'm not dreaming." Callie turned the paper so it faced the others.

Kathie came off her chair and knelt in front of Callie, then read the paper.

Princess Callie,

I would be honored if you'd grace me with your presence at the ball tonight. If you agree, tie the ribbon to Sweets's collar and send her out, and I'll pick you up at your cabin at seven o'clock. If Sweets appears without a ribbon, I will assume you have other plans and wish you a lovely evening.

Your hopeful prince,
Wesley

PS: I will arrange for your fellow princesses to be picked up as well.

"Callie, I'm so using this in a book. He's the most romantic man I've ever known in real life." Kathie read the invitation again.

Callie heard Wes's voice in the hallway, and Sweets bolted out of the room.

"No!" they all yelled in unison.

"Oh no! He'll think I'm refusing the invitation." Tears sprang to Callie's eyes. "He did so much and I messed it up."

Bonnie snagged the ribbon. "No, you didn't." She tied it around Callie's neck, spun her around, and pushed her out the door.

Callie stumbled into the hallway and stopped at the sight of Wes kneeling beside Sweets, his neck bowed.

With her heart in her throat and her friends pushing her forward from behind, Callie took a few fast steps, desperate to clear up the misunderstanding. She fingered the ribbon around her neck as Wes lifted his eyes and rose to his feet. Their eyes met. He took a step forward and opened his arms as a smile formed on his lips. She sprinted into his arms.

"You enjoy giving me heart attacks, don't you?" He laughed, but she heard the shadow of his momentary disappointment from finding Sweets without a ribbon around her neck lingering in his voice.

She kissed his lips. "No. God, no. I would be honored to go to the *ball* with you tonight."

He laughed, loud and deep. "Hear that, Sweets? She's going to the ball with us."

Sweets barked, and the girls collectively *aww*ed.

"You're amazing," she said.

"No, I'm just a guy in love."

Chapter Twenty-Four

CALLIE WAS THE last one to shower. She finished drying her hair and went to her bedroom to change into her outfit for the dance. Her head was still spinning from their magical day. She heard a knock on the front door and she froze. A quick glance at the clock confirmed that she wasn't running late.

"Callie! You've got to come down here," Bonnie called.

"Just a sec. I need to get dressed," she answered.

"Forget getting dressed and get your butt down here," Christine said in her tough voice.

Callie rolled her eyes as she descended the stairs. "What on earth is so—"

The girls were each holding up a fluffy ball gown. Bonnie shoved the box at her feet across the floor with her foot.

"Oh my God." Callie ran down the steps. She reached into the box and withdrew an off-the-shoulder yellow ball gown complete with a white petticoat and layers of fine silk.

"I think you're supposed to be the belle of the ball, like in *Beauty and the Beast*. She had an off-the-shoulder yellow dress, didn't she?" Christine glanced at Bonnie. "Bonnie's dress looks like Ariel's, and Kathie's looks like Rapunzel's."

"And yours is Merida." Callie fingered the satin dress. "This is—"

"Crazy," Christine said. "I don't even look like Merida. She has red hair."

"I think it's metaphorically speaking," Kathie said. "Rapunzel was studious, Belle was a smart literary type, and Ariel gathered things to help save her kingdom. Bon, you're our mother hen. This makes perfect sense. And, Christine, think about it. Merida was a tomboy, and you're pretty much the tomboy of our group. I think I love your boyfriend, Callie."

"Yeah, well, get in line," Bonnie said.

"You'll have to fight me for him. We'll be the princesses of the barn dance." Callie could barely contain her excitement at what Wes had done. She felt like a real princess, being treated to such an extravagant day. "I'm changing!" She ran up the stairs with the dress bundled against her belly.

"Wait!" Bonnie yelled. "We're coming with you."

They dressed in a flurry of laughter and *Oh my Gods*, and Bonnie captured it all on film. When they were finally dressed in their gowns like four princesses, they went downstairs and sat on the couch like prim and proper ladies—save for their sexy cowgirl boots—with their hands folded in their laps, afraid to move for fear of messing up their beautiful gowns.

"How can we walk to the barn? The bottoms of the dresses will get ruined." Bonnie fingered the hem of the dress.

"He said we'll be picked up," Christine reminded her. "Maybe we'll take the four-wheeler. I heard that if a rancher lets you ride his four-wheeler, you're practically married."

A knock at the door brought them all to their feet. Callie rushed toward the door.

"Wait." Bonnie stepped in front of her. "Let the man make an entrance."

"Okay. Okay." Callie inhaled deeply, trying to calm her fluttering stomach. No such luck. She'd never been the focus of a man's attention in this way. She felt lavished and loved and like she might pass out, all at once.

Bonnie pulled the door open and her jaw dropped. She waved the girls forward. The full skirts of their gowns swished as they hurried to the door and huddled in close to look outside.

Wes stood beside a white horse. He looked striking in a blue velvet jacket with yellow trim, with a white ascot that covered his broad chest. He wore black slacks that outlined the curves of his muscular thighs, and sitting obediently by his booted feet, was Sweets, with a yellow bow around her neck. The horse was draped in blue velvet and her mane was braided with yellow ribbons.

Wes came up the steps and held out a hand for Callie. She was struck dumb. Her arms remained at her sides. When she finally caught her breath, Wes took her hand in his and kissed the back of it while Callie did nothing more than breathe him in and try to remain erect.

"You look stunning."

"Wes," she whispered. "You...this...today..." She swallowed against the lump in her throat and went with the first complete sentence she could manage. "You look so handsome."

"Then we make a perfect pair."

Callie realized that her friends were as awestruck as she was, except for Bonnie, who had somehow slipped away and retrieved her camera.

Bonnie aimed the lens at Wes's white horse and exclaimed, "Oh my God!" drawing everyone's attention toward the three men on horseback headed up the hill. Before Callie could register who was riding toward the cabin, Kathie had bundled the skirt of her purple gown in her hands and was running across the field. The heels of her cowgirl boots kicked up from beneath the fluffy layers of fabric.

Christine stepped onto the porch, her blond bob revealing her graceful neck and lean shoulders. Her tightly fitted dress clung to her slim arms and torso, with a skirt that didn't need frills or sheer covering. It was elegant and simple in deep velvet blue with threads of gold sewn throughout and adorned with gold appliqué along the bottom. A delicate brown belt with a round gold buckle hung low on one hip, with a swatch of blue silk hanging beneath.

"I wish I had taken that roping class. I'd lasso that man of mine right off the horse." Christine didn't bother to lift the skirt of her dress before taking the stairs two at a time and sprinting across the grass toward Billy. In one easy move, Billy lifted her to his horse and set her in front of him. Billy's dark hair brushed over the fancy tuxedo shirt he wore with his jeans and chaps. Callie wondered if Christine was calling him Tex. Billy kissed her so long, Callie's cheeks heated.

Bonnie shoved the camera into Callie's hands, gathered the sparkly green layers of satin in one arm, and flashed a wide smile before hurrying down the steps with her other hand out to her side in a ladylike fashion. Mark was fair-haired and blue-eyed. He looked more like a model than a lawyer, with high cheekbones and a sharp jawline. He dismounted the chestnut-colored horse, and Bonnie leaped into his arms. As Mark swung her in a circle, her dress bloomed around her legs.

Callie blinked several times to hold back tears at the sight of her friends' happiness. With trembling legs, she turned to Wes and grabbed the lapels of his fancy jacket.

"How on earth did you do this?"

Wes folded Callie into his arms. "If I told you, it wouldn't be a fairy tale."

Chapter Twenty-Five

THE BARN DANCE was always a favorite of the guests, with a live band, open bar, and the barn decked out in full country fashion, including bales of hay for seating and cowboy hats hung on metal hooks along the barn wall for guests to wear. Tonight the barn also had a flair of fantasy, thanks to Emily's and Wes's careful planning and Butch and the other ranchers' capable hands. Belts of satin swirled around the wooden support poles from floor to ceiling, and matching satin swatches were draped over tables at the far end of the barn.

Butch came to Wes's side and spoke quietly. "You must have seen the look that reeled you right in."

Wes thought about what Butch had said the last time they spoke. "Every look is that look with Callie. Thank you for your help with everything, Butch. The place looks great, and I now understand how great of a loss you feel for Roxy. I can't imagine a day without Callie. Please know that if I can do anything at any time to help ease your missing her, I'm here for you. Okay?"

"You help me by just being you, Wes. Friendship is as important as love. Speaking of which, it is Cutter who deserves your praise. The delivery truck got stuck this morning, and he drove out and met it. He didn't want to take a chance that your evening would be spoiled."

"Cutter? Well, I'll be damned."

Wes was mulling over that new information when he felt Callie squeeze his arm. She looked gorgeous in the yellow gown that dipped in at her waist and flowed full and thick to the ground.

The idea for the fairy tale evening had come to him the night Callie said she loved fairy tales, and after spending time with Callie and her friends and seeing how closely knit they were, he knew that the surprise would be ten times more special for Callie if Bonnie, Kathie, and Christine were included. The emergency phone numbers on the applications led him to their husbands. Three phone calls later, he had the women's dress sizes and three more guests for the dance. Thankfully, with his offer to pay whatever it took, Emily had been able to coordinate the outfits from a specialty shop in Denver and everything else he'd needed to pull off the fairy tale evening. He owed Clarissa, Butch, and the others a major thank-you. And now he would be adding Cutter to that gratitude list. Who was he kidding? Cutter and the others deserved a *permanent* place on that list.

He owed Emily big-time, and since she was due to arrive at the ranch either tonight or tomorrow, he'd spent the afternoon coordinating a surprise for her, too.

Mark and Bonnie were already on the dance floor, their bodies pressed close as they swayed to the music. Christine and Billy were lip-locked just outside the entrance to the barn. Wes envied them, but this night was for Callie to enjoy in other ways. They'd have the rest of their lives—he hoped—for intimate embraces and kisses that led them to explore every passionate fantasy they could dream of.

"Wes, I just wanted to say thank you." Kathie stood in the circle of Paul's arms. He was a tall, handsome man with thick brown hair and cat-green eyes, which were currently looking at his wife like he'd never seen anyone so beautiful. She reached up and touched Paul's cheek. "*We* wanted to thank you."

"Don't thank me. Thank Callie. If she had said her favorite thing in the world was mud wrestling or hog tying, I think you'd be looking at me a little differently." He set his attention on Callie. "Shall we?" He led her out to the dance floor.

Wes didn't consider himself much of a dancer, but at Clarissa's insistence, he and Chip had both taken dance lessons so they wouldn't look like losers at the barn dances with the ranch guests. Now, as Callie moved with skillful grace in perfect sync to his lead, he was glad he had.

Wes had never understood why women loved the idea of fairy tales, but as the details of the evening came together—and thousands of dollars were spent—he realized that for most people, fairy tales were unattainable. Something to dream about and hope for. Now he understood the thrill of hoping for something magical.

Callie lifted her eyes to his, and the love and gratitude in her warm, dark eyes told him he'd spurred a hope for something other than a fantasy in her future.

The hope of their reality.

Chapter Twenty-Six

THE MOON SPREAD a hint of romance and mystery over the warm evening like a beguiled mistress. Callie couldn't believe it was already time for her to leave. It felt like she'd fallen down the most wonderful rabbit hole of all. She loathed the idea of climbing back out and facing real life once again. Bonnie and Christine had already left with their husbands. Kathie's Cruiser was packed and ready to go. Callie drew in a deep breath as she scanned the grounds of the place where her entire life had changed. She wasn't the same woman she'd been when she'd arrived. *Nowhere near the same person.* She fingered the slick material of her gown and felt tears well in her eyes.

"How can it be so hard to say goodbye?" she asked in a shaky voice.

Wes stood beside her in his velvet princely clothing, looking handsome and charming and oh so sad.

Sweets barked and wagged her tail at Callie's feet. How could she say goodbye to Sweets? She crouched and reveled in her sweet puppy kisses. Callie tried to be strong against the sadness welling in her chest. Wes crouched beside her and took her hand from Sweets's head. He gazed lovingly into her eyes, and for an instant, she thought, *Forget work. I just want to be here with you.* But she could no sooner do that than keep Kathie waiting much longer.

"It's only twenty-four hours, even if it feels like forever right now. We can do twenty-four hours."

She nodded, afraid to try to speak for fear of letting loose a flood of tears. She felt silly for wanting to cry over being apart for such a short time, but as she wrapped her arms around Wes, whose strength and comfort had become as familiar as the fingers on her hands, she knew it didn't matter how silly she felt. She didn't want to spend one night apart from him or fall asleep without his arms around her. She had to own those feelings as she'd owned her fears over the past few days—and every other emotion Wes had drawn from her heart.

"I'll be back right after the interviews. Do you still want me to come by the library and pick you up there, or should I pick you up at your place?"

"The library, so I can see you sooner." She rested her forehead against his chest. "I sound so needy. I'm sorry. I'm just…I miss you already."

He lifted her chin and smiled. "I miss you already, too. I know I can't call you at the library, but do you want me to text you when I'm on my way?"

"Yes, and I'll check it when I get a break. You could try to call me at the library, but they frown upon personal calls, and I'm new, so…"

Wes folded her in his arms and took her in a deep, sensuous kiss that made her head spin and her body hot. *Oh God.* How could she have become so enraptured with him so fast? She gripped his lapels and saw his eyes dart to the truck.

"Know I love you. I don't want to cause trouble at your job, so I'll text when I'm on my way. We shouldn't keep Kathie waiting any longer."

"I know. Thank you for the perfect end to the most incredible day of my life. Well, almost the most incredible." She nibbled on her lower lip.

He arched a brow. "Almost?"

"I think the most incredible moment was our first kiss. But then there was the first time we…you know. And…" She closed her eyes for a second to stop herself from babbling. "This was the perfect end to an amazing few days."

After another kiss goodbye, Wes opened the door for Callie and she climbed into the truck. Kathie was scribbling in her notebook. She glanced at Callie and smiled.

"Ready?"

"I think so." She reached for Wes's hand one last time.

"Drive carefully, Kathie. You've got precious cargo." He gave Callie a quick kiss.

"Don't worry. She's safe with me." Kathie glanced at Callie again. "Buckle up, Belle."

"Okay, Rapunzel. I'm ready."

Callie watched Wes head into the lodge with Sweets on his heels as they drove down the long driveway away from the lodge. The light of the lodge disappeared into the darkness, and Callie sucked in air to keep from crying. When they reached the main road a few minutes later, Callie's heart was still slamming against her ribs as if she'd run the distance.

"Wait."

Kathie slammed on the brakes. "What's wrong? Did you forget something?"

"Yes. Can we go back?"

"Back?" Kathie wrinkled her brow. "What did you forget?"

My heart. I left it in his hands. "I'm sorry. I know you're tired, and waiting for me was the last thing you wanted to do, and I appreciate that. But…I just want to say goodbye one more time. Please?" She laced her fingers together and held them up under her chin, pleading for her to go back to the lodge.

Kathie shot a look at the clock. She had a long drive ahead of her after she dropped Callie off.

"Can't you text him?"

"Our cells don't work here, remember? I just need to see him one last time. I'll be really fast. I'll run in and run out. Just…I've never felt like this before about anyone, Kath. My stomach hurts and my heart's going crazy. Please? I'll never ask for another favor in my whole life."

Kathie rolled her eyes as she turned the Cruiser around. "It's fine, and yes, you will." She reached over and squeezed Callie's hand. "I've never seen you like this. Is everything okay between you two? Did something happen?"

Yes. I fell in love. "No. I can't explain it. I just need to see him one last time."

"Okay. Then you will."

At the lodge, Callie jumped from the car. "I'll be fast. One hug, one kiss, and I'll be back in three minutes. Promise." She closed the door, then opened it again and leaned in. "Thank you!"

"Go already." Kathie shooed her out.

Callie ran through the empty lobby looking for Wes. She hurried to the reception desk and gripped the edge.

"Hello?" she called with great anticipation, and was answered with silence. Callie held her breath and listened to a murmur coming from an office off the reception area.

Wes! She hurried around the desk, then slowed to smooth her dress and wipe the tears from her eyes. She reached up and finger brushed her hair, then closed her eyes for a second so she didn't fly into Wes's office looking like a lunatic.

"I can't wait to see you." Wes's voice was thick with emotion. She couldn't see him from where she stood beside the open door, but his words hit her like a brick in the face. "Yeah, I have to go back tomorrow night," Wes said. "You sure you can't come tonight? We'd have all night together."

Callie's stomach lurched.

"Okay. I'll see you tomorrow. You'll love the surprise I have in store for you."

Surprise? That didn't sound like an applicant. She pressed her hand to the wall for support.

"You deserve a little pampering after all you've done. Love you, too. Drive carefully."

Callie leaned her back against the wall, trying to keep her heart from shattering. *A little pampering? Love you? Oh God.* Is this what he did? Like some wealthy player who wooed women like her into believing they were special? She covered her mouth to keep the pain that gripped her from spewing forth, turned on her heel, and ran back out the front doors and into the truck.

"You okay?" Kathie asked.

No! "Can we go, please? Quick?" How could she have fallen for it hook, line, and sinker?

Kathie drove away from the lodge, stealing glances at Callie. "Hey, you must really love him to be this upset."

She didn't want to believe it. Wes couldn't be like that. He was so sincere, so loving. He was a good, honest man and she loved him.

She must have misunderstood.

Misunderstood, or was I too naive to see the truth?

She thought of the jealousy she'd seen in his eyes when she

was with Cutter and wondered if he'd just been reacting to that when he'd reached out to her. Maybe it was a joke at the ranch. *Hey, which guest will you bang?* The thought nauseated her. *Maybe I was just a conquest.*

No. He said he loves me, and—oh God—I love him.

"Cal? It's only a day," Kathie reminded her.

Callie couldn't say a word. If she repeated what she'd heard out loud, she would fall to pieces and die right there in Kathie's truck. *Oh God. Is this what Bonnie meant about reality kicking her in the ass?* Callie leaned against the window, arms crossed tightly around her burning stomach. Hot tears streaked her cheeks. She refused to talk herself into a tizzy. She'd talk to Wes, and she was sure he'd clear it up.

Wouldn't he?

Chapter Twenty-Seven

TUESDAY MORNING, CALLIE dragged herself from bed, gave a halfhearted effort to her Jillian Michaels workout, hoping it might take away some of her sadness. It didn't. She went through the motions of getting ready for work as if on autopilot, not bothering to pin up her hair. She called The Woodlands lodge, intending to leave a message for Wes to call her back so she could ask him about what she'd heard, but she lost her nerve and hung up. What if it really was all a big game to him? She didn't—couldn't—believe that, but she didn't have the courage to leave a message if there was even a slight chance that it was true.

She stopped in at the diner for coffee before work to try to inject a modicum of energy into her morning and stood by the counter, waiting for Margie Holmes, the middle-aged waitress, to fill her to-go cup.

"How was your weekend?" Margie was in a pink waitress uniform with a white apron tied around her waist. She wore her hair in a feathered style left over from the eighties.

"Good," Callie managed.

Margie handed her the cup. "So I heard."

How could Callie have forgotten that Margie was the eyes

and ears of Trusty? What could she possibly have heard? Callie felt a heavy hand on her shoulder and her body went rigid.

A friendly smile spread across Margie's lips. Her eyes softened with obvious recognition. "Ross. How's my favorite Braden?"

"You said that to Pierce when he was in here with me last week," Ross said.

"A woman can't limit herself to just one Braden man," Margie said with a laugh.

Callie wanted to shrivel up and disappear. She wished she'd gone straight to work and didn't know why she'd put herself through dealing with the heart of Trusty's grapevine.

"Hey, Callie. Good to see you again."

Callie kept her eyes on her coffee as she turned to greet Ross. "Hey." It took all her strength not to bolt for the door.

"We'll see you at Luke's this weekend, right?" Ross asked.

"Sure." Clutching her cup, she chanced a glance at Ross and her heart ached and softened at the same time. He had the same honest eyes as Wes. *I'm such an idiot. Of course there's a good explanation for what I heard.*

By the time she reached the library, she was second-guessing herself again. She was going to drive herself batty. She needed to concentrate on work, not fall apart because she'd overheard a conversation that might, or—more likely—might not mean something. This was not like her at all. She never jumped to conclusions. Then again, she'd never been in love before.

She was still fretting a few hours later, when she ducked into the ladies' room and stared at herself in the mirror. Her eyelids were heavy with fatigue, and the plain beige shift she wore made her look dowdy. The outfit had matched her feelings when she'd dressed that morning, hoping to remain insignificant and invisible and just make it through the day.

She leaned closer to the mirror.

"This whole thing is crazy," she said to her reflection.

"I love him. He loves me."

"More importantly, I trust him."

With that, she drew her shoulders back, scowled at herself one last time for being such a jealous idiot, and headed for the women's fiction aisle, hoping to find her next escape.

She came face-to-face with Tiffany Dempsey. This…was not…her day.

"Callie, I heard you had quite a weekend." Tiffany twisted a lock of her blond hair around her finger.

Callie's stomach knotted. She wished she'd worn something besides the plain and shapeless beige shift she'd chosen. It was bad enough that her heart was breaking into pieces and she had no chance at salvation until she could reach Wes, but to be faced with Tiffany Dempsey while her chips were down was just too much.

"Mm-hm." She walked farther down the aisle and pretended to look for a book, when in reality she was trying to figure out if she could dart out of the aisle fast enough to lose Tiffany.

Tiffany leaned against the bookshelf, watching her.

"Do you need help?" Callie kept her eyes trained on the books.

"Nah."

Then what the heck do you want?

Callie pulled two books from the shelf and walked past Tiffany. She heard Tiffany following her, and when she reached the next aisle, she clutched the books to her chest, gritted her teeth, and mustered her courage.

"Are you sure you don't need help?" Callie asked without

turning to face her.

"Oh, I need help, all right, but not with books," Tiffany said with an edge of humor.

The smile in her voice drew Callie's attention. She turned and faced Tiffany, and even though she'd heard the smile in her tone, she was surprised to see it in her eyes.

"I make you nervous, don't I?" Tiffany asked.

Tiffany was a few inches taller than Callie, with a small waist and large, full breasts. With long blond hair and blue eyes, and confidence that rivaled that of a supermodel, she could make Jennifer Aniston nervous. Callie's chest tightened under her steady gaze. The longer they stared at each other, the more Callie's discomfort turned to anger. She'd scaled a mountain carrying a dog, fished by a rushing river, slept in a goddamn tent, and now…Now, while she mentally battled jealousy—an unfamiliar and horribly uncomfortable emotion for her—she had to deal with *this*? If she could face all of that, she sure as hell could talk to some woman who wanted the only man she'd ever loved.

Or at least she hoped she could.

"You've never said two words to me. If you have something to say, just say it." Callie pressed her mouth into a firm line to keep Tiffany from seeing her trembling lower lip.

"You're right." Tiffany unwound her finger from her beautiful golden lock of hair. "When you moved into town and Wes started coming in to see you, everyone was talking about the two of you, and I thought, no way. You were nothing like the women he's been with." Her eyes softened as she said the hurtful words.

Tears sprang to Callie's eyes. She couldn't take another hit to her heart. Not today. Maybe not ever. She stumbled backward a step and grabbed the shelf for stability.

Tiffany narrowed her blue eyes. "But I watched the way he was with you. He was…different."

She smiled, and it took Callie by surprise. Callie wasn't sure if it was a sincere smile or a ruse for the claws that were about to come out.

"He was definitely interested in a way he never was with me," Tiffany admitted. "Maybe different than he was with anyone."

"Tiffany, please." Callie's voice was shaky.

"Let me finish. I didn't want to see you as the woman that you are. You're so petite and pretty, and you're obviously smart. That's tough competition."

Callie could hardly believe her ears. She had the urge to look around to see if she was being punked.

"Then I hear that you guys are like, *really* together. And I'm thinking, Wes has never been *really together* with anyone."

Wes has never been really together with anyone. Callie knew that, of course, from what Wes had told her, but the way Tiffany said it, like it meant something more, made Callie feel like a heel for doubting his fidelity.

"He's a good man, Callie. He deserves a good woman. I'm glad it's you. You're not petty and jealous like everyone else in this town. You never gave me dirty looks or said snotty things when I tried to get his attention." She nodded, and a genuine smile crossed her lips, making her entire appearance morph from vixen to something softer, friendlier. Nicer.

If you only knew what I've been thinking.

Tiffany leaned in and hugged Callie, but Callie was too shocked to reciprocate. She stood rigid beneath a cloud of shame for having judged Tiffany so hastily. And though she still didn't want to believe what she'd heard Wes say back at the lodge, she didn't know what to do with the worry—or how to escape it.

"Thank you," she finally eked out.

Tiffany waved her hand in the air. "*Tsk.* You need someone to have your back around here. Ever since his brother Luke went off the market, Wes has had twice as many eyes on him. Keep your chin up, and the gossip will turn to how cute of a couple you are, and then eventually it'll settle on someone else."

How cute of a couple we are?

Callie needed to get a grip on her emotions. After Tiffany left, Callie went into the back office, where her purse was stowed in her desk, and she grabbed her cell phone before heading into the bathroom to call Wes.

She listened to her voice mails while she paced the bathroom floor. The first was from Bonnie.

Hey, Cal. I emailed you the pics this morning. Had a great time, and I'm so happy for you and Wes. Call or text me tonight.

She deleted the message and listened to the next one, which was from Wes.

Hey, babe. I miss you. His warm, caring voice brought tears to her eyes again. *A group of twenty just registered for a day trip tomorrow. I need to stay for another night.* The pit of her stomach sank. *Call me at the lodge. I'll be here until three. Love you, and I'm sorry.*

She checked her watch. It was four o'clock. She called the lodge anyway.

Please be there. Please be there.

"Good afternoon, The Woodlands," a cheery voice greeted her.

"Hi, this is Callie Barnes. I'd like to speak with Wes Braden, please?" She slammed her eyes shut. *Please be there.*

"Hi, Callie. He's not here right now. Can I take a message for him?"

Yes. No. Oh crap. "Um. Yes, please. Can you ask him to call me when he gets a chance?" She gave the receptionist the library's phone number since she couldn't exactly carry her cell phone around. After she ended the call, she tried to talk her mind out of going down a crazy path of piecing together him staying another night at the lodge with the *I love you* she'd heard him say while he was on the phone.

Chapter Twenty-Eight

WES CROSSED THE property with Sweets trotting along beside him toward the barn. He wished he had heard back from Callie before leaving the lodge, but he didn't want to waste any more time after having spent so many hours interviewing applicants who seemed neither trustworthy nor experienced enough to fill Ray's position. None of them had the knowledge that Cutter had, and they were strangers. He had worked too hard to bring on a stranger who might take off right after they trained him. Then they'd be right back where they started. He pushed the thought away, stewing over the real issue that had the muscles in his neck and shoulders working overtime. He should have been leaving to go back home to Trusty, and instead he was hamstrung by the last-minute group that had scheduled an outing for the next day.

He walked by the barn office and saw Cutter working on the financial reports for the inventory. He went in search of Chip and was cursing under his breath about the inconvenience of the morning when Chip rode up on horseback, causing Sweets to run back and forth between the horse and Wes.

"Hey." Chip brought his horse to a stop beside Wes. "How'd the interviews go?"

"They were all shit." Wes ran his hand through his hair and looked off into the woods toward the boulder where he'd taken Callie the first night she was there. Damn, he wished he were on his way home to see her.

"Come on, Wes. You can't knock down everyone." Chip shook his head.

Sweets barked repeatedly.

"I'm not." *When did Sweets become a barker?* He slapped his thigh. "Sweets. Here."

Sweets came to his side and plopped down beside him. With her tail wagging and her butt wiggling, she looked like a spring ready to launch.

Wes continued. "Look, we got a few years out of Ray, and we knew him before we started. If we hire someone we don't know, we could train them, then lose them in a year or two, or whatever. I think we need to reconsider Cutter."

"Cutter?" Chip took off his hat and wiped his brow with his forearm. "You're an ass. You dismissed him from the get-go, remember? You said he was too vital to the ranch's everyday needs."

"He is." He clenched his jaw. "Damn it. This is a pain in the ass. Cutter handles the budgets, the inventory, and the barn. He manages the ranch hands and sees to the animals with meticulous care. I'm not sure how we'll fill his position, but he's reliable and respectful, and the guests love him. The truth is, he deserves this promotion. It was shortsighted of me not to see that. I think we're better off trying him out and then filling his position."

"About fucking time. Why the change of heart?" Chip set his eyes on Wes's.

"Truth?"

"No. Lie to me." Chip shook his head.

"I trust him explicitly. He's the best damn barn manager we could have. He's organized as shit. He's in the barn office right now, going over inventory spreadsheets and all sorts of shit that I can't even think about. Moving him up means getting new blood in that position, and that sucks."

Chip laughed. "Your fear of paperwork never ceases to amaze me."

He wasn't about to admit to Chip that in addition to his aversion to paperwork, he'd been jealous of Cutter and he had let that jealousy cloud his decision these last few days. Nor did he tell him that with a single look, Cutter had understood that his sights were set on Callie, and without question, Cutter had respected Wes enough to back off. That was more than the mark of a smart employee. It was a mark of a good friend. What kind of a friend doesn't promote a guy who more than deserves it?

"You're not just doing this so you can take off tonight and see Callie, are you?"

"Nope. I'm taking off and seeing Callie whether we promote him or not. I'll send Cutter *and* Butch on the trip if I have to." Wes hadn't made a conscious decision until that very second, and now he felt as though a great burden had been lifted from his shoulders.

"When were you going to clue me in on that change?" Chip asked.

Wes smiled at the prospect of leaving tonight. "I didn't even realize I was thinking about it until just now. You have a problem with it?"

"No, man. I don't. It's about time you did something besides work." Chip lifted his chin toward Wes's cabin. "I'm glad

Em made it up for a few days."

"Yeah. She needed a break. I'll go talk to Cutter after I touch base with her; then I'm out of here." Wes patted the horse, which brought Sweets to her feet again. She trotted back and forth beside them before following Wes up the hill toward the cabin.

He found Emily reading on the deck. She crouched to pet and love up Sweets, who wiggled with delight and lavished her face with kisses.

"She's so adorable. She almost makes me want one." Emily rose to her feet, and Sweets tried to climb up her legs. She was about as big around as a sapling, and in her shorts and sweat-shirt, she looked more like she was twenty-five than thirty-one.

"Sweets." Wes patted his thigh again, and Sweets hesitated, looking up at Emily with her big, sad eyes one last time before coming to his side.

"I don't know why you ever come back to Trusty. If I worked here, I'd stay twenty-four seven." Emily set her book down on the chair and hooked her thumbs in her pockets.

"Are you sure you don't mind if I take off soon?" Wes asked. He hadn't bothered to tell Emily about the last-minute booking and the trip he was supposed to go on, and now he was glad he hadn't. It alleviated the need for a complicated explana-tion.

"Oh God, no. Go see your precious new girlfriend. I love it out here with no phone or Internet. It's the only way for me to get away from work." She lowered herself into a chair, and Wes did the same.

"You can get both Internet and phone in the lodge."

Emily narrowed her eyes. "Shh. I'm going to pretend I didn't hear that. I like not being available for a whole forty-eight hours. Don't you?"

Sweets sat between his legs and he reached down and stroked her head. "I used to, but now? Not really."

Emily's eyes widened. "You know, out of all of my brothers, I was sure Ross would be the first to fall in love, and I always thought I would before any of you." She sighed. "But here you are creating fairy tales and dying to get home to see your girlfriend, and here I am, the same single girl as always." She flopped back in her chair and groaned.

"Well, you may be the same single girl as always, but…" Wes withdrew an envelope from his back pocket. "Now you can be the single girl who has seen the Poppi Castle."

Emily gasped and snagged the envelope from his hands. "What?" She tore it open. Emily was a year younger than Wes, and they'd always been close. Seeing her jaw agape as she read the confirmation paperwork for the trip he'd arranged made him smile. "Wes. My God, I can't accept this."

"You can, and you will."

She shook her head, as if clearing her vision. "You have to be kidding. I arranged for a day of pampering and some dresses, for God's sake. You're sending me to Italy? That's huge."

"What you did for me was huge." He rose to his feet, and Sweets followed. She ran to Emily for a quick head pet and snout kiss, then returned to Wes's side.

"Wes…"

"Hey, I'm your older brother. You can't win. Stand up and give me a hug and say thank you." He opened his arms and she walked into them.

"Thank you so much. I could have booked my own trip." Emily, as well as each of their siblings, had large trust funds that had been passed down for generations. But like Wes and their other siblings, Emily wasn't one to dip into it for whimsical purposes. He'd noticed that Emily had been a little down lately, which wasn't like her, and even so, she was always willing to pitch in for Wes or any of their siblings. The extravagant trip paled in comparison to years and years of her doing whatever anyone ever asked of her.

"Yes, but you haven't, and you won't, so just enjoy it. Besides, how long have you been talking about that villa you want to see?"

She ran her hand through her straight hair and pushed it over her shoulder with a dreamy sigh. "The one Gabriela Bocelli built. It's a dream come true. Thank you."

He pointed at her. "I don't want to hear that you can't take off work to go."

"Don't worry. I wouldn't miss this for the world." She hugged him again. "What time are you leaving?"

"Ten minutes. I'm going to talk to Cutter; then I'm heading back to Trusty. You sure you're okay here alone?" Emily was tough as nails despite her slight figure. He knew she'd be fine.

She waved him off and settled into her chair, reading over the confirmation document again. "You know I'm fine. Besides, if I need anything, Cutter's here."

Cutter. Wes felt like an ass for waiting so long before seeing the light where Cutter was concerned. "Hey, there's a guy for you." He was only half kidding.

"He's like a brother to me, not a real guy." Emily put the paper back in the envelope and pressed it to her chest.

"Not a real guy? I'll have to remember that when the guests are drooling all over him. Make yourself at home and just lock up when you leave. Hey, Em, I really appreciate all of your help."

"I know you do. It was fun for me, believe it or not. I can't wait to meet Callie this weekend at Luke's."

"You'll love her." He gave Emily another hug; then he and Sweets headed down to the barn to talk to Cutter.

BY THE TIME Callie left work, she felt like she had a devil on one shoulder whispering, *He's staying another night. Who's he with?* And an angel on the other side screaming, *It's Wes, for heaven's sake. What are you thinking?* She was exhausted, confused, and so in love with Wes that she wanted to drive up the mountain to The Woodlands and fall into his arms so he could dispel her worries. Of course, if her worries were valid, then she'd be driving right back down the mountain with even more tears.

She pulled over in front of the diner with the intention of picking up an entire chocolate pie to consume by herself. Her cell phone rang, and Bonnie's name flashed on the screen. Callie glanced through the diner window and saw Margie talking with a customer at the counter. If she went inside, Margie would probably ask about Wes, and Callie wasn't sure she could talk about him without bawling—so she threw the car into drive, pulled back onto Main Street, and answered Bonnie's call on speakerphone.

"Hi, Bon."

"Hey. You sound awful. Are you okay?"

Fricking dandy. "Yeah, just tired."

"Oh, well, with a guy like Wes, it's worth every sleepy moment, I'm sure. Hey, did you see the pics?" Bonnie sounded happy, and for some stupid reason, that made Callie even sadder.

"I couldn't look at work. I'll see them when I get home." She pulled around the corner and down the street, then turned into the parking lot of her apartment complex with a heavy heart.

"Are you seeing Wes tonight? Kath told me how upset you were on the way home. She said you didn't say two words."

How could she answer? Kathie was right. She'd remained silent the whole way home for fear of sobbing so hard she'd flood the truck.

"Cal? Why aren't you gushing over seeing him?"

She parked and turned off her car and headed upstairs to her apartment with the phone against her ear.

"Callie Jo Barnes, if you don't answer me, I'll climb through this phone and I'll drag it out of you."

She pictured Bonnie's brows furrowed and her lips pinched tightly together. She stepped inside her apartment, and when she saw her still-packed bag on the couch to her right and the yellow gown lying over her reading chair, she couldn't stifle the sharp inhalation that followed.

"Cal? Come on, hon. Tell me what's wrong."

The compassion in Bonnie's voice pulled Callie from her stupor. "Oh, Bonnie. I'm so messed up."

"Why?"

"I went back into the lodge to say goodbye to Wes, and he wasn't expecting me. He was on the phone, and..." She pressed the heel of her hand to her tear-filled eyes.

"Callie, take a deep breath and tell me what happened."

Callie drew in one deep breath after another and sank onto the couch. "I heard him talking to someone about coming down

for the night and how he had a surprise for them. He even…"
She clenched her eyes shut to try to stop the relentless tears from
tumbling down her cheeks. "He…he said, *I love you.*"

"And? Who was he talking to?"

Bonnie sounded calm and rational, which only made Callie
feel worse because she knew if she hadn't been living in some
fantasy world fueled by love over the past few days, she would
have asked him about the phone call instead of torturing herself.
Even if the answer might have crushed her, she normally wasn't
someone who avoided the truth. But then again, her emotions
were all-consuming right now.

"I didn't ask. I just left." She wiped her eyes and went to the
kitchen and opened the freezer.

"Why not, Callie? You can't seriously think he has some
other girl in his life after everything he did this weekend."

Callie pulled a quart of strawberry cheesecake ice cream
from the freezer and snagged a spoon from the drawer, then
returned to the couch, where she kicked off her heels and
hunkered down beneath a blanket.

"Of course not." She shoved a spoonful of frozen comfort
into her mouth and closed her eyes against the shock of cold. "I
don't think so, but…"

"Oh, Callie." Her name sounded like an embrace. "Callie,
Callie, Callie. What are you eating?"

Callie dropped her eyes to the ice cream carton. "Strawberry
cheesecake."

"Good. At least you have something worth the calories.
Now listen to me, hon. You need to talk to Wes. You know
there's a good explanation for this."

She shoved more ice cream into her mouth. "I know there's
a good explanation! That's why I'm having such a hard time."

She swallowed the mouthful of ice cream. "Oh, brain freeze!" She clenched her eyes shut until the pain subsided. "Sorry."

"Why haven't you called him?"

"I did. But his cell doesn't work there, remember? And he said he's staying another night, so that made me worry even more." Callie shoveled more ice cream into her mouth and tried to talk around it. "You know…" She swallowed the ice cream. "I'm not like this."

"I know, Cal. Listen. Set your ice cream down long enough to pick up your laptop. Let's look at some of the pictures. Maybe that'll knock some sense into you."

Callie reached for her laptop, knocked over the ice cream carton, and spilled pink ice cream onto her lap. "Darn it. I spilled the ice cream everywhere." With one hand, she scooped the ice cream from her lap back into the container.

"I told you to put it down."

"Whatever. At the moment it's my security blanket, okay? And I'm not giving it up." Her dress was ruined. She pulled it over her head and brought it into the bathroom, where she set it on the sink. Then she washed her hands, pressing the phone to her ear with her shoulder. "That stupid dress was ugly anyway." She went to her bedroom wearing her bra and underwear and threw on a T-shirt; then she climbed back onto the couch and put the ice cream container on her lap again.

"Are you all cleaned up?" Bonnie asked.

"Sort of. Okay, my laptop is open, and the ice cream is secure." She ate a spoonful.

"I thought you spilled it."

"I did. But I scooped it off my lap and tossed it back in the container."

"Oh, Cal. You're in bad shape. Want me to drive over to

your place? I can be there in—"

"No. I'm fine." She shoveled ice cream onto her spoon and clicked on the pictures. Wes's handsome face lit up the screen, and all her emotions tumbled forward again. She suppressed the urge to cry at the ache in her heart. In the picture, he was standing before her in his princely clothing with one hand outstretched. Callie's hand went to her heart, tilting the spoon and spilling the ice cream onto her shirt. Mesmerized by the slide show as it displayed one loving picture after another, she felt her heart swell. There were pictures of her and Wes hugging and kissing in various places throughout the ranch and profile shots of Wes gazing at Callie, his sensuous dark eyes filled with love. *How could I ever doubt you?*

"Are you still there?" Bonnie asked.

"Yeah." It came out as one long whisper as the pictures changed from frame to frame. "Bonnie, these are…Oh my God. You took pictures when we rode the horse up the trail together?"

"Girl, you were in your own little world. There are hundreds of pictures on that slide show, and you didn't even know about half of them. But let's focus on the important issue here. Do you really think Wes would cheat on you? I have always believed that we should trust our gut instincts, even if we don't want to, but this? Callie, I cannot believe this."

Callie shook her head.

"Callie?"

"Yeah?" Another whisper. She pulled the laptop onto the couch beside her and noticed the melting glob of ice cream on her shirt. She used the spoon to put it back in the container, then set it on the coffee table.

"Cal, do you really think he'd do that?"

No. "Aw." A picture of Wes kissing Sweets appeared on her screen.

"Callie!"

Callie startled. "What? Sorry."

"Listen to me. Do you think that he would hurt you like that?" Bonnie's tone was serious.

"No. That's the problem. I don't. There's no way he could fake the love in his eyes or his voice. Or his touch, for that matter." She pointed to a picture of Wes on the computer. "Look."

"Oh my God. You really are messed up. You're the one friend I have who never spaces out, and you are totally spacing here, Cal."

"Sorry." She paused the slide show. "I'm sorry. You know what, Bon? I needed this so badly. I definitely don't think he'd cheat on me. Thank you for making me see that."

Bonnie exhaled loudly. "I didn't do anything, but I'm glad, and I hope you're right."

"Oh my God, really? How can you say that?" She sank into the back of the couch.

"No, no, no. I didn't mean it like that. Are you sure you're okay?"

Callie looked down at her shirt. "Yeah, but my clothes have seen better days."

"Okay. Call if you need me, and, Cal, call him. Stop jumping to ridiculous conclusions."

Callie turned back to the computer and watched the slide show all the way through. Twice. She was already feeling much better and felt like a fool for worrying in the first place. Each time she watched it, she noticed something new, like the way Wes's smile quirked up a little higher on the left side than the right and how in every picture where they were in close enough proximity, he was touching her. He had his hand on her hip or her lower back, or they were holding hands, or his arm was draped across her shoulders.

She touched his image on the computer screen. "God, I love you."

A knock at her door drew her attention from the computer. Callie paused the slide show and peered out of the peephole, then fumbled with the doorknob and yanked it open.

Wes stood before her with the easy smile that made her knees weak. His eyes traveled down her body, darkening as they went, and with her next breath, she flew into his arms, sending him stumbling backward over Sweets, who scampered across the hallway with a few sharp barks. Callie pressed her lips to Wes's. He slipped one hand beneath her. The feel of his calloused hand on her bare thigh reminded her that she wasn't wearing any pants. Wes deepened the kiss as his fingers slipped beneath the lacy material and cupped her bare ass. She heard Sweets clawing at his legs, whimpering to get to her.

"I'm so sorry," she said against Wes's lips.

He kissed her again. "For the goop on my shirt or for greeting me in a way that makes me want to take you right here?"

She tried to pull back to look at his shirt, but he tightened his grip.

"You don't really think I'm going to let you down, do you?"

Sweets barked up at them.

"What are you doing here?" She kissed him again.

"Kissing you." He took her in another thought-stealing kiss.

"I think we better go inside before the neighbors complain." She pressed her lips to his as he carried her inside.

"I promoted Cutter." He kissed her again. "And I'm yours

for the next few days."

That sounded too good to be true.

Sweets ran from room to room as Wes closed the door, set Callie on the floor, and kissed her again.

She clutched his shirt in her fists. "I…"

He captured her words in his mouth, and when he deepened the kiss, a moan of pleasure escaped her lungs. She had to talk to him about what she'd heard him say, or she would be sidetracked all night. She forced herself to pull her lips from his.

"I have to ask you something," she said breathlessly.

He kissed her again and backed her up against the wall, pinning her there with his hips and once again stealing her ability to think clearly. She forced herself to draw back again.

"I need to tell you something, and it's embarrassing. Unless I'm wrong, then…"

When he lowered his lips to hers and kissed her again, her mind went blank. His hands found her hips, and she rocked into him.

Forget talking.

He drew back on a sigh. "Okay, tell me." He cupped her cheek and kissed her again, a soft press of his lips to hers. "You're more beautiful than I remembered."

She couldn't think, much less talk.

"Babe? What did you want to say?"

Kiss me again. She cleared her throat in an effort to clear her thoughts and ran her finger down his arm, then held on tight. "I'm a little afraid to tell you."

"Hey," he said quietly. "You can tell me anything."

She should just forget it, let it rest. She didn't really believe he'd do anything to hurt her, but there was still the inkling of needing an explanation. She forced the words from her lungs.

"The other night when I left, I came back to say goodbye one last time."

"Came back?" He drew his brows together.

She tightened her grip on his arms. "To the lodge. I went inside and you were on the phone."

"Why didn't you tell me? I would have hung up."

She drew in another deep breath. *I would have hung up.* That was her answer. She wished she could just say *never mind* and go back to kissing, but Callie knew herself too well. She continued with a shaky voice.

"I didn't mean to eavesdrop…Well…at first I didn't, but then I heard you say you couldn't wait to see whoever you were talking to, and…"

His eyes remained curious, but he didn't have the look of a man who was caught doing something wrong.

Callie forced herself to continue. "And then you said you had a surprise for them and that you…loved them." She lowered her eyes to keep him from seeing hers dampen.

"Oh, Callie," he whispered. He kissed the top of her head. "Have you been worried about this?"

She nodded.

He lifted her chin and kissed her forehead. "All you had to do was ask me who I was talking to. Don't you trust me?"

"Yes, but…"

He arched a brow.

She tightened her grip on his arms. "I do, but I haven't exactly been thinking straight lately. Everything happened so fast, and I'm glad it did, but then all of a sudden we were apart, and I heard you say that stuff, and…" She lowered her forehead to his chest.

He slid his hands around her waist and held her close. "Remember when I asked you to have a little faith in me?"

She nodded.

"You can trust me. I will never hurt you." He kissed the top of her head. "I was talking to my sister, Emily. She came down for the night, and she's at the cabin now. I did have a surprise for her, because she helped to coordinate your spa day and fairy tale night, and, well, she needs it. She's been bummed lately, and she's always done whatever my brothers and I ask her to do—and even what we don't ask her to do. And my family always says I love you. We just...do."

"Oh my God. Now I feel really stupid." Her face was still buried in his chest. "I'm so sorry."

"Babe, let's sit down and talk." He turned toward the couch. "Uh-oh."

Sweets lay in the middle of the floor, nose deep in the ice cream container. Callie couldn't help but laugh.

"Sweets," Wes said in a sharp voice as he slapped his thigh.

Sweets pulled her ice-cream-covered nose from the container, looking adorably guilty. Callie was so glad she hadn't seen *that* look in Wes's eyes.

Wes shook his head and shifted his eyes to the pink stain on Callie's T-shirt.

"You two make quite a pair."

Callie glanced down at her ice-cream-stained shirt and bare legs. Well, almost bare. There were a few drops of ice cream on them, too.

After they cleaned up Sweets, the coffee table, and the hardwood floor, Callie went into the bedroom to change her clothes. She took off her shirt and heard the bedroom door close behind her. Wes's hands circled her from behind. His lips grazed her shoulder, and a flash of desire pulsed through her.

She leaned her head back against his chest.

"God, I missed you," she said.

"I'd never hurt you," he whispered.

"I know."

"No, you don't." He turned her in her arms. "Babe, I don't blame you for worrying. I don't have a very good track record for you to put your trust in, but I made you a promise, and I intend to keep it."

"I've never been the type of person to jump to conclusions, but I was so hurt I could barely think. And I know I shouldn't have jumped to that conclusion, but…"

"I'm sorry you were hurt." He tangled his hand in her hair and gently drew her head back, just enough to clear her hair from her neck. He settled his mouth over the curve where her neck met her shoulder and sucked, sending a ripple of need between her legs. She sucked in a breath when he drew his mouth away.

"To be honest." He kissed her collarbone. "I probably would have thought the same thing if the tables were turned…" He kissed her shoulder. "Except I would have stormed into the office and demanded to know who the bastard was on the phone."

Hearing that he'd have had the same reaction helped her feel less like a confused, lovesick psycho and more like a normal person in love.

He kissed her and ran his hands up her back, then un-hooked her bra and dropped it to the floor. She closed her eyes as he kissed her again.

"Oops," he said with a mischievous grin before pulling off his shirt.

They were hip to hip, his hard length pressing against her as he lowered his mouth to her breast and teased her nipple with his tongue, sending a thrum of desire right to her center. He lowered her to the bed and positioned himself above her, so they were eye to eye.

"I love you, Cal."

The honesty in his eyes was all the assurance she needed to push away the worry until it felt like a distant memory and let her love for Wes take over. She wrapped her hand around the back of his neck and met him halfway for a deep, passionate kiss.

WES'S HEART WAS so full of love for Callie that knowing she'd worried about what she'd heard made him ache. He never wanted her to go to bed worried or upset again. In that moment, lying on top of her, in the bedroom where she laid her pretty head down to sleep every night, he never wanted to leave. He knew that he'd spend the rest of his life doing everything he could to show her he could be trusted.

"I don't want to just love you." He slid his lips to the edge of her mouth and kissed her there. "I want you to feel secure *and* loved." He brought her hand to his mouth and unfurled her delicate fingers, then pressed his lips to her palm. "Promise me you'll never hold anything back. I don't want you to worry. Ever. Talk to me. Let me in on all levels, Callie."

Her beautiful eyes darkened. "I promise."

It was only a whisper, but it rocked him to his core. There was so much more he wanted to say, to assure her, to assure himself of her, but he was powerless to force words from his lungs. He needed to love her. To claim her. He captured her mouth in a greedy kiss, and she pressed her hips to his, spurring him on. Still gripping her hand, he brought it to his mouth again and dragged his tongue down the center of her palm, to her delicate wrist, then traced the tendon down her forearm, feeling her shiver beneath him. He wanted more. So much more. He held her arm above her head as he took her in another sensuous kiss, as he took possession of her other hand, holding them both there together. Callie's eyes opened, dark and laden with desire.

"Yes," she said in one hot breath.

Holy hell.

He looked down at the goddamn jeans that had him trapped and bound. In three seconds, he freed himself of his boots and clothing. Callie hadn't moved. Her arms remained above her head, her panties, damp at the center, rode low on her hips, and it just about did him in.

"Hurry," she urged.

Hurrying was the last thing on his mind as he drew her legs apart and her knees fell open. He licked her through the silky material, tasting her sweet juices as she arched to meet his tongue. She reached down and pushed at her panties. Wes grasped her wrist and held tight. He knew what she wanted, and it was all he could do to draw it out, but hell if he would be rushed through experiencing every inch of her.

Wes took his cues from Callie, and he quickly learned that with him, she was uninhibited, and he knew, somehow just knew, that she had never been like this with anyone else. He sucked her fingers into his mouth and pulled them out slowly, and when she used her slick fingers to caress her breasts, he wanted desperately to bury himself inside her while she did it.

But he repressed the urge, moved her panties to the side, and slid his fingers in instead. Callie gasped, and he used his tongue to soothe her as she tightened around his fingers. He circled her sensitive nub with his tongue, and she moaned for more, clutching at her breasts, rocking her head from side to side. She was so wet. He had to get rid of those damn panties. When he withdrew his fingers to tear them off, she groaned in frustration. He buried his fingers deep again, bringing her quickly up to the edge. She clutched the sheets, panting in fast spurts of sexy, breathy need as he quickened his pace. Her thighs flexed, and her back and neck arched as she hit the peak. Every little pulse landed against his tongue.

"More," she said in a raspy voice. "Touch me more."

He lifted his eyes and met her hungry gaze. She reached for her center, begging for more. He rolled her onto her side, placed her leg over his shoulder, and brought his mouth to her again. She was completely open to him and so deliciously sweet he groaned with need. She shifted, pushing him onto his back with her knee, and in the next breath, her sweet center was above him for the taking, and boy was he going to take. Callie groped at her breasts as he gripped her ass, holding her above his mouth. When he licked the tender skin around her sensitive folds, she arched back and he took her right over the edge again. It was too much for him. He *needed* her like he needed oxygen. She must have read his mind because she slithered down his body, settling between his legs, and licked and stroked him into a goddamn frenzy until he was about to come.

"Callie. Sweet Jesus. Please. Stop."

She was relentless, sucking and stroking until he couldn't take it anymore, and he lifted her onto his hard length with a groan of satisfaction. She rode him fast, lifting and gyrating her hips until it did him in, and he wrapped his arms around her, buried between her breasts, and grunted through his own fervent release.

Chapter Twenty-Nine

CALLIE AWOKE TO a wet lick on her cheek and a furry body pressed against her right side, and one masculine—and gloriously naked—body to her left. She'd worried that she might feel an inkling of leftover worry this morning, but all she felt was love for the man beside her and the pup who had wiggled and snarfed her way into her heart. She closed her eyes for a minute to soak in the comfort of them and relish in the memory of the evening before. After they made love, they'd looked at the pictures that Bonnie sent and ordered a pizza, because apparently sex made them both so hungry they thought they might die. Wes had set up a bed of blankets on the floor beside the bed for Sweets, but she wanted no part of it, and within minutes she was lying across the bottom of the bed fast asleep.

Wes shifted beside her.

"That won't work, you know," he said quietly.

Sweets crawled over Callie's stomach and covered Wes's face with puppy kisses.

"See? She knows we're awake, and she has no snooze button." He shifted onto his side and pulled Sweets against his belly, then moved closer to Callie and kissed her.

"That's okay. I have to get up for work anyway. She's a good alarm clock."

Sweets wiggled free from Wes's arms and licked Callie's cheek.

"Oh, I've got a great alarm clock. I keep it below my waist." He rolled on top of her, inching Sweets out of his way.

Did she really have to go to work today? Oh, how she'd love to laze around all morning, making love with Wes, maybe take Sweets for a walk. She didn't care what they did as long as they were together. Coming home had been like culture shock after being close for so many days.

She felt the tip of his arousal between her legs, and heat coiled down low in her belly. She pressed on the back of his butt, hoping he'd take the hint. He was good at taking hints, she'd learned—and loved.

His eyes darkened. "Good morning, beautiful. No nooky for you until I hear you promise again that if you're worried about something, you'll talk to me right away. I don't care if I'm on the phone or out on the trail. Find a way. Call the lodge. Have them track me down. Use a skywriter if you have to. Just promise me you won't let things stew and cause a valley of doubt between us."

"I promise."

On her words, he filled her. *Completely.* Heart, body, and soul.

Chapter Thirty

WES AND CALLIE had spent every free minute together since Tuesday evening. It was Saturday, and Wes could hardly believe that they'd been together only a little over a week. He loved living in Callie's world, staying at her apartment and watching her get ready for work in the mornings, and the feeling that came over him when Callie stayed at his house was overwhelming. Sweets had settled right in, too, enjoying their evening walks and curling up with them when they snuggled together on the couch, reading or talking, or sometimes doing nothing at all but being together. Wes had known from their first night together that he wanted more with Callie. He wanted her to move in with him, and today, before they went to Luke and Daisy's for the barbecue, he was going to ask her to do just that.

Wes paced Callie's living room floor while she spoke to Bonnie on the phone in the bedroom. Every once in a while she'd laugh and draw his attention. He caught snippets of their conversation, breathy sighs, and comments about how happy Callie was. He didn't need confirmation of her love. He saw it in Callie's eyes and felt it in her touch. She didn't worry when he went to the ranch to work, and for that he was thankful. He loved her too much for her to worry about nonsense.

"Sorry I took so long." Callie came into the living room and crouched to pet Sweets. Her love of Sweets got to him every time.

"Don't be. We have plenty of time." He reached for her hand and drew her to her feet. In her flat, strappy sandals, she barely came to his chest. Just another thing he loved about her. She wore her femininity like a veil, so sweet and graceful in her mannerisms and what she let the world see, but with Wes, whether they were behind closed doors or catching a moment of seclusion in a grocery store aisle, she was seductive and surprising. The combination was intoxicating.

"Is this okay to wear to meet your family?" She took a step back and twirled in a circle, looking cute as hell in a salmon-colored halter dress that stopped midthigh.

"I don't know. You might look too sexy. I do have brothers, you know." He pulled her in close and kissed the pink blooms on her cheeks. "You look gorgeous."

Half an hour later, they parked Wes's truck and walked across the grassy knoll of Trusty Town Park. There were a handful of picnic tables and covered pavilions scattered throughout the park. Families picnicked on the grass, and couples walked hand in hand down mulched paths that ran like veins through the lawn. Edged on the far side by a burgeoning forest, with a spectacular view of the mountains on the opposite side, the park had a welcoming feel.

"Is this anything like the park where you grew up?" Wes asked as they followed a path between a grove of trees.

"Yeah, sort of, but the park where I read had a man-made lake, too. This is nice, though. There was always goose poop around the lake."

She crinkled her nose, and Wes had to lean down to kiss the

tip of it.

"We'll try to avoid goose poop." It had been a while since he'd been in the park, and he didn't remember it feeling quite so good. He pulled Callie close. Everything felt better with her.

Her eyes danced over the verdant foliage, and when the path turned and a marble sculpture came into view, Callie's eyes widened.

"What is that?"

Wes had spent so much time by the sculpture that he knew every crevice by heart. "It's an abstract piece. What does it look like to you?" The white marble sculpture stood about ten feet tall and five feet around. It was carved into thick, ropy strands that wrapped around an indiscernible shape in the center. The top was rounded, and just below was another curved shape seemingly engulfed in more ropy strands.

Callie walked closer and touched it with her fingertips.

Sweets put her front paws on the base of the sculpture and looked up at Callie.

"These things are like tentacles, or arms, or something. It makes me think of being bound together, I guess." She walked around it with a thoughtful, assessing gaze and stopped to read the information plaque. "It says it's called *Behold*."

She was so beautiful when she was deep in thought, as she was now, with her thin brows knitted together.

"What do you feel when you look at it? Anything or nothing?" he asked.

She hooked her finger in the waist of his jeans. "What do *you* feel?"

"You're a clever one, aren't you?" He pulled her close and drew in a deep breath. He was always bringing her in closer, like she was a part of him, and without her, he didn't feel whole.

He'd never told anyone how the sculpture made him feel, but it felt natural to share this piece of himself with Callie.

"It makes me feel like I'm looking at a warm embrace." He shifted his eyes to hers. "Before you say anything, I know that sounds...girlie. But ever since I was a kid, it felt like I was looking at someone enveloped by another person." He shrugged. "This was always one of my favorite spots. I'd hang out over there and read, or cool down over whatever happened to piss me off as a kid." He pointed to a small patch of grass between two tall, full trees.

Callie took his hand and led him to the spot on the grass where he'd pointed. "Let's sit. I like it here. I like knowing *you* like it here."

Sweets plopped down beside them.

"I could see myself coming here to read," Callie said.

Wes had the feeling that this was the perfect time to ask Callie to move in with him, even though he still had no idea how to ask her. It was an impulsive request, but in his heart, nothing had ever felt more right.

"Coming here from where?" he finally managed.

"Home. Work. Wherever."

His pulse quickened as he withdrew a small black velvet bag from his pocket.

"What's that?" Callie asked.

He opened her hand and placed it in her palm, then closed her fingers over it.

"If you'll have me and Sweets as part of your future, it's a key to my house."

She blinked several times, as if he'd spoken a foreign language, but he knew Callie well enough to understand that she was letting the words sink in.

"Wes?"

"I know you love your apartment, but I'd love it if you would move in with me." He glanced at Sweets. "With us."

She ran her thumb over the velvet. "Move in with you?"

He nodded. "That's when two people live together, you know? They come home from work and know the other one is there. They fall into each other's arms at the end of the day and wake up with their bodies tangled together, and in our case, with a furry girl between us."

Wes took her trembling hand in his. "You don't have to answer now. Take your time. Think it over."

"Take my time? Yes, Wes. Yes, with every piece of my heart. Yes, yes, yes." She threw her arms around his neck, and he felt as though he could finally breathe again.

"THIS IS TOTALLY unfair, you know," Callie said to Wes as he pulled into his brother Luke's driveway with a big grin on his face. "I'm going to look like a fool. I can't stop smiling." She was still holding the velvet bag that contained a key to his house.

"Good." Wes parked behind Ross's truck. "They'll think we just did something naughty." He slid his eyes to hers and she knew he'd said it just to see her blush, which she did. "Come here." He kissed her, and Sweets pushed her snout against their chins and licked them. "I swear she's jealous."

"No, not jealous. She just wants to get in on the love." She kissed Sweets's head. "Don't you, baby?"

"Your brother's property is gorgeous." A wide front porch

graced the front of the cedar and stone two-story house that sat at the end of the long driveway. They stepped from the truck, and Callie turned at the sound of horses whinnying in a pasture off to their right, where several horses stood by the fence. They were gorgeous, with thick feathering covering their hooves and lush, full manes and tails.

"Are those Clydesdales?" she asked.

"Gypsy horses. Luke breeds them for a living. The mares in that pasture are his *girls*. I swear he spoils them like they're his kids." Wes led her up toward the house.

"Like you and Sweets?" she asked.

"No," he said sarcastically. "Okay, maybe it runs in the family a little."

They followed the sounds of voices around to a patio in the backyard. Callie tightened her grip on Wes's hand. She'd met Ross, of course, and over the last week Wes had filled her in on all of his siblings, but the knowledge didn't quell the butterflies that gathered in her stomach over meeting his family for the first time.

"They're here!" A slim, dark-haired woman wearing a short sundress and flats ran across the patio with her arms open wide. "Wes!" She hugged him, then turned that welcoming enthusiasm on Callie and threw her arms around her. "Callie! I'm so glad to finally meet you." She stepped back and looked between them, then rolled her eyes. "My brother stinks at introductions. I'm Emily."

Emily! She swallowed a wave of shame leftover from having been jealous after overhearing their conversation. "Hi. I've heard a lot about you."

"I bet," Emily said as she took Callie's hand. "You don't mind if I bend her ear, do you, Wes?"

Sweets ran from person to person, licking them as they crouched to greet her.

"Who are you kidding? He has no choice." All of Wes's brothers were tall, dark, and handsome men. Wes had shown her pictures of them, and she knew that Luke and Ross could be twins, save for the five-year age difference. This brother had straighter, shinier hair than the others, and Callie knew he was Pierce, Wes's oldest brother.

"I'm Pierce. Nice to meet you." He wrenched her from Emily's grasp and embraced her. "Saved you from the clutches of my little sister."

"Your only sister, genius," Emily teased.

Callie thought of how Wes had described Pierce. *Imagine an eagle-eyed brother who would let me have fun until he thought I'd get in trouble; then he'd yank me back in and lecture me until I understood whatever lesson he thought I needed to learn.* Wes had said it with a thoughtful gaze, each word thick with emotion. Looking at Pierce's serious eyes, she could envision him doing those things.

Pierce wrapped Wes in his arms. "Good to see you, bro."

Callie recognized Daisy Honey as she crossed the patio carrying a large salad bowl. She was one of those women who made a person take a second look, with white-blond hair and a figure to die for. Ross was walking by, and he took the bowl from her and carried it to the table. Behind Daisy, a woman who could only be Wes's mother came out of the house.

Wes had a funny way of describing his family. He didn't describe how they looked. He focused on who they were as people, their mannerisms, and the things they'd done over the years. He'd said his mother was the rock of the family. She'd raised them alone, and he had very few memories of her ever being anything other than *a bright light*. The description had made her wonder, and now, seeing the way she smiled at the sight of her children, and the pride and warmth that radiated from her almond-shaped eyes, Callie understood his description. She also realized that she'd seen her in the library several times.

Emily waved her over. "Mom, come over and meet Callie."

Wes reached for Callie's hand. "Cal, this is my mom, Catherine. Mom, this is Callie."

Catherine smiled warmly as she embraced Callie. "How wonderful to finally meet you."

"It's a pleasure to meet you, too," Callie said. "I've seen you in the library."

"Yes. I hear we're both avid readers," Catherine said.

"Okay, let me in here." Daisy gently nudged Catherine and Emily aside. "This family can be a little overwhelming. Just take a deep breath, Callie, and you'll get through it fine. I'm Daisy, Luke's girlfriend." She hugged Callie.

"Nice to meet you, Daisy. I've seen you around town." They welcomed her with genuine smiles and warm embraces, and Callie realized that the butterflies in her stomach had settled down.

"Where is my baby brother?" Wes asked Daisy.

"Don't let him hear that," another brother said from across the patio. He had a deep tan and shorter cropped hair a shade lighter than all the others. He, like the others, was easily over six feet tall, with at least two days' growth on his cheeks. He opened his arms. "Get in here, bro."

"That's Jake," Wes said to Callie as he let go of her hand to greet his brother.

Another brother, who Callie knew had to be Luke because he looked just like Ross, only younger, dove at Jake, and they both tumbled to the ground. Sweets barked and circled their thrashing bodies.

"Oh my gosh." Callie reached for Wes as he and Pierce eagerly jumped onto the pile.

Emily sighed, like she was used to seeing four grown men wrestling on the ground. "They're such boys."

"Shouldn't we stop them?" Callie watched them roll and tumble. Jake flipped backward, taking Luke along with him.

"They're fine." Ross put an arm across Callie's shoulder and hugged her. "Nice to see you again."

"Why aren't you in the…rumble?" Callie's heart thundered in her chest at the sight of them, in stark contrast to Wes's sister and mother, who were calmly setting the table, and Ross, who was sipping a beer.

He held up a hand and splayed his fingers. "Can't do surgery if my hands are messed up."

Wes broke free of the wrestling match, brushed the dirt from his jeans, and came to Callie's side. "Ross is just a wimp."

Ross shook his head. "Hardly."

"That's enough, boys," Catherine called.

"Aw, Mom." Luke wrinkled his brow.

"Luke," Daisy chided him. "We have a guest, and now she probably thinks you guys are all nuts." Daisy and Emily dragged Callie from Wes and brought her over to the table while the men brushed themselves off.

"I swear they'll never grow up," Emily said.

"Emily, Wes told me that you helped him coordinate the manicures, the dresses, and all that stuff he did for me and my friends. That was the most incredible day of my life. Thank you."

"Oh, it was nothing. I had fun with it." Emily tucked her

hair behind her ear. "Did Wes tell you what he surprised me with?"

"Yes, and I nearly fell to my knees," Callie said.

"Speaking of that, the next time he wants to do something, can you have him call me?" Daisy smiled at Callie.

"I know, right? I tried to tell him that it was too much, but you know Wes. There's no arguing with him when he gives you something," Emily said. "Tuscany? How lucky am I?"

"Actually, I think I'm the lucky one," Callie said, looking across the lawn at Wes, who was talking with Luke and Jake. He shifted his eyes and smiled at Callie.

"I think he's the lucky one," Emily said. "I've never seen him so happy."

"Can I join the party?" Catherine asked. She handed Callie a glass of wine. "My boys are falling in love, and for a mother, that's a wonderful thing to see."

"Well, I wish some of whatever they're doing would rub off on me," Emily said. "I want to feel that wonderful feeling."

"Oh, you will, Em. Your guy must be very special to remain hidden for this long." Catherine glanced at the men. "I never thought I'd see the day that they settled down. I thought Ross, maybe, because he's not quite as rambunctious as the others. Then again, love's a powerful emotion, and when it hits, there's no turning away."

Watching Wes with his brothers, and hearing his mother talk about love, Callie was beginning to understand the passion she heard in Wes's voice on a daily basis. A man couldn't love others if he himself wasn't loved, and it was obvious how much his family loved one another. Pierce joined Wes and slung an arm over his shoulder, then leaned in close. A minute later, Wes threw his head back with a hearty laugh.

"Let's join them before they get crazy again," Catherine said.

"I hear that you climbed down a mountain to rescue Sweets," Daisy said. "You're braver than I could ever be."

The memory of how scared she'd been sent an icy shiver down Callie's back. "I wasn't really brave. I just did what I had to do."

"No. *Doing what you have to do* is going to work every day, or eating so you don't starve to death. Climbing down a mountain and carrying a dog back up is brave," Daisy said. "Trust me on that."

Emily tapped her on the shoulder. "If you ask me, bravery means being willing to put up with one of these guys for days on end."

"*Tsk.* You might be right." Daisy laughed as Luke came up behind her and kissed her on the neck.

"Right about what?" Luke asked.

"That it takes bravery to be with a Braden man," Daisy answered.

"Hell, yeah, it does. We're all a pain in the ass." Luke spun Daisy in his arms and kissed her. "But then again, we're worth it."

"Speak for yourself," Wes said. "I'm not a pain in the ass."

"Wanna bet?" Jake took a pull of his beer. "All I know is that there's no way in hell I'm doing the whole monogamous relationship thing. I'm having too much fun."

Pierce said. "I'm with you. No way, no how."

"Hear, hear." Ross lifted his glass.

Emily rolled her eyes. "You guys are so stupid. Look how happy Luke and Daisy are, and Wes and Callie. The heck with fun. I want love."

Callie wondered if hearing his brothers' comments gave Wes any regrets about asking her to move in.

As if he'd read her mind, Wes folded her into his arms, pressed his cheek to hers, and whispered, "They have no idea what they're missing." He leaned his forehead to hers, as he'd done so many times before, and said, "You're my happily ever after, Callie, and I hope I'm yours."

"You always were."

Ready for more Bradens?

Fall in love with Pierce and Rebecca in
ROMANCING MY LOVE

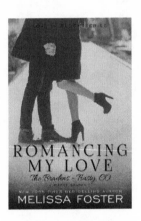

Chapter One

PIERCE BRADEN NEEDED to relax. He'd had a damn hard day. He'd sat through too many meetings, strategizing over the potential acquisition of the Grand Casino, a local property that he'd been eyeing for three years. Not to mention that he'd forgotten to turn on his phone that morning and missed calls from both his mother and one of his brothers, and when he'd called them back, they'd given him crap about it. The last thing he needed was to be fawned over by his employees, but when you owned most of the happening digs around Reno, and several more around the world, there weren't many places he could go unnoticed. King's Bar was a dive on the outskirts of town, and he hoped, a place he could just fucking relax.

He was crossing the dance floor to the bar when the scent of Curious—a perfume he hadn't smelled in a decade—wafted past, trailing a hot, curvy ass, which was attached to a woman blazing a path toward the door. He didn't blame her. The place reeked of alcohol and testosterone.

Some drunk guy stopped her, and Pierce watched as she turned on the guy. Holy shit. She was a hell of a lot more than a great ass. She was scorching hot, with dark—and at the moment, angry—eyes, heavy breasts, and a sweet little waist.

Another greasy-haired, sweaty guy grabbed her, and Pierce circled back, fire rushing through his veins. He couldn't watch drunken assholes manhandle a woman. He took a step toward helping her as the guy leaned in close, his lips about to assail hers.

Through gritted teeth, she said in a low growl, "Let go of me."

Before Pierce could push through the gathering crowd, the woman kneed the asshole in the groin, and when he doubled over with a loud groan, she grabbed his massive shoulders and slammed his face into her knee. His friend stepped in behind him, and the woman clocked the guy who was doubled over with a right cross to his chin, sending him sprawling backward against his friend. They both stumbled into a group of people. Pierce set a threatening, narrow-eyed stare on the asshole, then grabbed the woman's arm and dragged her toward the door before the guy decided to retaliate or the manager kicked her out. She flailed and fought against his grip. Her body was trembling, and when the cool night air hit her, she blinked several times, as if she were trying to regain control. After what he'd just witnessed, he knew she could protect herself, but it was the momentary flash of vulnerability in her eyes that kept his hand on her arm.

"Let me go," she demanded. "God, what is it about men grabbing me tonight?"

"I'm sorry. I was just trying to help by getting you out of there before the manager called the cops." Pierce released her arm.

"Oh, he would have loved that. The jerk." She shook her head.

"You're shivering. Here, take my shirt." He took off his Armani dress shirt and draped it over her bare shoulders, covering her tank top and leaving him in his undershirt.

She shrugged off the shirt and stepped back. "I'm fine."

Pierce caught the shirt in one hand as it sailed toward the ground. "Okay. I just thought you might be cold. Can I get you a cab?"

She looked up and down the street, giving Pierce a moment to assess the feisty brunette. Her hair had been pinned up when he first noticed her inside the bar, and during the fight the messy bun had slipped to the nape of her neck. She had sharp features—a pointy chin, high cheekbones, thin lips, and a nose that perked up at the end. They might have looked harsh, or on the opposite end of the spectrum, perhaps elfin, on any other woman, but her dark eyes were big and round, softening all those sharp edges into a mask of angry seduction.

"Cab? No, thanks." She drew in a deep breath and put her hands on her hips.

He wanted to put his hands on her hips.

Pierce was thirty-six years old and had more money than he could ever spend and more women than nights to pleasure them. He was the supreme bachelor. He'd give his own life to protect his family, but when it came to women outside of his family, they had always been expendable.

Ever since two of his younger brothers, Wes and Luke, had fallen in love, and he'd watched their lives transform into blissful coupledom with women they adored, he'd begun to wonder if he was missing out. Now, this delicious, angry, slightly vulnerable woman was sparking a familiar spike in adrenaline, tugging at the protective urges that were reserved for his family, and he couldn't let her just walk away. She seemed anything but expendable.

She walked away while he stood there in a fog of confusion over the instant desire to protect her when she obviously didn't need him. He caught up to her a few steps later.

"Okay, no cabs. My car's in the garage around the corner. I could drive you home."

She continued walking at a fast pace. "Thanks. I really appreciate it, but I can walk." Her tone was still incensed. She shoved her hands in the pockets of her jeans, and her slim shoulders rounded forward against the chilly night air. It was just after eleven, still early by Reno standards.

Why on earth he couldn't walk away when she clearly wanted him to was a mystery to him. She was gorgeous, but hot women were a dime a dozen in Pierce's circles. He wasn't used to being turned down, even for just a drink or a ride, and could barely believe she had done so. Pierce was a man who was used to getting what he wanted, and she was too fine to give up that easily. He could think of no reason for her to turn him down, except...He wondered if she thought he frequented that dive of a bar and was judging him by those surroundings. *What the hell was she doing there, anyway?*

"I don't usually hang out there," he explained.

She stopped walking and finally turned to face him. He didn't even know her name, but when he saw that the anger in her eyes had been replaced by a well of sadness, he wanted to fold her into his arms until the sadness that turned the edges of her lips down disappeared. He thought of his younger sister, Emily. If Emily looked as sad as this woman, he hoped someone would be there to make her feel safe without any ulterior motive.

"Look, you seem like a nice enough guy, but I'm not a damsel in distress, okay? Some jerks took the brunt of a really bad night." She shrugged as if it were commonplace for her to deck a guy in a bar. "I'm fine. They didn't even call the cops, so he must be fine. Go do your thing and I'll go do mine, okay?" Her words were strong, but her voice wasn't quite as determined, and her eyes—those big, beautiful, sad eyes—gave her heartache away.

"How about I make sure you get home okay?" Pierce offered.

"You don't have to." She began walking again.

"I know. But if you go around decking every guy who bugs you, your arms are bound to get tired." They turned down another street. "You'll need backup."

She smiled, and the tension around her eyes and her sweet lips eased. He felt her resolve softening. She rubbed the goose bumps that pebbled her arms. "I have pretty strong arms."

"No doubt, but it's chilly out. How about if I buy you a cup of coffee?"

She stopped walking again and tilted her head. In the fluorescent lights of the main drag, her eyes changed again. Pierce had never met such a chameleon. She no longer looked angry or devastatingly sad; she looked feminine and a little fragile. But he already knew better than to say that to her.

"Look..."

"Pierce," he said.

"Pierce? Is that your real name or some kind of casino or stage name?" She crossed her arms and jutted one curvy hip out to the side.

He ran his hand through his thick dark hair. "Apparently, my mother thought I needed a casino name." *Most women dig my name.*

She smiled again, and it shot a strange sensation to the center of his chest. "Well, *Pierce*, I really appreciate your efforts to help me. I'm sorry if I seem ungrateful. It's just been an *interesting* night. But really, I'm not looking for a guy to buy me a drink, or to hook up, or any of that." She dragged her eyes down his body. At six three and two hundred and ten pounds of solid muscle, Pierce knew he was irresistible to women, and now that she'd finally looked at him, he readied himself for her acceptance of his offer.

"Besides, my mother warned me about men who look like you." She drew in a deep breath and blew it out slowly. "So, I thank you, and I bid you a good night."

Are you fucking kidding me? Your mother warned you? He forced his ego aside for a second before he said something he shouldn't and focused on her choice of words, which were equally as surprising.

"Bid me? Now who belongs in a casino?"

"Good one." She walked backward, lengthening the distance between them.

"Just tell me your name," he called.

She narrowed her eyes, and her mouth quirked up at the

edge, taking her from sexy to goddamn cute and making her even more intriguing.

"Rhonda Rousy," she answered, then spun on her heels and disappeared around the corner.

Rhonda Rousy, my ass. Rhonda Rousy was one of the best mixed martial arts fighters, and attractive as hell. *You're one hundred times as pretty and one hundred times as clever.*

He headed back toward his car, wondering how in the hell he'd concentrate on anything else with "Rhonda's" sassy personality and her red-hot image seared into his mind.

REBECCA WALKED BACK toward the parking garage where she'd left her car, thinking about Pierce and forcing the memories of the terrible night away before she collapsed to her knees in a puddle of tears—or boiled in fury and punched someone else. *God, I punched a guy—and Pierce saw it all.* When he'd dragged her from the bar, she couldn't hear past the blood rushing through her ears, but she'd sensed people moving away, and she'd seen fear and surprise on their faces; then everything blurred together as Pierce dragged her quaking and shivering self out of the bar and into the night.

He'd been as determined to change her mind about the drive home as she was to stand firm. She'd almost caved under the weight of his beguiling dark eyes. That tight undershirt left every drool-worthy muscle on display. Not to mention that all six feet something of pure male sexuality beckoned to her private parts, which she thought she'd turned off years ago.

Pierce. What type of name was that, anyway? *Pierce.* She

rolled it over in her mind, imagined saying it in a dark bedroom atop satin sheets, with his thighs pressed to hers.

Don't even go there, Rebecca.

She hadn't had a social life of any sort in three years. It was kind of hard to focus on anything other than the business classes she took and caring for her ailing mother, especially toward the end of her mother's life. Not for the first time in the last six weeks, her eyes teared up. It wasn't because of the fight she'd had with her boss, or the fact that she told him he could shove the damn job up his scrawny ass. No. That was nothing new in Rebecca's life, either. She was thinking of the last moments with her mother, before she closed her eyes for the final time and the last puff of air left her lungs. Before Rebecca was left alone in this crazy world.

Magda Rivera had always been the picture of health, at least from the outside. But that had been an illusion. Cancer was an unfair assailant that snuck in when they weren't looking and stole pieces of her mother, consuming her until her very last breath. Now her mother's ashes lay in an urn in the safe of her previous landlord's office. Mr. Fralin had been nice enough to hold the urn for her until she found a permanent place to live.

She took the elevator in the Astral resort parking garage to the fifth floor, where she'd left her car. She loathed this part of the evening. The parking garage was at least ten degrees colder than the street, and even though Rebecca had been coming *home* to it for three days now, she knew it would never lose the icy chill of concrete. She surveyed her surroundings as she crossed the dimly lit parking garage and noticed a man getting out of his car at the far end of the lot. She slipped into the driver's seat of her 1999 Toyota Corolla and waited for him to enter the elevator before putting up the sunshades on the windows and reclining her seat. She'd only been staying in her car for three days, since she'd had to give up her apartment for lack of rent money, but three days of worrying about being caught in her car felt like three years. She had excuses at the ready, just in case security banged on her window in the middle of the night. *I didn't want to drive after drinking too much* was her favorite excuse. Who could argue with that in the garage of a casino?

As soon as she had enough money saved, she'd find a room to rent. She missed the privacy of her tiny efficiency. Before her mother's illness, when Rebecca had rented her own apartment and had a normal life for a twentysomething woman, she'd made it a practice never to take men back to her apartment. Her home was her private oasis, and she liked to keep it that way. She thought about how nice it would be to go home at the end of the day and kick her feet up on her own couch, in her own living room. Now that she'd quit her job, finding a room to rent would be pushed back for God only knew how long. She could have kicked herself for quitting. Why hadn't she just shut her mouth and let Martin the asshole yell at her for the millionth time? Her mother's voice floated through her mind. *Because*, mi dulce niña, *you matter.* She closed her eyes and rested her head back, wondering what her mother would think of her *sweet girl* living in her car.

Rebecca didn't rue her circumstances. Mr. Fralin had been kind enough to allow her and her mother to stay in their apartment rent free during the final two months of her mother's life. Rebecca had been at her side every minute until the end, making it impossible for her to hold a job, and her mother had earned so little money when she was healthy that even her disability didn't cover their bills. Not to mention that her mother hadn't realized she was responsible for paying taxes on the disability income because her employer had paid for the insurance premiums. Rebecca was still working to pay off the debt her mother had accrued during her illness—it was the least she could do for the woman who gave up so much of her own life for her. Luckily, Mr. Fralin was a generous man, and he'd allowed Rebecca to remain in the apartment for almost six weeks after her mother had died, while Rebecca tried to pull herself together. Mr. Fralin did all he could, but he needed the rent money, and once again, Rebecca did what she had to in order to survive. Not wanting to be any more of a burden on Mr. Fralin, she found the pride she'd set aside to ensure her mother's comfort, and she'd moved out of the apartment and into her car.

While Rebecca didn't rue her dire circumstances, she did have a bone to pick with God, or whoever, or whatever, powers that be had stolen her mother away like a thief in the night.

To continue reading, buy **ROMANCING MY LOVE**

Have you met the Seaside Summers friends?

Fall in love on the sandy shores of Cape Cod Bay, where true love, good friends, and happiness come together. Seaside Summers is a hilarious and sexy series featuring a group of friends who gather each summer at their Seaside cottages.

Fall in love with Caden and Bella in SEASIDE DREAMS

Chapter One

BELLA ABBASCIA STRUGGLED to keep her grip on a ceramic toilet as she crossed the gravel road in Seaside, the community where she spent her summers. It was one o'clock in the morning, and Bella had a prank in store for Theresa Ottoline, a straitlaced Seaside resident and the elected property manager for the community. Bella and two of her besties, Amy

Maples and Jenna Ward, had polished off two bottles of Middle Sister wine while they waited for the other cottage owners to turn in for the night. Now, dressed in their nighties and a bit tipsy, they struggled to keep their grip on a toilet that Bella had spent two days painting bright blue, planting flowers in, and adorning with seashells. They were carrying the toilet to Theresa's driveway to break rule number fourteen of the Community Homeowners Association's Guidelines: *No tacky displays allowed in the front of the cottages.*

"You're sure she's asleep?" Bella asked as they came to the grass in front of the cottage of their fourth bestie, Leanna Bray.

"Yes. She turned off her lights at eleven. We should have hidden it someplace other than my backyard. It's so far. Can we stop for a minute? This sucker is heavy." Amy drew her thinly manicured brows together.

"Oh, come on. Really? We only have a little ways to go." Bella nodded toward Theresa's driveway, which was across the road from her cottage, about a hundred feet away.

Amy glanced at Jenna for support. Jenna nodded, and the two lowered their end to the ground, causing Bella to nearly drop hers.

"That's so much better." Jenna tucked her stick-straight brown hair behind her ear and shook her arms out to her sides. "Not all of us lift weights for breakfast."

"Oh, please. The most exercise I get during the summer is lifting a bottle of wine," Bella said. "Carrying around those boobs of yours is more of a workout."

Jenna was just under five feet tall with breasts the size of bowling balls and a tiny waist. She could have been the model for the modern-day Barbie doll, while Bella's figure was more typical for an almost thirty-year-old woman. Although she was tall, strong, and relatively lean, she refused to give up her comfort foods, which left her a little soft in places, with a figure similar to Julia Roberts or Jennifer Lawrence.

"I don't carry them with my arms." Jenna looked down at her chest and cupped a breast in each hand. "But yeah, that would be great exercise."

Amy rolled her eyes. Pin-thin and nearly flat chested, Amy was the most modest of the group, and in her long T-shirt and underwear, she looked like a teenager next to curvy Jenna. "We only need a sec, Bella."

They turned at the sound of a passionate moan coming from Leanna's cottage.

"She forgot to close the window again," Jenna whispered as she tiptoed around the side of Leanna's cottage. "Typical Leanna. I'm just going to close it."

Leanna had fallen in love with bestselling author Kurt Remington the previous summer, and although they had a house on the bay, they often stayed in the two-bedroom cottage so Leanna could enjoy her summer friends. The Seaside cottages in Wellfleet, Massachusetts, had been in the girls' families for years, and they had spent summers together since they were kids.

"Wait, Jenna. Let's get the toilet to Theresa's first." Bella placed her hands on her hips so they knew she meant business. Jenna stopped before she reached for the window, and Bella realized it would have been a futile effort anyway. Jenna would need a stepstool to pull that window down.

"Oh...Kurt." Leanna's voice split the night air.

Amy covered her mouth to stifle a laugh. "Fine, but let's hurry. Poor Leanna will be mortified to find out she left the window open again."

"I'm the last one who wants to hear her having sex. I'm done with men, or at least with commitments, until my life is back on track." Ever since last summer, when Leanna had met Kurt, started her own jam-making business, and moved to the Cape full-time, Bella had been thinking of making a change of her own. Leanna's success had inspired her to finally go for it. Well, that and the fact that she'd made the mistake of dating a fellow teacher, Jay Cook. It had been months since they broke up, but they'd taught at the same Connecticut high school, and until she left for the summer, she couldn't avoid running in to him on a daily basis. It was just the nudge she needed to take the plunge and finally quit her job and start over. *New job, new life, new location.* She just hadn't told her friends yet. She'd thought she would tell them the minute she arrived at Seaside and they were all together, maybe over a bottle of wine or on the beach. But Leanna had been spending a lot of time with Kurt, and every time it was just the four of them, she hadn't been ready to come clean. She knew they'd worry and ask questions, and she wanted to have some of the transition sorted out before answering them.

"Bella, you can't give up on men. Jay was just a jerk." Amy touched her arm.

She really needed to fill them in on the whole Jay and quitting her job thing. She was beyond over Jay, but they knew Bella to be the stable one of the group, and learning of her sudden change was a conversation that needed to be handled when they weren't wrestling a fifty-pound toilet.

"Fine. You're right. But I'm going to make all of my future decisions separate from any man. So…until my life is in order, no commitments for me."

"Not me. I'd give anything to have what Kurt and Leanna

have," Amy said.

Bella lifted her end of the toilet easily as Jenna and Amy struggled to lift theirs. "Got it?"

"Yeah. Go quick. This damn thing is heavy," Jenna said as they shuffled along the grass.

"More…" Leanna pleaded.

Amy stumbled and lost her grip. The toilet dropped to the ground, and Jenna yelped.

"Shh. You're going to wake up the whole complex!" Bella stalked over to them.

"Oh, Kurt!" Jenna rocked her hips. "More, baby, more!"

"Really?" Bella tried to keep a straight face, but when Leanna cried out again, she doubled over with laughter.

Amy, always the voice of reason, whispered, "Come on. We *need* to close her window."

"Yes!" Leanna cried.

They fell against one another in a fit of laughter, stumbling beside Leanna's cottage.

"I could make popcorn." Jenna struggled to keep a straight face.

Amy scowled at her. "She got pissed the last time you did that." She grabbed Bella's hand and whispered through gritted teeth, "Take out the screen so you can shut the window, please."

"I told you we should have put a lock on the outside of her window," Jenna reminded them. Last summer, when Leanna and Kurt had first begun dating, they'd often forgotten to close the window. To save Leanna embarrassment, Jenna had offered to be on sex-noise mission control and close the window if Leanna ever forgot to. A few drinks later, she'd mistakenly abandoned the idea for the summer.

"While you close the window, I'll get the sign for the toilet."

Amy hurried back toward Bella's deck in her boy-shorts underwear and a T-shirt.

Bella tossed the screen to the side so she could reach inside and close the window. The side of Leanna's cottage was on a slight incline, and although Bella was tall, she needed to stand on her tiptoes to get a good grip on the window. The hem of the nightie caught on her underwear, exposing her ample derriere.

"Cute satin skivvies." Jenna reached out to tug Bella's shirt down and Bella swatted her.

Bella pushed as hard as she could on the top of the window, trying to ignore the sensuous moans and the creaking of bedsprings coming from inside the cottage.

"The darn thing's stuck," she whispered.

Jenna moved beside her and reached for the window. Her fingertips barely grazed the bottom edge.

Amy ran toward them, waving a long stick with a paper sign taped to the top that read, WELCOME BACK.

Leanna moaned, and Jenna laughed and lost her footing. Bella reached for her, and the window slammed shut, catching Bella's hair. Leanna's dog, Pepper, barked, sending Amy and Jenna into more fits of laughter.

With her hair caught in the window and her head plastered to the sill, Bella put a finger to her lips. "Shh!"

Headlights flashed across Leanna's cottage as a car turned up the gravel road.

"Shit!" Bella went up on her toes, struggled to lift the window and free her hair, which felt like it was being ripped from her skull. The curtains flew open and Leanna peered through the glass. Bella lifted a hand and waved. *Crap.* She heard Leanna's front door open, and Pepper bolted around the corner, barking a blue streak and knocking Jenna to the ground just as a police car rolled up next to them and shined a spotlight on Bella's ass.

CADEN GRANT HAD been with the Wellfleet Police Department for only three months, having moved after his partner of nine years was killed in the line of duty. He'd relocated to the small town with his teenage son, Evan, in hopes of working in a safer location. So far, he'd found the people of Wellfleet to be respectful and thankful for the efforts of the local law enforcement officers, a welcome change after dealing with rebellion on every corner in Boston. Wellfleet had recently experienced a rash of small thefts—cars being broken into, cottages being ransacked, and the police had begun patrolling the private communities along Route 6, communities that in the past had taken care of their own security. Caden rolled up the gravel road in the Seaside community and spotted a dog running circles around a person rolling on the ground.

He flicked on the spotlight as he rolled to a stop. *Holy Christ. What is going on?* He quickly assessed the situation. A blond woman was banging on a window with both hands. Her shirt was bunched at her waist, and a pair of black satin panties barely covered the most magnificent ass he'd seen in a long time.

"Open the effing window!" she hollered.

Caden stepped from the car. "What's going on here?" He walked around the dark-haired woman, who was rolling from side to side on the ground while laughing hysterically, and the fluffy white dog, who was barking as though his life depended on it, and he quickly realized that the blond woman's hair was caught in the window. Behind him another blonde crouched on the ground, laughing so hard she kept snorting. *Why the hell aren't any of you wearing pants?*

"Leanna! I'm stuck!" the blonde by the window yelled.

"Officer, we're sorry." The blonde behind him rose to her feet, tugging her shirt down to cover her underwear; then she covered her mouth with her hand as more laughter escaped. The dog barked and clawed at Caden's shoes.

"Someone want to tell me what's going on here?" Caden didn't even want to try to guess.

"We're…" The brunette laughed again as she rose to her knees and tried to straighten her camisole, which barely contained her enormous breasts. She ran her eyes down Caden's body. "Well, *hello* there, handsome." She fell backward, laughing again.

Christ. Just what he needed, three drunk women.

The brunette inside the cottage lifted the window, freeing the blonde's hair, which sent her stumbling backward and crashing into his chest. There was no ignoring the feel of her seductive curves beneath the thin layer of fabric. Her hair was a thick, tangled mess. She looked up at him with eyes the color of rich cocoa and lips sweet enough to taste. The air around them pulsed with heat. Christ, she was beautiful.

"Whoa. You okay?" he asked. He told his arms to let her go, but there was a disconnect, and his hands remained stuck to her waist.

"It's…It's not what it looks like." She dropped her eyes to her hands, clutching his forearms, and she released him fast, as if she'd been burned. She took a step back and helped the brunette to her feet. "We were…"

"They were trying to close our window, Officer." A tall, dark-haired man came around the side of the cottage, wearing a pair of jeans and no shirt. "Kurt Remington." He held a hand out in greeting and shook his head at the women, now holding on to each other, giggling and whispering.

"Officer Caden Grant." He shook Kurt's hand. "We've had some trouble with break-ins lately. Do you know these women?" His eyes swept over the tall blonde. He followed the curve of her thighs to where they disappeared beneath her nightshirt, then drifted up to her full breasts, finally coming to rest on her beautiful dark eyes. It had been a damn long time since he'd been this attracted to a woman.

"Of course he knows us." The hot blonde stepped forward, arms crossed, eyes no longer wide and warm, but narrow and angry.

He hated men who leered at women, but he was powerless to refrain from drinking her in for one last second. The other two women were lovely in their own right, but they didn't compare to the tall blonde with fire in her eyes and a body made for loving.

Kurt nodded. "Yes, Officer. We know them."

"God, you guys. What the heck?" the dark-haired woman asked through the open window.

"You were waking the dead," the tall blonde answered.

"Oh, gosh. I'm sorry, Officer," the brunette said through the window. Her cheeks flushed, and she slipped back inside and closed the window.

"I assure you, everything is okay here." Kurt glared at the hot blonde.

"Okay, well, if you see any suspicious activity, we're only a phone call away." He took a step toward his car.

The tall blonde hurried into his path. "Did someone from Seaside call the police?"

"No. I was just patrolling the area."

She held his gaze. "Just patrolling the area? No one *patrols* Seaside."

"Bella," the other blonde hissed.

Bella.

"Seriously. No one patrols our community. They never have." She lifted her chin in a way that he assumed was meant as a challenge, but it had the opposite effect. She looked cuter than hell.

Caden stepped closer and tried to keep a straight face. "Your name is Bella?"

"Maybe."

Feisty, too. He liked that. "Well, Maybe Bella, you're right. We haven't patrolled your community in the past, but things have changed. We'll be patrolling more often to keep you safe until we catch the people who have been burglarizing the area." He leaned in close and whispered, "But you might consider wearing pants for your window-closing evening strolls. Never know who's traipsing around out here."

To continue reading, buy **SEASIDE DREAMS**

More Books By Melissa Foster

LOVE IN BLOOM SERIES

SNOW SISTERS
Sisters in Love
Sisters in Bloom
Sisters in White

THE BRADENS at Weston
Lovers at Heart, Reimagined
Destined for Love
Friendship on Fire
Sea of Love
Bursting with Love
Hearts at Play

THE BRADENS at Trusty
Taken by Love
Fated for Love
Romancing My Love
Flirting with Love
Dreaming of Love
Crashing into Love

THE BRADENS at Peaceful Harbor
Healed by Love
Surrender My Love
River of Love
Crushing on Love
Whisper of Love
Thrill of Love

BAYSIDE SUMMERS
Bayside Desires
Bayside Passions
Bayside Heat
Bayside Escape
Bayside Romance
Bayside Fantasies

THE RYDERS
Seized by Love
Claimed by Love
Chased by Love
Rescued by Love
Swept Into Love

THE WHISKEYS: DARK KNIGHTS AT PEACEFUL HARBOR
Tru Blue
Truly, Madly, Whiskey
Driving Whiskey Wild
Wicked Whiskey Love
Mad About Moon
Taming My Whiskey
The Gritty Truth

SUGAR LAKE
The Real Thing
Only for You
Love Like Ours
Finding My Girl

HARMONY POINTE
Call Her Mine
This is Love
She Loves Me

THE WICKEDS: DARK KNIGHTS AT BAYSIDE
A Little Bit Wicked
Wicked Aftermath

WILD BOYS AFTER DARK (Billionaires After Dark)
Logan
Heath
Jackson
Cooper

BAD BOYS AFTER DARK (Billionaires After Dark)
Mick
Dylan
Carson
Brett

HARBORSIDE NIGHTS SERIES
Includes characters from the Love in Bloom series
Catching Cassidy
Discovering Delilah
Tempting Tristan

More Books by Melissa
Chasing Amanda (mystery/suspense)
Come Back to Me (mystery/suspense)
Have No Shame (historical fiction/romance)
Love, Lies & Mystery (3-book bundle)
Megan's Way (literary fiction)
Traces of Kara (psychological thriller)
Where Petals Fall (suspense)

Acknowledgments

Nothing is quite as exciting as receiving emails and messages from readers. Thank you for inspiring me to continue bringing you more Love in Bloom novels, to take care when crafting my characters, and to dig deeper to bring you unique stories. I enjoy hearing from you, and I hope you will continue to reach out.

I'd like to thank Shanyn and Earl Silinski, for guiding me with all things ranch related, and Nowell May, ranch manager at Black Mountain Ranch, for answering my questions about running a dude ranch. I hope to make it to Black Mountain Ranch someday. Thank you, Aurelia Kucera, for answering all of my questions about puppies and for being patient when I kept coming back for more information. I took many creative liberties in *Fated for Love*. Any and all errors are my own and not a reflection of others. The towns of Trusty and Weston are fictional, as are the comedian and architect mentioned in the book.

Natasha Brown and Clare Ayala, thank you for your extraordinary patience and attention to detail. Christine Cunningham, jokester extraordinaire, provided many of the jokes in this manuscript. Thank you, Christine, for always being ready and willing to dish out a few laughs.

My editorial team deserves a lifetime supply of chocolate for their patience, persistence, and meticulous attention to detail. Tremendous gratitude goes to Kristen Weber, Penina Lopez, Jenna Bagnini, Juliette Hill, and Marlene Engel.

Lastly, thank you to my family for giving me the time to bring my worlds to life.

Meet Melissa

www.MelissaFoster.com

Melissa Foster is the *New York Times, Wall Street Journal,* and *USA Today* bestselling and award-winning author of more than 100 novels. Her books have been recommended by *USA Today*'s book blog, *Hagerstown* magazine, *The Patriot,* and several other print venues.

Melissa enjoys discussing her books with book clubs and reader groups and welcomes an invitation to your event. Melissa's books are available through most online retailers in paperback, digital, and audio formats.

Shop Melissa's store for exclusive discounts, bundles, and more. shop.melissafoster.com

Melissa also writes sweet romance under the pen name Addison Cole.

Manufactured by Amazon.ca
Bolton, ON

41256505R00199